Murder on Camac

Joseph R. G. DeMarco

LETHE PRESS
MAPLE SHADE, NJ

This trade paperback edition published by
Lethe Press,
118 Heritage Ave,
Maple Shade, NJ 08052.
lethepressbooks.com   lethepress@aol.com

Cover by Niki Smith
Book design by Toby Johnson

ISBN 1-59021-213-4 / 978-1-59021-213-4

Library of Congress Cataloging-in-Publication Data

DeMarco, Joseph R. G.
  Murder on Camac / Joseph R. G. DeMarco.
    p. cm.
  ISBN-13: 978-1-59021-213-4 (trade pbk. : alk. paper)
  ISBN-10: 1-59021-213-4 (trade pbk. : alk. paper)
  1. Private investigators--Fiction. 2. Catholic authors--Crimes against-
-Fiction. 3. Catholics--Fiction. 4. Gay men--Fiction. 5. Philadelphia
(Pa.)--Fiction. I. Title.
  PS3604.E449M87 2009
  813'.6--dc22

                                              2009031198

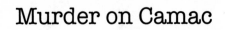

Murder on Camac

Murder On Camac

Chapter 1

Benny Rippa was a liar. I can spot a liar ninety percent of the time. The other ten percent, I'm usually suspicious and always right to be. I'm also Italian which gives you a proclivity to being distrustful. It's how I was raised.

Being skeptical comes in handy for a P.I. So when Benny's call came whispering through on voicemail, I knew he was lying. Again.

"They tried to kill me, Mr. Fontana. I need your help." He always whispered, every one of his five calls. I guess he felt it was more dramatic.

Benny's a bouncer at the Come Back Bar. Bouncers make enemies but not Benny. Fact is, he's a sweet giant and everybody loves him. He was never in any danger, I'd checked that out after his first call. Benny just had a thing for me and when he couldn't attract my attention any other way, he resorted to pretending he was in danger.

I hit the delete button and made a note of the call. Then I shouted out to my secretary.

"Olga, how'd you like to take a case for me?"

"Is Mr. Benny? Bouncing man? No, thank you! I am having enough to do."

Olga's stolid Russian personality didn't mean she had no sense of humor. She was smart. Smart enough to have been married four times and survived.

Which was more than anyone could say about her husbands. They were, all four of them, in the ground. They'd left Olga financially comfortable. Especially number four. When he died is when I met Olga. She was on trial for murder and her lawyer hired me to find out the Truth. Which is what I do and there's little more satisfying.

Turned out Olga's fourth husband had a sister who thought all his money should be hers. She'd hired a hit man to take him out. She'd also planned well. The frame-up was nearly perfect. Nearly. But I found the flaws and the Truth. Olga came to work for me shortly after the charges were dropped.

I grabbed a file but before I opened it, the phone rang. Olga put the call through without asking.

"Fontana," I said, fiddling with the file.

"Someone's trying to kill me," he said. No introduction, no nothing. My antennae went up.

"Who is this?"

"My name is Helmut Brandt." I noticed a slight German accent. The name seemed vaguely familiar.

"I'm listening."

"Someone… you must believe me, Mr. Fontana. This is no joke."

"Believe what?"

"Someone wants me dead. For what I'm about to expose in a book I'm writing."

"How about coming in to my office to talk?."

"Have you heard of Opus Dei, or P2, or the Roman Curia?"

I'd heard of two out of three. Not bad.

"These are the people trying to kill you?" If he thought so, I knew exactly which shrink to refer him to.

"Someone wants me out of the way. I'm in possession of documents which people would kill to keep secret."

"Has there been an attempt on your life?"

"You've got a right to be skeptical, Mr. Fontana, but I assure you I'm telling the truth. Look me up on Amazon or Wikipedia, you'll see why certain people want me buried. Maybe you'll find that more convincing." He paused and I heard him breathing. "I'll come to your office tomorrow. Ten in the morning."

He hung up. I didn't really want to talk to him again, let alone take his case. I'd had my fill of paranoid nut cases. But he'd given me homework. Something about his voice and his name made me curious about why he'd have potentially lethal Christian organizations trying to skin him alive.

As I was about to type his name into Amazon's search bar, the phone rang again. I wondered why Olga put yet another call through without asking, then I heard the voice.

"Marco, we've got a minor problem which you apparently caused." Anton said.

When Anton used the word 'minor' I knew it meant trouble. What he considered minor was usually an eight-point-five on anyone else's earthquake scale. His unflappable nature was why he helped manage StripGuyz, my other source of income. StripGuyz, an ever-growing troupe of male strippers and go-go boys, was a business I'd started a few years back.

"Cal's being a diva again? The baby spots are not the right color or what?" I felt happy to have something other than paranoid people to deal with.

"Cal and Bruno are sulking and it's almost showtime. They both expect to be the Feature this weekend. Said you promised them. Did you promise both of them, Marco?"

"Me? Anton, you know I nev…"

"What I know is, that when a pretty boy bats his eyes at you, you kinda forget the promises you made to the pretty boy who came before." Anton's tone was world-weary and accusatory.

"And I thought you liked me. Just a little."

"I keep hoping you'll like *me*, Marco. But that's another story."

It certainly was another story. Anton was interested in a relationship. With me. And I was equally interested. All right, maybe not equally. But I was interested. The timing wasn't right. There were too many unsettled things in my life. I also had to be sure. Trouble is, with Anton it was all or nothing. We could date but he wouldn't allow us to sleep together. Kissing, cuddling. Everything but rolling in the hay. He wouldn't let that happen until I was ready to commit. It was actually sweet and one of the things I liked about the beautiful hunk.

Anton was far and away the favorite with the crowds when he danced, which was rare now. He was my first dancer and had become my right arm in the business. Even as my manager, Anton was still popular. How could he not be? His sultry, golden, Eastern European looks almost literally hypnotized men. He'd had his share of guys. But no one ever tempted him to settle down. Except me. And I just wasn't ready.

"Anton, you know how I feel about you."

"Anyway, Marco, I need you here." A wistful note threaded its way through his words making me feel small and alone. "Both Cal and Bruno are threatening to go on strike. I'm not sure they know what the word means but they're threatening. They might take others with them. If you don't get down here and fix things, we'll have an empty stage tonight."

"I'm on my way, Anton."

I hung up the phone, stashed the file, and found my cell phone hiding under some papers. On the way out I grabbed my jacket, October was colder than expected but I enjoyed a chill in the air. It woke me up, brought me to attention.

"You are going to stripping guys?" Olga kept her eyes glued to the computer monitor. "Another emergency is arising and they need Daddy to handle?"

"I'm not old enough to be anybody's daddy," I said and opened the door. Unless thirty-two was daddy territory, I was still safe.

"You will be back?"

"Not tonight. It's almost seven. I'll deal with the boys at Bubbles then get something to eat. Why're you here so late?"

"Is personal project," she said.

I took the stairs to the street. The too-small elevator was not quick enough. The peeling paint and cracked walls reminded me that I'd promised myself to look for a new office as soon as I cleared a few more cases.

It was chillier than I thought which made me glad Bubbles, the bar where StripGuyz is based, wasn't far. The suede jacket I wore was more fashionable than warm. I'd struck up a friendship with Stan, the owner of Bubbles, several years before. When I started the troupe, he was only too glad to let Bubbles become my base of operations. My guys brought in business. Lots of business. Like my office, the bar was smack in the middle of the gayborhood. With four floors of fun, a restaurant, lounges, and a small twenty-four hour café, Bubbles was as complete a setting as you can imagine. My StripGuyz office occupied a small, microscopic was a better word, space at the rear of the second floor. There was also a large locker-dressing room with lots of accoutrements to keep the boys happy. The dressing room was near the back stairs which only my guys were allowed to use to move from floor to floor without being disturbed.

Ty, the afternoon bartender, was setting things up for the night shift when I walked through the first floor bar. Short and muscled, he had a face like a prize fighter who'd been at it a long time. The rough manly look made him wildly popular.

"Hey, Marco." Ty turned to smile at me. "Situation upstairs?"

I always unconsciously touched my face when I saw his broken nose and this time was no different.

"Yeah, Ty. Too many divas and not enough stage. That's why I want you to work for me." I wasn't joking. Ty was a natural. His innate grace along with his dark hair and olive complexion made his rough exterior even more appealing. I could see him pulling down a few hundred on weekend nights. No problem.

"I might just be another diva." He winked and continued stacking glasses.

Nearing the locker room, I heard the buzz of angry voices. I entered without knocking. The glare of dressing room mirror lights was calculated and necessary. These boys needed to see their flaws so they could figure out how to fix or disguise them before going on stage. Some just loved seeing themselves. I squinted until my eyes adjusted.

"Marco!" Cal turned from his place at one of the mirrors. No shirt, smooth chest, low rise jeans revealing the flattest of stomachs, he had a fresh, innocent face. Cal was anything but. He was nice enough but was savvy, could be manipulative, and never let anyone best him.

He threw an arm around my shoulder and seductively pulled me to him.

"You're gonna clear this up, right, Marco?"

"Yeah, you *will* clear this up," Bruno rumbled from a far corner. His dark Puerto Rican looks made him appear fierce and wildly sexy. At that moment he smoldered with anger. He was usually polite, courteous, and a willing worker. But anyone could see that beneath the civil exterior, there was more going on, a suppressed slow burn.

"Marco's a great fixer." Anton smirked.

I didn't remember promising feature status to either guy yet each had the impression I'd given him the nod. Being the feature meant more money. A bigger paycheck from me as well as a lot more in tips. Everyone wanted to be featured. I had a system for rotating them. Usually. Something went wrong this time. Boy, had it gone wrong.

I had to come up with something quick.

"Well, Marco?" Anton smoothed his hair and stared at me as if I had the magic answer. Sure enough it came to me. Maybe it was his stare, maybe I'm just used to talking my way out of things.

"Someone's not remembering something," I said.

"You got that right." Bruno's soft accent and lingering anger colored his words.

"Doesn't anybody remember that tonight is Auditions? We never have a Feature on Audition night." Which was true. I had five guys who'd applied to become dancers. I let applicants work for tips to see how they performed. Not everyone could hack it. Bruno made a ton of money when he'd auditioned.

"Oh, auditions! Right. How could I forget?" Anton fell in with me. Not to save my ass, I was sure. He wanted to keep the dancers happy and working, without a lot of unproductive competition.

"Saturday and Sunday are Amateur Nights. We don't do a Feature those nights either," I said and heard Cal sniffle softly in the background. "But I'll tell you what."

"Yeah, boss man?" Bruno said.

"I'll let you and Cal have top billing Saturday and Sunday. You can host the Amateur contests and dance between their sets. I'll make sure Anton schedules each of you for your own feature-weekends later. How's that?"

Bruno grunted; even his grunts were seductive. The man exuded a sexual power that drew the customers to him like few other dancers.

Cal sniffled and hiccupped which I took for agreement.

I knew they were happy, they just had different ways of displaying it – after a while you get to know your guys well. They're great at hiding things from an audience – even though they bare it all for a living. But privately, when they get to know and trust you, there's little they can hide or want to. With all my own trust issues, lots of people had no trouble trusting me and I never violated that confidence. Having people trust me was paramount. It ranked right up there with loyalty. In the stripper troupe, trust was all there was at times. The guys had to confide in someone and they knew they could count on me. I was something between a house mother and on-scene psychologist. They came to me with all their problems. It was nice being needed.

"Great," Anton said. "In fact, Marco, you and I will work on that schedule now. Right?" Anton raised one eyebrow, a trick I'd never mastered.

"Yeah, sure. We can work it out right now." I agreed. Anton hated handling diva moments. I knew my office was going to feel a lot smaller once he got started in on how I needed to manage the group better.

Anton moved to the door. Holding it open for me, he said, "After you, boss." I didn't like the way he emphasized the word 'boss.'

He unlocked my office and held the door for me again. I was in for a lecture.

"Well," he said, leaning on the door, leaving me no escape. "Quick thinking, Marco. Even I have to admire that. But you weren't here when it all hit the fan. I was. I had to listen to Cal whine and Bruno rumble like an old car."

"I'm sorry... really." I moved closer to him, which wasn't saying much since the office was like a sardine can made for two. "How can I make it up to you? Tell me what I can do." I took him in my arms and was about to kiss him.

"Here's what you can do," Anton said, not pulling away, but not accepting the kiss, either. "Promote me to Manager."

"Of the whole shebang?" I was taken aback. Anton was good but I wasn't about to give up complete control of StripGuyz.

"No, tiger." Anton said and stroked my cheek with one long finger. "Just of deciding schedules and features. That way, I won't have to call you for every little thing. We won't have to have auditions when we didn't plan to. And you won't be allowed to make promises you can't keep. Sound fair?"

I had to admit it was fair. It would take a lot off my back. Anton liked keeping things orderly. Not that I ran a sloppy show. I just had a different management style, kinder and gentler, you might say. After working with some of the low life types I met in my investigative work, dealing with my strippers allowed me to indulge an entirely different side of my personality.

"Sure, it sounds fair. But I can't promise I won't interfere once in a while." I laughed. Pulling him tighter to me I nuzzled his neck and savored the clean fragrance of his flesh.

"But…," he moaned, a small guttural sound filled with longing. Then he caught himself and cleared his throat. "But not often. Promise?"

"Promise," I said and made my smartest Boy Scout salute.

He pecked me on the cheek, pulled away, and opened the door.

"What? You're going?"

"Why? Is there more to discuss?" He was all business now.

"I thought maybe we could have dinner?"

"I've got a lot to do before the show tonight." He was almost out the door when he turned. "Give me the list of guys who want to audition. I'll call them. Curtain's up in three hours."

"Sure. I told them we'd call when we were ready."

I wanted Anton in my arms but he had his rules and even my saddest puppy-dog look wouldn't have made a difference.

We stood awkwardly outside my office, me wanting to hold him and cover him in kisses and me wanting to pull back and tell myself to slow down. It was tough being me.

Before I could move, Ty rushed up the stairs, his face drained of color.

"There's been a shooting. On Camac. Some guy was killed…" Ty was breathing hard and sat down on the top step. "This is crazy. That's the way I go home every night. It coulda been me. Shot dead on the street."

Chapter 2

Taking a left turn out of Bubbles, I headed for Camac. Twilight had darkened the sky and a sad, cold breeze blew papers down the street. October ushers in the dark months and melancholy. Too many memories associated with that month for me. Not all of them good.

The shooting focused my mind. Shootings aren't common in the gayborhood so I had more than a professional interest in seeing what had occurred. I hoped it wasn't someone I knew.

The streets were calm. The nippy air had people wearing jackets but there are always those few guys who insist on wearing shorts until their legs turn blue. No one seemed in a hurry, no one seemed disturbed at all. I don't know what I expected, people running around screaming? Probably most of them didn't even know anything had happened, let alone a murder. There were guys strolling while holding hands as if the world would never end. Singles on the prowl. Ragged, drug-ravaged hustlers trolling for hungry men. A typical night.

Jane and Dierdre, a couple who lived in my condo building, were sitting at a crowded outdoor café and waved as I rushed by. I smiled without stopping. They know me well and probably figured I was on a case.

There was such an air of calm and order that I wondered if Ty had been mistaken. Nothing seemed unusual. Until I reached Camac Street south of Cypress.

The red, blue, and white flashing lights of a police car blocking the other end of the street signaled trouble. Police officers and a small knot of people gathered where I stood. Camac is a small street – in Philadelphia we call it a street, in some places it might be called a back alley. It was never well traveled.

Except for tonight. It teemed with people. CSIs literally crawled around searching for evidence. Cops, detectives, people I assumed were witnesses, and onlookers made the normally quiet street a mini Times Square.

Ronnie Larkin, a familiar face, stood guard near the yellow tape roping off the crime scene. She and I went back a long time, since before my abortive attempt to join the force. She'd become a cop and had encouraged me to join. Things didn't work out but we'd remained friends and drinking buddies. I could always count on her when I needed information not easily squeezed out of other "friends" in the ranks.

"Hey, Ronnie." I kept my voice appropriately low.

"Fontana." She ducked her head in salute.

Behind her, by the light of street lamps, I saw a man, sprawled on the cobblestones. Dark blood pooled around the corpse and had filled the gaps between the paving stones. The guy was face down and a CSI probed around, picking up trace evidence, taking photos, before turning the body over.

"What happened, Ronnie? Any witnesses?"

"Mugging. Overheard a witness say a guy with a gun runs up to the victim, shouts something, takes the vic's bag. Then he opens up, puts three rounds into him, and runs away."

"Just like that?"

"Flash of an eye. The vic was walking with a friend. Friend says they were going to dinner at the Venture. Then this guy runs up and pops the man. Are you, like, an ambulance chaser now, Fontana? Need cases that bad?"

"I'll ignore that, Ronnie." I smiled. "He shot without the other guy struggling? He took the guy's bag? That was it? Didn't even try to shoot the friend?"

"I'm just on crowd control. They tell me nothing. For all I know, he coulda tried to shoot them both. Maybe somethin' scared him off before he could. I didn't hear everything. I don't even know who the vic is... was." She winced. She was still the Ronnie I knew from way back, tough but compassionate.

"If you hear anything, let me know, will you Ronnie?"

"Sure thing, Marco. You got a personal stake in this?"

"When it happens on your doorstep, it's kinda personal." I gave her a nod, looked over the scene once more, and left.

I wouldn't get more information right then and it wasn't my case in any event, but I liked to know things. Force of habit with me. Can't help asking questions, poking into everybody's business, picking up odd facts. You never know when some detail will come in handy. That's why so many men I've dated tell me they feel like they're being interviewed, or, grilled is more like the word they use.

My stomach grumbled reminding me I'd only eaten half a turkey sandwich for lunch. I pulled out my cell phone, forwarded office calls to the cell, and walked home.

The gayborhood gets larger every day, adding more businesses, condos, and people. A new café, HavaCup, with the cutest staff and the best muffins, was quickly becoming my place of choice for out of office experiences. Maybe their muffins only tasted good because the staff was so hot. All I knew was that I found myself there almost every day. Just across the street, a small and very chic bar, named Secrets, had taken the place of an old music store. The walls were enclosed sheet fountains which created the illusion of privacy. Secrets had dozens of spaces made for that private tête á tête with a special guy. Observers could see only shadows and outlines. Very sexy.

You never knew who or what you'd find in the gayborhood.

I'd managed to get a condo close to it all, in Lyric House which made living in the city very easy. The building was like a small town with about eight hundred condos and who knows how many people? The residents were amazingly varied, from the outgoing and pushy to the solitary and rude. I guess I fell somewhere in between. Except for the rude part.

The automatic doors whisked me in and I saw people chatting in the marble-clad lobby, Nosy Rosie at the center of the group as usual. She was a gossip magnet and I'd even thought about hiring her to ferret out information, except she couldn't keep anything to herself. I passed her without being seen. Rosie was too busy finding out details of Mrs. Cooperman's surgery to notice me.

Carlos was on the desk. Dark and sultry, Carlos loved kidding the denizens of Lyric House. Teasing with his natural good looks, his intense eyes, and his broad smile. Even on my glummest days, he lifted my spirits. Of course, he could lift my spirits in more ways than one if he wanted to.

"Marco! You on a case, man?"

"Always on a case, Carlos." I laughed wondering if he knew I'd love to be on his case. Even though he was a flirt, he gave all the signs of being straight. Oh well, someone had to do it.

The elevator zipped me to the forty-first floor. It wasn't the highest floor but damned near and the view from my balcony took my breath away every time. I turned on a few lights, put a Lean Starts dinner into the microwave, and flipped on the radio. All news, all the time. Not a bad thing while nuking food. I'd gotten a lot of leads over the years, listening to them drone on.

"At the top of the hour, we have word the hostage situation at Hopewell Mall in New Jersey has been resolved peacefully. KYW will bring you the police briefing live. Philadelphia returns to normal after the fifteen day transit strike and Andrea Fitchell will have that story. Talks to discuss parochial school closings are set between Mayor Stroupe and Cardinal Galante. After months of speculation, a list of inner city Catholic school closings has been announced. The Mayor hopes to reduce that list. Cardinal Galante, a leading voice in the Roman Catholic Church, still recovering from double knee replacement surgery, offered no comment on Archdiocesan plans. In other news, authorities have uncovered an identity theft ring on Rittenhouse Square. Arrests have been made. But the hour's top story is the murder of local author Helmut Brandt. Witnesses say an armed man confronted Brandt as he and a companion strolled down a quiet center city street. The assailant then fled on foot. Brandt, author of Vatican Betrayal: The Death of John Paul the First, was returning from a book signing at Giovanni's Room, a gay and lesbian bookstore. The author, a noted gay pundit and activist, revealed plans for a new book in which he claimed there would be further information on the death of the one they call the Thirty Day Pope. Police released no further information on Brandt or the assailant who is still at large."

I could hardly believe what I'd heard. The microwave bell dinged but I didn't move. This had to be some kind of mistake. I'd just talked to Brandt and pegged him as a paranoid nut. This had to be a coincidence. And maybe I was going to be elected the next pope. How many times does a guy tell you he's going to be murdered and then actually turns up dead and it's a coincidence? The answer is none. I'd have to look into this case, if only for my own satisfaction.

I pulled my dinner from the microwave and set it on the table. Closing my eyes for a moment, I took a deep breath. I had the rest of the night to get through and the day already seemed a week long. Staring at the meager portion of what Lean Starts laughingly calls roast pork, I lost my appetite. It looked like cardboard cut to simulate meat and the tiny serving of vegetables resembled bits of brightly colored rubber. I looked out the sliding glass doors dominating one wall of my apartment. The eastern quarter of the city was splayed before me, thousands of lights glimmered in the October darkness. The air was clear, bringing things into sharper focus. Lights twinkled and shone making it seem nothing could be wrong in the world. I knew different. Beneath the glistening surface, cruel things happened. Was it human nature to want things so much you'd kill to have them, to hate others so deeply you'd trample on anyone to insure your superiority? In my investigative work, I dealt with the consequences of that behavior and it was never pretty. Still, what I've seen and the people I've worked with never spoiled the view from my lofty floor. That's just the way the world is, lots of glitter and tinsel hiding slimy imperfections. It's one reason I do what I do.

As I contemplated a forkful of pork, my cell phone rang. I didn't recognize the number and almost didn't answer. Then I remembered the new LCD television I wanted and snapped open the phone.

"Fontana."

"Mr. Fontana? The detective?" The unfamiliar voice sounded tired, beaten down.

"Yes."

"I... I need your help. My partner... he...." His voice caught in his throat and he struggled to keep from crying.

"It'll be all right, whatever you have to tell me, go ahead, Mr....?"

He fought to regain control. Probably another wayward lover. Like I needed one more of those cases. Why did people do these things to one another? Why did people bother to make a commitment if they didn't feel deep down they could keep their end of the bargain? And Anton wondered why I avoided committing to him.

"You OK?" I asked when I heard him clear his throat.

"I'm... I'll be all right. Please pardon me, Mr. Fontana. It's all so terrible and ...," he struggled again but took control quickly this time. "I always feared something like this would happen. And now it has."

"Relationships can be difficult even at the best of times. What's your partner done? How can I help?"

"No, Mr. Fontana, you misunderstand. My partner is dead. He was murdered."

"Murdered?"

"I'm certain of it."

"First you've got to call the police. There's no question. I can't do anything for you until... Let's start with your name."

"The police know all about it. They say they're working on the case. But I know that isn't true. There are so many murders in the city, what's one more mugging? No, I don't think they're working on it. Nor do they intend to."

"But, they consider the case open?"

"I suppose. But for how long? I need someone like you to look into this for me. I can pay, if that's what concerns you."

"Not exactly. Give me some time to check with the police. I'll need some information from you. Then I'll see what they have."

"When?"

"As soon as I can. Probably tomorrow," I said. I'd check with Ronnie and others who could get me up to speed. But they wouldn't be happy about a shadow investigation if they thought they had a chance to make the collar.

"Time is of the essence in these cases. Isn't that what they always say?"

"That's true. I'll do what I can." I promised. The poor guy sounded unhinged. I sympathized with him. I've lost people in my life and loss can do dirty things to your mind. It's never fair. Never.

"There are things you should know, Mr. Fontana. You should know them now. Before you contact the police. It's more urgent than you think." He sounded stronger, more serious, less off balance.

"Why so urgent, Mr.... um?" I realized he still hadn't told me his name.

"Hollister. My name is Timothy Hollister," he said. The name rang a very tiny bell way at the back of my consciousness. But I couldn't pull up the details. "My partner is... was Helmut Brandt. We must meet tonight, Mr. Fontana. "

When I could pick my jaw up off the ground I agreed to meet with him in an hour.

Chapter 3

Finishing dinner was next to impossible. Not just because it tasted like soggy cardboard. Hunger was displaced by curiosity about Hollister and the call I'd received earlier in the day from Brandt.

I poked at the faux meal. It was bad enough forcing myself to eat nuked food "fresh" from the microwave. Having to do it after it'd gotten cold was downright masochistic. Counting calories was crucial, though. Managing a troupe of strippers gave me the incentive to keep my thirty-two year-old body looking good. The boss can't look worse than his guys. If I do say so myself, my body keeps up just fine.

After tossing out the plastic tray, I dashed out the door. I needed to get to my office before Hollister. I intended to look authoritative and in charge.

My office building, if you could call it that, had been someone's elegant home more than a century before. Now, it was a sad-looking pile of brick, housing offices and apartments on four floors. Late Nite Videos occupied the ground floor and contained the world's largest collection of gay films. Drew, the twenty-eight year old owner, was a geek but I liked the intelligent look. His shy, self-effacing manner was engaging. Drew also kept an eye out for whatever seemed unusual in the neighborhood. I'd gotten a few leads from him.

As I went by I noticed him rearranging shelves, arms filled with DVD cases.

I took the stairs two at a time. The wooden stairs creaked and sighed as I bounced from one step to another. I heard a TV blaring news as I passed the floor with two of the apartments. The fragrance of cabbage and curry and something I couldn't name wafted up the stairs as I reached the top. Fontana Investigations took up the small fourth floor. The reception area, my office, and my private quarters which held file cabinets, a cot, and whatever I'd need if I had to stay in the office for a while.

Outside a siren blared as an emergency vehicle tore down the street. The sound grew smaller allowing an eerie silence to settled in around me. I unlocked the office door, flicked on the lights, and walked through the reception area. Without Olga, a spark was missing. She brought the place to life. Unlocking the door to my office, I headed for my desk, sat down, and waited. Olga had left a pile of messages for me but I pushed them aside. I needed to do some background research online before Hollister arrived. I wanted whatever I could find on Brandt and his work.

I could only imagine what Hollister was going through. Seeing someone you love gunned down in front of you had to be crushing. That's one reason I wanted to meet the guy and let him get things off his chest. Probably no one else wanted to listen.

It was that way for me when Galen disappeared. After a while, people didn't want to hear how I felt. They just wanted to forget and they wanted me to put it behind me so that they could forget. People aren't good at dealing with emotional pain, especially if it isn't their pain. I was only twenty-seven and didn't realize just how uneasy people are when it comes to dealing with other people's suffering.

Maybe my friends didn't get it about me and Galen. We weren't lovers but we were closer than lovers ever could be. Galen was more than family to me and when he disappeared, I was lost. No one understood. They certainly couldn't fathom that I still needed to find out what happened to him.

I glanced at my digital clock, the one with numbers the size of a Times Square marquee, one of Olga's touches, and realized Hollister was overdue. I considered how long I should wait.

Just as I'd decided he wasn't coming, I heard the elevator creaking its way to the fourth floor. That elevator was the only modern thing about the building, other than heat and electricity. And it was none too modern, which is why I usually opted for the stairs. The creaking stopped and the door rumbled open. Then the soft padding of feet. I saw a man standing at the outer door.

"Mr. Hollister? C'mon in." I called to him.

The man strode into the room with the casual air of someone who had money and no worries. Tall and aristocratic, his age, evident in white hair and wrinkles, did not affect his ramrod posture. And that face – at once tainted with arrogance and pain.

"Mr. Fontana? I'm Timothy Hollister." He extended a pale white hand which, when I shook it, was dry as dust and nearly translucent.

All of a sudden it came to me. I knew who he was. Long ago, when the gay movement was still in the streets and I wasn't born yet, this guy had been a priest fighting for the rights of gays and lesbians in the Church. But the Catholic pooh-bahs were having none of it. They tried silencing him but he became more militant. Eventually Hollister came out, was kicked out of the priesthood, and became instrumental in Dignity, the organization for gay Catholics.

Mine was a different view of the Catholic Church. Italians are more practical when it comes to religion. They follow to a point. When religion gets in the way, oops! Time for confession. And I do think there's something to the old proverb, "Familiarity breeds contempt." The Pope lives smack in the middle of Rome. Being that up close to the man, Italians have a more nonchalant approach toward him and his organization. Sure there are plenty of old ladies dressed in black, shedding tears when a pope dies, but Italy is loaded with actresses who never made it to the right stage. The world is their theater.

That Italian attitude was part of me. I could never take their rules and regs seriously. Though I parted company with the institutional Church, I retained an inner spirituality. I still had a fondness for all the incense, chant, and Vatican intrigue. And I knew how much it all meant to my older relatives.

When I came out, the approval of the Church was the furthest thing from my mind. Even if I wanted the Church to change, I never wanted back in.

But Dignity and Hollister did want the Church to accept them. I left the closet behind more than twenty years after Dignity got started and those guys were still doing their imitation of a battering ram using their own heads. When I learned about this group of gay men and lesbians pounding their collective skull against the doors of Mother Church, I was turned off. I mean, if an institution hates you and doesn't want you around, how pathetic is it to keep begging to be let into the party? As far as I was concerned, Dignity and Hollister kept fighting a losing battle.

As I watched the elegant Hollister, former priest, current activist, and bereaved lover, a wave of mixed feelings hit me. I smiled and shook his hand.

"Nice to meet you, sir. You're something of a legend, aren't you?" Flattery never hurts, but I meant it. Whatever I thought of him and his efforts, he was a legend. He'd been brave to come out when he did, forsaking everything he'd ever wanted. Now, he was broken, alone, and in need of help. My help. "Please accept my deepest sympathy. I know those words don't change anything for you, but…"

"Thank you, Mr. Fontana. I don't feel legendary and words do change things. They got Helmut killed." His voice was hoarse. He cleared his throat but it took him a while to regain his composure.

"Are you… all right?" I kept my own emotions in check.

"I've never felt uncomfortable in this neighborhood. It's been our home for years," he said. "We've lived here so long. But now…"

"It's understandable after what you've experienced." I shook my head. Hell, I didn't know if I could get over something like that happening right where I lived.

"You're right, of course. But now everything feels sinister, threatening. Every face I see looks as though it harbors some evil plan."

"A normal reaction. It's all too fresh."

"Yes, yes. I suppose it's so. Still, coming here it felt like I was under everyone's scrutiny. It was as if someone were following me." He held up a hand to stop anything I might be going to say. "I know. I know. It's all in my mind. Logically I understand that. After what happened..." He bowed his head and kept silent for a moment.

"Do you think maybe you want to wait a few days before we talk about this?"

"If you think I'm in shock, you're right, Mr. Fontana. If you think shock has clouded my cognitive powers, you're wrong. I've been through a lot of things in my life. This might be the worst but it's times like these when I've found I need to do something," he paused. "Besides, there are things you should know. Before any more time passes, before anything else happens. In fact, I know Helmut would insist we speak tonight."

"I received a call from him this morning. He wanted to talk."

"I was there when he called you. There's little that we don't share." Hollister paused. He seemed to drift away on some thoughts. If I had to guess, I'd say those thoughts were about what his life had been like with Helmut. And what it might be like from here on out. "Of course, sometimes Helmut thought he was protecting me by not telling me every detail. But it was I who should have been more protective. I shouldn't have gotten him started down this path."

"How long were you two together?"

"Quite a while," he said, a wistful smile crossed his lips. "Helmut was considerably younger than I. A source of jokes for some, I'm sure. But his affection was genuine. After all, an ex-priest has little to offer someone in the way of money, prestige, or most anything else."

"How old was he? I don't think they mentioned that in the reports."

"You're really asking how old I am. I won't be coy, though an aging gay man has little currency in the community unless he has real currency in the bank. Wouldn't you say?"

"I'm sure Helmut didn't feel that way about you."

"You're right, Mr. Fontana, but he was a different kind of man in many ways. I'm eighty. Helmut was a baby, just forty-five. But here I sit and there he is in the morgue." He heaved a deep shuddering sigh and looked up at me. The expression on his aristocratic, gray-complexioned face made it appear that he could take no more. But he sat up straighter.

"Life never seems fair," I mumbled. How many times had I reminded myself of that? When Galen left, when my closest friend on the force was killed. The list just grew. Life never worked out to being fair, it was just life. I sometimes felt like a lab rat running a maze, wondering what the hell I was doing.

"Life had been quite decent up until today," he said. "All things considered, I'd been luckier than most. I guess you could say life was more than fair to me. I had the luxury of making choices. I chose to come out. I chose to leave the priesthood. I chose to live by what I believed. Being able to make your own choices and live your beliefs, that makes life appear pretty fair." He looked at me with those watery blue eyes and I saw tears glistening at the edges. "Then I met Helmut. That was fifteen years ago, he was thirty and I..., well, you can't deny that life was being fair to me then. More than fair. What's more he even loved me. The poor boy. He loved me and I couldn't understand any of it."

"Fifteen years is a long time. He must have loved you very much."

"The irony is that maybe... I don't know... maybe I got him killed. Indirectly. But ultimately it was my fault." He looked at the floor.

"The police say it was a random mugging. You can't blame yourself. You could never have known." I watched him try to compose himself. He was like a rag doll with all the stuffing pulled out. Slowly he sat up straight and peered at me.

His eyes were different, more focused, more intense.

"It wasn't a mugging. It was an assassination. His work shed light into dark corners. He had to be stopped. That's what one of the callers said. He had to be stopped."

"There were actual threats?" I hadn't quite believed Brandt when he'd called. "Didn't you call the police?"

"What would they have done? Exactly nothing. We'd called them before but they treated us as if we were insane or paranoid. Those threats made me regret I ever got him started on that project. The calls weren't the only thing. Church leaders condemned his work. Tom Quinn, another writer, claimed he'd been working on the same idea for years. Even Opus Dei weighed in on Helmut's book. And I started it all."

"Sounds like a real tangle," I said. I knew the guy was grief stricken, but Opus Dei? He'd read one too many thrillers. I resolved not to judge the guy until I'd heard him out. "How did all this begin? What made it so dangerous?"

"All right, Mr. Fontana," he said and cleared his throat as if getting ready to begin a long story. "Everything I tell you will be placing you in danger as well." He looked at me as if there were spies everywhere.

"Call me Marco. If we'll be working together, we can skip the formalities."

"Does this mean you'll look into the matter for me?"

"I said 'if.' Let me hear more and see where it leads. I won't take your money if I don't think there's anything to be discovered." I was mostly convinced I'd discover this guy was a conspiracy nut.

"I appreciate your honesty. Hear me out, then, and see what you think."

"My time is yours, Mr. Hollister. At least for the next hour or so." I'd have to get over to Bubbles at some point. I never knew when something crazy would happen making it necessary for me to get on stage and finish the show. Not that I wouldn't draw a crowd. I had fans who wanted to see me dance. But I wasn't ready to become known as 'the Naked P.I.' just yet.

"You'll have what you need by then," Hollister said and resettled himself in the chair. "When Helmut and I met, he was already a rather successful, widely known journalist. For a man of thirty that was something. He was a young gay man with a unique perspective, willing to talk about things no one else would touch. That opened a lot of doors. He was featured in a number of prominent publications, The New Yorker, Atlantic Monthly, you know the list. Then he wrote his critique of the gay obsession with youth and muscle and became a talk show regular. Throwaway Men was a bestseller that kept him in the public eye."

"It was on the lists for quite a while, if memory serves." I remembered Brandt more clearly now. When his book came out I was nineteen or twenty and not long out of the closet. I'd bought the book at Giovanni's Room because I thought the author was cute when I saw his picture on the dustjacket. Never did get around to reading it. But I did see Brandt when he had a reading at Giovanni's Room. He was cuter than his picture. His looks coupled with his astonishing achievements had me tangled in attraction and awe. That had been more than ten years ago. I was young and starstruck back then so almost everything gay impressed me for a while.

Brandt came rushing back into memory and I felt a twinge of sadness for that intelligent pretty boy. Literary superstar. Heartthrob. Victim. His murder felt more personal now.

"Yes, it was on the lists for a while. But the celebrity never went to his head. That's just the way Helmut is." Hollister stopped himself, probably remembering that "was" would be a word he'd have to get used to from now on when it came to Helmut. "He wanted to do good things with his money and fame. That's when I stupidly made the suggestion that ultimately got him killed."

"And that was what, exactly?" I asked.

"I encouraged him to write a book on the murder of Pope John Paul the First." He sighed.

"Surely he wouldn't have done this just because you said so? He was a prominent person by then, a celebrity in his own right."

"No, no. Of course not. Helmut was born in Munich and had been raised a Catholic. Bavaria is the Catholic stronghold in Germany, you know, and that was his home during his formative years. He grew away from Catholicism but Church workings and politics still engaged him. When we met, the fact that I'd been a priest fascinated him. He wanted to know everything. Wanted to help me in my work with Dignity." Hollister looked me in the eye. "I filled him with stories of my priestly life, of my training in Rome, how I hobnobbed with some of the big guns of the Roman Catholic hierarchy." His eyes got that teary look again and I imagined that his past was rushing through his mind. Faces, places, sounds, and sights.

"It all seems innocent enough," I commented when he remained too long lost in thought.

"You might think that. But for all his fascination with the Church, Helmut had a burning anger over the Church's treatment of homosexuals. He could never forgive them for what they'd done over the years and for what they continued to do and refused to do."

"I don't see how this could have..."

"Gotten him killed? There's more to the story. There's always more, isn't there? When I told Helmut about Albino, that's when I saw the fire grow in him. I realized then, that I'd started something I'd never be able to control. Albino Luciani became Pope John Paul the First, as you no doubt know. Telling Helmut that I'd known the man, and what I knew about him, well, that's what put Helmut on the road that led him to his death."

Hollister took a deep breath.

"You actually knew the Pope?"

"Not when he was the Pope, of course, but before that. Long before that. I knew him and knew what kind of man he was. I told Helmut everything. It came spilling out after all those years. Perhaps because Helmut was so intrigued and such a willing listener. Maybe because it was all I could offer the boy. I had little else but who I had been. Albino's beliefs were compelling and out of the conservative mainstream. When I told Helmut what Albino had said about the Church's treatment of women and homosexuals, that it was abysmal and beneath contempt, Helmut was incredulous. He couldn't believe anyone so highly placed in the Church could hold such views. But it was true. Albino intended to change a lot of things if he ever had the chance."

"He almost did, didn't he?" I said. I'd never known that much about the man. He was just one of those sympathetic figures. Every time I saw his picture I couldn't help feeling sorry for him, thinking how he must have been stunned by his election to the papacy. Elated by the sudden ability to do things he'd only dreamed about. And then he was gone.

"Almost. But they wouldn't let him get anywhere." Hollister said 'they' with startling vehemence. "They killed him as surely as I'm sitting here. I knew people back then. People who knew things, people who knew others. In Italy, many things depend on knowing someone who knows someone. It's the way it's been since before Augustus rebuilt Rome. But I did know people who knew the truth of what went on inside those walls. And they knew Albino was murdered."

"There've been a lot of theories," I said. I didn't want to insult the guy but conspiracy theories were as common as pasta in Italy. "But I don't think there's been any hard evidence. At least that's what I've been led to believe."

"Along with everyone else. That's what Helmut intended to correct. He wanted to provide hard, incontrovertible evidence. I gave him all my old contacts in Rome, anyone who knew anything. Helmut was relentless in his pursuit of the truth."

"I've searched out reviews and they said there wasn't anything new in his book. Certainly no solid evidence." I hated having to say that but it was the truth.

"Vatican Betrayal was his opening salvo, that's how he thought of it. At that time, he hadn't yet obtained the unassailable proof he sought. He was a consummate journalist, though, and knew the value of publicity, of keeping a story in the arena of discussion and speculation. So he produced Vatican Betrayal as a sort of prologue. I think he also wanted to see just what his earlier book would bring out into the open. He continued to dig for new, more serious evidence. Eventually he claimed he'd found previously undiscovered documents. This new work was what got him killed. I'm sure of it. I trust my feelings. I always have."

"It all sounds intriguing, Mr. Hollister. But you haven't given me a lot of solid information so far. On the surface it appears there's some connection to Helmut's death. But I'll need more if I'm going to try and get to the truth."

"I'm sure you've seen people killed for less. I assure you, there's more. The new documents, for one thing. He kept hinting that his new work would have some startling revelations. I don't doubt he was telling the truth."

"You have those documents? Or anything that gives someone a motive for murder? Something that connects his work to his death?"

"Helmut has a laptop filled with information. But he keeps that out of sight and hidden, away from the house. He doesn't have much in the way of paper files. Some old clippings, drafts of old works, nothing sensitive or secret. His workplace was sacrosanct. I never entered that room, never used his computer, or looked through his files."

"So you don't know for certain there was anything real in the way of documents? Anything that added more weight to what he'd been claiming?"

"That's just it. He said he had something new. Secret documents. He'd just returned from Rome and told me about information that had been kept hidden for thirty years. But he was never specific. I suppose he thought he was protecting me. When it was he who needed protection."

"I see." Having those documents would help me determine a few things for myself. "Is there any chance I could get a look at his files and computer?"

Before Hollister could answer, the phone rang. I noticed the caller ID screaming Anton's number. I was tempted to answer but I hated interrupting meetings to take calls.

"I'll let it go to voicemail. As I was saying, is there a way I can…"

The phone stopped ringing, then started again. Anton's number appeared.

"Hold on, Mr. Hollister. I apologize." I picked up the receiver.

"Marco?! Is that you?" someone other than Anton said.

"Who is this?"

"Anton needs you! Somethin' weird is goin' on here."

Chapter 4

Whoever had used Anton's phone to call me made my already overactive imagination kick into high gear.

"I know there's more you wanted to tell me, Mr. Hollister," I said as I ushered him to the elevator. "We'll talk when I come by in the morning to see Helmut's work." My thoughts were really on Anton and whatever was going on at Bubbles.

"Call around nine, earlier if you like." Hollister shook his head. "It's all unreal. This isn't happening. Is it, Mr. Fontana?"

His question was so child-like I wanted to cry. I knew how he felt. None of it seems real. Not even when you're standing over that hole in the ground and they're shoveling dirt over someone you've cared about. Reality takes a lot longer to get used to.

"You need rest and you probably haven't eaten anything. Get a meal and get some sleep. Nothing will seem real for a long time."

"You'll call in the morning?" Hollister pulled his jacket tighter around his thin chest as we walked together.

"It's a promise." We approached Bubbles and I wondered when he'd peel off. "There's a great café in Bubbles – in case you wanna take my advice and eat something."

"A friend called earlier about having something to eat. I think I'll take him up on it. I don't want to face an empty house. Helmut was the life of the place. I'm too old to pretend he's away on one of his trips. I'm too old to pretend anything." He pulled a cell phone from his jacket pocket. Waving goodbye, he sadly tapped a number into his phone. He looked alone and wretched.

Hollister's sad figure stirred up an image of Helmut Brandt. A hazy memory from long ago of a beautiful young man, with a rich accented voice and compelling enthusiasm. Brandt had seemed to me like some kind of gay, journalistic demi-god. The feelings I'd experienced back then still echoed and I felt that sense of loss I always get when remembering the past.

Hollister's presence reminded me of that past. Even if he was a conspiracy nut, he deserved an answer to his questions.

Kevin, the bouncer at Bubbles, was tall and burly. Bouncers never seem to come in any other package. But Kevin's appearance was deceptive.

"Marco." He lifted a hand in salute. "When am I gonna MC one of your shows?" Kevin winked, subtly folding down his shirt lapel to reveal a lacy, pink undergarment. Beneath all the brawn, Kevin was a drag queen ready to strut. "Or, have you forgotten me?"

"How could I forget? But Anton handles scheduling now. I'll remind him I promised you a night." Kevin, or, as he was known when in drag, Germaine Shepherd, had been dying to MC our Top Cheeks night, a best buns competition that a drag queen always hosted.

"Promises! Men are all alike." Kevin smiled, then Germaine blew me a kiss.

It was after nine and Bubbles was crowded. Not unusual for Friday nights but it seemed louder, more frantic. I waded through the sea of men, bumping here and touching there. I flinched when someone goosed me. When I turned around, everyone looked innocent and engaged in conversation or cruising.

I hiked up to the second floor. Whatever was happening in the dressing room hadn't spilled over into the bar. Happy voices floated up from the bar. But tension filled the hall ahead. It was purposely dimly lit – so as not to encourage customers to "explore" the terrain. Tonight the hall was filled with guys – my guys. My Friday night strippers. There were fifteen or more standing around in their thongs, one or two were bare as babies. Some paced back and forth, their sculpted bodies tense. Angry looks darkened their faces. Phoenix, the softest, most vulnerable of my dancers, hugged himself in a corner while Nick stood by the dressing room door clenching his fists. As I got closer the tension raged, then it was like a dam broke.

"Marco!" Trey approached me. "This isn't good, dude."

The guys crowded around grumbling, swearing, and shivering without their clothes. I noticed with relief that no one was hurt.

"What's happening? Fill me in."

"Marco, I'm so glad you're here. It's awful. They're in there." Phoenix threw his arms around me. I gently peeled him off.

"Who's where? What's happening?" I asked.

"Anton and Nando…" Trey started.

"And that other guy!" Nick spat out the words.

"He's got our clothes and costumes," Phoenix complained.

"Whoa. What other guy? Who is he? Who let him in? How did this happen?"

"Nando's ex," explained Trey. "He came begging Nando to get back together. But Nando didn't want to hear anything. I told the guy to get lost."

"I remember him. Didn't look dangerous to me," I said nonchalantly, wanting to keep them calm. Dancers are high strung and, especially before they're about to go onstage, they're always jumpy. The least thing could throw them off and ruin their mood. Which would have a domino effect – ruined mood, bad performance, low tips, depressed dancers, more ruined moods. I couldn't have that.

Nando's ex was a cute, love-sick, puppy of a guy, who'd been haunting the place on nights when Nando danced. He'd just stand at the back and stare. Once I noticed him crying. Sometimes he'd sit at the bar and silently stuff Nando's g-string full of dollar bills. Nando took the cash, no fool Nando, and kept moving.

I'd thought he was harmless since Nando never complained.

"What're you gonna do Marco? I'm standin' here balls in the wind. Get me in there and I'll fuck him up. He's got all my stuff," Strider said. He didn't mind being naked in public, that much was clear. But he couldn't go onstage like that.

"Let's see what I can do." I paused. "Anybody know if the guy is armed?"

"Armed? You mean like with a gun or something?" Phoenix always got right to the heart of the matter.

"Of course he means a gun," Nick said. "Nah, he wasn't packin' and I can tell." Nick liked playing the tough guy, claiming his roots in South Philly gave him all sorts of mob connections. But everyone knew he was a pussycat.

"He must've had something," said Phoenix. "Or why would we all be out here? One minute we're all in there getting ready to go on, the next we're out here because he came in shouting and waving his arms. Maybe he had a gun. Or a knife. Or something. Or we might not be… out… here. Would we?" Phoenix had managed to confuse even himself. Which wasn't all that difficult.

"Okay, I'm going in. I'll take care of this," I said. If that guy wasn't carrying, I was. I never knew what would come up.

I pulled the door open and the guys behind me craned their necks to get a peek. I slipped in quickly and shut the door.

The room was stuffy and smelled of sweat, fear, and cosmetics. Anton sat in a chair off to the side, his hands propped on his head as if he'd been told to keep them in sight. Nando and Zegg, naked as plucked chickens, hugged each other as they huddled in a corner near Anton. All of them were chalky white and looked ready to faint.

On the other side of the room stood the source of their fear. "The guy" as everyone outside called him, braced himself against a table, gun in hand, tortured expression on his face. Short, smooth-faced, dark-haired, his intense eyes were filled with despair.

"Marco!" Anton sounded relieved.

The guy whipped around to look at me.

"You! You took Nando away from me." His gaze shifted from me to Nando and back to me. He kept us all at bay with his gun. All I noticed was his face – the picture of a man in a lot of pain.

I said nothing.

"Tell Nando to come back to me. Tell him this kind of life's no good for him." The poor guy was a mess, dark circles under his eyes, hair like a fright wig, and clothes that looked as if he'd left them in the dryer too long. He was a walking wrinkle.

"What's your name?" In his disheveled state, he was still appealing, but even the cute ones can be crazy. Looks are no guarantee of anything. I didn't move, not wanting to spook him. "What's your name? How can I tell Nando anything if I don't know your name?" Of course, that made no sense. But I didn't suppose the guy was thinking straight anyway.

He looked confused. Whipped his head back and forth looking at us. The hand with the gun never wavered.

I inched forward while he wasn't noticing. I felt the weight of my gun in its holster but it wouldn't do me any good here so I didn't reach for it.

"C'mon, what's your name? Maybe we can all sit down and talk this out."

"K-Kent," he said. The pain in his eyes seemed to grow. "Nando and I were happy before he met you."

"Kent, right?" I waited for him to respond.

He nodded and grunted.

"Kent, listen to me. It's not gonna be long before someone calls the police and then this is all outta my hands. Right now we can keep it between us. You put that gun down, we'll talk. Wait too long and the police won't be so friendly." I inched forward. His face was a map of warring emotions.

He obviously hadn't thought about the consequences of holding people hostage. He'd hoped Nando would waltz out with him and they'd continue the happily-ever-after that existed only in his mind.

"You'll call the police anyway."

"No. No I won't." I meant it. I could keep this all under control if he'd just give up the gun. "And no one will press charges." I glanced at Anton, Nando, and Zegg. "Will you?" They all shook their heads furiously, mumbling "No. No."

Kent remained silent but I saw him relax. The pupils of his eyes, his jaw muscles, his breathing all said he was calmer. Even his grip on the gun softened.

"C'mon, Kent. Whaddaya say?" Another inch closer. "You don't really want to shoot anyone, do you?"

"N... Yes. If Nando doesn't come back, what's the use?" Kent asked. "Then..." He looked at us all with those pained brown eyes and put the gun to his head. "I don't want to live. Nando is my life. If he doesn't love me, there's no point."

See, this is why children and guns don't mix. This kid was definitely not in any emotional shape to be handling firearms.

"Kent!" My voice was sharp. I wanted to startle the little drama queen. And I did. He stiffened and held the gun on me now instead of himself.

"Don't try to stop me. I'll shoot you then I'll kill myself anyway." He kept the gun trained on me.

"I don't care one way or another if you shoot me and I care even less if you shoot yourself." I moved forward again. "What I do care about," I said, as I crept toward him, "is the mess you're gonna make for these boys and for the club."

I was almost close enough to reach out and grab the gun away. But that would have been foolhardy and stupid.

"Don't make a lot of trouble for everybody. You kill yourself, you're givin' up any chance you have of getting Nando back. I'm not saying you have a chance but if you do, being dead kinda changes your odds."

Now he looked even more confused.

"But..." He put the gun back up to his head. "Make him say he'll come back. I don't have anything but him."

"Please don't do this, Kent." Nando said in an accented voice so weak it was almost a whisper.

I looked at Nando for a moment. He shivered and held onto Zegg like a lifeline.

"You hear the pain in that voice?" I asked Kent. "If you do, you understand what I'm tellin' you about the trouble you're gonna cause."

Kent's hand trembled, he brought the gun down to point at me again.

"You took him away." Kent sounded as if all the troubles in the world were on his plate. "You filled his head with talk. About dancing and men and money."

I edged forward. I stood directly in front of Kent, the gun nearly touching my chest. I held myself as still as I could manage.

"Let it go, Kent." I slowly brought my hand up to the gun. "Let it go. Give yourself a break."

I touched Kent's hand and he flinched. His hand trembled.

"Give me the gun."

He looked into my eyes. For a moment I wasn't sure if he'd drop the gun or pull the trigger. But he relaxed and placed the gun into my hand.

I gulped in some air realizing I'd been holding my breath waiting for whatever would happen to happen. Before I said or did anything else, Kent promptly crumpled into a heap on the floor.

Nando, Zegg, and Anton rushed over to me. Nando pushed the others out of the way and stood in front of me.

"I don't believe what you juss done. You are so brave, papi. Thank you, thank you, Marco." Nando threw his arms around me, gave me a long hug, then kissed me lightly on the cheek and whispered into my ear, "You're the best, papi." He turned to look at Kent lying on the floor. "Can I... should I help him?"

"Why not?" I said. Maybe it wasn't a great idea but I sort of thought it might be good for both of them.

"Hot shit, man, you are somethin' else. Wait'll I tell everybody. Hot and heroic. I'm proud to be workin' for you," Zegg said. The tough, little blond moved toward the dressing room door.

Anton waited until Zegg threw open the door and told the others what had happened. Then Anton moved closer, wrapped his arms around me, and hugged me as if I'd been gone for a long time. I thought I heard a sniffle but maybe it was my imagination. I'd never seen Anton get emotional.

"You're stupid, Marco Fontana." Anton stood back, holding me at arm's length. "Stupid and very brave. I've never seen anything like that." He held me tightly to him again and it felt good. All the tension in my body melted away. "Maybe that's why I can't get you out of my head. You're perfect."

"Then why not take me home and tuck me in bed?" I nuzzled his neck. I felt the guys watching us. Their eyes on the boss and his second in command hugging like lovesick teenagers. "I live not far from..."

"I know where you live. And you know the answer to your question, Marco."

And well I did. Before I could say anything, Nando gasped as Kent woke up.

"I've got him, Nando." I knelt down to help Kent. "You go out there with the others. Anton will take care of everything. I looked up at Anton, who, from this angle, looked like a blond demi-god: strong, shapely, square jawed, blue eyes sparkling. I stared at him a moment. "You get them set up. I'll take care of Kent."

I bent over the kid and helped him up. He shivered and I saw his eyes fill with tears. But he held himself together and didn't cry.

"Are…are you gonna call the police?" Kent asked.

"No one got hurt. And you came to your senses. I don't need to call them. Unless you want me to?"

"No! No. Please." His voice was choked. "I'm… sorry. I was… it was crazy."

"Let's you and me have a talk. I'll buy you a drink."

"S-sure." He nodded.

"Listen to me, the boys are going to look at you as if you've got three heads. Just ignore them. You're with me. And it'll be all right."

We walked into the hall between two rows of my guys. They glanced at Kent but what surprised me was the way they looked at me. There was something like awe in their eyes. Every step I took, they moved to clear a path. They were silent. A few of them stared as if I'd burst into flame. I could get used to this kind of treatment.

I kept my arm around Kent's shoulder to guide him but mostly to keep him from bolting. I wanted to watch him for a while, make sure he was all right. I guess I wanted to see if I could help him. Anton says that's my soft spot and tells me it'll get me into big trouble some day.

I didn't really think Kent was trouble. He was just a love-sick mess. Now that I got a better, calmer look at him, I thought he might even make a nice addition to StripGuyz. Maybe he'd open up and learn a thing or two about himself while he danced for the customers. But that would come later, right now I'd have to bring him back down to earth and reality.

We were about to sit in a quiet corner of the second floor bar, when my cell phone rang.

"Fontana," I said into the phone.

"Mr. Fontana?" Hollister's voice was familiar now. But he sounded frantic. "I've got a problem, can you get here right now?"

I got Stan the owner to keep Kent with him until I could get back. As the door closed behind me I stepped into a quieter world. A place more dull and less exciting than the fantasy world inside.

But Hollister's last words, pushed me to move fast: "I think someone's broken into my house and I don't want to go in alone."

Chapter 5

Hollister's townhouse was on Latimer, a pint-sized street, studded with ginkgo trees, in the middle of a tangle of tiny streets common in downtown Philadelphia. I navigated my way there quickly.

The more I thought about the case, the more I was convinced that finding the mugger was a key to the whole thing. Brandt had angered people. He'd been threatened. And now he was dead. There are no coincidences and finding the so-called mugger would prove that.

In less than five minutes I was at the head of the street and saw Hollister standing midway down, one hand to his mouth, staring at his brightly lit house. I waved him over and watched him carefully step over the cobblestone paving and smelly ginkgo seeds, seemingly afraid to trip.

"Somebody's in there." His voice was just above a whisper. I noticed alcohol on his breath. If I were him I'd have had more than a few drinks, too, after what had happened.

"Did you see anyone?"

"All the lights are on," he said, swaying side to side. "When I… we… left this morning, we didn't turn lights on and we don't have timers. Somebody's in there."

"Wait here." I reached for my gun then eased up to the house. Sneaking a look through a window, I saw the empty living room. The place was still and quiet. Didn't mean it was empty, though.

No choice but to go in. I signaled Hollister that I was going and indicated he should hang back. Didn't really look like he'd be sprinting up in any case. He had all he could handle standing upright.

I climbed the three marble steps slowly, holding my breath. Standing to the side, just in case, I pushed at the door.

It squeaked open a crack. I pushed it all the way. Gun in hand, I entered and swept the room. No one. Cautiously moving from room to room, I cleared the place including the second floor and the basement. There wasn't a soul in the house. But it'd been tossed.

I poked my head out the door and signaled Hollister in.

"Nothing. Nobody's here." I kept my voice down but noticed a few neighbors peeking through blinds or curtains. Living on a tiny street you're everybody's business, which is bad and good. I'd canvass for witnesses.

Hollister wobbled carefully through the maze of cobblestone treachery beneath his feet. He gripped the railing and hauled himself up the steps and into the house. When he saw the mess, the look on his face told me he was sobering up real quick.

"Why would anyone do this?" He drew in a breath and a tear ran down his cheek.

I led him to a chair and sat him down. I figured he'd been holding himself together all day and this was probably his first opportunity to let go. But he just stared in stunned silence. There was no way to read what went on beneath the surface.

The place had been ransacked. Someone wanted something bad. But Brandt had been a careful guy, according to Hollister. He wouldn't leave sensitive materials around the house. If he did, they wouldn't be easy to find.

Every shelf had been emptied, books and objects lay everywhere. Some books had been ripped apart, delicate figurines had been smashed. Drawers had been pulled out and overturned. Paintings and photographs had been torn from the walls, some lay face down, their backing ripped apart, some were sliced. The kitchen was a mess of pots and pans, utensils and dishes.

I decided to give the second floor a better look.

The ancient stairs creaked. These houses had been built in colonial days. It gave me goosebumps when I moved and heard a creak or groan. Lights were on in every room. I went into what had probably been Brandt's office. It'd been torn apart worse than the rest of the place. Papers and files everywhere. There was no evidence of a laptop other than a power cord on the desk. The bedroom was just as torn up. So I headed back down.

Hollister sat where I'd left him, he looked about a hundred years old. His whole body sagged under the weight of his loss. He stared ahead as if he could see through walls.

"Mr. Hollister?" I placed a hand on his shoulder and he felt slight, almost as if nothing were there. "Mr....?"

"I want to get these... people, Mr. Fontana... I want them to pay." Hollister seemed revived by his anger.

"We'll find them, Mr. Hollister." I guessed I'd be taking the case after all, though there were still a lot of pieces missing. The ransacking might have been connected to the killing. Or, someone might've taken advantage of the tragedy to steal valuables. Thing is, I didn't like the feeling I got. Things didn't add up to a simple solution. "Let's call the police."

"No! I won't have them here. The way they treated me today. The way they brushed off Helmut's murder... No." He paused to take a breath and swipe a hand over his face. "We don't have to call them, do we?"

"Not if you don't want to. It's up to you. For insurance, a police report will be helpful."

"Insurance. They dropped us after the third time we'd reported some water damage they should have covered. So, no, I don't think I'll need a police report."

"You have someplace to stay tonight?"

"You think they'll be back?"

"No. No. I just think this is an awful mess for you to be around." Actually, I thought it was entirely possible whoever did it might come back. If they hadn't found what they were looking for, they might try beating it out of Hollister. But he didn't need to hear that. "I'll have someone come and help you clean up in the morning."

"I'd rather not be alone anyway. Give me a minute to call a friend."

* * *

Next morning, I walked to Hollister's place the long way. October mornings reminded me there would be a mad rush to the end of the year and before I knew it I'd be on vacation, standing in a bar in Ft. Lauderdale, toasting the New Year with a bunch of people I hardly knew.

As I walked, I enjoyed the bracing air, it made me more aware of my surroundings. It also cleared my mind and I needed to think about the case and review things with Luke before I talked to Hollister.

Luke was a little younger than I and a lot more successful. Owner of one of the city's largest housecleaning agencies, he'd made a fortune. There was even a group of his cleaners who did it in the buff, if the customers requested. Naturally they got loads of requests. Luke himself had started out as a cleaner, though not of the nude variety, and that's how we met.

My housekeeping skills being less than satisfactory, according to my mother, I'd figured it would be a good idea to hire a housekeeper. Even better if he'd be naked when he cleaned. When Luke showed up at my door five years before, I was caught off guard. A gorgeous Chinese man, slightly shorter than my five feet eleven, with dark hair and the darkest deepest eyes I'd ever seen. He was shapely, had a lilting smile, and a seductive manner. I could see him working for StripGuyz not cleaning houses. I was sold.

That day, five years ago, he and an assistant, cleaned house and made it look like I'd just moved in.

When my mother saw the job he'd done she said, "Che bello! Come pullito! What's his name, this cleaning guy?" When I told her, she just said, "Marry him." And not another word on the subject. If I didn't know better, I'd have thought they were collaborating since Luke made it pretty clear after a few months, that he wouldn't mind playing house permanently. He wasn't as coy as Anton about showing me just how much he wanted it.

Since then nothing has cooled off between us. Luke even helps out with investigations at times. Like this one – Hollister wanted his place put back together and I needed someone I trusted to go through the papers and give me a report. So, I'd called Luke and explained everything.

Luke brought Chip, the employee he trusted most and one I'd known a long time. Chip was a man in his seventies and no one's fool.

Anton also agreed to help out and arrived at the same time. Since I knew how that Eastern European mind worked, I realized Anton was keeping an eye on how Luke and I were getting along. His blue eyes never missed details. But that was the point, he had an eye for anything out of the ordinary which is why he often helped with cases I worked. He and Luke were both detail-oriented.

Luke knew how to put the place back together and I told them what to watch for that might help the case. Hollister hovered over them and I knew that'd have to stop. So, I took him aside.

"Can we talk somewhere away from here?"

"Don't they need me here?"

"Luke will get your place in order. Take a break. Besides, I've got lots to ask you."

Hollister nodded slowly, the dark half-moons under his eyes gave him a grave, clerical appearance. Turning, he plucked a jacket from the closet.

"Won't you be cold?" He looked me up and down.

"I'm Italian. Hot from the inside out," I joked. "I like this temperature. Keeps me alert."

"The young," Hollister said and shook his head. "You think you'll live forever. You won't, you know. No one ever does."

"The café on the corner has great coffee, but I guess you already know that."

"Actually, I never drink coffee. I'm a tea man," Hollister commented. "But we did go to the café quite often. Brandt would work on his projects, I'd read. It was always so peaceful."

"Would you rather we talked somewhere else?"

"No. I shouldn't avoid places. Anyway it might bring back those moments for me and that would be good." He breathed in the cold air and lightly thumped his chest. "You're right about the cold, Marco. It makes you feel alive."

The café was relatively empty at eight on a Saturday morning. The fragrance of fresh baked pastry filled the air and I breathed it in, trying to resist temptation. Hollister took a table at the rear and I bought us both something to drink.

"So, you'll take the case?" Hollister stirred some sugar into his tea.

"Looks that way, Mr. Hollister." I poured half and half into my coffee and tore off a piece of my croissant. It tasted like ones I remembered eating in Provence. For just a moment I was far away from Hollister and Philly and everything.

"What convinces you?"

I heard Hollister ask me the question but it was as if he were on the other end of a very sketchy connection. I sipped my coffee and the bitter flavor brought me back to the café in the gayborhood.

"I'm not saying you're right and there's some grand conspiracy. But I don't believe in coincidences. It wasn't just a mugging. There's more to it than that."

"You'll find out just how much more there is. And it won't be small."

Now he was getting all conspiracy crazy on me. I ate another piece of croissant and sipped more coffee.

"I have to ask some questions you may not like, Mr...."

"It's Tim. Now you're taking the case, just call me Tim. All this mister stuff makes me feel older than I already am."

"I've got to ask some difficult questions. They might bring back memories you'd rather not think about."

"Ask. How much more can I be hurt? They took away my life last night and then they ransacked my home. After a while, you become numb."

"The mugging..."

"The assassination, you mean."

"Did you get a good look at the shooter? Can you remember anything about his face or voice, or anything. Anything at all?"

"The man who..." Hollister closed his eyes, drew in a breath. "The man who took Helmut's life was just so ordinary. A face in the crowd. Nothing you'd remember if you spent hours standing in front of him. There was fear in his eyes. That I remember. He was a frightened man."

"No attempt to hide his face?"

"Only minimal, a cap and his jacket collar. But I could see his eyes."

"The color of his hair? His height? What he was wearing?"

"I can't remember. It was all so fast, so shocking. One minute we were laughing, the next Helmut was on the ground."

"Did the shooter say anything?"

"He asked for Helmut's bag then said Helmut had better stop what he was doing. No explanation. Just stop. Then he fired and Helmut went down. The man glanced at me and, for a second, seemed confused. The next thing I knew he was running away and people were screaming. Helmut was bleeding to death on the ground. I was lost in an ocean of silence."

"I'm sorry. Truly, Tim. I'm sorry." I placed a hand over his, it was cool and seemed unreal. Hollister appeared strangely unmoved.

"It hasn't all sunk in yet," he said. "And I'm confused."

"About what?"

"What's so important…?"

"About the shooter? If this is about Helmut's work, and that's looking pretty likely, then the mugger is important. If we're right, somebody hired the shooter and he can tell us who that was." I was convinced it was no ordinary mugging but I was still skeptical that there was a huge conspiracy behind everything.

"Ah. I see." Hollister mulled this over.

"I'm sorry you can't remember more. It would have made things a whole lot easier."

"Then, how will you find him? There were other witnesses. Maybe they can do better. Maybe they'll recall more detail."

"Let me worry about it. That's why you hired me." I looked him in the eye which seemed to reassure him. "Can you handle a few more questions?"

"I want you to find Helmut's killers. Ask what you need to ask. I'm stronger than I look, Marco."

"Last night you mentioned rivals and others."

"There are all sorts of people I can name."

"Outside of his work, who else might have wanted to hurt Helmut? Was there anyone he fought with?"

Hollister held his teacup in his hands as if gathering the warmth to himself. The man looked ragged and tired and the day had hardly begun.

"A man like Helmut, with opinions on so many things, has enemies. He had a long list. Few of them were the killing kind."

"So we all think. Let's start with the worst and work our way down. What were his most recent problems?"

"There's not going to be anything dramatic, Marco. Nobody threatened Helmut in public like in some low grade drama. There were quiet arguments. Academic struggles, I suppose. Some weren't so quiet. Religion raises hackles."

"And the worst of those with their hackles raised?" I asked, unable to help asking myself what the hell hackles were anyway.

"Tom Quinn, a writer who's doing similar work. They had a skirmish not long ago and Quinn promised to get even with Helmut. Helmut never gave it much thought."

"Did Quinn threaten Helmut physically?"

"No. He claimed he'd get even in print or he might tell Helmut's publisher some dirty little secret. Undoubtedly he'd have made something up to suit his purposes. He's a vile man."

"Others on your list?"

"There's Franny, oh, his name is really Francis Clifford but we all know him as Franny. He doesn't like people to remember what he was like when he was called "Franny." He's connected to both Opus Dei and the Archdiocese."

"Connected? How?" Again with the Opus Dei stuff. These conspiracy guys never let go when they get an idea in their heads. And they say Pit Bulls have strong jaws.

"He works for the Archdiocese. Some sort of low level functionary. As for his Opus Dei connection, he isn't publicly a member. But he sometimes has an Opus Dei boarder in his home."

"He has an Opus Dei boarder?"

"Franny lives in a large house in South Philadelphia and often has one or two boarders. I've heard he has one living there now. That kind of fits one Opus Dei pattern. Frankly, I don't understand how the man tolerates Clifford. There must be some connection there."

"And Clifford argued with Helmut recently?"

"Argued is too strong a word. Franny never argues. He just condemns with quiet words and evil glances. He met Helmut on the street and told him in so many words what he thought of his book and the harm it would do the Church."

"No threats?"

"Not so you'd notice. But Franny has his own way. He told Helmut that his new work would never see the light of day. That he would destroy Helmut's name."

"Sounds like a threat to me."

"If you knew Franny you might not think so, but with the weight of Opus Dei behind him, who knows?"

"That's the list?"

"And one Peter Wren from the Archdiocesan public relations office. He had a meeting with Helmut that turned into a screaming match. It never got violent, people like Wren never get violent on the surface. But he told Helmut that his work was damaging the moral authority of church leaders. Making them seem like conspiratorial murderers. Helmut said he'd laughed it off."

"That probably lit Wren's fuse."

"The man flew into a rage and said that Helmut would burn in hell for his work and that he, Wren, would see to it."

"Certainly sounds like a threat."

"Until you see Wren. The wizened little creature can hardly keep himself upright in a chair, let alone credibly threaten someone."

"Still. I'll want to talk with him."

"I'll keep thinking if there are others. Is that it?"

"I don't quite know how to say this." I felt the color rising in my face. I wasn't ashamed about the question, it was just bad timing.

"Then just ask. I've always found that to be the best way to do it."

"Okay, was Helmut involved intimately with anyone else? Did he have other lovers? For that matter, were you involved with anyone else?" There's nothing wrong with fooling around, in my book. Of course, Anton would have a different take on the subject.

"I suspected you'd ask that. It's no secret. We both had our dalliances. What couple who've been together so long doesn't? At least we were honest with one another." Hollister seemed defensive. Maybe he didn't feel Helmut had always been honest with him.

"I don't want details, just names. I'll need to check them out."

"If you feel that's necessary." He seemed stung.

"You can write up a list at the house. No need to dwell on it now."

* * *

Back at the house everything looked better. Luke, Anton, and Chip had gotten a lot done. Paintings on walls, drawers in their places, books on shelves. The three of them were sorting papers at the dining room table.

"You guys are miracle workers!" I said "Great work, huh?" I turned to Hollister.

He looked pleased but there was a sadness to his smile.

"Helmut would be impressed. He always said we should hire someone to do the housework."

"How's the upstairs?"

"Oh, piece of cake," Anton said. "We finished putting everything back."

"But these papers…," Chip said, running a hand through his white hair, making it even messier. "It's like a bizarre jigsaw puzzle."

"We're working on it," Luke said. "We'll have it figured out soon."

"I'll check back later then. You guys'll be all right for a while?"

"Where're you off to?" Anton asked, a smile twisting the upper left corner of his mouth. It was an unconsciously sexy movement that drove me crazy.

"I need to see somebody down at the police district office. Then, I want to check out a couple of characters at the Archdiocesan building."

"Right into the mouth of the lion. You're a brave man." Luke smiled. "Last time I was there I swear I could feel the building shudder when I entered."

"Wish me luck, then."

Chapter 6

Walking into the Center City police district office felt odd. My short stint trying to qualify for the Force hadn't been the greatest time. Being rejected for some arcane reason which no one has ever fully explained left a sour taste in my mouth. Somehow now I felt above it all, maybe even lucky not to have gotten trapped in police work.

Though I knew a person or two at the district, very few were ever willing to stick their neck out for me when it came to something big. But squeezing information out of them wasn't always difficult. Depending on the person being squeezed.

Clark "Obie" O'Brien, a few years short of retirement, sat at a desk directing visitors. Obie had been one of my supporters when I was at the Academy. He'd aged since then. His hair was thin and uneven, and he looked overworked. His usually pink face appeared dry and rough, like a pumpkin left out in the weather.

He smiled broadly when he saw me. Obie was a smiler but I knew when the smile was genuine and when it wasn't.

"Marco! Good to see you. How's the P.I. business?"

"Can't complain. And you?"

"Things are good. Retirement looks better every day, but this ain't so bad." He passed a hand over the desk. "So what can I do ya for?"

"Who's working the Brandt case?"

"The mugging in midtown?"

"That's the one. Who caught that case?"

Obie's smile disappeared and that wasn't good. I stared at him and waited.

"Giuliani." Obie looked at me as if I'd lost my dog and he couldn't do anything about it.

"Shit."

"Not the word I woulda used, but you got it. She'd rather chew on your liver than help you out. And she don't even care about this case. 'Just another friggin' mugging.' That's what she said."

Gina Giuliani was a cop who wanted to be Commissioner. She was on a mission. Little cases and people like me had no business getting in her way. She hated all P.I.s but me in particular. I'll never really know why. Could have something to do with the fact that she'd dated one of my brothers who dumped her for a hot French-Canadian guy he'd met on one of his buying trips. I'd always thought she was bigger than that. Anyway, she'd moved on and gotten married.

She had a good chance of moving up in the ranks. I was happy about that because she was smart, hard working, and dedicated. But she was too transparent. It's great to be ambitious, you just can't look too hungry. Giuliani always looked like she was starving.

"Well, Obie, I gotta give it a try. Do me a favor?"

"Anything, kid."

"If it sounds like it's getting rough in there, call the cops."

I left Obie laughing and coughing as I made my way to Giuliani's door. Seeing her name on the frosted glass door gave me the willies. She was good at what she did, knew her stuff, and handled things well. But she hated me.

Opening the door after knocking, I seemed to have surprised her. She looked up quickly from something she was writing. Her expression went from startled to stony in less than one second.

"Who let you in?"

"Uh, taxpayer." I pointed to myself. "Remember? I pay your salary? I get to come see you now and then." I hated being a wise ass but how much more could she hate me?

"Leech is more like it. A boy playing adult games. What can I do for you?" As she moved, her voluptuous dark hair arranged itself in elegant waves down to her shoulders. She was a looker. That didn't matter on this job but she had everything else that did.

"How can I resist such a kind offer of assistance?" I smiled my best and brightest. It was no use. My brother looked too much like me and I almost saw the memories replaying themselves in her head. "I could use some help on a case. The Brandt murder. Guy named Hollister was his partner. But I guess you know that. Anyway, he hired me."

"We've interviewed him and whatever witnesses we could find. That's all I'm gonna say, Fontana. It was another mugging that went bad. In case you don't watch the news, we've got a murder rate ready to break five hundred and the year still has eleven weeks to go."

"Wouldn't clearing this case help?"

"We've got a few more than that to clear, Fontana. And we don't need your help."

"Makes sense, I mean, you wanting to end the year with a lot of open files so you'll have something to do come January. But this case is a little personal."

"How's that?" she said, turning back to her paperwork, obviously not really interested.

"Long story. Anyway Hollister is hurting. Some closure would help the old guy."

"Since when have you started doin' good deeds? You a Boy Scout again?"

"They don't want my kind. I just want to question the witnesses. Hollister can't really remember anything."

"Case is still open. I can't let you have any of that."

Which I knew wasn't entirely true but she was calling the shots.

"You and I both know you could let me take a look at the jacket."

"You and I both also know that I wouldn't let you look at anything remotely connected to what I do."

"Hey, Gina. It's Marco standing here, not Dario. My brother didn't handle things so well with you. But I'm not him. I'm trying to do something good here. How about I get a break from you?"

"Funny, I hadn't thought about that little piece of shit for a long time," she said and I knew she was lying. I always know.

"Then…"

"I don't want to think about him. Then you come in and it's like Dario standing there. You look too much alike. But that isn't why I don't like you."

"It isn't?"

"I just don't like you. I don't like P.I.s and you're a P.I. Even worse, you're you." Her deep brown eyes glittered with something way at the other end of the scale from happy.

"You have guys looking into this case? Could I at least tell Hollister…"

"We've got priorities, Fontana. Other things come first."

"It wouldn't have anything to do with the fact that this happened to a gay guy in the gayborhood."

"Don't even pull that card on me, mister. You know as well as I do there's a priority list. My history with your brother hasn't affected my judgment."

"Glad to hear it, Gina. Since it's low priority, maybe I can give you guys a hand?" It was worth one more shot.

"Take a hike. And don't give your brother my regards."

"So, that's it?"

"That's it, Fontana. Now I gotta get back to this work you taxpayers expect me to do." With that she went straight back to making notes on papers and ignoring me. The silence in the room pressed in on my ears.

"Gotcha, chief. Be seein' you." I turned toward the door.

"Not if I can help it, Fontana," she murmured in a soft slurry way.

I gave Obie a salute on my way out.

Strike one. I'd have to try and find the witnesses on my own which wouldn't be a hell of a lot of fun.

I headed for the Archdiocesan offices. Boatload of fun.

* * *

The headquarters of the Archdiocese on Race Street is located in an awful, coral colored, granite-clad building behind the cathedral. The two buildings presented a contrast. The Italianate cathedral was tasteful. The boxy, ribbon-windowed headquarters showed all the marks of bad taste.

I approached the entrance and felt my heart thumping. Above the entryway, the coat-of-arms of the current cardinal was inelegantly placed inside the glass, which no one had bothered to clean for a while. For some reason, just passing through those plate-glass doors made my heart pump even faster.

The Church still had a shadowy hold over me, not enough to force me into services on Sundays or even Christmas. But it was as if an invisible power loomed over me in this building allowing old fears to bubble to the surface. Years of having been taught by nuns and priests and pious lay people left their mark. I felt their presence humming around me as I moved across the marble floor. Here I was, walking into their lair. At least, their bureaucratic lair.

An insipid little guy, dressed in an ill-fitting gray uniform and sitting at the information desk, told me Clifford was out that day and directed me to Wren's office. As for information on Opus Dei, he told me to try the Cardinal's Office for Public Information. Two out of three wasn't bad. But if I was going to see Clifford that meant I'd have to return to this den which didn't put a smile on my face.

I crammed into an elevator packed with priests. The fluorescent lighting made all of us look pale and not very pretty. I couldn't shake the sensation that someone was about to slap me for being me. The presence of the Church and its power was everywhere in this place.

Before long the elevator spit me out on an institutional-looking floor. Nothing special or elegant, nothing remarkable save for the odor of disinfectant. In fact, it all looked drably cheap, just like the exterior. A directional sign pointed me to Wren's office; I squared my shoulders, took a deep breath, and walked in.

The cool silence, plush crimson carpet, and expensive-looking dark wood furniture had me feeling I'd entered another world. The shabbiness of the corridor was replaced by a princely style I expected only in offices of the highest Church officials. A deathly stillness filled the place, like the feeling in a vast, empty cathedral. Nothing moved, nothing felt alive. Gave me the creeps. The fragrance of incense and candle wax in the air completed the illusion that this was a holy place where solemn things got done.

A secretary appeared seemingly out of nowhere. Short and wispy, her face conveyed innocence and suffering. The long-suffering type, biding her time here on earth, waiting for a better place. But she would never admit that. She played her part well as one of the smiling faithful, a good example of those filling low paying secretarial jobs at the Archdiocese.

"Good morning. May I help you?" She took her seat as she spoke and plunked some papers onto the desk.

"I'm here to see Mr. Wren." I smiled.

She looked at me with curiosity. My faded jeans, my clean but wrinkled designer shirt, and my hair which needed to be cut. She frowned her disapproval.

"Do you have an appointment?"

"No. I'll be honest, this is a spur of the moment, mission of mercy kind of thing. I was hoping Mr. Wren might just give me a small bit of his time," I said as politely and piously as I could manage.

"Well," she mused and flipped through pages in an appointment book on her desk. "He doesn't have an appointment for another hour. Let me ask him...What did you say your name was?"

"Fontana, ma'm, I'm a private investigator trying to help someone find closure in a murder case."

"And Mr. Wren can help?" I don't know whether she sounded shocked, or proud, or both. "Wait here a moment."

She slipped out of her chair and went through a polished oak doorway recessed into the wall: The inner sanctum. If some flunky of a press guy got this kind of office, I couldn't wait to see the offices of the bigger hoo-hahs.

After a few seconds, she opened the door and looked in my direction.

"He'll see you." She held the door wide for me.

The inner office was as plush as the outer. This pious man enjoyed living well. Red carpeting, dark paneled walls, windows with elaborate treatments. His desk was massive and dark. Everything on that desk reeked of money spent. Sitting behind it all was a reedy man, with hair darkened with dye and skin that looked well hydrated but tight. He was probably as old as Chip but his cosmetic efforts made him seem a bit younger, if plastic.

He stood.

"Mr. Fontana… was it?" He extended a hand. There was a studied wariness about him. Undoubtedly used to dealing with all sorts of people and situations, caution was a good opening gambit.

"Yes, that's right. Thank you for seeing me." I waited for him to ask me to sit. He didn't. I knew then what kind of game player he was.

"How can I help you? My secretary wasn't very clear." His tone was disdainful

"I'm looking into the murder of Helmut Brandt." I watched for a reaction. Other than a slight twitch at the corner of one eye, there was nothing. "He was a local author. I understand you knew the man."

"Whoever told you that was mistaken. I'd heard of him. Is that all, Mr. Fontana?" His expression of distaste stretched his already taut skin.

He was lying and I knew it.

"You'd only heard of him? Didn't his book shake things up in your circles?"

"The Vatican book? It was nonsense. All of it. I'm in a position to know. I work in public relations, I am privy to a lot of information."

"Were you happy his book gave you a chance to put all those conspiracy theories to rest?"

"Happ… I wasn't happy at all. It was a scurrilous book. Filled with lies and hate. He obviously had an axe to grind."

"Okay, you weren't happy. That why you two had a shouting match a while back?"

"We had a meeting." That little twitch pulled at the corner of his eye again. "To characterize it as a shouting match is…" He paused, gathered himself, and looked me in the eye. "What is it you want, Mr. Fontana? I have better ways to spend my time than to quibble."

"Like I said, I'm looking into Brandt's murder. I'm talking with anybody that had a beef with him."

"A beef? Listen carefully. Mr. Brandt was the sort of man who wanted to tear down the Church at any cost. I don't know his motivation." Wren pulled out a handkerchief and dabbed at his forehead, even though it was three degrees cooler than a morgue in his office. "Part of my job is to nurture the image of the Church in the media. Brandt was shredding it. He was undermining confidence in the hierarchy, casting aspersions on people whose lives are above reproach. Unlike his own."

"How was he not above reproach?" This I wanted to hear.

"He was a homosexual. A homosexual who was unrepentant, proud, and vicious. The men whose reputations he was intent on destroying were saintly. Men who helped people without regard to themselves."

"Okay," I said. And if I believed his load, I'd probably be working somewhere in this building myself. "Is it fair to say you wanted Brandt silenced?" Nice word, "silenced." It covered so many bases.

Wren squirmed. "If you're implying that I would soil my hands in any way... That I had anything to do with his unfortunate murder... and yes, it was unfortunate. Anyone's death is. Particularly a person like Brandt, unrepentant, filled with vitriol. I don't expect they look too kindly on that in the afterlife. I'm sure he's burning in Hell. It could have been avoided."

* * *

I told Wren I'd be back when I had more information to share. He told me to be sure and make an appointment the next time. Yeah, right. I'd let him know I was coming so he could duck out.

Now I wanted to know about Opus Dei. Not that I for one minute believed they had any involvement. But Hollister thought so and he was paying the bills. He'd need reassurance that Opus Dei wasn't a player. Then I could get on with the real investigation.

In the hall outside Wren's office, I waited for the elevator, feeling as if I'd been exiled to a shabbier corner of the universe. A soft tone signaled the elevator's arrival and the doors whooshed open. I stepped in, stood to the side, and noticed an extremely handsome young priest across from me. Over six feet tall, soft blond hair, blue eyes, and a face which could stop traffic. He glanced briefly in my direction, nodded politely, then stared at the doors as if trying not to engage me.

I almost forgot to hit the button for my floor but when I looked, it was already lit. Meaning he was going to the same floor.

That was confirmed when the doors opened and he allowed me to exit first. He headed off toward the right while I searched the directory for the office I wanted. As it turned out I was going the same way. He walked ahead of me with an odd, twisting gait. We moved down one hall then turned onto another. There was only one door at the end.

He glanced over his shoulder.

"I'm not following you. Honest," I joked.

He laughed and it was a rich throaty chuckle. I liked this man.

"Unless you're lost, we're going to the same office." His voice gave me a pleasant tingle. It was sexy but comforting and soothing. Almost hypnotic.

He opened the door and, once again, waved me ahead of him. Another plush office. This one even had stained glass windows giving the place an eerie, devout atmosphere. The odor of incense and candle wax floated through the air making it smell like a church. I sank up to my ankles in red carpeting as I approached an elegant reception desk of polished light-colored wood. Behind the desk sat a man – late twenties, dark hair, deep dark eyes, and a smile so white it had to be bleached. The stained glass, the red carpets, the dark oak paneling, and the overall atmosphere gave the guy an otherworldly look. I wouldn't say angelic, though.

"Good morning Monsignor," he said to the priest who disappeared down a hall after giving us both a curt wave.

I stood waiting for the receptionist to turn his eyes on me.

"May I help you?" Finally. The deep voice fit his appearance. He stared at me and I felt naked.

"I was told I could speak to someone in this office about Opus Dei."

"They were mistaken, this isn't Opus Dei headquarters. We don't have any information."

"Why would they send me here?"

"Because they send everyone here when they don't know where else to send them." He was a bit officious which didn't blend well with the tough-guy exterior.

"No one here can give me any information?"

"Fr. Marlon is the Public Information Administrator. He might be able to point you in the right direction."

I waited. Obviously this guy needed prompting or was being a smart ass. I counted to thirty then took the plunge, "Well, any chance I can speak to Fr. Marlon?"

Just as I was asking, the tall, blond priest poked his head around the corner and smiled at us.

"Tony? We're gonna need some coffee," he said and that buttery voice filled the room. "And you can send the gentleman back, Fr. Marlon can answer his questions. I don't mind and it wouldn't be right to keep him waiting."

Hot, kind, considerate, and a priest! Was there no justice?

"Thanks," I said, catching his eye. I wondered just who he was and how he'd heard what I was asking.

"Sure thing, Monsignor," Tony answered with a studied submissiveness. When Tony turned to me, the tough guy was back. "You can go in. But keep it short, they've got work to do." A cute frown knit his thick dark eyebrows together and the twinkle in his eyes was unmistakable. He rose from behind the desk and I noticed that he was small and powerfully built. Kind of an odd choice for a receptionist.

"Thanks, Tony." I said. "Who's this other guy?"

"That other 'guy' is Monsignor Kusek, the Cardinal's personal adjutant. He's here making office inspections. He's got a lotta juice in the Archdiocese. Don't cross him or you'll never get your information."

Things were looking up. A hot priest with power. Never know when that would come in handy in an investigation.

Tony trotted off to get the coffee and I knocked on Marlon's solid oak door and waited. After a moment Kusek held the door open for me. I entered and was in another lavish office with a sleek modern desk at its center. A computer, a printer, and other technological devices sat on counters built into the walls around the office. One short shelf of books took up another side of the room.

At the desk sat a squat, African-American man. His shaved head shone in the light filtering through the stained glass windows.

"Good morning, good morning," Marlon said and stood to greet me. Except you'd never guess he was standing. The man was so short, he looked as if he were still seated. "What can I do for you, Mr.... uh?"

"Fontana. Marco Fontana, Fontana Investigations." We shook hands.

"And this is Monsignor Kusek." Marlon indicated the tall blond.

Kusek extended his hand. "Nice to meet you again," he said, then explained to Marlon how we'd met in the corridor.

Marlon indicated I should sit, so I did.

"I'm here on behalf of a client. I'm looking into the murder of Helmut Brandt."

"I heard about that on the radio," Kusek said.

"Yes, yes. I did, too," Marlon chimed in. "Tragedy. A young man, quite young. A senseless tragedy. This city is drowning in crime."

"My client doesn't believe it was a random act," I said. "I'm investigating every possibility. I was hoping you could help."

"Help? Well, certainly, of course. But I don't know how I can be of help." Marlon stroked his chin and looked concerned.

"I think, Father, that Mr. Fontana is looking for information on Opus Dei. If I overheard correctly." Kusek smiled at me. "I couldn't help hearing. You were asking Tony as I came around the corner. I hope you don't mind."

"As long as it doesn't become a habit." I laughed. I caught his eye and noticed a certain something there. Oh, I'd be in trouble if I went any further down that path.

"Why Opus Dei?" Marlon lost some of his clownishness.

"The nature of Brandt's work brought him into contact with a lot of groups. Unfortunately his work also made quite a few people angry."

"What… oh, yes, now I remember what that young man was all about. You think Opus Dei had something to do with this? Opus Dei?"

"I need to track every lead."

"Brandt was a provocateur. A provocateur. It must have been in his nature to provoke people. Any number of people were angered by his ravings. Even I…" He stopped himself abruptly.

"You were saying…?" I prodded.

"I'm sure Fr. Marlon was about to say he found himself getting upset at what Mr. Brandt postulated in his book. He was, after all, an activist with an axe to grind. He wanted people to react. Am I right?" Kusek looked at me for an answer.

"I suppose so," I said. He'd used the same "axe to grind" phrase as Wren.

"He managed to get a rise out of lots of people. Even my friend here. Right, Father?" Kusek was smooth, transparent, but smooth.

"Yes. Of course. Of course I was angry. Certainly. I was upset. Many people were upset. Any number of people could have... I mean, anyone might have been... Well, it was upsetting. That's all. No one was happy." Marlon was hopelessly tangled in his thoughts.

"You see my point, then, Father? Everyone was upset. Even the folks at Opus Dei were probably unsettled."

"I suppose someone might have mentioned they were. Yes. I suppose so."

"All I'm doing, is tracking down leads and opinions. Never know where they'll take you."

"Well, Mr. Fontana. I don't know, I don't really know what I can tell you. I mean, Opus Dei. Goodness, Opus Dei. A controversial group. We have no control over them." He paused and pulled some sort of book from a small rack on one side of his desk. I saw the word 'Directory' as he opened it.

"You won't find much in the Directory, I'm afraid. Not much at all." He turned to a page and showed me the entries. "See? Nothing. Their headquarters are out of state. They are their own prelature. Which means they aren't governed by these offices. They have their own bishop. You'd have to..."

"He's right, you know. The Archdiocese has no authority over Opus Dei. The Cardinal's office, other than offering an opinion, can't do much in Opus Dei matters," Kusek added. "They're not a rogue group, you understand. But they do act on their own authority. We have no control."

"You've gotta know someone involved in Opus Dei in this city. Someone who's part of that community, who liaises with the Archdiocese. There must be a leader of some sort." I was going to hold their feet to the fire until I got something out of them.

"Well, Monsignor, do you think...?" He glanced at Kusek. As the Cardinal's representative, I guess the guy controlled Marlon's tongue.

"I don't see any reason we couldn't give out some information. Do you?"

"I'm a little concerned that this is a murder investigation. Murder. They won't take kindly to being implicated in anything like murder. Don't you agree?"

"I'm not accusing anyone of anything," I insisted. "I'm following possible leads."

"I don't see the harm," Kusek said. "Especially if knowing more will bring comfort to your client."

"That's the point, Monsignor," I said. "Knowing for sure Opus Dei wasn't involved will go a long way to bringing my client some peace of mind." Not to mention my own peace of mind. I was itching to get out of this rabbit hole. Everything was beginning to look upside down.

"There is a fellow. Nice fellow, really, despite what they say. He's a good man, you know. Does a lot of good works." He paused, placing the Directory back on the rack.

There was a knock at the door and Tony entered carrying a tray with a silver coffee service. Everything was laid out nicely. Bone China cups, silverware, even a small torte and plates.

I watched Tony move as he set down the tray, gave each of us a cup, and poured the coffee. He was amazingly fluid for the little muscleman he appeared to be. I found myself judging him as a potential member of StripGuyz and had to mentally slap myself back to reality.

"Shall I cut the torte, Monsignor?" he asked Kusek. I noted that he directed most of his attention to the blond. Tony was either currying favor with the powerful or he had a thing for Kusek. I was betting on the latter.

"That's fine, Tony. You've got your own work to do. But take a cup of coffee for yourself." Kusek smiled, a little too widely.

Tony happily took a cup, poured some coffee, then left, shutting the door quietly behind him.

"You were saying, Father?" I prodded. His attention was riveted on the torte and I really didn't have time for tea and crumpets. On the other hand, I found it interesting that they didn't defend Opus Dei even when murder was involved. I was well aware that the Opus Dei people ruffled lots of feathers.

"Yes, I was going to say there's a man you might talk to. What's his number? I have it here somewhere," he mumbled as he riffled through an address book. There's a Father Bidwell at the New York offices and locally there's Francis Clifford. He's not in Opus Dei but he lets them board at his home. Maybe he can help." He took a piece of paper, scribbled something on it and handed it to me. "Their numbers. Tell them I gave you the information. Now, look at this pastry. Lovely isn't it?" Marlon bubbled.

* * *

I got out of there before allowing myself a piece of pastry. There was something odd about sharing niceties with priests. After one more exchange of glances with Kusek and shaking hands all around, I was on my way.

October got chillier by the day. It made me melancholy watching the light die early, seeing the trees give up their leaves, knowing another year was about to close. At the same time there was a sexiness to the chill in the air. I can't explain it exactly but there was something about the onset of Winter that made me think sex and romance.

The walk back to the gayborhood gave me a chance to guy-watch. In Rittenhouse Square, I spotted Kent. Poor, lovesick, lost, Kent. Sitting on a bench in the Square, he looked as if no one cared.

"Hey," I said sitting next to him.

He hardly moved and stared at the ground. I heard him sniffle.

"Kent?" I placed a hand on his shoulder. He trembled. "Look at me."

He turned his face to me and his eyes were red. He mumbled something incoherent. I gave his shoulder a squeeze and watched a tear tumble down his cheek. But he held himself together, drew in a deep breath, then exhaled.

"Things will get better, you know. You can't let this destroy you."

"I know. But…"

"Whaddaya say we get something to eat?" It had to be lunch time or near it and I knew the kid could use company. "My treat."

"O-okay… uh… but… I don't really feel hungry."

"Sure you do. Or you will when we get there. We'll go to Woody's. How's that? You and I can have a talk. Something I want to ask you."

"Sure."

A few people lounging on other benches had watched both of us closely. One reedy man with huge glasses shook his head disparagingly. And a young guy sitting across the way looked at us in a dreamy way, imagining, no doubt, that he'd just witnessed a pair of lovers reconciling.

We walked most of the way in silence. Kent seemed lost in thought. As we reached Thirteenth Street, he looked at me.

"You think things are gonna be all right?"

"How do you mean?" I wasn't about to make any promises.

"Am I gonna make it all alone? I don't wanna be alone. I can't."

"Hey, listen. Alone is what we are most of the time. You have to learn to like what's inside you, Kent. Then being alone won't feel so bad. Anyway, a looker like you won't be alone for long. Be happy with yourself and you won't be so afraid of being alone." Great advice coming from a guy who had his share of afraid-to-be-alone times. I hadn't yet learned the trick to being totally happy with me. But I was making progress. There were even times I enjoyed being by myself.

"Marco!" Anton called out from across the street.

"You guys finished at the house?"

"We're breaking for lunch. But there's some stuff you should see. It might help with the case."

"What are we talking here?" I asked and tried to shelter Kent from Anton who I knew was still understandably upset about the night before.

"E-mails, letters. All of them threats, death threats."

Chapter 7

I told Anton I'd meet them after lunch. The death threats weren't going anywhere. Kent was in need of more immediate help. He didn't seem to have anyone else to talk to and something about him made me want to hear him out. Besides, I think everybody deserves another chance.

It was just shy of lunch hour so Woody's was relatively empty. We took a window seat and I reevaluated my opinion of Kent. I'd thought he was a loony stalker. Now I wasn't so sure. He'd come to see Nando before last night but had never bothered him. He'd probably felt lost, alone, and scared. Nando was his lifeline and he couldn't face losing him. The more I observed, the more I wanted to help him. I'm no saint, but some people tug at my heart strings. Still, I wasn't going to baby the guy.

Kent's movements were shy, his body language tending toward the defensive, as if he needed to protect himself. "I've never been here before. To eat, I mean."

"Nice place. Besides I didn't think you'd want to eat at Bubbles right now."

"How is... how's Nando doing?" His voice was laced with pain. "I miss him."

"He's okay. Right now, I wanna talk about you." I gently rattled the menu. "What're you having for lunch?"

"I'm not really hungry. Just coffee," he mumbled.

"I'm Italian, we can't stand to see somebody not eating. Seeing people enjoy food makes life worthwhile. So, you're gonna eat, right? Or do I have to force feed you?"

"Okay, okay, what're you having?"

"There's a hamburger with my name on it in that kitchen. I'm having it with the works." I smiled. "You?"

"A hamburger sounds good." He looked over the menu and then at me. "Yeah, I'll have a hamburger. And coffee."

I caught the waiter's eye and we ordered.

"What kind of work do you do, Kent?"

"Still a student. At Temple. I can't wait to finish." He sat up straighter.

"What're you studying?"

"Hotel management. Hospitality."

"Like it?" At least he wasn't majoring in Business, or worse, Psych.

"I love it. Really. Just… right now, things aren't going great. Since Nando's been gone, I can't concentrate."

"I understand," I said and I did. When Galen disappeared I was lost. We weren't lovers but we loved one another. He left a big hole in my life.

"You do? Guy like you can have anybody he wants."

"You think it's all that easy, huh? I've been left, too. More than once. But there was one time it hurt more than all the others put together."

"You're just shittin' me so I'll feel better."

"Listen, after what you did last night, I should be jackin' you up in some alley, teaching you a lesson. Last thing I thought I'd do was play nice."

"See? You are shittin' me with all that talk."

"What's my motive, Kent? Why would I be sitting here with you?"

"Yeah, well, it's kinda strange. I had a gun pointed at you and now…"

"You did and I should'a knocked you into next week. But I decided to give you a chance. Somebody does that, you should act more grateful."

"It's just… why are you bein' so nice? Nobody's ever that nice." He paused, looked at the table.

I said nothing.

He looked up at me, guilty and confused. "I'm sorry about last night. I acted like an idiot."

"Can't argue with that."

"I don't know why I did it. It was like another person doing it. Not me."

"Put it behind you, Kent. Sometimes pain makes us do stupid things. I understand or I wouldn't be sitting here. But it's over now."

"I'm really sorry. I don't know how to say it better than that. But I owe you. You coulda turned me in and you didn't."

"You do owe me and that's another reason we're sittin' here talking. I want you to consider working for me."

"As a detective? Are you…"

"No. I don't have enough work to keep me busy. Though you might be able to help some time. I was more thinking about StripGuyz." I just casually dropped that in his lap and waited.

"StripGuyz! Are you…? Are you asking me to..? 'Cause I won't, y'know. I won't. I'm not taking off my clothes." His eyes were all confusion and something else, like fearful curiosity.

Tom, the waiter, brought our coffees just as Kent said he wouldn't take off his clothes. Eyebrows were raised.

"You tell him, sweetie. Besides, if anybody's taking off his clothes for Marco, it'll be me. Right?" Tom looked at me.

"Would I ask anybody to take their clothes off? Me? Would I do that?"

"Yeah, you're right." Tom smirked. "You've never asked me. I've been waiting. I've even offered for chrissakes."

"See, Kent? I'd never ask you to do that." I'd wanted to, because he'd make a great addition to StripGuyz, but I knew he'd react the way he did.

"Anyway, sweetie," Tom addressed Kent. "If the nice man asked me to take my clothes off for him, I'd be naked in a flash. You might give it some thought." He sauntered away without looking back.

"Seriously, Kent. I'm not asking you to strip. Though I think you'd be terrific. Actually I'm wondering if you'd like to help with crowd control, keep an eye on the audience." I'd have to get Anton to agree. I respected him too much not to. And, Nando, of course. He'd have to agree. But I had a feeling there wasn't as much space between Nando and Kent as there appeared. If I could bring them back together it'd be worth it. In any case, Nando only worked certain nights. I'd schedule Kent when Nando wasn't dancing.

But Anton's approval had to come first. Convincing Anton would probably mean dinner at Le Bec Fin and a trip to New York to see a show. Seeing the pain in Kent's eyes, I thought it would be worth it.

"I wouldn't have to strip?"

"You think I force people to be a part of the troupe? You've got to want to do that. If you don't it shows and you wouldn't make a dime."

"What if I bumped into Nando? He wouldn't mind? If I was there, I mean. He wouldn't think I was hanging around just to be with him?"

"Would you be?" I stared into his eyes daring him to lie.

"I… I don't know," he said and hung his head.

"That's at least honest. I wouldn't have believed anything else," I said and placed my hand over his.

* * *

Lunch lifted his spirits and mine, too. There was something about him, despite what he'd done the night before. I guess I'm a sucker for a kid in need. Anyway, he agreed to consider my offer and to not do anything foolish. Like come back to the club with a gun. Or, hurt himself.

We parted company on Spruce and I walked to Hollister's place. Some large clouds scudded by blocking the early afternoon sun and creating an eerie atmosphere. A chilly breeze kicked up, just right for October, but I felt the weight of the case hanging over me. I entered the Neverland of tangled little streets and eventually found Hollister's place. It was almost as if you weren't in Philadelphia once you were folded into this hidden enclave.

"Hey, Marco." Chip greeted me as I entered the house and saw them all working. Hollister helping Chip sort papers, Anton cleaning, and Luke making sure everything was where Hollister said it should be.

"Marco." Luke and Anton sounded off simultaneously.

I went over to Hollister and knelt on one knee. "How're you doing, Tim?"

"I'm better than I appear probably," he said and looked me in the eye. "You didn't have any success at the Archdiocesan offices. Right?"

"Been a frustrating day so far." I stood, squeezed Hollister's shoulder, and turned to the others. "Tell me you've got some leads."

"Couldn't have been too frustrating a day," Anton said, disapproval in his tone.

"Oh? Meaning?" I knew but I wanted him to say it.

"I saw you huddling with Kent," Anton said. "That can only mean one thing."

"What's that?" Luke asked.

"That I want him to work with StripGuyz. If you approve." I had to drop the bomb some time. Letting Anton know while there were people around was good. It would give him time to think about it before we spoke.

"You and I will talk later," Anton said as calmly as I've ever heard him. That could not be good.

"Right now, you should take a look at this, boss," Chip said and held out a bright green accordion folder stuffed with papers. "It's some of the threats we found."

I took the folder which was heavier than it appeared. Hollister would be the best person to review it with but I knew it'd be painful.

"Tim, this won't to be easy but…"

"If you want me to look those over with you, don't worry. I've read through them before, with Helmut. He laughed the threats off, of course." Hollister rose to his feet, and it appeared to be a painful effort. Grief can do that sometimes. I've seen people literally bent over with the pain of grief. The lucky ones get through it.

"How about the kitchen? It'll be quieter." I headed back to the tiny kitchen which barely held a table and three chairs.

I sat and pulled the papers out of the folder. The pile was three inches thick.

"All threats?" I asked.

"Veiled threats, death threats, lawsuit threats, you name it. Helmut shoved them all into the folder and joked about putting an appendix into his next book with all of these." He sat next to me and placed a hand on the pile. Shutting his eyes, he took a deep breath. "Why didn't you listen to me, Helmut?"

I waited. He was far away, talking to someone even farther away. I let him have his moment. Then his eyes fluttered open and he looked down at the papers.

"Will you be all right?" I asked.

"What can be harder than what I've already been through? I'll be all right. I want to see this through."

"Let's divide them into e-mail and snail mail. Then we'll read through them."

We spent a few minutes separating papers; e-mail was by far the larger pile. Makes sense since it was easier to be a coward in cyberspace. If you knew what you were doing you could hide, at least from non-techies. Old-fashioned mail could contain fingerprints or other trace evidence.

"It's impossible," Hollister said after reading a few. "How can anyone tell which are real threats and which just the ravings of religious lunatics?"

"There may be key words or phrases, screen names, things that repeat, almost anything," I said, placing a hand on his arm to calm him. "Let's look together."

* * *

After ninety minutes of poring over the mail, I was bug-eyed. Some were angry and righteous, some were outright loony, some were well-written arguments.

"A lot of people threatened lawsuits," I commented.

"Quite a few people wanted to take him to court after that first book. But nothing ever came of it. When word got out he was working on a follow-up, the legal posturing began all over again."

"Most of them are just blowing smoke," I said and rustled a letter or two for emphasis. "Just people saying they'll hire a lawyer. How about the ones from actual lawyers demanding he stop his work or be sued for libel. Anything ever come of those?"

"No. But, one of the letters comes from a lawyer connected to a firm the Archdiocese uses."

"That so? Was Helmut concerned about that?"

"It names a client but I'd never heard of him. Seamus Scanlan. We both just supposed he was either connected to the Archdiocesan PR office or was someone who used the same lawyer."

"No such thing as coincidences in a murder investigation. Can't be just an accident that someone chooses the same law firm as the Archdiocese."

"I suppose not. The Archdiocesan public relations people were always full of bluster. Always looking for a good story for their so-called diocesan newspaper. They're not above creating a controversy by suing an author."

"People who hire lawyers are usually serious. They'd be intent on stopping Helmut. It's worth looking into."

"The lawyers won't tell you a thing."

"Maybe, but then again...." I knew he was right. I also knew it was possible to learn things you never thought you'd find out. You had to keep your eyes and ears open.

We fell into silence again as I made my way through some messages that sent chills down my spine. The actual death threats. These didn't call for Brandt to burn in hell. That would have been too neat and easy. The people who sent these e-mails had much more insidiously horrible things in mind. I'd need expert help tracking the e-mail.

I stood and stretched. The tiny kitchen was cheerful and the afternoon sun managed to find its way into the small window brightening things even more.

"It doesn't seem fair," Hollister mumbled as he stared into the sunlight streaming through the window.

"What's that? These letters...?"

"That the sun is out, that the world just goes on as if nothing happened. Helmut is dead and my life... my life is empty now. Seems like time should have stopped, or the sun should have gone into hiding, even for just a little while."

"It'll take a long time before anything seems right," I said and placed a hand on his shoulder. He was bony, fragile.

"If we get to the bottom of this, it'll go a long way toward helping. I'm sure."

"Yes," I answered but I'd already started thinking about what I'd have to do next. I poked my head into the living room. "Luke, can we talk?"

"Sure," he said and popped up off the couch as if he had springs in his shoes. "Here… or, outside…?"

"Here's fine. Any clue about the laptop? Brandt claimed he had new documents or evidence or something like that. Find anything like that?"

"Mr. Hollister said Brandt usually hid the laptop outside the house when he wasn't actively working on the book. Could be stolen but Hollister seemed sure it was hidden somewhere. As for papers… who can tell what's new or what's old? That'll take a different set of eyes. We can't tell what's what."

"I can," Hollister said looking up at us. "I may not know much about his other work, but the Vatican papers I know well. I worked with Helmut on that and I'd know if there's anything new."

"Sweet," Luke said. "Then let's…"

"Of course," Hollister continued. "He hid the laptop and odds are the papers are hidden, too. Most likely in the same place."

"Sure, that follows. Unless it was stolen." I said. "Wouldn't he have left a way for you to find the papers and the laptop in case anything happened to him?"

"I don't think he ever really felt anything terrible would happen. But as confident as Helmut was that all these threats were nonsense, he wasn't stupid. I'm sure he left a way for me to find the papers. He just never told me what that might be."

"How do we figure that out?" Luke asked.

Chapter 8

"We'll put our heads together. He can't have made it impossible. Can he?"

"Helmut was fond of secrets and liked his privacy," Hollister said. "But he never really hid anything from me exactly."

"Exactly?" Did Hollister doubt his partner's truthfulness or did grief make him question everything? Maybe he realized things about Helmut which only death made clear. "I think we all need a break. In the meantime I'll check out the law firm and see what I can dig up on this Scanlan character."

"We're pretty much finished," Luke said. "We can be outta here in an hour or so. I'll drop everything off to the Fortress of Geekiness on my way home."

"Be kind. Those geeks have saved my ass a number of times. Tell them I'll have a laptop for them to crack. As soon as we find it." The high tech crew was a real boon but dealing with them was sometimes like the Mad Hatter's tea party.

"I've got to get going," Anton announced. "It's Amateur night at Bubbles and you so nicely said Cal and Bruno could co-host. I've got to get there and set up. And maybe place myself between battling strippers."

"I'll be there later, you know I wouldn't let you down." I stroked his back. We usually made joint decisions on amateur candidates.

"You have a verdict on the gunslinger?" Anton said, the sarcasm in his voice was like molasses.

"Kent?" I'd almost forgotten. "It's your call. If you say no, then it's no."

Anton was about to open his mouth to say something I probably didn't want to hear.

"He's waiting for my call," I said, trying to stave off a lecture. "I wouldn't hire him without you agreeing. I hope you know that."

"You're playing on my forgiving nature," Anton muttered.

He hugged Luke, pecked me on the cheek, waved a good-bye and left.

"Got your work cut out for you, huh?" Chip commented.

"You can say that again." I laughed and turned to Hollister. "Well, Tim, what do you think?

"They've done a great job, Marco but...," Hollister paused, unable to speak, then he cleared his throat. "Putting the house in order isn't... well... it doesn't answer any questions, does it?"

"I understand, Tim. You want things resolved. I promise we'll find answers for you." I looked around. Everything was back where it belonged, with one exception and he could never be replaced. I wondered again about Hollister's safety. "Tim, I'm thinking maybe you should stay with friends, until I make some headway."

"You think someone..."

"We've got to assume the break-in was connected to Helmut's death. They may not have found what they wanted. These guys obviously don't play well with others. They'll likely be back."

"Mygod, haven't they done enough?" Hollister sat back down looking defeated.

"It's only for a while. I don't think it's a good idea for you to be alone anyway."

* * *

Once I'd made sure Hollister would stay with friends and out of sight, I took off. The day wasn't getting any younger so I headed over to scope out the law firm Scanlan had hired. Might be a coincidence, Scanlan and the Archdiocese using the same law firm. Could also be true that Mars was inhabited by skinny gray men with big eyes.

One Liberty Place was elegantly modern and gave Philly's skyline an air of sophistication. Liberty reminded me of the Chrysler Building in New York. Very classy. Inside, a world of glass, chrome, and blue marble whisked you out of the mundane and into serene solemnity. Law firms located in Liberty Place didn't come cheap. Since the Archdiocese always played for keeps, it figured they'd have a high powered firm.

I stepped into a sleek elevator that swept me up to the fifty-second floor. If I thought the lobby was elegant, this floor was the epitome of elegance and taste. Blue marble peacefully coexisted with black granite, glass walls, dramatic lighting, and hushed tones. I pushed open the huge glass doors marked O'Herlihy, Specter, O'Brien and Horowitcz and told myself that barging in without an appointment wasn't a bad thing. After all, the words 'murder investigation' had a way of getting people's attention.

The receptionist didn't look like a receptionist. She appeared to be a high-level executive who just happened to have her office on the front line. She was young, stiff-backed, and stern-looking. Her dark-blonde hair was piled tastefully on top of her head. I marched up to the desk as if I belonged there.

"May I help you?" Her voice was one part honey, two parts vinegar. She eyed me suspiciously. She wasn't going to buy anything I was selling. Not easily anyway.

"My name is Marco Fontana. I'd like to speak with Mr. Dreier." I waited for the inevitable.

"Do you have an appointment?" That was it. The first line of defense in every office. The appointment gambit.

"I'm investigating a murder and Mr. Dreier may have some pertinent information." I threw all my cards on the table. No use holding back. The murder card was my strongest move.

"He's… Just wait a moment." She stood, looked down a hall then back at me.

Nothing like having the word 'murder' uttered in a lawyer's office to make things happen.

"I can wait," I said politely as she walked off down the hall. She was tall and moved with authority.

The silence was eerily formal and ominous. Maybe that's the way expensive law offices felt. I didn't like it.

Pricey red-leather club chairs dotted the reception area along with tables holding floral arrangements that probably cost a small fortune. A long black leather couch stood against one wall and a dark wood console table against another. Atop the console table were several majolica pieces which looked like they cost real money. Probably antiques. The legal fees had to be astronomical to pay for it all.

Situated around reception were what I supposed were conference rooms. Glass walls separated dimly-lit rooms which appeared solemn and funereal. The walls didn't leave much in the way of privacy. You could see into all of them at once. Long, lacquered-wood conference tables, leather chairs, side tables with silvery carafes and crystal glasses. Made me want a reason to have a conference with one of these lawyers.

I sat in one of the club chairs and was glad I did. The leather was so soft I wanted to sink in and fall asleep. But I heard voices and sat up expecting the receptionist to shoo me out. Instead, a man ambled into the reception area. Tall, with a ruddy complexion and thinning blond hair, he wore glasses. His shoulders-back, military gait was impressive. But his face was soft and pasty. He glanced around the room, his gaze falling on me. For a moment, he stared as if about to speak. Instead, he turned and marched out the door.

The silence returned and I resumed waiting. Just as I was about to fall into a trance, out walked the secretary, her face unrevealing. She stood a short distance away and peered at me.

"Mr. Dreier will see you briefly. I'll show you to a conference room." She moved off as if I were to follow and be grateful for small favors.

Opening a room, she let me in without another word. The door closed and I felt as if I were in an observation cage. I was able to see into other conference rooms, the recessed lighting giving them an atmospheric importance. I felt as if I were waiting for sentence to be passed or for guards to come and escort me to some more sinister place.

The door opened and a man entered. Average height, with coppery hair and a face that looked cosmetically touched up. His expensive, tailored suit moved with him as if it were part of him. His perfectly coiffed hair was sprayed into place. The pleasant, if totally manufactured exterior, held together a man who obviously had lofty things on his mind. His eyes told the real story and spoke of suspicion and controlled impatience, maybe even anger.

I stood and noticed as he turned a latch on the door. Instantly the glass walls turned smoky and translucent. I couldn't see out and no one could see in. I'd encountered this kind of thing on a smaller scale, in bars and restaurants.

"Marco Fontana." I extended my hand. He took it reluctantly.

"Sam Dreier. What can I do for you, Mr. Fontana?"

"I'm investigating the murder of Helmut Brandt." I watched his face for any flicker of recognition. He was good but there was a slight movement in his eyes. His makeup didn't crack but he knew what I was talking about. "You sent a letter on behalf of your client a Mr. Scanlan, asking Mr. Brandt to cease his activities. Is that right?"

"You've obviously seen the letter." Dreier was slick.

"I wanted to be certain you'd actually sent it."

"We sent the letter. Mr. Scanlan is a client." His eyes shifted to the left, toward the door. Was he hoping I'd get out or was he inadvertently indicating something else? "You understand, of course, I can't say anything more. Attorney-Client privilege."

"Not even an address? I'd like to see if Mr. Scanlan will talk to me."

"I'm afraid I can't do that, Mr. Fontana. Now, if there's nothing more…"

"Exactly what activities did the letter refer to? Brandt's writing or something different?" I needed to know if Brandt was engaged in something else.

Silence. The lawyer did a great imitation of a clam.

"Your firm works for the Archdiocese. That right?"

"What's that have to do with Mr. Scanlan?" Dreier sounded annoyed.

"That's just it, Mr. Dreier. I was wondering if there was some connection."

"Neither Mr. Scanlan nor the Archdiocese has anything to do with your case. Now…" he stopped and looked at his watch, an expensive-looking gold lump on his wrist. "I need to prepare for a client. I trust there's nothing else you want."

"For now." I waited at the door.

"I can assure you Mr. Scanlan is an upstanding citizen," Dreier said as he turned the latch which slowly cleared the walls, returning them to their crystal clear state. "It's unfortunate you came all this way for nothing."

"Oh, it wasn't far and I wouldn't say I got nothing." I smiled. Never hurts to keep them guessing. "Thanks again, Mr. Dreier."

The elevator whisked me down to the lobby and I waited for my stomach to catch up to the rest of me. Not that I don't like the thrill of a fifty floor drop. It tickles in the right places.

Dreier wasn't much help but I'd figured as much going in. I wanted to see how he played the game. I didn't expect much more. But I always gleaned something from these meetings. That was no lie.

*** * ***

I bumped into Nina the computer geek on the way back to my apartment. She was a gorgeous, dark-haired Latina who hid her looks behind large glasses and baggy clothing. The tattoo running up her left arm and spilling onto her neck was an unusual double headed Aztec serpent. Its large fanged jaws nipping at her elbow and throat.

Nina was incredible. With a brain the size of Alaska, she knew anything anyone *could* know about computers. If a computer could do something, she knew about it.

"Marco," she said, staring from behind those glasses like a fish in a bowl.

"Nina! You look great! Did Luke get in touch?"

"He did and you have a gold mine with all those e-mails, *jefe*. Gonna give me and my chicas a lot of work."

"Good. I'm counting on you."

"It's gonna cost you."

"No problem. But I need it yesterday."

"No can do, jefe. These things take time."

The oldest maneuver in the techie playbook, say things will take a lot of time, then finish early and look like miracle workers.

"You can do it, Nina. How about I throw in tickets to Cirque du Soleil when they're in town? And a free Olympus spa treatment for you, Hallie, and Deena?

"Thought that was guys only."

"Gotcha there, it's coed and Stavros will have Electra take care of you."

"Massage, facials?"

"The works!"

"You got a deal, Marco."

She walked off without saying good-bye, probably already thinking about the work.

I reached my building and strode across the lobby. The elevator was crowded. The Cell Phone Sheriff towered over the rest of us. An imposing woman with dramatic frizzy brown hair, she absolutely hated anyone who even openly held a cell phone in an elevator. A young woman pulled her cell phone out when it started ringing and I cringed. Instead of answering, she silenced it. I felt the Sheriff stirring, ready to lash out. She was undoubtedly disappointed at not being able to take off yet another head. Then it was my turn to exit.

I heard the phone ring as I entered my place, then a voice came through the answering machine. "Mr. Fontana, this is Francis Clifford, I understand you want to speak with me."

I snatched up the nearest extension. "Mr. Clifford. Thanks for calling. How did you know to get in touch with me?" I'd never left a message for him.

"That's not important. What's essential is that I'll be happy... well, happy is not the word... I will talk to you about the Brandt case. An unfortunate incident that needs to be handled with discretion and sensitivity."

"Oh?"

"Your case is not about what you may have been led to believe. The Church isn't interested in scandal or in destroying the reputation of innocent men. Even though Mr. Brandt was hardly what we might call innocent. Wouldn't you say?"

"I'd say let's meet and talk. When can you see me?"

"How does tomorrow suit you?"

"The Archdiocesan offices aren't closed on Saturday?"

"The Church never sleeps. But I'd much rather meet away from the office."

"There's a great diner in town where we can talk without being interrupted. How about meeting there?" The diner was neutral turf.

"Where exactly? I live in South Philadelphia."

"Broad and Lombard. Right on the corner. Cactus Corner. Know it?"

"I've seen it."

"Meet you there at ten tomorrow morning?"

He agreed and I wondered about my sanity. I wouldn't get home until at least two after finishing up at Bubbles. A ten o'clock meeting would be painful.

Clifford's call got me thinking about the case even more.

Part of me wanted it to be all about Vatican intrigue, the machinations behind the crimson curtains of the Church. I wanted to know what had really happened to Pope John Paul the First. That was the appeal of Brandt's book. Everybody wanted the truth. They needed to know why a gentle soul only lasted thirty-three days in the Church's supreme position. Maybe that office wasn't made for nice guys. Maybe John Paul the First was in over his head and his heart knew it before his brain. And that heart gave out, just like the papers said.

Nah, life wasn't that neat and convenient. There was always something more sinister going on. At least that's what my Italian nature taught me to believe and it was right most of the time. But this case was about Brandt's death. That was the personal part for me. I'd actually seen Brandt and been inspired by him. I was too young to even remember John Paul the First, though I'd read about him and I'd been moved. I'd never forgotten what I'd read and always wanted to know more. Brandt's case held that as an additional lure for me. But no one keeps secrets better than the Church. The Vatican's basement is full of skeletons and not just the saintly kind.

Would be nice to get my hands on that particular secret. It'd do wonders for business. I could see the headline: "Philly P.I. Closes Coldest Case of the Last Century"

Who was I kidding? More likely Brandt was murdered by someone with a different motive. An angry publisher, a jealous writer, a fanatic, a lover, a thug, or who knew what else?

The phone rang and my daydreams vanished.

"Fontana."

"Mr. Fontana?"

"Kent!" I recognized the voice immediately. How can you forget someone who held a gun to your chest? "Hey, still interested in that job?"

"I've been thinking, Mr. Fontana…"

"You're not going to bug out on me, are you? And, call me Marco."

"N-no. No. I…"

"Anton will let me know tonight and I'll call you. He's gotta be on board." I wasn't so sure he'd been convinced that the guy who'd held him at gunpoint was really a sweet kid.

"I understand." He let out a small sigh. "I just wanna say thanks, even if it doesn't work out."

It all depended on Anton now.

Chapter 9

Bubbles was crowded. Amateur nights always packed them in despite the cover charge.

"Hey, Fontana!" One of the regulars waved me over. Dale, a stocky, middle-aged guy had been coming to Bubbles for years. He was observant, clever and, most of all, generous. The dancers loved him and not just for the fifties and hundreds he sometimes handed out. He actually treated them like people.

"Here to take your pick of the newbies?"

"I gotta admit it's exciting seeing them start out."

"How many years've you been coming to Amateur Night?"

"Since…," he said and stroked his chin remembering. "Since the first time you had one'a these nights. Never missed yet."

"How'd you like to be a judge?"

"A judge? You mean, choose the winners? Me?" The red blush rising in his face was visible even in the dim lighting.

"Only hitch is you gotta stay until it's over."

"Hell, yeah!" Dale exploded with a hearty, never-thought-this-would-happen-to-me laugh.

"I'll get you when we're ready." Patting him on the back, I snatched a shot glass and placed it upside down in front of Dale, a signal for the bartender to give him free drinks the rest of the night.

Outside the dressing room, Bruno strutted in full military camo duds. Impressive, but then Bruno was impressive in and out of clothes.

"Hola, jefe," Bruno said.

"Learning Spanish from your new boyfriend?"

"We're history. Don't you get the news? Anyway, I knew Spanish before I met the pendejo."

"Where's Cal? Wanna go find him for me?"

"Oh, I get it. You wanna be alone with Anton. Ain't gonna happen. There's more amateurs in there than flies on shit. They been arrivin' for an hour. It's like Nerve City, that's why I'm out here. Don't need them to throw me off."

"Gotcha."

I entered the dressing room. It was wall to wall guys, dressed and undressed. All vying for mirrors and lights. They primped, pulled clothing on and off, tested tear-away pants, brushed their hair, and inspected every inch of their bodies. Some practiced their moves: gyrating, wiggling their asses, or thrusting their hips forcing their pouches to bounce temptingly.

Anton stood in the middle of this beauty tsunami. Head and shoulders above most of them, he glanced in ten directions at once. Chaos was not his thing, he insisted on order and control. I got his attention and waved him over. It was fun watching him wade through all the manflesh, pushing well-formed asses out of the way, nudging this guy and that, slipping his hands around enviable waists, gently moving them out of the way, until he stood in front of me.

"It's hot in here, let's go to my office," I said fanning myself.

"Cute, Marco. You're a laugh a minute." Anton smiled. "Did you do some special advertising? This is the biggest group we've had in years."

"Maybe it goes in cycles," I said. "The male psyche is set to want to strip every so often and sometimes there's a convergence of individual cycles causing them to rip off their clothes all at the same time. Or, maybe there's a full moon, no pun intended, and we benefit."

"You're full of it. As usual." Anton opened the door. In the hall he turned to me, eyebrows raised. "You weren't joking, it's ten degrees cooler out here."

"It's the men. All that muscle packed together in a small space. There's bound to be heat."

"There are a lot of hot prospects. We can expand the ranks of StripGuyz and maybe I can think about retiring earlier so I can finish school."

"Retire? You can't. You have fans, admirers. They're just waiting to give you their money. Every time you're out there your g-string is packed with loot! How can you think about retiring?"

"It's getting to be…"

"Besides, it's the only time I get to see you nearly naked."

"You can see and even have the whole package. Just say the word."

"You mean two words, right? 'I' and 'do'?"

"Exactly the words I had in mind. See, we even think alike. We're made for each other." Anton laughed. He kept trying. Maybe one day he'd get the answer he wanted.

"Yeah, yeah. But we're not thinking alike on retirement. Besides, don't you need the money?"

"Who doesn't need money? I just don't need all the pawing and prodding and people wondering if I'm just the sum of my cock and balls."

"I know." I placed an arm around him. "Anyway, I know how smart you are and just how valuable you are to me."

"As a business asset."

"Lots more than that, Anton. As well you know."

I kissed him and neither of us came up for air for a long while. He felt warm and smelled like clean forest air. I didn't want to let go.

Someone knocked on the door. The two of us broke apart like teenagers caught by parents.

"C'mon in."

The door swung open and Kent stood there looking lost and alone.

"Kent!" I said a bit more enthusiastically than I'd intended. Out of the corner of my eye, I saw Anton grimace.

"H-hello," he said concentrating on me. Then he turned to Anton. "I w-wanted to say I'm sorry. For the other night, I mean. I'm really sorry."

"Kent," I repeated.

"I know I was supposed to wait. But... look... even if Anton doesn't want me to work here... I just had to apologize in person. I was dumb. I could've hurt you and I never wanted that. I can't tell you how sorry I am." His voice quavered.

"Hmmm..." Anton murmured.

"I'll get going." Kent turned around.

I said nothing but cast a sidelong glance at Anton and watched him soften. Anton was tough and competent but he was also genuinely compassionate. He was the best and I was lucky to know him.

"Hold on," Anton said. His tone was commanding and Kent froze.

"Y-you're not gonna call the police, are you?"

Anton walked over and placed a hand on Kent's shoulder.

"What you did the other night was monumentally stupid."

"I... I know. I'm not gonna make excuses."

"Now you're back and..."

"I'm... I'll go. Honest. Just wanted to tell you myself that I'm sorry. I won't bother you anymore."

"It's pretty brave of you, coming here," Anton said. "I admire that."

I kept silent and watched as Anton's protective nature took over.

"You gave me a few white hairs," Anton continued. "But I know what it's like to be desperately in love."

"I was an idiot. I shouldn't have done it."

"Then you won't mind if I pat you down?" Anton laughed and I knew everything was okay.

"Sure. Go ahead. I understand." Kent swung out his arms so Anton could check for weapons. "Go ahead. Pat me down. I don't have a gun. Or a knife. Want me to take the position so you can feel and see?"

"It's tempting," Anton said. "Very tempting. I'll reserve the right to feel for weapons any time I like. Deal?"

"Deal." Kent laughed.

"Next thing I know you'll want to strip search him," I said.

"I might do that. Jealous?" Anton teased.

"Let me get Kent settled."

"Did you pick a judge for the contest?" Anton asked.

"Yep. Dale."

"Dale? The Dale who's never missed a night since I started working here? That Dale?"

"Your most loyal fan."

"Great. He'll be good. No one pays closer attention than he does." Anton turned to leave the room. "I'll talk to the contestants. You get Cal and Bruno started."

I gave Kent some papers to fill out and told him to meet me at the bar.

Downstairs, I approached Cal and Bruno waiting in the wings.

"Did you toss a coin to see who goes first?" I asked. Cal wore his sailor boy costume which was about as tight as clothing could be without being sprayed on. It was his most popular outfit. Bruno had changed into workman's overalls with a tank top and an orange neckerchief.

"He'll go first," Bruno said.

"You lost the toss?"

"Nah, we didn't need to toss. I'm lettin' him go first." Bruno grunted.

Cal stood there humming, trying to look innocent.

"Okay." I didn't want to know what that was all about. "Ready, Cal?"

"As I'll ever be." He wiggled his buns.

I stepped out front and took the mike, tapping it to make sure it worked, and cleared my throat.

"Welcome to Bubbles and StripGuyz Amateur night! Where you get to give a boost to guys who wanna be part of our gang. We've got a huge group for you tonight. Really huge. Your work's cut out for you. The judges are depending on your reactions to the dancers. So, if you like 'em, let us hear it."

The crowd clapped and cheered, hooted, and hollered.

"That's what I mean, guys. Just sittin' there doesn't help. We've gotta hear how much you like these boys."

I paused.

"The newbies are getting ready. While you wait, we've got two, yes, two feature dancers tonight. First up is Cal…" I waited while the audience applauded and whistled. "Cal is back from his stint on the USS Below the Belt. The sailors there were sorry to see him leave, even if they did like watching him walk down the gangplank. Put your hands together for Caaaaaalllll!"

Cal's music began for his routine in the small staging area. After that, he'd hop up onto the bar to get up close and personal with the customers.

I watched for a moment, as Cal gyrated, twirled, and moved his body like a pretzel in heat. It was mesmerizing and the audience was as entranced as I was.

"Uh, Mr. Fontana."

I heard the voice and felt the tap on my shoulder and realized I wasn't just another customer. I had responsibilities. Kent was one. He waited patiently for me to break free of Cal's spell.

"Finished the paperwork?"

"It's on your desk."

"Well, let's get started." I looked at his fresh, innocent face. He stared back, confused.

"Um, okay. What am I gonna do?"

I placed an arm around Kent's shoulder and he tensed up. The boy was one scared puppy. But brave. To come into an unfamiliar situation, with people you hardly knew, to do something you had no idea about, couldn't be easy.

"You'll help keep an eye on the crowd. Watch for potential trouble. People who look like they don't fit; guys too drunk to keep their hands to themselves. When the dancers are on the bar, you'll make sure that when customers tip, they don't put their hands where they're not supposed to."

"What'll I do if I see someone who's trouble? Hustle him out of here?"

"No. First few nights, come get me. I know a lot of the guys and you can observe how I handle things. There's lots of ways to deal with situations. That's what I'll show you. If it comes to it, we get Kevin, the bouncer, to do the heavy lifting. You'll get the hang of it. You can always ask me or Anton if you aren't sure about something."

We walked the length of the huge main floor bar and around to the other side.

"See that guy, backpack at his feet? You wanna keep an eye on things like that," I said, pulling Kent back so the customer wouldn't hear. "You just never know what they've got hidden. Trick is, don't let customers feel they're being watched even though they are."

"Gotcha, Mr. Fontana."

"If you're gonna work for me, call me Marco." I winked.

"Okay… Marco." Kent was appealingly shy.

"Gotta get back to the stage. Stay here and I'll show you what to do when dancers are on the bar."

Adding Kent to the other eyes I had on the floor would make life easier. Not to mention I hated being the guard dog on premises. But that was the deal I'd made with Stan, the owner.

"Give it up for Cal, guys. Anybody feel like joining the navy?" I waited for the applause to subside. "Now you're gonna get a chance to see just how convincing Cal can be when he's in your face. Remember, tips are welcome, wandering hands aren't. Place your tips in the side of the g-string only." That announcement was usually made a few times throughout an evening.

I went back to Kent who watched Cal move onto the bar.

"This is when you really have to have three heads and keep your eyes looking in several places at the same time."

As Cal danced on the bar, I glanced at Kent staring intensely. He was probably remembering Nando doing the same thing.

"Okay, now see…" I pointed to a customer attempting to place a hand into Cal's g-string pouch along with a dollar. "That's not allowed."

I moved behind the customer. Cal knew what to do, but backup from management never hurt. Cal deftly brushed away the guy's hand and I leaned in, lips near the customer's ears and whispered, "State law, no touching the dancers in certain places. Tips go into the side of the g-string only."

I stepped back before the startled guy could react.

"That's it? What'd you say?" Kent asked, giving me a strange look.

"Just told him the rules. Keep an eye on him the rest of the night. He'll know we're watching."

"They really can't touch dancers like that?"

"State Liquor Control Board has regulations. They send spies to make sure we're complying. Never know when they're here to test us."

"I didn't know," Kent said. I had a feeling he had a new appreciation for Nando's work.

"I've gotta introduce Bruno. Then it's Amateur time. You'll really have to be sharp. Customers try to get away with doing more with amateurs. Keep your eyes peeled."

"Gotcha, Marco."

Back at the mike, I saw Bruno was ready, rubber hammer in one hand, clipboard in the other.

"And now, gentlemen, to rev you up for the amateurs, here's a real pro. He brought his tools and he's ready to fix your problems. Give it up for Bruuuuunoooo!"

Bruno was a crowd pleaser and he knew it. He strutted onto the stage, teasing the guys with his eyes, exuding confidence and pure sex.

As Bruno began, Kent tapped my shoulder again. I thought about getting mini-walkie-talkies.

"We've got a situation, Marco." Kent sounded official. "In the corner. Looks like it might get outta hand."

"Show me." I placed the mike back under the counter.

Kent led me to a couple that seemed in the middle of a heated argument. One of them gesticulated angrily. The other fended off the first guy's advances. It was dim and I couldn't be sure, so I edged closer, pretending to watch Bruno and Cal. I only heard certain words as the two customers argued.

"He's... not anymore!... dead and gone... back... with me," the first guy said putting a hand on the younger man's shoulder.

"...fuck... away! ...you hear?... get... from me!" The younger guy roughly swiped the other man's hand away.

I moved in before it became a full fledged fight. As I approached I realized the older of the two was the same guy I'd seen leaving Dreier's office earlier that day. Except now he seemed more arrogant and sinister.

He looked up, saw me, and his eyes narrowed in anger. Glaring at the younger man, he stood and made for the door.

"Kent." I waved him over. "See if you can find out who this guy is." I pointed to the man sitting at the bar. "I'll be back."

I followed the other guy out and onto the street.

"Hey!" He never turned to look back as he quick walked. "I just want to ask a question."

I caught up to him at Broad Street. It was too busy for him to cross and he wasn't happy. When the light changed, he moved and I fell in next to him. Finally, outside the Hyatt, he turned to face me.

"Stay out of this. It's none of your business. People have already been hurt," he spat out the words and turned to go.

"Hold on." I'd caught the corner of his lapel and pulled him around. He didn't put up a fight but anger burned in his eyes.

"Get your hands off me. Don't press your luck," he snapped. The guy was wired and on fire. "Keep outta my business. He's mine and…"

"Who's yours?"

He jerked himself away and walked off. Over his shoulder he shouted at me, "Stay away from him. Or you'll pay, too."

Chapter 10

"The guy you chased is named Scanlan. Seamus Scanlan." Kent was excited to be helping. The look in his eyes said it all. The same sparkle I'd seen in Anton and Luke whenever I brought them in on a case.

"Where's the boyfriend?"

"He booked as soon as I was done talking with him," Kent said. "Sorry."

"Don't be. Did you get a name? Anything about him?"

"Said his name was Jared Beeton."

"What was the fight about?"

"He said Scanlan was tryin' to convince him to get back with him." Kent smiled weakly. "Sounds familiar, huh?"

I thought it was a good sign that Kent could poke fun at himself.

"Did the kid say anything else?"

"Nope, gulped his drink and shot outta here," Kent said. "I'll get back to work."

"Yeah." I checked the time. "The amateurs start in five. Keep your eyes open."

I'd track down Jared and Scanlan and see what I could find out. But that would have to wait.

* * *

The alarm screamed at nine, waking me from a dream involving a giant hamster rampaging through my building's lobby. He'd gnawed his way through the reception desk and ripped the pants off Carlos who stood there, every inch of flesh exposed. I was about to help Carlos when the damned alarm broke the dream and left me breathless.

Eyes wide, body wondering why I tortured myself getting up early on a Saturday, I remembered my meeting with Clifford at Cactus Corner, then with Luke at the Fortress of Geekiness, after which I'd recruited Kent to come along to canvass for witnesses.

I took the longest shower I could. It's a way for me to relax into the day. I try not to think about anything but the water and my body. Today that wasn't easy. Clifford's cryptic aside that the case wasn't what it appeared to be made my thoughts race.

He knew I was working the angle that the murder was related to Brandt's work. Which still topped my list. But talking to Hollister and hearing Scanlan's threat, I knew there were other potential scenarios. I wondered which lead Clifford would endorse. According to Hollister, Clifford himself had something to hide.

I left the apartment in plenty of time to get to the diner. On my way through the lobby I glanced at Carlos to make sure he wasn't being menaced by a giant rodent. He wasn't. Unfortunately he still had all his clothes on. The way he smiled at me, though, made me wonder if he knew what I was thinking.

Cactus Corner was bustling when I arrived and I took a booth at the back. Broad and Lombard had been a grim intersection bordering the center of town. With the advance of what the city called the Avenue of the Arts, even that area benefited. The Avenue was Broad Street moving from City Hall to the south and lined with five or six theaters, music venues like the Academy of Music and the Kimmel, educational institutions like the University of the Arts and a high school for performing arts. With even more coming, it lived up to its name.

Clifford sauntered in exactly at ten, wearing the brightest orange sweater I'd ever seen along with a green jeff-cap. He resembled a walking citrus.

Waving to him, I wondered what in hell he was thinking when he dressed that morning. He smiled broadly when he saw me. Making his way toward me, several people greeted him and he responded extravagantly. Lots of the customers seemed to know him. There was something familiar about Clifford but I realized quickly that he was a type. A type I'd known since I came out: the campy uncle who knew everything and everyone. A good-time Charlie with a purposely bizarre sense of style meant to make people notice and remember. It was difficult imagining him working for the Archdiocese.

He took my hand when I stood to meet him.

"Mr. Fontana," he said, looking me up and down. "So nice to meet you. You're the very picture of a Private Eye. In fact, you're better. Not grungy or decadent."

"I'm kinda disappointed. That I don't look decadent, I mean." I felt his eyes scanning me. "Thanks for meeting." I sat back down and motioned the waitress over.

"My pleasure. More fun for me to talk away from the office. So formal and stuffy there."

"Scrambled eggs and a short stack, Angie," I said to the waitress.

"What'll you have, gorgeous?" She asked Clifford. "The usual?"

"Um, oh…" Clifford eyed me as if I were the Food Police. "No, hon, how about black coffee and some toast."

"Whatever you say, doll." Angie stared at him as if he'd lost his mind. She glanced at me and smirked. She probably figured, as I did, that he was trying to impress me with his Spartan habits. But Sparta wasn't exactly the place you thought of when you looked at him.

"How long have you worked for the Archdiocese?" I asked.

"Oh… on and off about thirty years, I suppose. In one position or another." He winked when he said that but I pretended not to notice.

"Right now you're…"

"I help out in the PR department and I circulate from office to office doing whatever they need done. They aren't swimming in money for staff. I do what I can."

"I guess Brandt's book caused quite a stir there? You probably heard about it everywhere you went."

"A stir? You could call it that. An open wound is more like it," he said as if he'd just sucked a lemon. "You don't produce work like that and expect accolades. The man hurt a lot of people."

"But he hadn't named names. At least not in that book."

"He came darned close. He implicated supposed 'friends' of the late Pope, higher ups in the Vatican hierarchy, officials of the Church. It wouldn't take much to put two and two together and come up with the answers he hinted at."

"And those answers were…?" I coaxed.

"Naughty, naughty. I don't tell tales out of school."

"Who seemed most upset?" I didn't think he'd answer but I had to try. The guy was cagey despite dressing like a clown.

"Now Mr. Fontana, even if I knew, would you expect me to implicate innocent people?" He paused and looked me in the eye. "Especially when I know there are others who had even better reasons to want Brandt out of the way."

"So you said on the phone. Any chance you're gonna let me in on your little secret?"

"Far be it from me to name names, detective." Clifford rolled his eyes. "I'm not that kind of guy."

"What kind are you, Mr. Clifford? The kind who lets a man die for writing a book? Or, the kind who likes to play games in order to obstruct justice?"

"I'm just a person who knows what he knows. And I know Brandt had been fooling around with someone else's man. That didn't sit too well with the offended party. Didn't sit too well at all."

"That's it? No names, no nothing?" Even gossip columnists gave hints. "I'll need more than that. You could be talking about someone halfway around the world."

"No. Just around the block, so to speak."

"Meaning?"

"You do like to press, don't you? This isn't mere gossip. That I'll tell you. It's a very real… or was a very real situation. Brandt came between two people who loved each other. Of course, Brandt didn't care one whit about that. He was all about his own pleasure and gratification. Whether it was the pleasure of destroying good people with false accusations or the pleasures of the flesh which he took with anyone he pleased. Didn't matter to him."

"Did you dress him down with that same speech when you and Brandt argued on the street not long ago? Was it satisfying calling him a liar and worse in public?" I stared at him but there was little reaction. "You seem angrier than anyone else I've spoken to, Mr. Clifford. Considerably more incensed over Brandt."

"What? You'll put me on your little list of suspects?"

"You sure seem to have some personal grudge."

"Nonsense."

"That little dust up on the street a while ago, it wasn't because you were angry?"

"I ran into Brandt downtown. No law against going shopping, is there?" He paused, mostly for effect I guessed. "I was coming out of Mikey Leto's and Brandt was there, window shopping."

"So you took the opportunity to give him a piece of your mind?"

"Something like that. We'd met before through his friend Hollister. But Brandt pretended not to recognize me."

"That when you let him have it?"

"I asked him why he would write a book of harmful lies and he turned on me. Like a dog. Said he remembered me and knew I worked up close with all the big boys. He said I should know why he wrote what he did because I saw what they did every day. I told him he'd hurt a lot of people with his distortions. That only made him angrier and he implied that because I worked for the Archdiocese, I was responsible for covering up the truth. He said I worked for a hypocrite and I was one, too. He actually said he cared about the Church. That the Vatican had hurt it more than his books ever could. And I'll never forget what he said next, never. He said, 'People like you rob the Church of any power to do good.' That's about when I lost it and screamed at him, told him he was a liar and a destroyer. Which is what he is… was."

"Seems like he was dedicated to his work."

"Dedicated to destroying the Church is more like it."

"Who did he mean when he said you work for a hypocrite? Who do you work for exactly?"

"I told you, I circulate" Clifford's eyes shifted down and to the left. It wasn't difficult to tell he was evading the truth. "I don't work for anybody in particular. I'm not important. Just a cog in the works. I respect the Church, I'm not tearing it down like Brandt. Despicable. That's what he was. A despicable, narrow-minded man bent on hurting a lot of people for his own glory."

"Sounds like you've got a pretty big axe to grind. Maybe I should look into you for his murder."

"I would never have anything to do with violence. I may have despised the man. But I would never…"

"Then who? Your Opus Dei boarder?"

"What? What are you…"

"Your boarder. Maybe he was behind this."

"John?"

"Yeah, John." I said, not really knowing the guy's name but Clifford had slipped and I intended to make him go further. "Maybe John is a violent zealot who organized this whole thing. Maybe he even did it himself."

"John Navarro is a man of God, a peaceful soul. He would never…" Clifford stopped himself. "Forget him. He's not the one you should be looking for. I told you…"

"Well, who is this phantom couple you seem to think is involved?"

"Now, now. I just wanted to point you in the right direction."

"Then give me a map. Give me names."

"I can't be expected…"

"How about I give you a name? How's Franny hit you?" I knew from Hollister that Clifford wanted to keep his past buried. According to Hollister, the days he was known as Franny, were times he'd rather put behind him. I'd easily gotten the dirt on his past. It wasn't pretty.

"Never heard of him."

"I know people who know Franny well. Pictures and everything. Pretty hot stuff."

"Who… you couldn't know…"

"But I do."

"You're as bad as Brandt. An ugly man with an ugly soul."

"Franny can stay buried, but I need more on this phantom couple."

Clifford squirmed and gripped his butter knife. I knew he wanted to cut my heart out with it.

"Well….?"

"One works for the… Archdiocese."

"At the Race Street building?"

"Yes."

"Who?" I glared at him. "Who?!"

"Scanlan. Works for Wren. Scanlan can be dangerous." He didn't bother waiting for his breakfast. He snapped his cap back onto his head and rushed out, not even stopping to speak to his astonished friends. I didn't get to ask about his Opus Dei boarder.

I got more than a few angry stares from Clifford's friends who'd obviously heard the heated exchange we'd had. But Angie smiled when she brought my food and that's what counted.

* * *

After breakfast and a stop at the office, I made my way to meet Luke at the Fortress of Geekiness where Nina and her team worked the electronic fields of cyberspace with sophisticated computers.

Nina was incredibly savvy. With shrewdness and savings, she'd managed to buy property in Olde City, part of Philly's historic district. A large, serene, red-brick, three story house became her home and headquarters. From web design to research to helping with investigations and just about anything else you could do or want done with cutting edge technology, Nina and her gang could do it.

At the moment, Nina's company, InfoMonkeys, was composed of Nina, Hallie, and Deena. If they couldn't find what you were after, it couldn't be found.

Luke turned the corner just as I arrived from the opposite direction.

"You're looking good this morning," I said. "The new haircut is interesting."

"You don't like it?" Luke said. He enjoyed experimenting with his appearance. But since he was beautiful, everything looked good on him.

"Didn't say that. It looks good. You look suave. Worldly." I smiled. "It emphasizes your face, makes your eyes appear darker and deeper. I like it."

"Who can believe you? You're only interested in one thing."

"You ought to work at Quantico. They need more behavioral analysis guys like you." I gave him a hug. "Got the papers?"

"Right here." He patted the messenger bag which he always carried. Even I didn't know exactly what he kept in that bag.

"Well, let's gain entrance to the Fortress and see what Nina says."

Luke pressed the bell and I waved to the hidden, to most everyone else, camera.

There was a metallic whisper of locks pulling into themselves, of a bolt being thrown, then the door swung open. Luke and I stepped into the vestibule and the door gently shut itself behind us. We went through another door which unlocked only after the first was secured and they had a chance to see exactly who was in the entry.

The first floor consisted of an elaborate, high tech array of computers, lots of sleek flat monitors, a whole room devoted to the latest in surface computing, and an experimental 3-D monitor. I was sure in six months there'd be even newer cutting-edge technology. Nina never let cyber-grass grow under her feet.

I saw Nina at the surface computer, shifting pictures and maps, arranging information in patterns that would make it easier to find what she was looking for. Neither Hallie nor Deena were around.

"Right on time," Nina said without turning around. "What've you got for me?"

"Where's everybody else?" Luke asked.

"Hallie and Deena don't work on Saturdays unless we're on deadline. I'm here because I live upstairs and you guys need me. Not to mention Marco promised me some extras if I take this job."

"Oh, he did?" Luke smiled.

"A spa experience with the works," I said.

"So." Nina turned toward us. "What's the deal? Got the laptop?"

"Not yet. We've got to find it."

"You lost it?"

"Nope," Luke said handing her the accordion folder. "Brandt probably hid it before he was killed. Nobody has a clue."

"Not yet," I said. "But, there's a stack of e-mail I'm hoping you can track for us."

"You mean find out who wrote them?"

"The all-mighty Nina can do anything. That case last month? I thought it was impossible, but you did it."

"The Twining case? Ha! Did that in my sleep."

"That's what I mean. You're good. The best."

"Save the flattery for your pretty boys. It's lost on me." She eyed Luke and suppressed a smile.

"But you can do this. Right?"

"Finding out who wrote e-mails is another story, Marco. I can get you to a machine maybe."

"Take a look at some and see what you think." Luke pulled some papers out of the folder.

"What've we got?" Nina riffled through the papers. "Weird names. Templar1098@yahoo, VaticanMilitia@gmail, SecularVengeance@gmail, Ciliceguy@gmail, MensEcclesiae@hotmail. What is all this?"

"Threats, warnings, hate mail. Brandt inspired it all with his book."

"These sound like religious nuts." Nina was contemptuous.

"Probably," I said.

"These people dangerous?"

"I won't lie, Nina. One of these people could've killed Brandt or ordered the killing."

"Cool! It'll be like that other case, then." Nina grinned. Her Aztec serpent tattoo seemed to smile.

"That doesn't bother you?" Luke asked.

"It's exciting." Nina's brown eyes flashed.

"All righty then," I said, not wanting to know just how much of a risk freak Nina was. "What do you think you can do with this?"

"There's some stuff I can try. And I see gmail accounts here." Nina flipped the pages again.

"And that means...?"

"That means I might, just might, be able to get some inside information."

"Should I ask how?"

"No. It's not criminal. I know a guy. Cerberus. We used to hang together online. Hackers have a code. And this is a murder case, right? Information wants to be free. I help free it. So, lemme see what I can do while you find that laptop."

* * *

Luke lived nearby in a condo on a high floor; whenever I was there it seemed as if we were in the middle of the clouds and far away from everything. We'd be meeting Kent later to canvass the gayborhood for witnesses. But that was later.

"Lunch?" Luke asked. "Hungry for leftovers?"

"You're no leftover, mister." I looked at him and the glance we exchanged said lunch would come a distant second to other things.

The elevator, a high tech affair with recessed lighting and a small LCD TV broadcasting CNN, zipped us to his penthouse apartment. The housecleaning business had been good to him.

His condo was sleek and modern. He believed in the minimal look. Everything neat, tidy, and in its place. It smelled like clean linen. Of course, that was easy when you had a team of guys doing your housework. He'd offered to have some of his guys clean my place free but Luke was the only one I trusted to roam around my apartment poking into the intimate corners of my life and work. Not that he hired untrustworthy guys, it was my own skittishness and natural lack of trust.

I threw my jacket over a chair and flopped onto the couch. Luke didn't waste time with niceties, instead he ripped off his clothes and straddled me as I savored the beauty of his body and the elegance of his movements. Then he placed his lips on mine and the rest of the world was blotted out.

* * *

"I had three doors slammed in my face. Seven people told me to mind my own business and three guys said they never saw a thing but gave me their numbers," Kent said. "I might use those numbers. So it wasn't a total loss."

"Not for you," I said. Canvassing for witnesses was never fun. But sometimes, like Kent, you get lucky.

"I have numbers for five people who say they'd be willing to talk." Luke handed me a page from his book. "I wouldn't count on some of them to be telling the truth."

"Why's that?"

"One of them invited me in and wanted to get cozy before he'd say anything."

"Did you? Get cozy, I mean."

"I don't kiss and tell. Did you have any luck?"

"One guy says he might've seen something. A few dollars helped him remember. But he said nothing new."

"A washout, huh?" Kent asked.

"Sometimes it's like that."

"I thought this would be more exciting," Kent commented. "Like on TV."

"I'd say getting three numbers is pretty exciting," Luke commented.

"Yeah, well, there's getting and there's getting." Kent chuckled. "We'll see what happens."

"I'm exhausted and I still have schedules to make out." Luke zipped up his jacket.

"Why don't you two take off? I'll hit one more spot."

I watched the two of them walk off, chatting like old buddies, amazed at Kent's resilient capacity for change. I knew hiring him wasn't a bad idea.

The Venture Inn was next. That's where Hollister and Brandt were headed and I thought maybe one of the regulars might've witnessed something. The Venture was a very old bar and a great restaurant. Quiet and cozy, it had a loyal following. The rush of the outside world disappeared when you entered. I'd started going there regularly after Galen disappeared and it felt like home.

Everyone at the Venture has his own story. Lots of them know loss and heartbreak. When someone eventually coaxed me to tell about my friend Galen's disappearance, he let me talk as long as I wanted. It felt good to get it out and left me with a fondness for the Venture.

Zack, the bartender, set me up with my usual, a mojito.

"Been a while," Zack said as he washed glasses. "You lead one of those glamorous lives catching bad guys, shooting guns, getting all the hotties." He sighed dramatically.

"Yep, really glamorous, always a hottie on my arm, always a gun in my belt."

"That's what I thought." Zack laughed. "You don't look like you're here for a good time. Something up?"

"That shooting the other night. Were you here?"

"When am I not here? Do I look like I have a life? I was here and scared shitless. That guy was killed right down the street."

"Anybody mention they saw anything?"

"You know what the guys are like. Come back in two weeks and everybody here will claim they were witnesses."

"That night, you remember anybody coming in who said they saw the shooting?"

"You're workin' this case, aren't you? I knew it." Zack smiled and I saw all over again why he was so popular with Venture's crowd. "I hate to disappoint you, Marco, but nobody said anything to me about it."

"Said anything about what, Zacky?" A grizzled older guy, two seats down, slapped a twenty on the bar.

"That writer who got shot, Chaz. Remember?"

"Gimmie a Rolling Rock. Shooting? The other night? I wasn't here. Don't know much about it."

"You hear anybody else talk about it?" I asked. The guy looked at me like I'd just dropped in from Saturn. "Marco Fontana." I held out my hand.

"Chaz," he said, his voice like a gurgle. "What's your interest in that shootin'?"

"I'm a P.I. Hired to investigate."

"Just a muggin' that's what they said. You tellin' me it wasn't?"

"Because the police said it was a mugging doesn't mean it's the truth."

"Not the police, man," Chaz said and took a long pull from his beer bottle. "There was two guys here who said they saw it. Can't remember what they said because there's so much bullshit tossed around here I don't bother keepin' it all in my head. If you catch my drift…"

"But you remember who said it, right, Chaz? Tell me you remember." I stared hard at the man, hoping to jog his brain cells.

"It was Artie and… uh… Jordan. Ain't that right, Zacky?"

"Hey if you say it was them, it was them. They were here that night."

"You know them?"

"We all know 'em," Chaz said.

"Yeah, they're regulars," Zack confirmed. "But they're not here tonight."

"Shit."

"They'll be in tomorrow. They always come in on Sunday because it's Trivia Night. They love trivia. Any kind of trivia. They love showing off. And if you mention I said that, I'll spike your next drink and take you home over my shoulder."

"Sounds tempting, Zack."

Chaz laughed until he started coughing.

"Have some water, Chaz." Zack placed a glass in front of the guy.

"You sure they'll be in tomorrow?"

"If they're not, you can take *me* home over *your* shoulder." Zack winked at me. "Aw, you can take me home anyway."

Chapter 11

Working at Bubbles after the day I'd had wasn't exactly on my top ten list. But the boss had to interview the newbies. Besides, Kent said he'd encouraged Jared to return. He could be persuasive even without a gun. I wondered what kind of encouragement he'd used. If it worked and I could question the guy, I didn't care.

Before anything else, though, I'd promised to check in with Hollister. Voicemails he'd left had a note of exasperation and I didn't have much progress to report. But on the principle that something is better than nothing, I called him.

"Is Tim around?"

"Hold on, I'll get him. Who should I say is calling?" The guy sounded upbeat and cheery. I wondered if Hollister was in the mood for a host like that.

"Marco Fontana."

"Oooohhh, I've heard about you. You're the handsome detective Tim's hired. Well, hold on, I'll get him."

I waited and heard muffled voices, even what sounded like a giggle.

"Marco? I'm glad you called." Hollister sounded tired, maybe a little tipsy. "You think it's safe for me to get a few more things from my place?"

"Can it wait until tomorrow? I don't want you going alone."

"Certainly. And, Marco...?" Hollister paused.

"I don't have answers, yet, Tim. I'm working on some leads."

"But, you think..."

"We'll get to the bottom of this. Whatever happened we'll know why and who. I promise." It was a promise I intended to keep, not only for Hollister but for that beautiful, fresh-eyed author I'd met long ago who was kind enough to be nice to me. Maybe I was even keeping the promise for that Pope I never knew. He deserved a little justice, too. "I don't make promises lightly, Tim. We will find out what happened."

* * *

I stripped off my clothes, put a ManSized Chicken Dinner into the microwave, and poured a glass of merlot which would take the edge off the day.

The sofa was soft and I melted into it hoping the wine would lull me to sleep. I watched darkness engulf the city and lights twinkle to life illuminating the night and making the river shimmer. A happy, drowsy, wine-induced peace was about to help me forget for a while. Not.

The microwave's bell and the warbling telephone broke through the buzz.

Dinner could wait, I picked up the phone.

"Fontana," I said, my voice betraying how utterly relaxed I felt.

"Tom Quinn, here. I understand you're investigating Brandt's death." The man's voice was grating. Hollister mentioned he wasn't pleasant.

"That's right." Word was getting around fast.

"You'll want to talk to me but I have nothing to tell you."

"Why're you calling me, then, Mr. Quinn?"

"You think I'm involved with Brandt's murder. Don't beat around the bush."

"Never said that, Quinn." He was obviously an attention hog and wanted to be on my suspect list. Or, maybe that was his way of deflecting suspicion.

"You think I'm involved. They all think I had something to do with it. After all I have a good motive. The bastard stole my work. Filched my research. And twisted it into something that is patently a lie."

"When can we meet face to face, Mr. Quinn?" I had to stop his rant.

"Never. I've done nothing wrong. Nothing! But I know my name will surface in this investigation. Which is why I called." His breathing was labored and wheezy.

"You want to defend your reputation, I understand." It felt like I was talking to a child. "No one's forcing you to come forward. But…"

"But what? Now you're going to threaten me. Like if I don't talk to you, I'll just have to talk in court. Or, if I don't talk to you, then some bigger goon will come and beat it out of me. Or, maybe…"

"Not at all, Mr. Quinn. You're a respected author," I said, my voice oozing honey. "You may be able to help both yourself and the investigation."

"Good." He sounded as if he were ready to listen.

"You'll have the opportunity to tell your side in your own words. I'm handling the investigation, you can talk to me. I'll get your story to the right people. Even the media."

"How can I be sure you'll tell the truth? How do I know you'll report exactly what I say?"

"We can record the conversation."

"No." He said with a swiftness I found paranoid. Then, "That won't be necessary. If you're willing to go that far, I'll have to trust you. No recordings. Do I have your word on that?"

"You got it. When can we talk?"

"This evening. I'm free now. Next week will be quite busy."

The Man-Sized Dinner was getting colder by the minute, the glass of ruby-red merlot beckoned, and I wanted to hang up the phone. The sound of Quinn's wheezing breath was annoying. Then I remembered promising Hollister I'd do everything I could.

"Give me an hour. Where do you want to meet?" I sighed.

"The café at Twelfth and Walnut, across from Starbuck's. Know it?"

"I know it well. One hour?"

"Come alone. No cameras, no recording devices. And no tricks. Understand? I'll be able to tell."

"One hour, Mr. Quinn."

He hung up without a word.

The microwave is my friend. I punched the buttons and reheated the food. The aroma, when I opened the door, was enough to make my stomach growl. The chicken was dry but I was hungry and in a hurry.

I freshened up, got dressed, and left.

Carlos didn't work the desk on Saturdays. Instead, Grace, as fierce a guardian as there was anywhere, stood watch. A barrel of a woman, she had bulldog intensity in a sweet-faced package. She peered at me with her sensitive, liquid eyes as I passed.

"What's up, Grace?" I smiled.

"You all right, Mr. Fontana? I mean, you been havin' any trouble?" Concern creased her face.

"No more than usual," I said and laughed. "Did I forget to pick up a package?"

"No. It's not you, exactly. There was a guy in here looking for you earlier," she said. "Don't worry. I didn't give him anything. Not a word. No apartment number. Nothing about your schedule."

"But he asked all that?"

"Said he needed to talk to you, something urgent."

"He leave a name? A number? What'd he look like?"

"Didn't leave a trace and looked like hell," Grace said. "Short. Wouldn't even come up to your shoulders. Dark hair, really dark eyes, and, whatta' they call it? Three days growth. Grungy clothes. Didn't stink, just looked dirty. Kinda tired lookin' and scared, too."

"How old?"

"Impossible to tell. Not too young, not too old."

"Anything else?" I asked as I made notes.

"Jittery. Really jittery. Kept walkin' up and down, up and down. I finally told him to leave. I wasn't gonna let him ambush you. I didn't know what he'd do."

"Thanks, Grace. You're a life saver."

"Tried to call you, but I guess you were out. Exciting. Your P.I. work, I mean."

"Sometimes. If that guy should to turn up again, you know what to do."

"You bet." She laughed.

The café wasn't far. On the way I spied a lone squirrel, acorn in his mouth, darting up an oak tree with yellowing leaves. Another sign the seasons were rapidly changing. But Quinn was on my mind and I was steeling myself for the meeting. He sounded annoying.

The café wasn't crowded when I entered, which wasn't surprising. This time of day, people were at dinner or doing other sensible things, not meeting with cranky writers.

I saw a guy I figured had to be Quinn. His face was wreathed in dour frowns matching the voice on the phone. He was a tall, long-limbed, wiry man in his fifties. Thick black-framed glasses, stringy gray hair, and rumpled clothes completed the picture. Wrinkles set his sour expression into permanence. His swarthy complexion served to intensify the dark and brooding cloud hanging over him.

He saw me staring and glared. I went up to him, introduced myself and invited him to sit with me. He grunted assent, chose a place way in a corner, and sat with his back to the wall.

I got us each a coffee and sat across from him.

"You and Brandt go back a long way?" I emptied some sugar packets into my coffee, stirred, and waited for him to reply.

"What's that got to do with anything?"

"Hey, pal, you called me. You want me to know your story, then answer my questions. I need to understand Brandt and why his work made people hot under the collar. You both worked on similar projects. You can give me some insight into him through his work. That way I learn about you, too."

"I can tell you that he was a johnny-come-lately to the subject. Hollister put him on to it. I'd been working on it far longer and had far better sources. I just didn't have the breaks, or the pretty face."

"Tell me about your work. Then you can tell me where Brandt had it wrong."

"I was and still am investigating the death of John Paul the First," he snapped. "It's taken years to develop sources, dig out materials, compile documents, get people to give me any scrap of information or leads no matter how seemingly insignificant. I have amassed files. I was close to what I know must be the truth, when Brandt comes along with his piece of crap book."

"Why crap?" I asked and watched his face morph from one emotion to another.

"It's innuendo and unsubstantiated material. It may have the ring of authenticity, some of it is based on the same material I've used. But Brandt spins off into directions nowhere near the truth."

"Does anyone really know the truth?"

"You're too young, aren't you? Too young to have been aware of that Pope and what he meant to people. You're too young to know what a stir his death caused, how it echoes down the years." Quinn's breathing was rapid. I realized he was just winding up.

"I only know what I've read. He was an unusual man with unorthodox views."

"That's what they'd like you to believe. They want you to think the conservative factions killed him. They didn't."

"The money people killed him? It was all about the Bank scandal?"

"Wrong. It was the liberals. They had to stop him. The money guys, that was just the surface. He would've taken the lid off that, too. But not for the reasons you might think. He was set to expose everything, all of them. They hadda stop him. And they did."

"How does anyone even know it was actually murder?"

"The evidence! That's how they know. The evidence. They were all in on it. The Bank, the Masons, the Curia, and some of the Cardinals. But not the ones they think." His brown eyes flashed with a malevolence I could feel.

"The Masons?" I knew he was flying on one wing. Next he'd mention the Knights Templar. "What about Opus Dei?"

"Opus Dei? You're kidding. They're the right wing. They wouldn't side with the liberals if that was their only choice."

"You've got a point. But…"

"What about the undertakers? Huh?" He leaned in and glared.

"The undertakers? Whose undertakers?"

"The Pope's undertakers. The Signoracci brothers. A family business. Four brothers. They were called in to deal with the Pope's body."

"Standard procedure, right?" I asked and realized Quinn sounded wackier by the minute.

"They were called in before anybody knew the Pope was dead. You want unusual? They were put in a limousine an hour before anybody discovered the Pope's body. That unusual enough for you?"

"I'd say it was," I mumbled. Now he mentioned it, I vaguely remembered reading something like that.

"You don't have to believe me. Other people have written about it."

"No one's ever offered hard evidence, though. Unless you've got some."

"Hard ev… are you crazy? You think people like that are gonna leave solid evidence? Cardinals, Bankers, Masons? They're gonna leave a trail to their front door? You gotta be kidding me."

"Almost all of them are dead. Easy to say anything now they can't defend themselves. Am I right?"

"You think I'm making this stuff up?" He rose to leave.

"Hold on, Quinn. You got me out here, make it worth my time. All I'm seeing right now is a jealous competitor. For all I know, you're trying to cover your ass."

He reluctantly sat back down.

"Nothing I'm saying is made up, Fontana. You hear? I don't have what you like to call evidence, but I can prove my case."

"That's what Brandt said. He had new evidence to prove his case." Nothing I'd read, including Brandt's book, offered anything in the way of a smoking gun, or in this case, a tea cup with poison residue. Which is how they say it was done.

"Showboating. That's all it was. Brandt had hoity-toity inside contacts thanks to Hollister but they didn't provide anything more than what I have. Anyway, they're on the other side of the fence."

"How so?"

"They're a bunch of fag liberals who want to prove Papa Luciani was a homo who would accept them all. That he was gonna end the prohibition on birth control and endorse women's rights."

"That was all in Brandt's first book." I tried to restrain myself from punching Quinn for what he'd said. "Nothing new in what you said.

Everybody knows all of it. Old news floating around since the day the man died."

"But that's my point. There wasn't anything new in Brandt's first book. Maybe he added in the homo stuff. All the other crap was there before Brandt knew how to get milk from a tit. The only new thing was he claimed he had proof on paper. Something that would make his case airtight."

"And you don't believe him?"

"You see the proof? You have the papers he bragged about? Nobody has. All hype for his next book. I'd love to get my hands on that pack of lies and prove Brandt was nothing but a charlatan."

"What would you do if you found the papers and they proved Brandt's case?"

"That won't happen."

"Did you, by any chance, take a look through Brandt's stuff? At his house?"

"His house? What're you talking about?"

"You tell me, Quinn."

"It's getting late." Quinn drained his cup and stood.

"I'll have more questions."

"You know where to find me. But there's nothing else I can tell you." With that he pulled his jacket tighter around him and left. The draft from the closing door wasn't the only thing that gave me chills.

✳ ✳ ✳

Later that night, I found myself walking to Bubbles, wanting to be at home, eating popcorn and watching a movie. It'd gotten chillier and the moonless night seemed sinister and unfriendly. I still loved October with its promises of holidays and cheer. But tonight I was loving it just a little less.

Bubbles was crowded, it hadn't gotten cold enough to keep the guys away. I saw Zegg performing in the staging area. Kent sat in a corner chatting up Jared, the guy from the night before. Whatever he'd used to charm the kid, it worked.

In manager mode now, I greeted old time customers and new faces. I air kissed off duty strippers and generally turned on the charm. I noticed the looks in customer's eyes, wishing they were in my shoes. If they only knew. I smiled anyway and went up to my office, needing to relax before the interviews began.

Anton was waiting for me behind my desk.

"Taking over, Anton?" I gave him a kiss.

"It's a rough, dirty job but somebody's got to interview these naked men. When I didn't hear from you, I thought maybe you weren't coming in. I was worried."

"About doing the interviews? You're great at that."

"No. About you. This case is dangerous. People getting shot, houses ransacked."

"No more scary than a lot of other cases you've worked with me. Remember the one in South Philly?"

"No need to remind me. I still have a scar on my leg."

"I'm all in one piece. See?" I turned like a fashion model and dramatically opened my jacket a la the runway set.

"OK, fashionista, the first interview will be here in fifteen minutes."

"I've got time to get some coffee. Want some?"

Anton nodded. I dashed down the stairs and out the door. The bartender made the worst coffee in the universe. I knew an all night place around the corner that rivaled the best cafés.

I returned with a bag containing three coffees and some doughnuts. Anton would yell about calories and fat and then he'd tear into at least one. And I needed two cups of the coffee to keep my eyes open after the day from hell.

Re-entering the bar, I waited until my eyes adjusted. Out of the corner of my eye I noticed a flurry of activity. Jared was leaving with another cute guy. All of a sudden it registered. The other cutie was Tony from Marlon's office at the Archdiocese. Interesting. I tried following but a large customer, wanting a better look at Zegg, barreled into me and nearly threw me off my feet. It was all I could do to keep the bag from flying onto the bar and creating a mess.

By the time I got to the door, Tony and Jared were gone.

Chapter 12

A young soldier entered the cozy room and sat next to me on the loveseat facing the fireplace. Sleek and tan with deep brown eyes, he pulled me to him, taking my face in his hands. Our lips were about to meet when…the phone rang.

"Fontana," I slurred into the phone. "What's up, besides me?" I stayed in bed as I spoke. If it wasn't important, maybe I'd get back to sleep and recapture that soldier.

"It's Tim." He sounded hesitant. "I woke you didn't I?"

"I was getting up anyway. I've got a lot on my plate today." I inelegantly suppressed a yawn. "We're meeting later, right?"

"That's why I called. I'm headed to the Cathedral for mass and thought you might like to join me. We can go back to my place afterward to pick up some things."

"Mass? The cathedral?" This had me wide-eyed. I hadn't been in a church, at least not for a service, since I-don't-know-when.

"I don't usually go either. But in light of things… Sometimes the old forms bring me comfort. It isn't the mass so much, it's just being there, in the church. The murmur of prayers, the smell of beeswax, the choir. I stopped listening to their message a long time ago but the forms, the rooted memories always do something for me." He paused. "Having you there, knowing you care about helping... that would make a difference."

How could I say no? The guy was in pain and I did care about the case. "Sure, Tim. When and where?"

"I'm ready to leave but I'll wait for you. I know it's last minute..."

"Give me a few to shower. I'll head over and meet you in half an hour?"

Forty minutes later, I reached the corner where Hollister waited. My quick shower took longer than I'd figured. The night before had been long. Interviewing fifteen potentials for StripGuyz may not sound like work but open-ended conversations with hotties, one after the other, in the close quarters of my office, can take its toll. Being sluggish in the morning couldn't be helped.

"Marco!" Hollister seemed genuinely glad to see me. "Perfect timing."

"Ready to go?" I noticed the fluttering blinds of the bay window out of the corner of my eye. Hollister's host was trying to get a peek at his houseguest's detective. I nearly turned and waved but realized that sneaking looks through blinds was a guilty pleasure all its own. Better to pretend I didn't notice.

"We should make it before it's all over. The eleven o'clock is usually the big show." Hollister smiled sadly.

"If you feel the foundation trembling as I cross the threshold, let's get the hell out." I laughed and Hollister joined in.

We were a few long blocks from Sts. Peter and Paul cathedral. The air was cold. October remembered that it was really Fall and not late Summer any more. It was bracing and shattered my lingering sleepiness.

The verdigris dome of the cathedral came into view, poking at the sky. It reminded me of Italy and had actually been modeled after a church in Rome. Seeing it always moved me in some way. Pride? Nostalgia? Past memories? I'd received a medal there when I was a Boy Scout. I remember walking the huge, echoing length of the main aisle to where a bishop waited to pin the medal on me. I'd felt small and gigantic at the same time.

The lights were bright in the basilica and more people than I expected filled the place. Puffy pink-skinned women, some wearing head scarves, dotted the congregation. Parents fidgeted with restless kids. Leathery-skinned old men knelt in prayer. An occasional lone hottie peered at the altar. People of all stripes found their way to the cathedral looking for something. Solace? Forgiveness? Peace? They all seemed wrapped in their own struggles or pain.

I felt uncomfortably like an outsider. These people believed in the Church, or, at least that it was their path to something greater than themselves. I believed in a different path but I also maintained a deep conviction about respecting the beliefs of others.

A buttery voice floated through the PA system asking congregants to consider personal sacrifice and willing forgiveness. The voice seemed familiar but we were so far back, all I saw was a tall, dark blond standing at the lectern. I concentrated on the voice and realized it was Kusek, the monsignor I'd met in Marlon's office.

The tall, handsome priest, wearing subdued green vestments, finished his sermon, closed the book before him, and folded his hands in a prayerful pose.

There was a long way to go before the service was complete and I felt as fidgety as some of the kids. The organist played a chord and Kusek started the Credo at which point the choir took over.

It drew me back to my days as an altar boy. No one was as pious or as lazy as I was about studying what an altar boy had to know. I liked the cassock, the surplice, and the pageantry but not much else. Remembering where I had to be on the altar was always filled with comic possibilities. Priests or other altar boys had to point to where I was supposed to stand or kneel at any given time. In fact, parishioners had a good chuckle when I found myself in places I shouldn't have been. Ah, the good old days.

I tucked it all away and concentrated on the good-looking Kusek whose graceful movements on the altar made me wish I could throw on a cassock and join him. I noticed Fr. Marlon and another priest celebrating the mass along with Kusek.

"Does the Cardinal ever show up for these things?" I whispered to Hollister.

"Sometimes. The eleven o'clock is usually when he'd show up. Why?"

"Just asking." I wondered how seriously the high and mighty took their roles.

Hollister, on the kneeler and leaning on the pew in front of him, had seemingly gone into a deep meditative state. Healing comes in a lot of ways.

I tried focusing and was dazzled by Kusek singing the Sanctus and the Consecration prayers. His eerily beautiful voice matched his good looks, sending a chill up my spine. I was transported and wanted to know more about him. I felt almost guilty when a rush of lust ran through me as he sang.

I mentally slapped myself back to attention and studied the ornate side altars and shrines. But that voice continued to haunt me.

Before I knew it, the altar boys, the reader, and the priests processed up the aisle and toward the doors. I turned to Hollister who had come out of his prayerful silence and stood. I expected his knees would be stiff from all that kneeling but he moved like a kid.

Kusek smiled vaguely as he passed by. He threw a blessing our way making the sign of the cross in the air and moved out the door. Marlon, on the other hand, grinned when he saw me.

Most of the congregation hesitated before moving which allowed us to beat the crowd. At the doors, Kusek shook hands with people while Marlon hovered at his side.

"Fr. Marlon, nice to see you again." I extended a hand. "This is Timothy Hollister. Helmut Brandt's partner."

"I've heard a lot about you, Mr. Hollister. I'm sorry for your loss. Truly." To give the guy credit, he seemed sincere.

"Mr. Fontana, isn't it?" Kusek's memory wasn't bad. "I saw your face as we moved up the aisle but…"

"You never expected to see me in church. Right?" I returned his smile. "The walls didn't even tremble when I entered. Think that's a good sign?"

"There's room in God's house for a lot of people." He was diplomatic as well as good-looking. A sure sign he wanted to move up in the church hierarchy. Maybe even get himself a red hat. Though I have to admit, I don't remember any cardinals ever looking like this guy. "What brings you to the Cathedral?"

"I'm accompanying Mr. Hollister," I said and introduced him.

"Of course, I've heard your name. I've seen the reports on TV. I'm so sorry for your loss. I can't imagine your pain, Mr. Hollister." Kusek, placed a hand on Hollister's shoulder as they shook hands.

"Thank you," Hollister said. The emotion in his voice was palpable. "You're very kind. Thank you."

"If you ever need to talk, Mr. Hollister. Call my office and ask for me."

"Thank you. I'll remember your kindness. Thank you, again, Monsignor."

"You're quite a guy, Monsignor," I said to him.

"Good luck with your work, Mr. Fontana." He smiled modestly and it was even better than his voice.

Hollister seemed buoyed by the mass and the brilliant sun as we returned.

"I'd like to know more about Helmut's work, if you wouldn't mind talking." I glanced over at him as we walked.

"It was his passion not just his work. And if I don't talk about it now, who will? You think it might help your investigation?"

"It'll help me know him better to know what drove him. Everything helps."

"You don't believe his work had something to do with his death. Do you?"

"Not saying that exactly. I can't discount any possibility. I'm following every lead. Which also means I still have a few questions for you."

"Me? Oh... you're still thinking about dalliances with other men." Hollister chuckled. "You can ask, of course. I'm afraid it won't be very exciting or helpful."

"I'd like to know more about why Helmut was so passionate about John Paul the First's death. The guy's been dead for thirty years."

"My fault. It was all my fault. The Pope's death haunted me. Neither I nor my friends ever believed it was a natural death. I filled Helmut's head with stories and theories. I knew he loved learning about the inner workings of the Vatican. Maybe I hoped he'd uncover the truth," Hollister said. His walking slowed as he spoke and I imagined he was going over every last thing he'd said that got Helmut interested in that research. "God forgive me. I probably got him killed."

"No, Tim, you didn't. Tell me you know it wasn't your fault." I peered at him.

Hollister nodded. "In my mind I know that. In my heart... well, my heart says I should have known better."

"He wanted to tell that story as much as you wanted it told," I insisted.

"Helmut wanted to do it before any more time passed. He thought this might be the last chance to bring the truth to light. We both knew there weren't many still alive who had inside information. Only they could corroborate evidence that will bring the truth to light. I'm not sure who'll take up Helmut's cause now."

"All the principals are dead?"

"As far as I know. Cardinal Villot, the camerlengo who took charge of the Vatican after the Pope died. He's gone. Paul Marcinkus, the archbishop who headed up the Vatican Bank, recently dead. Roberto Calvi, one of the bankers in that scandal, dead. The older cardinals are all dead including Cody of Chicago. The main players are gone. Some of the people at lower levels may still be active or at least alive. Some of them may have inside information. People like the nun who supposedly found the body. She's dead. But there must be others at that level still alive."

We walked in silence and I contemplated the possibilities. It was difficult for me to believe anyone could be crazy enough to kill over the possible murder of a pope thirty years before. Quinn was petty and envious but he was nuts, or was he? He had motive. I'd have Olga dig up information on Quinn.

If it was Brandt's work that pushed someone over the edge, then any fanatic with enough motivation could have engineered his death. So far, only Quinn fit that bill. Clifford intimated the motivation was entirely different. He'd pointed the finger at Scanlan. Said he was a jealous guy and I'd seen evidence of that. Love was a powerful motive. The only thing I knew was that Brandt's death was no accident. The mugging was a cover for something else.

Hollister nudged me, breaking my train of thought.

"We're here, Marco." Hollister looked up at his house.

"I was thinking about the case."

"I could tell." He placed a foot on the first step.

"Let me go first," I said. "Just in case."

Hollister handed me the key. I unlocked the door and entered. The place was silent and empty. I pulled my gun and did a quick sweep.

"It's clear."

"This will only take a moment. I just need a few things. How much longer do you think I'll have to stay away?" he asked, slowly climbing the stairs.

"Can't really tell. If I knew who tossed your house and why, it'd help. Take enough for a week. I can't promise it'll be wrapped up by then, though."

The tiny enclave was so isolated and quiet, it was almost like being in another town. The only sound was Tim rooting around upstairs. I sat on the sofa facing the windows. The translucent blinds allowed bright sunshine to filter into the room giving it a tawny glow.

At first I thought my imagination was playing tricks on me. The silence, the warmth, and the feeling I needed to be on guard heightened my senses. I thought I saw someone outside trying to look through the blinds. I stared at the window, not moving. There he was again. Just a silhouette. But definitely trying to see in. I rose, moving silently, edging my way toward the door. He hadn't moved by the time I reached for the doorknob.

But the sound spooked him. When I opened the door all I saw was a blue blur rounding the corner. I chased after him but he was lost in the warren of tiny streets. I poked around as many corners as I could, then headed back to Hollister's house.

As I let myself back in, Hollister came down the stairs pulling a small, wheeled suitcase behind him.

"Something wrong, Marco?"

"Thought I heard something. Just checking it out. Hope I didn't give you a start."

"Not at all. I'm more hardy than you imagine."

"Got everything?"

"Yes. But I have something I want to give you." Hollister moved into the kitchen. "A bottle of liquor. A liqueur actually. Something you might like."

"No need, Tim, really."

"I insist, Marco. I never opened the bottle. It was something I bought on a lark thinking I'd like it. I was told to keep it in the freezer." Hollister opened the freezer compartment. "There it's been ever since. I'd like you to have it. It's Italian. Made in southern Italy, I think. Limoncello."

"Haven't had that in a while." The one time I'd tried the stuff, it had tasted like poison. It was a pretty yellow and the idea of a liqueur made from lemons was appealing. But the bitter taste lingered on my tongue for a long time.

"When this is all over, I'll come to your condo and we'll have a drink together. How's that?" As he pulled the bottle from the freezer, other things tumbled out.

Frozen dinners, a box of frozen waffles, a few icy freezer bags filled with unrecognizable lumps, and a box of frozen fish sticks.

I picked up the boxes and the fish sticks box rattled strangely.

"Doesn't sound full but it looks sealed."

Hollister shook the box and tore it open.

"What's this?" Tim retrieved an envelope from the box and handed it to me. "Hold that a moment."

He replaced everything in the freezer and held out his hand for the envelope.

"I'd heard about people hiding things in freezers. I just never thought anyone I knew did it." Slipping a wizened finger under the flap, he opened the envelope and removed a piece of paper. Unfolding it, he read to himself.

"Tim?"

He handed me the paper in silence. There were two sentences, "This is just in case. Never forget that I love you. H." Beneath that was an odd key taped to the paper.

"I never knew it was there." Hollister had that faraway look. "Do you suppose he knew something like this would happen?"

"Like you said, Helmut was a careful man. He wanted to keep his work safe. If he was like most of us, he never really thought…" I left the rest unspoken. Obviously Helmut had worried about something happening.

"A careful man. That's what he was. But he never told me about this letter or the key. I suppose he thought I'd figure it all out."

"Maybe he just didn't want you to worry. So he hid this away and knew you'd eventually find it."

"He never realized how helpless I can be. What if I hadn't found it? What then? He was very stubborn and too secretive for his own good. He made me angry sometimes." Hollister's voice quavered and his eyes became glassy with tears. It would take longer than he probably imagined for him to feel anything like normal again. "I'm s-sorry. Helmut was a good man… really."

"Anger isn't a bad thing, Tim. Have you called anyone for counseling?"

"Counseling?"

"Grief therapy. I know someone good."

"Maybe later, Marco. It's all too raw… I can barely think."

"Promise me you'll consider it?"

"When this is all over."

"Let's take a look at this." I slipped the key from beneath the tape. It wasn't your ordinary key. The fancy, cloud-shaped bow had a golden hue and the stem was engraved with a lightning bolt. There was something familiar about it. But I couldn't place it.

"Do you recognize the key?"

"Not in the least." Hollister shook his head.

"Well he hid something there. Maybe his laptop or those papers. Unless he had something else he was keeping safe for you? A will?"

"Our wills are on file with our lawyers. This has to be related to his work."

"The key's distinctive. Somebody's bound to know what it is." I flipped it into the air and caught it. "This could be a break."

* * *

I'd asked Luke to meet me at Nina's place. I wanted to check on her progress and show Luke the key.

Walking to Olde City gave me a chance to think. Nothing added up yet. Brandt was dead and someone had ransacked his home. The fact that someone tossed the house raised lots of red flags. But, if they were after his work, they couldn't have gotten it because the laptop was hidden.

Brandt's death was not the result of a mugging but was it related to his work or to something different? Lots of people didn't like what Brandt wrote about, including all the nuts who'd sent threats. But his death might easily have been connected to an affair he was having or something else.

Indefinable things just out of reach made me suspicious of everybody in this case. When I get that feeling, there's something moving under the radar. I needed to adjust my settings to see it.

Finding Brandt's laptop and those documents might help. I held the key in my pocket and traced its odd shape. I had the feeling I should know where it was from.

When Luke fell in beside me I smiled. He was a looker and I could never get enough of him.

"You seemed deep in thought." he said. "Which planet were you on this time?"

"Planet Who-Did-It. Not a nice place. You can't trust anybody there and everyone has a hidden agenda."

"Come back with any clues?"

"Of course not." I laughed. "But I promised Hollister I'd get to the bottom of things and I will. Whatever the outcome."

"Maybe the geek people have found some leads."

"Something about this case makes me a little crazy. Maybe the answer is just out of reach. Or, maybe I'm missing something right in front of me."

As we reached Nina's townhouse, the door opened and Deena popped her head out. If you don't know Deena, she's a bit of a surprise on first sighting. Unless you're used to purple hair in the strangest, stand-on-end pigtails and the special lavender spots she had tattooed on the sides of her face and running down her neck, which had something to do with a Star Trek character. Her dazzling green eyes made her child-like face look happy and sad at the same time, but mostly vulnerable. I'd learned never to let her surface innocence fool me. She was tough as concrete and twice as hard.

"Didn't expect you two," she said. Her small, high voice disguised even further her toughness. "We don't have hardly anything for you."

"Hello to you, too, Deena," I said.

Luke, never a fan of Deena's appearance, was silent but all smiles.

"You got Nina tied in knots." Deena held the door open. "She really wants to help but you gave her nothing to work with."

"I've seen you work miracles with a few scraps of information."

"Right now, we're comin' up dry, Marco."

She led us deep into the heart of the lair. Hallie was on the surface computer, arms flashing and images moving at lightning speed. Nina seemed to be going over notes. Neither of them noticed us.

"Company!" Deena called out.

Nina jumped up as if she'd been awakened from a deep sleep. Hallie continued working but waved over her shoulder.

"Marco, didn't know you were coming," Nina said.

"Any results yet?"

"You didn't give us much," Hallie snapped. She and Deena were protective of Nina. "So don't expect much."

"I've got some answers for you. I squeezed every bit I could out of what you gave me. Cerberus is seeing what he can come up with, too."

"Sounds good."

"You okay, then?" Deena asked Nina.

"Don't worry, Deena. I'll play nice. Nina is safe with me," I said.

"What I hear, nobody's safe with you." She moved to Hallie's side. Every once in a while she'd glance over at me.

"So, let's see," I said to Nina.

Nina picked out a folder from a rack on her desk. "I did a global search on the names you gave me." She riffled through the papers in the folder.

"And...?"

"You gave me Templar1098, VaticanMilitia, SecularVengeance, Ciliceguy and MensEcclesiae."

"Sounds right."

"Sounds like a bunch of nuts," Luke said.

"It gets better." Nina chuckled. "Two of them, Ciliceguy and MensEcclesiae, are all over the place on the web. They appear in forums on a lot of Catholic sites."

"Catholic sites?" Luke asked.

"Yeah, y'know, sites about what else? Catholics. Or about issues they get into. DogmaLeague, CatholicVoice, Domus Dei, Conclave and that's just some of the sites and blogs. There are lots and these guys show up on most of them. Doesn't look like they have a life. And they use the same names on all the sites. Stupid."

"What kinds of topics do they get into?"

"I made a list of links. Mostly conspiracy weirdness, pro-life stuff, and all that kinda crap. At first, I thought, who cares? But then I looked and there are thousands of them." Nina seemed either impressed or appalled.

"Candidates for padded cells," Luke said.

"You got that right," Nina commented.

"You didn't find all the names?"

"I haven't found Templar 1098. Yet! But the Vengeance guy and the Militia dude, oh man, they were in the darkest sites."

"Meaning really dangerous?"

"Dangerous is not the word. These freaks are into murder, torture, and suffering. They talk about weird ways of hurting people. Everything is a conspiracy. They are fucked up. Seriously fucked up."

"Well, Marco's on top of it all, right?" Luke said.

"The more you find out, the faster I can put this case away."

"Get me more to work with, then. But watch your back, Marco. These guys are insane. You could be in real trouble."

"Hey, Fontana," Hallie said, moving to Nina's side. "Nina said there's a laptop? Bring that in and we'll find you all kindsa shit."

"We're working on it. Let me have what you've got so far. When we find the laptop, it's yours."

Nina handed me a disk. "It's all on here. These guys are religious nuts. I'm gonna love it if I help put 'em away."

Luke and I stepped out into the dusk. A cold breeze eased leaves off the trees.

"You don't think these nuts will get to Nina, do you?" Luke looked apprehensively back at the house. "Or... or get to you? They won't, will they?"

"I learned a long time ago never to be sure about anything, Luke. Last time I was sure about something, I was left high and dry."

* * *

The Venture Inn was moderately crowded when Luke and I sat down to dinner. I had to wait for the witnesses to show, so I suggested we have dinner.

"You ever see anything like this?" I asked Luke after placing the key on the white tablecloth. "Does it look at all familiar?"

Luke stared at the key. He put out one delicate finger and touched the key as if it were a flame. He picked it up gingerly and turned it over and over, studying it.

"There's something familiar about it, but I've never seen anything like it. Looks like it opens something expensive. What is it? Other than a key, I mean."

"Hollister found it in the house when I was with him."

"Can't be important. If the guys who tossed his place left it behind, it must be worthless. Right?"

"Could be. But I don't think they even saw it. The key was in the freezer, wrapped in paper, placed in an envelope stuffed into a box of fish sticks."

"Oh." He placed the key back on the table. "I don't think I've ever seen a key like that. And I've been in some classy places."

This was true. Luke enjoyed luxuries and liked spending his money. He spared no expense. His success enabled him to be extravagant if he chose.

"If you know the guy who that belongs to, give him my name," said Charlie, the waiter who'd come to take our orders. "Looks like it's from someplace swanky. And this girl needs swanky. I been waitin' tables long enough."

"Never saw a key like this, huh? With all the places your ass has been." I teased.

"I'm proud of all the keys I've been given. It's a testament to the trust my men place in me." Charlie pretended to be aggrieved. "What'll you two lovebirds have?"

"Lovebirds?" Luke looked at me. "What've you been telling people?"

"Oh, hon, he's got plans for you. Didn't he tell you?" Charlie winked.

We placed our orders and Charlie smiled as if Luke and I were getting engaged. Charlie's long face was creased with dimples that twenty-five years ago must've made him cute. Now, they made him look dour which he was anything but. I couldn't help thinking he resembled a basset hound. Mousy hair, big droopy eyes, and dimples-gone-to-wrinkles screaming sad sack. When he opened his mouth, that illusion was blown all to hell.

"You think that key leads to the laptop, don't you?" Luke said.

"There was a note with the key, but it wasn't specific. Brandt said 'Just in case.' He also said he loved Hollister and that was it."

"Sad," said Luke. His expressive eyes showed he was moved.

"It is, but for Hollister's sake, I'm hoping it gets us the laptop."

* * *

Dinner was fun. We avoided talking about anything to do with crime or Catholics. We both had the new version of the house special, Chicken Livermore, which had been on the menu since George Washington lived in Philly.

"Unfortunately I've gotta meet Artie and Jordan. But you don't have to wait."

"I have a staff meeting at 7:30 tomorrow morning. But let me do this," Luke said pulling out his cell phone. "Put the key on the table."

I detached the key from my key ring and put it on a spot I cleared. Luke snapped open his phone, pressed a button and took two photos.

"For your scrapbook?"

"I'll show it to my staff. They get into all sorts of places, see all kinds of things. One of them might recognize it."

"Is it any wonder why I love you?"

"You only love the help I give you. Now I've gotta go." He gave me a peck on the cheek and a hug and was out the door.

"Now we can be alone," Charlie whispered as he cleared the table.

"Afraid not, Charlie. I'm meeting two other guys tonight."

"Two? You're hogging all the good ones." He frowned as he cleared the table.

I wandered to the bar where Zack was pouring drinks.

"Let me know when Artie and Jordan get in, will ya?"

"Trivia starts soon. They'll be here." Zack fussed with glasses. "The usual?"

"Sure."

As Zack set down the mojito, he glanced over my shoulder.

"Artie, Jordan! Right on time," Zack said. "I've got someone who wants to meet you two."

I turned around, anxious to see my possible witnesses. Artie was short, slender, and in full drag. His make-up was so thick he looked like an escaped mannequin. His chic black dress fit his slender form well. Petite, with a sleek blonde wig, he was balanced on the line between middle age and something more. The dim lighting helped. He smiled tightly, a safe bet since his make-up might've cracked otherwise.

His friend, Jordan, shrieked money from his professionally coifed silver hair to his cashmere sweater to his expensive Italian shoes. He was tall with a face that'd seen far too much sun and now did a fairly good imitation of parched soil. It was a wonder no one had told him about the benefits of moisturizers. But Jordan's eyes had the sparkle of a youthful personality, mischievous and knowing, belying his bland expression.

I stood and offered my hand. I towered over Artie but Jordan nearly edged me out in height.

"Marco Fontana." I smiled.

"Artie," said the blond. His hand was as soft and smooth as velvet. This man knew moisturizers.

"Jordan," the other said. "What can we do for you? Trivia will be starting soon."

"Won't take a minute of your time. I'm working a case and need your help."

"A case," Artie drew a hand to his mouth and his mascaraed eyes widened. "Are you a police detective?" There was a lot of Mae West in him as he moved close to brush up against me. "Brush" isn't exactly the word for what he was doing.

"Private investigator. I'm not with the police."

"Well, that's a relief," Jordan sighed and I wondered what he meant. I'd do a little digging later.

"I understand the two of you were around the night of the shooting?"

"The...? Oooh, the shooting," Artie cooed. "Yes, that poor boy. Handsome guy. A shame really. He's dead, you know. I saw..." He stopped himself.

"You saw something? Can you recall what you saw?"

"Why? What do you need this for? Am I going to have to testify? I can't go to court. I mean, I can go to court but not for... well, no, court is out. I can't do that. So, if you want me as a witness, forget that. I told the police that I didn't see anything." A Southern accent hung on his words like a dying echo.

"Artie doesn't like getting involved," Jordan said.

Tell me something I can't guess, I thought. But said, "Really, Artie, you won't have to testify. I'm not the police."

"You could be undercover," Artie said.

"No, Artie. I'm investigating the murder because I think the police don't care much and because there's a guy crying his heart out since his lover was killed."

"We could help, don't you think, Artie?" Jordan sounded moved. "I think we can help you, Mr. Fontana."

"Were you both there?"

"I was meeting someone for dinner. Jordan, too." Artie smoothed an eyebrow. "I avoid the major streets. I always walk the little streets, it makes me think of Europe. And when I got to that street... that street will never be the same for me now, you know. I'll never be able to walk there again without remembering what I saw. It'll play over and over again in my mind. That little twerp ruined it forever."

"What did he look like? The little twerp, what did he look like?"

"He wasn't little, I can tell you," Jordan said. "He was tall, like you. He wore a hat down over his eyes and a jacket collar pulled up, so you couldn't see his face."

"He was not tall, don't listen to him, detective," Artie insisted. "The man was small, I thought it was a kid at first. Person in my position has to be careful, so I notice things. Especially kids, they can be cruel and rough. When I'm out I pay attention. This guy was small, wiry, and had a gun."

"At least you're right about the gun," Jordan said. "He was far from short but he did have a gun."

"He went right up to the cute young man and mumbled something. I think he must've asked for the guy's briefcase. Because the young man handed his briefcase to the *short* guy." Artie jerked his head definitively, flouncing his blonde tresses.

"Then," Jordan continued the story, "he shot the young man. Just like that. Shot him. No warning. Didn't even show any emotion. I hit the pavement before more shots were fired."

"Did you see the same thing, Artie?"

"Like Jordie said, when those shots rang out, I closed my eyes and ducked. I wanted to drop to the ground but I was wearing my best silk dress. A pretty pale green number, makes me look like I have a wasp waist."

Jordan tried to suppress a laugh. Artie caught him and turned a deadly eye on him.

"As it happens I did hug the asphalt, while Mr. Lancelot, here, just let me shred my pantyhose on the street. Did nothing to help. I nearly peed myself."

"So neither of you saw the guy's face or anything?"

"It wasn't like you could really see anything," Jordan said. "As I told you, he covered his face pretty well."

"I didn't see his face either, but…" Artie stopped and stared at the wall across the room. It was as if he were trying to remember something that kept trying to escape.

"Anything you remember, Artie. Anything could help."

"I remember a tattoo. At least I think it was a tattoo."

"How could you see a tattoo?" Jordan sounded miffed, as if he wanted to be the one who'd remembered something. "You're reaching, Artie. There was no tattoo."

"Was, too. I saw it. I saw something."

"Where was the tattoo?" I asked.

"On his hand. The one he held the gun with. I don't remember what it was like. From where I was it looked like a smudge. But it was a tattoo."

"Trivia starts in one minute, guys," said one of the waiters. "No late entries."

"We gotta go." Artie slipped elegantly off his barstool. For a moment, the illusion was almost complete.

I gave them both a card.

"Call me if you think of anything else. I owe you guys."

Chapter 13

When Monday dawned, I was glad. Since Friday it seemed I'd been on the run for a year and what I had so far was a list of names, a key, and determination.

Olga, squat and alert like a pug on the prowl for food, was at her desk. She had an air of authority and efficiency about her like a glowing aura. Her face had begun to melt into comfortable and comforting wrinkles, but the sparkle in her eyes showed that age meant nothing.

"Morning, boss." She looked up from her monitor. "You have solved case?"

"Olga! It's only been three days."

"You are miracle worker, I have seen you."

"Any messages?"

"From girl. Nina the Greek is calling."

"The geek. She's a geek not a Greek."

"Nina, da. Is wanting to know if you are having laptop for her." Olga waved a pink message slip in the air. "One other calls and hangs up."

"I'll call Nina later. Right now, my sweetness, I have a chore for you."

"As if I am not having enough to do." Olga laughed, throaty and rich.

"I need some information on a Jared Beeton. Anything and everything you can find." I wrote down his name for her. "I'm guessing he lives in Philly."

"It will be done." She turned to her computer and went silent as she got caught up in the search. She was like that, focused like a bird on a worm. Wouldn't come up for air until she was done.

I took refuge in my office to sort things out. There weren't any leading suspects. Suspicious characters, sure. But no one looked like a murderer.

Clifford mentioned that Scanlan worked for Wren at the Archdiocese. Which meant another visit. I wanted to talk with Tony anyway, since I'd seen him with Jared at Bubbles.

I dialed Nina's number first.

"InfoMonkeys," said a voice that could only be Hallie's.

"Hey, Hallie. It's Marco." I waited but there was no reaction. "Nina around?"

"Yeah she's here. But she…"

"I'm returning her call. Can you get her for me?"

There was silence at the other end, then a rustling, and I heard someone mumbling as the phone was picked up again.

"Marco! Hey. Got that laptop? I kinda need it, if you want more results."

"Not yet Nina. But soon." I hoped.

"I did get another a name for you. Sort of a name anyway."

"Great!"

"I called in a few favors for you, jefe. You owe me big time."

"I'll make it up to you, chica."

"You're not my type. But if you had a sister…"

"Okay, I get it. So, what's the name?"

"It's not exactly a name, jefe. More like another code. The one who calls himself Ciliceguy, when you look deeper, he's got another name he uses: Serviam! With an exclamation point. I don't know what it means exactly but…"

"It's Latin."

"I know that. I meant I don't know what the significance is. That's your job, if I'm not mistaken. Don't forget the laptop. Gotta go."

* * *

The Archdiocesan building, like a stubby soldier, stood guard behind the Cathedral. I felt suffocated even before I went through the door. I'd called ahead to see if Wren and Tony were in but didn't leave my name. When they don't expect you is when they sometimes slip and talk.

Wren's office was quiet. His secretary sat at her desk, a ceramic pumpkin with a candle inside reminded everyone Halloween was coming. Other than that, the plush elegance of the place remained intact.

"May I help…," the secretary said looking up. "Oh… I know you. Don't I? You look familiar. Don't you?"

"Marco Fontana." I nodded and smiled. "I spoke to Mr. Wren last week."

"What can I do for you?"

"I have some information he'll be interested in hearing."

"Did you make an appointment?" She sounded wary. I'll bet Wren made her squirm for letting me in the first time.

"This just came up. It won't take a minute and I'll be on my way."

"I don't know…"

"I'm sure he won't mind."

"Can't I just give him the information?"

"He wasn't pleased about my last visit, was he?"

"I really can't discuss that. I'm sure you understand."

"All right, then. I can just as easily turn the information over to the police. They'll be even more interested than Mr. Wren."

The stricken look in her eyes was painful. I truly didn't want to make things difficult for her, Wren probably did that plenty. But I needed to talk to the man.

"H-hold on," she said and stood. She hesitated, turned back then forward. "I… I'll let him know you're here."

After a moment, she was back and waving me in.

Wren, a withered string bean, sat behind his massive desk which nearly overwhelmed him.

"What's all this about the police?" He glared at me, then glanced at his secretary who stood in shocked silence. "You can leave, Gladys. I'll deal with Mr. Fontana."

"Nice to see you again, too," I said.

"I distinctly remember asking you to make an appointment to see me again."

"That you did. But I'm forgetful. Especially when people give me orders. Always had trouble with orders."

"What is it you want this time?" He took his glasses off and cleaned them furiously.

"Seamus Scanlan. He works for your office."

"Who?"

"Don't let's start off on the wrong foot, Mr. Wren."

"I won't discuss office matters with you. This is a private organization and as such we don't have to bow to your demands or subject ourselves to your questions. Now, please show yourself out."

"Sure, sure. I'll go. But, uh… in case you happen to know anyone who works with this Seamus Scanlan character, maybe they should know something."

I waited but the guy refused to let on he wanted to take the bait. I could tell that his antennae were tuned in though. So, I let him hang for a few before I continued.

"People should know this guy Scanlan is an author of some note. He's written some really threatening e-mails to someone who later ended up on a slab at the morgue."

Wren flinched. He dropped his glasses on the desk but continued pretending he was deaf.

"That's not all. I've been told, by people who know, that Scanlan's poison pen e-mails can be traced to a specific computer in a specific building. Let's say this one, and this office. You know, we're just doin' a hypothetical. We're supposing Scanlan works here. He takes time from his work to threaten somebody. Using one of your computers. You have computers here, right?"

The blood drained from Wren's face faster than water through a sieve.

"Just doing my civic duty, Mr. Wren. If you know anybody who knows Scanlan or maybe works with him, you should pass on the information. I know the police will be hot for the info."

Wren was silent a few moments but I watched his façade crumble. His eyes darted back and forth so quickly it was almost unnoticeable. But I noticed.

"What is it you want?"

"Anything you can tell me about Scanlan. And I wanna talk with him. Now."

"You can't." Wren seemed pained.

"Well, I'll be leaving. I may have to turn off my cell phone when I get to Police Headquarters, so you won't be able to reach me." I made as if to leave.

"You can't talk to him because he isn't in. He didn't show up for work today. Didn't call. I don't know where he is or I'd make him talk to you. Right now." Wren was kind of pathetic once his bluff was called. Weak and thin, bent over his desk like a man with unimaginable burdens.

"Address? Phone numbers? Put 'em on a paper. I'll find him. It's what I do."

"I'll do what I can." Wren pulled a piece of paper from a pad and wrote.

* * *

I remembered the way to Marlon's office where Tony worked. The corridors were quiet and the elevator empty. The doors opened and I walked down the lonely hall.

Tony sat hunched over his computer screen like a large dark bird examining prey.

"Hey!" I said.

Tony reluctantly tore himself away from the screen, when he did, he blinked a few times before he recognized me. He was sensual, no doubt. But the sultry look was trampled by surprise. His dark eyes went wide, his lips moved but no sound came out.

"Saw you at Bubbles the other night but you were too fast for me. By the time I got to the door you and Jared were gone." I figured I'd unload both barrels, Bubbles and the fact he'd been with Jared, and watch his reaction. It didn't take long.

Tony's eyes searched the air obviously trying to figure out what he should say. His eyes narrowed.

I raised my voice. "I wanted to talk but you ran out of the bar with Jared so quickly." Guaranteed to make him uncomfortable. I'm sure he didn't want everyone knowing his business.

"Look, I don't know what you're talking about but this isn't the place. I'm working. Fr. Marlon doesn't like me conducting personal business here."

"I understand," I said. "When's your next break? We can meet in the hall and maybe you can help me clear up some things. How about it?"

Tony glanced around as if Marlon would pop out of the wall to scold him. I knew the look, I even knew the feeling. Not being out on the job took its toll especially on someone as young and vital as Tony.

"Ten minutes is all I get. I'll take a break now." He fiddled with his keyboard. "Let me set the phone to voice-mail. There isn't anyone to sub for me."

I waited patiently, partly glad he'd agreed, partly sympathetic to what he was going through. But I had to keep Brandt in mind. Tony was just feeling uncomfortable, but Brandt was dead. Big difference there.

When he was ready, we walked into the corridor. Marlon's office was at a dead end around the corner from the main hallway. It was private and quiet.

"Why'd you hurry off when you saw me at Bubbles?"

"I wasn't at…"

"Tony, let's not waste time. First off, I read you the first time I saw you, there was no doubt in my mind that I'd eventually run into you at Bubbles or Woody's or Bump, or somewhere. Why'd you run when I spotted you?"

"I… Jared… Jared didn't wanna talk to you. He's afraid." Tony licked his lips, his gaze slipped off to the side. I knew he was lying. But I wanted to hear what he had to say. The best liars sow a little truth here and there. Makes a more convincing story.

"Why would he be afraid? Other than the fact his boyfriend wrote threatening letters to a man who was later murdered. Did he have something to do with that?"

"No!" Tony's eyes widened and he looked pained. "No. Never. Jared's great. He'd never hurt anyone. That's why he's leaving Seamus. That's why he has to get away. Seamus is violent and possessive."

"You and Jared involved? Is that why he's afraid? You must be scared, too."

"No. You've got it all wrong. I've got a boyfriend, Niko. He's the best. Jared and I are good friends. He and Niko go back a long way, too. We asked him to stay with us until he figures out what to do. But he won't."

"Why would Scanlan be jealous?"

"Jared was in love. With Helmut. He couldn't think straight when it came to Helmut. Jared claimed they'd move in together as soon as Helmut could work it out."

So, Jared and Brandt were an item but moving in together, that wasn't in the rules according to Hollister. I'd have to confront Hollister with it. This threw a different light on things. Hollister himself could be on my list. Jealousy makes people do crazy things.

"And Scanlan? What'd he do when he heard?"

"He threatened Jared. Gave him a black eye and nearly broke his arm. Weeks and weeks ago. Then Scanlan turned his attention on Helmut. Jared said Seamus sent e-mails every day. He even saw a lawyer. Jared was worried what Seamus might do."

"What was Jared's reaction when Helmut was killed?"

"It nearly destroyed him. He could hardly talk."

"Yet there he was in Bubbles several times."

"Grief hits people in different ways. Jared may have seemed okay but inside he was crying. I know. We've been friends since we were kids."

Tony wasn't that far from having been a kid. Our perspectives on time and our own lives are strange. I wasn't a whole hell of a lot older than Tony yet I felt old as the hills when I talked to him.

"So you and Niko want Jared to stay with you for a while?"

"Niko and Jared are tight, best of friends. He wants to keep Jared away from Scanlan. I'm handling it." Tony nodded curtly, the swarthy beauty of his Italian features was strong yet refined. "Niko's got a lot to do. Working two jobs and taking courses."

"I understand. What kind of work does Niko do?"

"Works at a gym and his uncle's place. But Scanlan's the one you wanna talk to."

"There were others in this building who weren't too thrilled about Brandt either. Am I right?"

"That's true." Tony glommed onto this line. "There was a lot of anger around here when Helmut made his latest splash."

"Who for instance?"

"My boss, Marlon, wasn't happy. Ranted for days. Monsignor Kusek had to tell him to cool it. He told Marlon that the whole Brandt thing would peter out and making a fuss would only bring more publicity."

"Smart man."

"Kusek is more than smart. He's on top of everything and knows how to handle people. He made Marlon see how he was making things worse."

"Anybody besides Marlon blow up over Brandt?"

"Well, yeah. Everybody in the building. That guy Wren really went ballistic. Sent out a mailing to everyone about Brandt's book and how we should handle questions from the public. Felt like he had some personal thing with Brandt. People like Clifford and Scanlan got bent out of shape, too. But the Cardinal ordered everyone to cool it and not create more publicity for Brandt. He sent around a memo saying the more we fight these things, the more they stay in the public mind."

"But somebody decided Brandt had to be silenced."

"Don't look at me. I don't think anybody here… maybe Scanlan because he's so violent. But nobody else. I know these people." Tony looked as if he were searching his memory for possibilities. "Helmut was a nice guy. Jared really loved him and he was good to Jared. Poor kid hasn't had it easy in the love department."

"Tell him I'd like to talk to him, will ya?"

"I can ask. But whether he'll do it is another story."

"Think your boss has time for a question?"

"Break's over. I'll let him know you're here."

I marched into Marlon's office when Tony signaled me.

"Fr. Marlon, good to see you again."

"Mr. Fontana, a pleasure." He smiled so broadly I thought his face would split. "How can I help you?"

"Got a question. I came across a Latin word. I know what it means. I went to Catholic school and did my homework like a good boy. But I don't know the significance of the word in terms of what bearing it might have in the Church."

"What's the word?"

"*Serviam.* That's it. Just *serviam.* Any ideas."

"Well, let me think. *Serviam.* Meaning 'I serve'or 'I will serve.' Where have I heard that before? Seems to me I heard it… oh yes. I remember. Opus Dei. That's where. Members often say the word aloud when they get up in the morning. '*Serviam!*' They make themselves ready to serve the Lord another day. They say it aloud so they and God and anyone else knows they're ready to do the Lord's work."

"Thank you, Father. Thank you very much."

I thought about it in the elevator. It made a lot of sense and now I knew I'd have to visit Clifford's house in South Philly to interview his boarder, the Opus Dei member. Why did that organization make the hairs at the back of my neck stand up and scream?

Chapter 14

On my way to Anton's place I reviewed what I'd ask Navarro, Clifford's boarder, when I met him. It'd have to be a surprise visit. Alerting Clifford might cause problems I didn't need.

But I still needed to identify that damned key and find the laptop.

Anton was at home when I'd called to say I'd be dropping by. He was someone I could always count on. He never seemed too busy for me despite finishing up a degree, working as a trainer, and helping to manage StripGuyz. Anton was my right arm at Bubbles but he was also part of my heart and I didn't quite know how to handle that.

His jobs afforded him an apartment in a decent building almost next door to Woody's. The front desk people knew me on sight and always buzzed me in without hesitation. Dahlia was on the desk and I smiled. An older black woman, she could fix you with a stare and make sure you did as you were told. She was also great at spotting liars and we often traded tips.

"Marco, you're a sight for sore eyes. Been a real freak show here the last couple days." Her voice was like a big bell.

"Welcome to my life," I said. "You wouldn't believe what it's been like."

"Honey, sittin' on this desk and seein' what I see, I'd believe anything you told me." She laughed again. "Anton is in, least as far as I know. Didn't see him go out."

The elevator rattled me up to his floor and I knocked my usual number so he knew it was me.

"Well, if it isn't my boss." Anton swept open the door. "I've got pictures of the new guys and I've rated them on the back so as not to influence you."

"Good morning to you, too." I hung my jacket over the back of one of his dining room chairs. The Italian-made, wooden dining room suite fit perfectly in his compact one bedroom apartment. The fragrance of fresh-baked cookies wafted through the air and my stomach rumbled.

"It's afternoon," he said. "In case you haven't noticed."

"Feels like morning." I sprawled onto his couch.

"Sexy pose, but you're not here to seduce me. Or, are you?" Anton stared at me intently. "It won't work, you know."

"I know the rules and I've sworn to uphold them." I placed a hand over my heart.

"Good. I'll be here if you're ever ready." Anton smiled sadly.

I stood, took him into my arms, and hugged him. He nuzzled my neck which sent a shock through me. I kissed him, gently at first. His pink lips offered little resistance as we sank onto the couch locked in an embrace. I wanted to meld with him, lose myself and float. His forceful, emotional response took me by surprise. We'd done this hundreds of times but this was different. It left me breathless.

"Wh-what was that all about?"

"Just how I feel." Anton hugged me and looked into my eyes. His were so blue and hypnotic that I felt myself falling. But there was a sadness in those eyes. "I'm never going to have you all to myself, am I?" His voice was a raspy whisper.

"Anton," I started.

"Don't say a thing. I'd like to believe there's still a possibility. I know there's still a possibility." He sighed. "Don't say anything." He placed two fingers on my lips to quiet me. They were soft and warm and he was sweetly gentle.

How do you talk business after that? It was my fault. I pulled him into an embrace, I kissed him. Was I leading him on? A guy might see it that way. But I did have feelings for him and they were deep. I've known him a long time and over the years those feelings have grown. You could say we'd become comfortable. But I couldn't get myself to make that final leap. And why did I think of it as a 'final' leap anyway? Why not think of it as the first step on a different path? Why couldn't I give myself to him entirely? He was gorgeous, intelligent, thoughtful. Kind and considerate. What was not to like? Why was I hesitating? Was it Luke or the idea there might be someone else? Or was it just me?

I felt awkward, speechless. I took my keys from my pocket tossed them from hand to hand. Anton didn't always have this effect on me but the look in his eyes and his question derailed me.

"What's that new key?" Anton snatched the keys and inspected them.

"That's what I'd like to know." I recounted how I'd come by the key.

"How romantically sad." Anton's voice was low. "You think this is where Brandt put the laptop?"

"Could be. Hollister said all their other important papers were in a bank vault. This may be where Brandt hid his work."

"From the looks of the key, he didn't hide it somewhere shabby like a train station locker," Anton commented. "Or any other kind of public access locker. None of them would spend money on keys like this."

"You're right, of course, but then, where? You don't recognize it at all?"

"I'd love to say I did and make you pay for the answer with another kiss." Anton laughed. I knew his laughter disguised his real feelings.

* * *

After Anton took off for his job at the gym, I realized I hadn't eaten a thing all day. The hollow feeling in my stomach wasn't entirely due to the fact I was hungry. Kissing Anton had made me wonder what I was doing with my life, at least as far as Anton was concerned. Eventually I wandered into an upscale hamburger joint, deciding that a late lunch would at least solve one problem. Then I returned to my place.

Since it was still too early to visit Clifford's boarder, Navarro, I called Hollister who asked me to meet him at his friend's apartment. The fact I always had more questions never bothered Hollister, he just wanted to know the Truth.

I freshened up and was on my way.

Hollister's friend lived on Spruce near twentieth. That neighborhood, I was told, was the center of gay life in the seventies. What was now the gayborhood wasn't then. Most of the gay bars were west of Broad Street and most of the residents of those neighborhoods were gay. It was before my time but I'd read about Philly's gay history enough to know. Not that there was a shortage of gay men and lesbians living in those neighborhoods now, it just wasn't the epicenter.

This friend of Hollister's must have lived there in the old days and stayed put as the gayborhood drifted east. Visiting his place would give me a peek into history.

The house was a large four story greystone that had been carved up into apartments at some point. Sad. Stately old homes reduced to being inhabited by apartment dwellers.

Bancrofft was the first name on the tenant list. I pressed the buzzer and was admitted. Inside was as posh as the exterior was elegant. New carpeting, fresh paint, walls hung with oil paintings, stylish mirrors, and Art Deco-style lighting fixtures.

Hollister obviously had wealthy friends. He himself was well-to-do, but never came off as being moneyed.

As I moved down the hall, the wood floors beneath the carpeting creaking and moaning, a door opened and a short, slender old man with super white hair and very pink skin, gazed at me. Clean shaven and dapper, he smiled broadly.

"Mr. Fontana?" He wore a short-sleeved, lime-green, linen shirt and pressed khaki pants. Ramrod stiff, there was an elegance in his movements. "I'm Lyman Bancrofft." He held out his hand.

"A pleasure, Mr. Bancrofft," I said as we shook.

"Timothy told me you were attractive, but he never said how attractive. I've always had a thing for Italians, but who doesn't?" Bancrofft was the definition of forward.

"Stop embarrassing my detective." Hollister had come up behind Bancrofft and opened the door wider. "Let the man in, Lyman."

I stepped into the apartment which occupied the first and second floors judging from the staircase off to the side. It was tasteful in a rococo way, the opposite of the restrained gracefulness of the hall. Paintings lined the walls.

There was lots of gold and crystal. Marble statues and objets d'art were placed all around. It was dizzying. This was not my style. With Luke's help, I'd come to appreciate a more minimalist approach.

"I'll put the kettle on. You'll have some tea, won't you?" Lyman asked, punctuating his question with a suggestive wink.

"Of course." I turned to Hollister. "I need to talk a bit. Maybe if I jog your memory, we can identify this key." I held it out.

"That looks, awwwwwfully familiar," Bancrofft said drawing out his words. "I know I've seen something like that before."

"If you could remember, I'd really appreciate it," I said and Bancrofft smiled with calculated coyness.

"I'll think on it while I make the tea." He bustled out of the room.

"We can talk in here." Hollister indicated I should enter a room at the front of the apartment, where the bay window overlooked the street. "Don't worry about Lyman. He's my closest friend and had a lot to do with me and Helmut being together. He's just as intent on getting this resolved."

The room was an eighteenth century antiques fair. I couldn't tell if any of it was real but it certainly looked good. Hollister sat in an overstuffed wing chair and offered me the bergère chair across from him. It more or less swallowed me up when I sat down.

"Have you remembered anything about the key?"

"I've thought and thought about it but I've never seen it." Hollister hung his head as if in defeat. "It's obviously significant. Helmut must've thought I'd know what it was or that I'd easily figure it out. He was wrong."

"What about his habits, places he frequented, people he knew, travel destinations?"

"He traveled a lot doing research. Italy mostly for this current work. When he was in Philadelphia, he was in his office. Ask me what he was doing in there besides his work and I couldn't tell you. Diddling on the Internet. Doing research, he'd call it. I suspected he was trying to meet other men. And…" Hollister held up a hand. "Before you say anything, I knew and it was all right with me. Whatever he did, he always came back to me at the end of the day."

"All right, what about when he wasn't in his office? Did he go to the gym? Did he have a favorite bar or café? Where did he hang out?"

"I didn't keep him under surveillance, Marco. He was an adult, a free agent."

"You must have known his habits."

"He did go to a gym. But which gym I couldn't tell you. As for his hangouts, I know he enjoyed sitting at different cafes in the neighborhood. He'd write and read in cafes. He'd also meet with friends and acquaintances. But he didn't like bars."

"Friends like who? Gimme a break here, Tim."

"Friends we had in common. Lyman, Harry who works at the Gallery down the street, any number of acquaintances. But no one who was that close, no one who knew or really cared about his work."

"How can you be certain of that? How would you know whether or not these people really cared?"

Hollister paused, he gazed at the wall over my shoulder as if he were searching his soul. The silence was broken only by the faint sounds of Bancrofft puttering in the kitchen. Crockery clinking, tea kettle whistling. The juxtaposition of the sounds of ordinary, everyday life and the silence of Hollister's sorrow was eerie.

"I... I suppose I don't really know. Any of them could have their own reasons."

"Or connections," I added. "What do you know about a guy named Jared?"

"Jared?" Hollister hesitated. "Jared. Yes, I remember the boy. He was young. Younger than Helmut's usual." There was bitterness in his voice. Whatever existed between Brandt and Jared Beeton wasn't something Hollister enjoyed remembering.

"His usual?"

"Helmut found mature men attractive. Men with a bit of mileage. Over forty at least. When he started up with Jared, I was taken aback."

"Did the two of you argue over Jared?" Because that's certainly what it was beginning to sound like.

Hollister was silent.

"If you argued, I'm sure you feel terrible about it now. But whatever you remember, no matter how painful, could help."

He remained silent, staring down at the darkly intricate Persian rug beneath our feet.

"Tim? Talking about it might help. You can let it go then. Put it away."

"We argued," he said, his voice almost a whisper. "A lot."

"How long did the affair go on?"

"Longer than Helmut pretended. He thought I didn't know or couldn't tell."

"Why did he have to hide it? You two had an agreement, right?"

"Because with Jared, he went too far. Our agreement didn't include falling in love, threatening to leave me, wanting to divide the household. Our agreement didn't cover that. I told him he would have to choose. Jared or the life we had together."

"He chose both? And covered it over with lies?"

"An accurate assessment. If a little blunt."

"We don't have time for niceties. Not if we want to get to the truth."

"Personally I don't think his affair had anything to do with his murder. I still think it was his work, Marco. I'm trying to keep an open mind but I don't think an affair with a young sl… man is what got him killed."

"What if Helmut's work and his affair were somehow connected?"

"Connected? How is that possible?" Hollister looked puzzled.

"I've found some odd connections and I don't believe in coincidence."

"What? How?"

"Seems Jared was the boyfriend of one Seamus Scanlan who works at the Archdiocese. Works for Wren, in fact."

"And you think…?"

"I think it's possible Scanlan had two reasons to hate Helmut. Jared and Helmut's work. Twice the motivation to want Helmut dead. Or, Scanlan might even have been doing someone's bidding."

"Like Wren?"

"Wren had nothing good to say about Helmut. But I don't figure him as the type who would dirty his hands on something like this."

"I can't believe… but it… it could be."

"Scanlan was about to take legal action against Helmut. That letter from Dreier on behalf of a client. Could have been Scanlan. I saw him at Dreier's office last week. By that time Helmut was already dead, so it might have been something else."

"Maybe he was making sure that whatever legal action he was planning was erased. And that lawyer-client privilege would protect him," Hollister said.

"It's all speculation right now. But you see what I mean about connections."

"I'll keep thinking. Jared was Helmut's latest and longest affair. There were others over the years."

"Whatever you can remember. I'm not looking to destroy his reputation, you understand that, right?"

"Whatever he did doesn't matter. What he represented and what he meant to me, that's what matters. The sooner you find out who killed him and why, the sooner I can mourn him properly."

Just then Bancrofft entered with a tea tray. The poor guy looked as if he'd fall over if a slight breeze blew through the room so I got up and took the tray from him.

"Good-looking, strong, *and* mannerly. Where were you when I was thirty-five?"

* * *

Tea with the guys was like something out of a nineteenth century novel. Bancrofft regaled us with tales from his wanton youth, as he called it. The man had a blast and still had lots of energy. Not to mention that he remained a force to be reckoned with when it came to flirting.

Unfortunately he couldn't recall anything about the key, though he said he'd pass the word around.

The walk home was like a walk through time. Bancrofft's place represented another era and not just in décor. The attitudes of those guys and their way of life was something out of the past. I'm sure it still existed in some subset of modern gay men, but whatever there was today would be a faded copy of what had been. Probably what existed in the sixties and seventies was a diminished version of what had gone on thirty years before that.

I strolled through town into the gayborhood where a whole new set of styles was coming into being. The wonder of it was that all these eras existed side by side at the same time and no one knew it. Worse yet, maybe no one cared.

Navarro was next on my list and that meant heading into a time warp of another sort altogether. South Philly.

My parking garage, where what they charge to park your car is more than some people pay to rent an apartment, wasn't far. The usual nameless crew on duty saw me coming and their dour expressions turned to smiles. One raced to get my car. I winced at the thought of them zooming down the ramps in my BMW. Even if it was old, used, and not the most distinctive car on the road, it was all mine. Midnight blue and in perfect condition, it served me well. A former client had offered it to me, for a lot less than market value, when she bought a newer model. So, I'd retired my old Taurus and bought it. The BMW was old and nondescript. When I tailed someone or parked in strange places, the car was hardly noticed.

I took my car from the smiling attendant and was on Broad Street headed south in no time. Clifford's house, where Navarro boarded, was way down on south Broad. That was dangerously close to family territory and guilt usually did its dirty magic whenever I entered the area with no intention of visiting my parents. But I was working, this was business, it allowed me to avoid getting tangled up with feeling guilty. Sure.

South Philly represented a lot of things for me but mostly a past I was reluctant to relive. Not that I had a bad childhood, I just needed to move on. Sometimes I felt like Al Pacino playing Michael Corleone when he said, "Just when I thought I was out, they pull me back in." For him it was the Mafia. For me, it was old memories. It was that feeling of suffocation I experienced whenever I traveled to my boyhood stomping grounds. As I drove down Broad Street, I struggled with the mishmash of emotions I'd resolved to coexist with forever.

I passed several landmarks of my youth. Uncle Savio's house, an old flame's apartment, the home of a boyhood friend. If Clifford lived any farther down, I'd pass even more things I didn't want to remember.

We all have baggage and sometimes it's best if it gets lost in transit.

South Philly was Halloween crazy. Reminders were everywhere. Orange lights flickered in the dim dusk, decorations festooned houses. Huge carved pumpkins, skeletons, vampires, you name it. If it said Halloween, somebody had put it in their window.

Clifford's home was bare of decorations, though his next door neighbor sported flickering orange lights and a grotesquely carved pumpkin more than two feet in diameter on his top step. Of course, there was no curb parking in front of Clifford's house and the middle of Broad Street was already taken up by any number of cars. Against the law, sure. But the law was not meant for South Philly. So I drove around the block and turned down one of the small East-West streets. I managed to squeeze my BMW between two mean-looking pick-ups. Every house on this block was covered with Halloween decorations. Orange and black streamers, goblins in trees, and more orange lights than anyone could ever hope to see. Ghosts, skeletons, vampires, and witches hung in every window. I got out of the car and looked at the particularly ornate window where I'd parked. Two vampires with gleaming fangs leered at me. Between them were three witches with glowing red eyes. The figures also had movement and, as I watched, I was amazed to see one of the witches break off from the rest and peer at me from a side window. I quickly realized it was the owner of the house. Frightening how much she looked like her decorations. She stared until I turned, locked my car, and walked away. It wasn't an unusual occurrence for people to stare down outsiders. South Philly residents generally felt they owned parking spots in front of their homes. They didn't, but that never stopped them trying to intimidate interlopers. Luckily I looked like I belonged, so she didn't run out screaming that the parking spot was reserved.

Clifford's place was one of the four-story brownstone buildings that lined a lot of south Broad. It was near Dickinson and close to the home of one of my brothers.

There was only one doorbell. Navarro was a boarder and not in a separate apartment. Most smart people divided these old homes into multiple units and made money. Clifford was either not smart or didn't need money.

I rang the bell. When Clifford answered, he looked as if he'd seen a ghost.

"What're you doing here?" he said. Same old hard ass attitude.

"Hey, Francis. I'm looking for Navarro. He around?"

"I didn't think I'd see your face after we spoke. Didn't I tell you…"

"I'm not here to see *you*, pal. I wanna talk to Navarro. He around or not?"

"I don't understand why you need to see him."

"Listen up. This is none of your business. Or, do you own your boarders?"

"Navarro's in his room. He doesn't get many visitors. It's part of the way he lives. You know, the Opus Dei way. You didn't call ahead. That's the polite thing to do."

"Do I look polite? Wanna let him know I'm here?"

Clifford reluctantly opened the door wider.

"I'll tell him. Don't get your hopes up. Wait in the living room and don't touch anything."

What a fusspot. I moved from the narrow vestibule into the living room. The smell of cabbage hung in the air. Sunday dinner. The living room was big. The décor was nothing special, neither lavish, nor threadbare. Just plain, tasteless furniture: a deep-red upholstered sofa, a couple of side chairs of indeterminate color, and a faux-leather recliner. A large flat-screen TV dominated one wall. Pictures, mostly photographs, covered other walls.

I like a wall full of photos. You learn a lot about people that way. They can't help but reveal something about themselves in photographs. Clifford was in a lot of them. There were some old, sepia-toned photos which I guessed were his family. There were a number of pictures of a much younger Clifford with some pretty hot guys. On a beach, in front of museums, standing in public plazas, or near monuments like Mt. Rushmore or Independence Hall. One other guy, a shorter blond kid, was in almost all the photos. He and Clifford invariably stood next to one another. Then, suddenly the blond was gone. He wasn't in any other photos. Clifford, growing older in each shot, posed with his buddies, but the blond was nowhere to be seen. A few more pictures down the line and Clifford appeared with a newer red-headed model. All very interesting.

"He's in here." I heard Clifford say and I turned around.

A medium height, balding man with sallow skin and slightly bulging brown eyes moved into the room behind Clifford.

"This is Mr. Fontana," Clifford said, his voice dripping venom. "I'll leave you to talk." He turned to leave then turned back. "I'll assume you know how to let yourself out." Then he was gone.

Navarro stood awkwardly for a moment then sat in one of the side chairs.

"What's this all about, Mr. Fontana? You've interrupted my prayers."

"I'll get to the point, then," I said. "You're familiar with Helmut Brandt?"

"I've read some of his work," Navarro said. "A dangerous mind, if you ask me. Wants to pull the world down around him."

"Wanted to. He's dead."

"Yes, I'd heard that. God works in mysterious ways, doesn't He?" He didn't exactly smirk, but there was a smugness about him, especially when he mentioned God. I guess if you were supposedly doing God's work, you know the deity's mind, otherwise how would you know what work needed to be done? That would make a person smug.

"Sometimes, He does," I countered. "And sometimes mysterious organizations work in not so mysterious ways."

"Oh, I see," Navarro clucked softly. "You're implying that Opus Dei had something to do with his death? You couldn't sound more ridiculous if you stood there quacking like a duck."

"Just call me Donald, then. It's not beyond the pale of reason that the powers behind Opus Dei would be incensed enough to want Brandt dead."

"You expect me to listen to this nonsense?" Navarro stood. "I've got much better things to do."

"Of course I don't expect you to listen, that doesn't fit the profile. But maybe if I said Ciliceguy, your ears might prick up. Sometimes you call yourself Serviam. Kind of a giveaway, wouldn't you say?"

I knew I'd gotten his interest because he dropped back into his seat and stared hard at me. Anger and suspicion framed his face, his dark eyes burning.

"I have no idea what you're talking about," he said, his mouth a thin line slashing his face, his eyes still boring into me. As if, with that stare, he could understand just what I knew and what kind of person I was.

"Threatening e-mails, Navarro," I snapped. "E-mails that went beyond the you'll-burn-in-hell variety. Way over into criminal territory."

"You don't know me, Fontana. I would never do anything like that."

"But you did, Navarro. You did, and you made the sorry mistake of thinking there'd be no trail to follow in the ether."

"You can't prove anything because there isn't anything to prove. I never wrote those e-mails. I never threatened anyone." He rose to his feet again, this time more confident.

"There's where you're wrong, Navarro. But I guess you need something less divine to show you we've got what we need."

"You'll excuse me, I need to get back to my prayers."

"You do that. You know," I paused and he stopped in his tracks. "It's only a hop, skip, and a jump from those threats to proving you were involved in Brandt's murder."

"You had better be careful who you accuse. A word to the wise."

* * *

Navarro had tried looking tough, but he was transparent. If Nina came up with something more, I'd nail Navarro to the wall with it.

One of the anonymous garage attendants smiled at me like a bobble-head doll on a dashboard, as I parked my car and walked to my condo.

I caught an empty elevator and savored the quiet ride. Once in the apartment, I threw off my shoes and prepared some food. I was about to sit down with a piece of salmon, some veggies, and a Beck's when the phone rang.

Caller ID said it was a restricted call. I hate restricted calls but in this business, you can't pass them up. At first no one responded when I answered. Then I heard someone clear his throat.

"Hello?" I always give them a few chances. Calling a private eye isn't the easiest thing to do and usually comes at a time of emotional turmoil. So, when they call, they're often nervous to the point of being mute.

"You the guy?" He was obviously trying to disguise his voice.

"The guy?" I asked.

"The guy who's investigatin' that killing? You him?"

"I might be."

"Well ain't you or ain't you?" His nervous impatience made him drop the attempt at disguise.

"What killing are you talking about?"

"The guy. Y'know. Look, I don't have no time to fool around," he snapped.

"You talking about the writer? The one shot in a mugging?"

"Yeah, 'ats the one. And it wasn't no mugging. I know."

"You willing to talk?"

"Maybe... but I need protection and money."

"I could arrange that. Tell me whe..."

"I'll call you with a time and place." He left me with an earful of dialtone.

Sitting back down to my salmon, I took a pull on the Beck's and shook my head. The caller was probably another nut job. But the more I thought about it the more I realized he could be on the level. For one thing, this was not a high profile case. As far as the police and the media were concerned, it was low priority. They called it a mugging. Tragic but that was that. They'd look into it when they got around to it which meant the day after never.

There was no way this guy could know I was on the case. Unless somebody connected to the case told the caller. Which meant somebody was becoming very nervous about something I was doing. I'd have to wait and find out.

Chapter 15

T he ball was in his court, whoever he was. He'd call me when he was ready. In the meantime, I had other things on my mind.

Anton expected me at Bubbles to help pair up newbies with veteran dancers. He'd hit upon the mentoring idea a while back and it'd worked well. The old hands taught the newbies about dealing with customers and cranks. Once in a while, the pairings resulted in a budding romance which sometimes ended promising careers. The partner acts were good for business bringing customers in on slow nights, which made Stan, the owner, happy. I wasn't about to fool with the formula.

It'd gotten colder, forcing me to wear a jacket. The sky was clear and dark and velvety. The few stars cutting through the city glare, were diamond bright. The moon was a perfect silver crescent. I felt like things would go my way as I entered Bubbles.

The first floor crowd was sparse but Kent was there patrolling.

"Hey, boss," he said. "Got any more odd jobs like the other day?"

"Bored here already?"

"Bored? You kidding?" Kent laughed. "This is the best work I've ever had. School is dull compared to this."

"I'll have other work for you, never fear. You did well on Saturday."

Kent smiled boyishly.

"Anton around?" I asked.

"Upstairs." Kent gently grabbed my arm. "Can I ask you something? Just between you and me?"

"Of course." I moved to where we wouldn't be overheard. "What's up, Kent?"

"It's Anton. Is that guy ever gonna like me? Not like me... I mean... just trust me. Be regular with me? Not look at me like I'm gonna stab him in the back."

"Give him time. He's been pretty nice to you so far."

"Yeah, but sometimes I wonder. I've been trying. I always say hello. I run errands for him. But he looks at me like he wants me on another planet or something."

"Anton's a great guy. But it was just last week you pulled a gun on him. That kinda makes people a little sensitive. Know what I mean?"

"I know." Kent frowned. "I was an idiot."

"You were in love and hurting. I've been there. Not that I held people hostage or anything. But I understand how you felt and so does Anton."

"I woulda never hurt him... or Nando. Never. I just felt so low." Kent's voice was barely above a whisper. "I'll make it up to him. Whatever he wants."

"He'll come around. I'll talk to him," I squeezed Kent's shoulder. "Everything okay down here?"

"I saw Jared again," Kent said. "He's scared."

"Because of the guy he was arguing with?"

"He says they're back together. Which I don't understand because the other night they couldn't'a been more apart."

"What's got him scared then?" This was a twist I hadn't expected after what Tony had said.

"Who knows? He left before I could find out."

"Well, keep your eyes open."

"Will do, boss."

* * *

The sunlight blazed into my bedroom like a wave from a fiery ocean waking me at seven thirty. I swore under my breath for forgetting to close the blinds the night before. I'd been tired when I got home from Bubbles. I'd stripped, gotten into bed, and fallen asleep forgetting everything.

There'd be no getting back to sleep now, even if I wanted to, which I did. Some days you just can't roll over and ignore the world. As I lay there everything seeped back into consciousness and I knew Hollister was depending on me. I had a list of angry, secretive people with things to hide. I'd have to pry their secrets loose.

I took a deep breath and threw off the covers. Unfortunately there was no one else under them. Some mornings I felt more alone than others. This was one of them. Two of the new guys had made passes at me. I generally don't mix business and pleasure. Generally. I'd have made an exception last night but Anton was there and it felt like I was doing something wrong. Hurting him. Which made me wonder. Maybe I cared more than I was willing to admit?

Even though I didn't exactly regret passing up those guys, I remember falling asleep thinking about the possibilities.

A hot shower always clears the mind. I let the water cascade over me a long time and soaked in the steamy warmth. The heat filtered down to my bones as warm fingers of water traced a path over my flesh. The shower signaled the start of another day, another chance to make things right. Shutting off the water, I slid back the glass door and the cool air made me shiver.

Morning ablutions over, I padded into the kitchen for breakfast.

One bowl of oatmeal laced with nuts, hot coffee, and I was on my way to winking at Carlos in the lobby, then heading to the office ready for battle. I stepped into a rush of autumn air filled with promise. I could do anything.

I caught sight of Drew puttering around his video shop as I passed by. He seemed blissfully unaware of the world outside. I envied that quality.

In the office building, I let the elevator cart me up to my floor. Its creaks and groans reminded me about searching for new office space. The lights were on and a Beethoven symphony floated on the air. Olga was already there.

"Good morning, luscious," I said as I closed the door.

"Is no use, this flattering. I am through with marriages," she said without looking up. "Informations on Jared boy I have been putting on your desk."

"Thanks, Olga. Are you sure you're through with marriage? I mean it hasn't been all that bad to you."

"Pffft, I am sure. Four dead husbands. Is this what I am wanting more of?"

"They weren't dead when you married them."

"And making of me a suspect in death of Igor? This is good thing? No. No more marriage. Not even for one who is looking like you."

"Aw," I groaned, placing a cup of coffee on her desk.

"No. Though…," she paused and looked me up and down. "You are good specimen of Italian men, no?"

"Me?" I suppressed a smile.

"Yes, I am sure of it. Boy with big glasses and bigger eyes has said you are… hot. Yes. He is saying to me other day that Marco is hot man."

"Big glasses?" I couldn't think who she meant. Then it dawned on me. "Drew? You mean Drew?"

"I am meaning boy who is working downstairs with films."

"Drew. Well, go figure."

"If you are not finding informations I have left, is because you are leaving such mess on desk. No one is finding anything."

"Don't worry, I know where everything is. If there's something new I'll find it."

My office was quiet and warm. When I shut the door behind me I felt alone and content. I liked my work and my office was my sanctuary.

I found the papers Olga referred to. The background check on Jared Beeton said the kid was squeaky clean. A transplant from Oklahoma where he'd lived until he was twenty-one, he came to Philly for grad school at Penn. He was no slouch in the intelligence department. He worked as a design assistant at Belasco and Dalgliesh, a pricey design firm.

The only address Olga turned up was the same one I'd gotten for Scanlan. Something wasn't right. Jared tells Kent he and Scanlan are playing house again. Jared tells Tony and Niko that he wants out. It was time I talked to Jared myself.

Belasco and Dalgliesh had offices near Rittenhouse Square and probably a load of clients there as well, since that's where a lot of money chose to live. These days, though, with New Yorkers moving into Philly like it was the cheapest borough they could find, the money spread itself around town.

Belasco's receptionist who answered the phone sounded as if she'd swallowed jaw stiffener. Her Main Line speech pattern was perfect for the firm.

"Mr. Beeton is not in today, sir. May I have him call you?"

"Do you know when he'll be in?" I coaxed.

"He's due back at the end of the week. May I take your information?"

"Thanks anyway."

I decided to try Scanlan's place and see if I could find Jared. If he'd taken a few days off, I figured he might be up to something. Like moving. Maybe I'd find him there. If Scanlan happened to be there, I'd kill two birds with one stone, so to speak. Given Scanlan's violent nature, Jared was probably acting when Scanlan wouldn't be around to stop him.

Olga rolled her eyes when I told her I'd be back soon. The number of times I'd said that and didn't return until the next day was anybody's guess.

Scanlan lived on Spring Garden, not far from his work at the Archdiocese and a long but easy walk for me.

Bright sunlight made everything look fresh and new. Outdoor plantings reached out with rich foliage. People wore the sun like a smile. I felt great and whistled as I walked. Something good was in the air.

Twentieth Street always seemed the longest part of the walk when I'd lived in that neighborhood. A wide boulevard, as streets go in Philly, Twentieth was lined with large impersonal buildings: An assisted living facility euphemistically named Sparkling Mews, a darkly brooding Anglo-Catholic church, sinister research institutions, monuments. Tall London plane trees stood guard along the way. Eventually the Franklin Institute loomed and with it memories of childhood visits when I'd test all their scientific paraphernalia. My favorite was the liquid nitrogen presentation in which a scientist froze, then shattered, roses. I'd always wanted to freeze Phil, the kid who teased all the girls in my seventh grade class. Shattering him would've been fun.

Then came the Ben Franklin Parkway, a wide early twentieth century boulevard where traffic zoomed treacherously in all directions. Confusing stoplights and drivers in a hurry often left pedestrians stranded in the middle of the street.

Once you reached the main Library, Twentieth Street turned human-sized and comfortable.

Another two blocks and I was at Spring Garden. Lined with nineteenth century homes and more plane trees, it was a neighborhood that'd seen better days. Most of the old homes had been turned into multi-unit apartment buildings. Scanlan lived in one of them.

The building was constructed of red brick, a Philadelphia trademark. But this house was in need of brick pointing and paint. The white marble steps had a century's worth of character and wear.

I noted a small U-haul truck waiting at the curb and I knew I'd been right. Jared was moving. He'd lied to Kent about Scanlan.

Scanlan's name was on the doorbell list. I pressed and the door buzzed open. A musty, cat-litter odor clung to the air in the hall. The threadbare carpeting needed replacing.

"Up here," came a thin, trembling voice.

I climbed the stairs slowly, wary about what I'd find. Walking into the middle of a crumbling domestic situation had its dangers. People's emotions were raw, their minds cloudy. Thoughts, if they had any, were often dark and vengeful.

At the top of the stairs I saw an open door at the end of the hall. I made my way slowly, the floor complaining under my feet.

When I reached the door, I saw Jared. His face red and swollen, his nose bleeding. He sat limply on the sofa and barely looked up when I entered.

I went to his side and knelt on one knee.

"Who did this? What happened?"

"Who-who're... you?" He winced when he spoke as if moving his lips was painful. "Wh-where are my friends?"

"Jared, right?"

"Yes, but... who are you?" He mustered some strength.

"Marco Fontana. A private investigator," I said and looked around for the kitchen. I wanted to get a towel, wipe up the blood, put some ice on his face.

"What're you doing here?"

"Let's get you cleaned up first." I found a clean towel on a rack in the tiny kitchen, soaked it in cool water and brought it to him.

He was too weak to protest as I wiped his bloody face. He'd been hit in the nose and there was a cut near his hairline which had made a mess. He winced a few times as I gently sponged his face but otherwise he seemed grateful for the care.

"The ER is where you should be, not here." I examined at his face. "You need x-rays. You could have fractures."

"No… no. I've got to get my stuff out of here. I've got to get out." His voice became stronger. "I have f-friends coming."

"That who you thought I was?"

"Yes…"

"Who did this to you?" Had to be Scanlan. But I wanted to hear him say it.

Jared shook his head. "I just want to forget. I want to get out of here."

"You really think he's gonna let you go that easily?"

Jared was silent. He hung his head down and I saw a few tears fall. I placed a hand on his back and let it rest there to reassure him.

"I can help, Jared. I can make sure this won't happen again. Tell me who did it."

"He said he'd kill me if I told anyone."

"How were you gonna explain your new face to your friends? To the people at work? And what makes you so sure he'll stop?"

"He said he'd stop. He said he…"

"They all say they'll stop. I'll bet he even said he was sorry, right?"

Jared nodded.

"They never stop. He won't quit unless we put an end to it. But I need your help."

Jared looked up, face wet with tears. His eyes looked as if they held more pain than he could bear.

"Just tell me who did this. I have to hear it from you."

"S-Seamus. Seamus Scanlan."

Chapter 16

Seamus Scanlan was more dangerous than his unassuming appearance led people to believe. Jared was proof of that.

As soon as Jared's friends arrived I figured I could leave. I recognized one, Niko, the suave, dark-eyed, Greek kid who helped out at his uncle's diner from time to time. He exploded when he saw Jared's face. I almost pitied Scanlan because Niko was built like a boxer, his clothes barely concealing his powerful muscles.

Niko attempted to get Jared to go to a hospital but he refused. He wanted to get the hell out of the apartment and put Scanlan behind him. When I suggested a formal police complaint, Jared went pale with fear. Which told me a bundle.

Finding Scanlan was on my mind big time as I headed to my office. He'd moved to the top of my list of suspects. If he could beat Jared to a pulp, what's to say he wouldn't have had something done to Brandt? Scanlan was the closest thing I had to someone with potential for real violence and a motive. Even Quinn hadn't proven he was actually violent.

The fancy key burned a hole in my pocket as I walked. A dead end so far. Maybe whatever the key protected would help nail Scanlan, maybe it would exonerate him. But I wasn't close to an answer.

Back at the office I called Tony. He was the only contact at the Archdiocese who might help trace Scanlan. The others played their cards close to the vest and I wasn't in the mood for games.

"Archdiocesan Public Relations. May I help you?" Tony's "official receptionist" voice.

"Tony, it's Marco."

"Oh," he sounded annoyed but he recouped. "What's up? I'm at work and Fr. Marlon is a hard ass about personal calls."

"I'll keep it short. I'm looking for Seamus Scanlan. And before you tell me to call Wren's office, Wren won't give me the time of day. So how about you do a little snooping for me?"

"Why should I help you? All you've been is trouble."

I hadn't caused him any trouble. Yet. Unless making him think about things he'd rather not consider was trouble.

"Because Scanlan beat Jared to a pulp. And I know he's your friend."

Tony was silent.

"Tony? You there?"

"I…I'm here. You sure about Jared?" Tony's breathing became rapid.

"I was just with him. I wiped the blood off his face."

"Shit. Fucking shit. That bastard is gonna pay for this."

"Let me handle it, Tony. Help me find him." Silence again. "Tony?"

"Yeah. I'm here. I'm just thinking."

"Find out what you can and call me back asap."

"Was Niko there?"

"Niko? There was a guy named Niko there. Why?"

"That's my boyfriend. I told you, he and Jared are close. He'd better not find Scanlan before you do."

"Call me when you know something."

* * *

"Scanlan didn't come in today." Tony's voice was tight when he called back later in the day. "The bastard is probably hiding somewhere."

"Who'd know where he hangs out?"

"He's a ghost. Nobody knows much about him. Only reason I'm aware of the guy is because of Jared and because he works for Wren. How Jared got involved with that scum ball is beyond me."

"What about Niko?"

"What about him? He doesn't know any more than I do."

"You never know. I'm not implying he'd keep anything from you. But if he and Jared are close, maybe they talk. Maybe Jared said something to Niko. Something Niko isn't aware is important. Understand?"

"I…"

"Could be something little. Something incidental. A throwaway line. Anything can help."

"I'll ask him."

"Where's Niko now? I'll talk to him. I'll know what to look for, what might mean something." I tried gaining Tony's confidence but it wasn't easy. He had all the natural suspicion any Italian is born with. But he was also gay. We were both members of the same club, so to speak.

"He works at Olympus. He's a trainer. He'll be there tonight until closing." Tony said. "I gotta hang up now. Marlon's on the rampage about something."

Olympus was a classy gym. More than a gym. It was a combination high-tech gym, all-male sauna, day spa, and boutique hotel. It'd been written up in the local rags and in some national magazines. The day spa was on the ten best list in Philly. It cost at least as much as a few days in New York but was worth it. I could attest to that. Of course, I was comped a visit so I couldn't complain about the price.

I knew the owner, Stavros, before Olympus was even a glimmer in his eye. He was a hard-working Greek with a huge family behind him. He'd always dreamed of opening a facility like Olympus and when he found the backers, he'd jumped on it.

One block outside the official boundaries of the gayborhood but still part of it all, Olympus sprawled over more than half a city block. It was popular and getting more so. Olympus drew both male and female customers to the gym and the day spa. The boutique hotel had a growing gay clientele. The all-male sauna was kept strictly separate from the rest of the facility. Stavros should have been happy. But he was searching for love and could never seem to cross that bridge.

Since Niko wasn't available until later, I decided to check in at my office.

As I read through files, Olga buzzed.

"Woman with beautiful voice is on phone," Olga said sounding dramatic.

"Olga, you've been watching too many movies. What's her name?"

"Name is making difference? You are not in market for women. But you are also not looking for business?"

"Of course I want business."

"So? You are wanting to talk to woman?"

"Put the call through, sweetness."

"Mr. Fontana?"

"What can I do for you, Miss…?"

"Palmer. Jane Palmer."

"How can I help you, Miss Palmer?"

"I know you're investigating the death of Helmut Brandt. And, well… I work for Thomas Quinn." Her voice was like cookie dough.

"I've met Mr. Quinn. Quite a character. Must be a trip working for him." Especially if you're not part of the tinfoil-hat set, I thought.

"You've no idea. He's a driven man. He won't stop until he gets what he wants. No matter what he has to do to get it."

"What's this have to do with me, Miss Palmer?"

"I wanted to warn you, Mr. Fontana. Quinn is unstable. You're in danger."

"I can handle Quinn."

"He said Brandt had information that he needs to complete his work. Quinn said he knows the information wasn't in Brandt's home."

"How does he know? Did he break into Brandt's house?"

"I don't know. He just knows the information wasn't there. He was angry, frustrated. Babbled all day about it."

"How does this put me in danger?"

"I suspect he's planning something."

"What's that exactly?"

"He wants Brandt's papers. I think he'll try anything to get them."

"Like…?"

"Forcing you or Mr. Hollister to tell him where that information is. He's convinced you have the papers. I overheard him. He's hiring someone to do whatever it takes to get the information."

"And you're telling me this because...?" I said.

"I won't allow him to harm anyone. After observing him for a while now, I've come to feel that he's capable of having someone killed. Maybe even Brandt. He'd do anything to get what he wants."

"Do you have proof he was involved in anything? The break-in, the killing?"

"Of course I don't have proof. I'd have gone directly to the police if I had. But Quinn knows things. And now he wants to force you or Hollister to talk. Isn't that enough?"

"Warning me could get you into serious trouble. If Quinn is as dangerous as you think, anything is possible."

"He's totally unhinged. I'm giving him my notice and leaving."

"If you know anything else that might help..."

"I wanted to warn you. Now I have."

The phone went dead. Her words echoed in my head.

* * *

On my way to meet Niko, I returned a DVD to Drew.

"Hey, Marco. Did you enjoy it?"

"If I could've watched it all in one shot, I think I'd've enjoyed it a lot more. You're looking happy." His happy was a kind of messy, unmade-bed look. Hair mussed, clothes awry.

"Crazy day, Marco. Just got rid of a really edgy kid. Bouncing off the walls. Didn't know anything about movies, but kept asking for recommendations. Wasted a lot of time."

"Lots'a crazies around."

"There was something funny, though." He pushed his glasses back up on his nose.

"What's that?"

"He kept looking at the stairs leading to your office. Like he was waiting for something."

Chapter 17

All the way over to Olympus, I couldn't shake the feeling someone was following me. But there wasn't anyone I could see. I'm pretty good at scoping out a tail. If someone was shadowing me, he had to be invisible or I'd have seen him.

The sun had just set and a violet glow suffused the sky. A twilight dimness took hold, giving everything a sinister cast. There were too many ghosts in my past; maybe that's what I felt following me. The lights on Broad flickered on and fought off the impending night. That didn't shake the feelings I had. When I reached Olympus and stepped onto the mini stoa, I moved behind one of the massive ionic columns and slowly panned the streets. Nothing out of the ordinary. Still I couldn't dodge the feeling I'd been tailed.

I shrugged and went through the glass and chrome doors with Spartan soldiers etched into thick glass panels. It was impressive. Walking through gave you the feeling you were entering a kind of temple, that you were an ancient demi-god. Once inside, you had no doubt. The colonnade leading to the reception area was stunning. Exquisite statuary stood between white columns. Statues of Greek and Roman gods and athletes gazed off into the distance or down at you as you passed. The green-gold marble floor was inlaid with an elegant ancient Greek pattern.

On the reception desk, a live version of one of the statues smiled as if he had the greatest job in the city. Dark hair cut short, dark eyes shining with dumb intensity, and a nose that was classical in every detail. There was no hint of doubt or diminished self-confidence in him. Dressed in dazzling white, his scoop-cut spandex top revealed a smooth torso and musculature that needed constant maintenance. His hours off the desk were, no doubt, spent on the gym floor working out and showing off.

"Hi, nice to see you again," he said. He certainly made it sound as if he really remembered me, which he didn't. "Can I help you?"

"I'm here to see Niko," I said nonchalantly, drinking in his perfect pecs.

"The trainer?" His face didn't register a question though his voice did.

"Unless you've got a dozen other Niko models stashed away somewhere."

"No, just the trainer, I'm afraid." He turned to a computer screen and tapped a few keys. "He's with a client. Do you have an appointment?"

"Not exactly. Just let him know Marco Fontana is here. Tell him Tony sent me."

At that I saw a tiny frisson pass through the demigod's body, like a transient electrical pulse, undetectable to most naked eyes. His hand paused over the keyboard then he glanced at me, his face cool and collected again, his brown eyes back to their calm, liquid state. He picked up a phone and, turning his back toward me, murmured something into it. All I saw was his rippling lats as he hunched into the call. Then he turned to face me again.

"You can wait in the Elysian lounge, Mr. Fontana," he said, his face flushed. He pressed a hidden buzzer and the wrought brass gate swung open for me. "Niko will be with you shortly."

If the entrance to this workout paradise was meant to impress, the interior was guaranteed to knock your eyes out. I'd been to the Elysian lounge before, but the demigod pointed the way and I nodded politely.

The circular room was lined with comfortable leather chairs. Small alcoves, inset into the cream-colored marble walls, held classical busts. Two people, a middle aged man and a youngish woman, sat drowsily waiting. I sank into one of the chairs and stared at the spectacular trompe l'oeil ceiling. A blue sky ringed with gauzy white clouds and winged nude men all gazing in awe as bolts of lightning sizzled through a billowy white cloud at the center.

Something about the scene nagged at me but I couldn't put my finger on it. Something danced at the edges of my memory. I leaned my head back and closed my eyes to think.

After a few moments I heard someone clear his throat. Niko stood there, a fine sheen of sweat glistened on his brow, eyes dark and brooding. From my vantage point, he was backed by the billowy cloud and the lightning bolts and looked like an Olympian deity come to life.

"Marco. What're you, stalking me?" He laughed. "At the diner, then at Jared's, now here?" Then his face darkened. "What's up? Why did Tony send you?"

"Is there someplace we can talk?"

He nodded. "C'mon, we'll go to the intake room. No one's there." He turned to go and I realized I'd never seen him in gym clothes. He always dressed in slacks and white shirts when working at his uncle's diner. This gym-look changed his demeanor. Totally self-possessed, he was the tough-and-in-charge trainer rather than the fawning maitre d' at a cheap diner.

At the end of another marble-floored hall, walls lined with torch-like sconces between which were pedestals topped with more nude male statues, we came to a door.

The intake office was an efficient sea of plate glass desktops. Recessed lighting pale restful colors, and lots of fresh flowers humanized it.

Niko took a seat behind a desk and offered me one opposite him.

"What's this all about, Marco?"

"Jared and Scanlan is what it's about. Tony wanted me to talk to you and I need some information."

"You know where Scanlan is?" His breathing quickened. The veins at his temples stood out as his anger ramped up. "Tell me so I can get my hands on that fuck face."

"I thought you'd have some idea where I could find him."

"Me? Why would I...?"

"Because you and Jared are close. Maybe you know their habits. Or maybe he told you things about Scanlan. Any of it could help me find him."

"What's in it for you? You don't even know Jared. Which reminds me, why were you there this morning?"

"For the same reason I'm talking to you now. I need to find Scanlan. He might be the best lead on a case I'm working."

"This have anything to do with Jared's new boyfriend? Or, he was gonna be Jared's new boyfriend before he got himself killed."

"You knew Brandt?"

"I met Helmut a couple of times."

"How'd he and Jared meet? How close were they?"

"They met some months back. Jared went to some event at the community center and Helmut was there."

"And just like that they…?"

"It wasn't exactly like that. Jared fell in love. He's always falling in love. It's like an addiction or something. That's how he got tangled up with Scanlan. They met and Jared fell for the guy." He screwed his face into an expression of distaste. "You ask me, a seagull wouldn't stop to pick Scanlan up and they go for anything."

"What about Brandt?"

"Jared got his phone number and pursued the poor guy. Called him nonstop until he agreed to a date."

"Didn't he know Brandt was involved with someone??"

"It's not that Jared didn't respect other people's relationships. He kinda couldn't help himself. If a guy ever told him once and for all to stop, Jared stopped."

"But Brandt never told him to stop."

"No. In fact he said he was falling for Jared. At least that's what Jared said."

"And you believed that?"

"No reason not to. I mean, yeah, Jared can get carried away. But if a guy keeps goin' out with you, what're you supposed to think? You're gonna think he must be interested. At least a little bit."

"I suppose. But there was Scanlan to consider. What did Jared say about…"

"He said Scanlan was too rough. Had slapped him around. He wanted to leave."

"Did you confront Scanlan?"

"Sure. But Scanlan denied everything, of course." Niko looked down at the desk and shook his head. "I pinned him against a wall and told him if he ever hurt Jared again, I'd serve him for breakfast at the diner. He didn't touch him again... until this morning."

"I saw the results. That's just one reason I want to find Scanlan."

Niko looked at me and it was as if I could see the synapses firing in his head, making connections between pieces of information, memories, suspicions, and guesses.

"You think Scanlan had something to do with Helmut being killed, don't you?"

"I wanna question the guy. But first I need to find him."

"I'd like to help you, Marco. But I don't know much about his life. Jared never said anything. It's like they lived separate lives when they weren't together and Jared never knew anything about Scanlan's life. My guess? He didn't care to know anything."

"Do you know where Scanlan liked to hang out? Jared ever mention bars or clubs? Did Scanlan ever drop any hints when you talked to him? You must've talked to him, time to time."

"Never talked to him except to say hello and goodbye. He gave me the creeps. I do remember hearing him talk to some of his buddies once. We all went to that high-tech bowling alley, Lucky Strike, I think. Jared likes to bowl. Go figure. Scanlan had some friends there, too. They all talked about goin' to Stella's after the bowling alley. Jared didn't like Stella's. Too many lowlife types. But Scanlan dragged him there anyway."

"Best place in town to get just about anything you're looking for. Information. Drugs. You name it," I said. I knew the place well. A private investigator doesn't just get to hang out at the quality joints, you have to slum it now and then. If you wanted contacts on the seamier side of life, Stella's was the place to go. Hustlers, johns, addicts, and people you'd never want to meet in a million years. Stella's drew them all.

I knew the bartenders there. Always good to make friends with the guy pouring your drinks. Sometimes they pour information, too. I'd made other acquaintances there, too, who'd helped me out on more than one occasion.

Everybody hated the place but sooner or later everybody showed up there. Fact is, when you went into Stella's, at least you knew up front what the guys wanted. Nobody played games. If someone came onto you, you knew it wasn't your body they were after. At least not just your body. And the only size that mattered was the size of your wallet.

"Yeah, great place, especially if you're looking to get your pocket picked," Niko said. "Jared was right. Stella's caters to the underbelly types. One of the guys Scanlan had with him at the bowling alley was a hustler who hangs at Stella's. Calls himself Beto. He's young and very hot."

Well that was something anyway. One name leads to another and another.

"What did he look like, this Beto?"

"Average height, dark wavy hair, beautiful face, dark eyes, and clear pink skin. But his eyes. They were always moving, always sizing things up."

"Anything else?"

"Can't think of anything." Niko looked over my shoulder. "I gotta get going. I've got a client coming and I need to get his charts out." He rapped his knuckles on the desk in a nonchalant way, as if he were punctuating the end of the meeting.

I stood and pulled a business card from my pocket and my keys spilled onto the floor at Niko's feet. He quickly scooped them up and was about to hand them to me when he took a look at them and whistled.

"What?" I said.

"I didn't know you were a member. And you've got an Olympian level membership. My cuz never told me. But he's protective of Olympian members."

"I'm not a member. What makes you think that?"

"This key, man. It's for a locker in the Olympian dressing room." Niko picked out Brandt's key.

I felt my heart beat faster and I'm sure my eyes widened. This was what I was waiting for.

"You sure about this? The key goes to a locker in this gym?"

"Marco, you kidding me? This is my cousin's place. I'm a member. Not at the Olympian level but I'm a member and I work here. I know this stuff. Believe me."

I gently took the key from him.

"I could hug you, Niko." I laughed.

"Not that I'd mind but Tony gets a whiff of that and I'm a dead man."
He smiled and his teeth sparkled whiter than white. "So why does this key
give you an orgasm?"

"It might crack this case wide open. We've gotta open the locker."

"You're gonna have to talk to Stavros. I mean, if it belongs to a member,
he protects their privacy. Especially Olympian members. They pay a lot and
they trust him."

"Well…" I was about to go into the details then I thought better of it.
"I'd better talk to Stavros. He around?"

Niko turned back to the desk and picked up a phone.

"I'll buzz him." He pressed a few buttons and waited. "Hey, cuz, Marco
Fontana is here. He needs to talk to you…. Sure… sure. I'll tell him."

I looked at him questioningly as he placed the phone back in its cradle.

"He says I should take you to the spa lounge. He'll meet you there."

"Lead on," I said.

If the gym was swanky, the spa was designed to make you feel like a child
of Zeus. The elevator opened onto a floor with a layer of fog wafting over it,
which gave the impression you were strolling over clouds. The fog machines
worked overtime and the expenditure on CO_2 must've been huge. Just part
of astronomically-priced spa services.

Everything in the spa had a golden hue. Soft pink and blue lighting
seemed to originate in mid-air. The floors were coral-colored marble, accented
with pale green marble. Delicate harp music hung in the air and the scent of
vanilla drifted lazily by. The place was geared to obliterating stress.

"Stavros will meet you in the lounge, Marco. Have some bottled water
or whatever you want." Niko turned to leave and with clouds underfoot, he
glided off in god-like fashion to engage in celestial pursuits.

The ethereal music wafting through the air calmed and relaxed me, so
that I wanted nothing more than to drift off to sleep. But the feeling I'd been
followed earlier snapped me back to reality. I pulled out my cell phone and
called Luke.

"What's up, Marco?" Luke's beautiful mildly-accented voice had
enchanted me from the moment we'd met several years before.

"Got some time to meet?"

"When?" I heard his keyboard clacking in the background as he multitasked.

"I'm at Olympus." I paused for effect.

"You joined and didn't tell me?! I'll have to join so we can work out together."

"Would I do that? I'm on the case and I need your help. Can you come down?"

"Be there in a flash. Where will you be?"

"Call me when you get here."

I'd formulated an idea to avoid mishaps on the way back, in case I'd been tailed. I needed Luke to help.

The refrigerated cabinet containing bottled water and juices was a wooden unit with satyrs and fawns, nymphs and centaurs cavorting around the frame. I pulled out a bottle of water. It was imported, of course. All the contents of the case were exotic and supposedly good for you.

"You gonna like that stuff, my friend," the raspy voice behind me said. Stavros had arrived. He stood there grinning, all five feet five inches, curly graying hair, bright gray eyes, and rippling muscles. His tight-fitting, teal tank top emphasized his powerful build. He wore warmth and friendliness like a badge.

"Stavros! Long time, buddy." I extended my hand.

"When you gonna join, Marco? You afraid what you gonna find here?" He pulled me into a powerful hug.

"Still got a contract with the old gym, Stavros. As soon as that's done, I'm yours."

"Gonna give you a special deal, Marco. 'Cause havin' you here is good for business." Stavros slapped me on the back. "And maybe we can work a deal for some'a them dancers to perform some time?"

He always had an angle. But he was a big hearted guy and I never minded his sales pitches. Besides, he did a lot for the community and fought hard to have his business here. A lot of the neighbors were none too happy when it was proposed. Of course, after it went up and people saw what a gem it was, tunes changed and suddenly there was no one around who'd admit to having been against the project.

He led me out of the waiting room and into the golden hued hall.

"Sure, Stavros. We'll talk. But right now…"

"You got a key? I hear you got a key to one of the Olympian lockers?"

I took my keys from my pocket and dangled them in the air. The Olympian key stood out from the rest like a tux next to tee shirts.

"This one of your keys?"

"Yeah, yeah. How did you get this? People, they find them, they sometimes drop 'em in a mailbox. We got a code on the keys."

"I thought that's what the number was but the Post Office would never part with that information. So, how can I get a look at what's in the locker?"

"I can't do this, my friend. My customers they depend on my discretion. On the safety of what they store in these lockers."

"How about if I tell you I know who the locker belongs to and…"

"Impossible. There is no way."

"What if I tell you he's dead and his partner wants what's in the locker?"

"Dead?"

"Dead. Helmut Brandt. He's dead and he left this key with his partner."

"I could not believe my ears when I heard this news. He was a beautiful man, Marco. Heartbreaking. In the bars they speak of this because they are afraid now. Pah! Little queens. Not a real man in the bunch. Helmut was a real man. He was afraid of nothing."

"This key could help solve his murder."

"Murder? I thought… It was not a mugging? The news says this. Everybody talks about the mugging. This is why they fear the streets."

"It was no mugging, Stavros. If you open the locker and let me take a look, we'll know more."

He hesitated. Shaking his head back and forth, he paced the floor and the fog swirled around him. The eerie lighting and the fog turned Stavros into an old satyr protecting his treasure.

"I'll let you talk to Mr. Hollister. He was Brandt's partner. Brandt left the key for him in an envelope. Obviously there was something he wanted Mr. Hollister to have."

"Maybe it's better if I talk to him first. Cover my ass, right?" He laughed and it sounded something like a cement mixer.

"Whatever makes you comfortable, Stavros." I pulled out my cell phone and was about to dial.

"Let's go to my private office, Marco. Too many ears here." He looked over his shoulder at the shapely young man and woman at the reception counter both of whom might have been mannequins except that once in a while they blinked.

He walked toward the elevators, the fog engulfing him. Vulcan making his way back to his forge. I followed in his wake and we entered the elevator.

His office on the top floor occupied one whole corner. Ceiling to floor corner windows gave him a spectacular view of the city. The office was larger than a lot of apartments I'd seen and was furnished with sofas, club chairs, and tables laden with magazines and statuary. It had a light and airy feel due partly to the windows but also to pale blue walls and blond furniture. It felt good just being there.

"You got the number?" Stavros sat behind his desk and punched something into his computer, then stared at the monitor.

I flipped open my phone and recited the number.

"Not the number in his record, my friend."

"Stavros, you don't trust me?"

"Greeks and Italians are too smart to trust anyone, my friend."

"The number's different because Hollister, his partner, has to stay with friends. Somebody broke into his house."

"They diiiid?" Stavros looked horrified. "What for? They can't leave this guy alone? His lover dies and they can't leave him be?"

"Somebody was looking for information. Brandt was a writer and had a lot of information that some people would like to see disappear."

"Ahhh, this makes sense."

"So, can you place the call?"

"This information? Is it valuable?"

"No, Stavros. Not in dollars. Just in secrets. He may have known things that some people would rather keep hidden."

"I seeeee," he said.

"Maybe the information is here." I held up the key. "If word gets out this is a possibility… they could come here." I paused for effect. I didn't expect Stavros to cave out of fear, but placing that thought in his head wouldn't hurt.

"We don't have to worry, my friend. We got protection. And alarms."

"Oh, I know, and I wouldn't be concerned about it either, if I were you." I smiled reassuringly. "What bothers me is that Hollister's heart is breaking right now. Helmut was everything to him. And when he found the note from Helmut giving him this key and telling him that he'd find one last gift here, well, I don't have to tell you, Stavros. My heart nearly broke when I saw the old man's face."

Stavros looked at me as if he were trying to figure out if I were telling the truth or making it up as I went along. I saw his internal debate in his eyes. Should he believe me, should he use the romantic tale to allow him to get rid of whatever it is someone would kill to have, should he just toss me out on my ass? Slowly a sympathetic smile crept across his face.

"My friend, who am I to deprive an old man of his love's last gift?" He wiped quickly at his eyes with his fingers. "Come, we'll go to the lockers."

"You don't need to call Mr. Hollister?"

"Why should I bother a man who is already steeped in sorrow? No. I will trust that you are doing the right thing."

As we left his office my cell phone rang and I saw it was Luke.

"Luke. Stavros is taking me to the Olympian lockers. Can you meet us at the elevators?"

"Luke?" Stavros said. "My favorite little Luke who is still not a member here either?"

I nodded and smiled to myself. "Little" Luke was several inches taller than Stavros.

"He's coming to give me a hand. If that's all right?"

"Of course. Of course. I like this Luke and I will make him the same deal as for you." Stavros winked at me, jabbing me gently with his elbow. "Of course, if the two of you, you know… I can give you a household membership. An even better deal."

Everybody wants to be a matchmaker.

"We will meet him at reception and return to the Olympian level. It's a special elevator." Stavros said.

* * *

Stavros stepped out first and held his arm across the doors to keep them from closing. Luke and I move into the softly lit entrance. Everything seemed to glow from the inside, from the gold-veined white marble floors to the walls covered in yellow man-made stone infused with sparkly flecks. The lighting seemingly emanated from nowhere causing the place to radiate with exclusivity and superiority.

Two muscled men in towels ambled by, followed by three older men, likewise wrapped in towels. They were draped with an air of ownership and entitlement. All of them glanced our way as if they were sizing up new prospects begging entry.

There was no way I could afford this level of membership, not in money or in snooty attitude.

I turned to Luke but his dark eyes took in everything as he judged whether or not it was worth the expense of membership.

"You boys should consider this," Stavros said. "It's up to your standards. Especially you, little Luke. I am aware what you expect in a place. You have exquisite taste, my friend. This, you will like."

"The lockers first, Stavros. Then we can take the tour."

"Always business, Marco. You must learn to relax. Give yourself a treat once in a while. We have masseurs with hands like silk." He shook his head and started off down a side hall.

Along the way, more men in towels, a few gorgeous towel boys, and a stunning trainer or two wandered by. The fresh scents of newly laundered towels, of soap and shampoo colored the air and the pungent odor of heated wood from the sauna lingered as we passed.

The special lockers were in a room off the main Olympian dressing area. I was distracted by several men in varying states of undress. You'd think I get to see more than my share in the dressing room in Bubbles. But it's never enough and it's always different.

"Here we are," Stavros said, his sandpapery voice tearing me away from the sights around me. "First I unlock this door." He ran a key card through a device on the wall and the little light blinked from red to green. The door, made to simulate an ancient wooden gate, swung inward.

We found ourselves in a slightly smaller room with banks of lockers each about a foot square, lining the walls.

"The key?" Stavros held out his hand and I placed the key in his palm. "Each has a number. You see?" He held out the key. "This one is in the back."

He led the way once more, turning a corner into a cul-de-sac. With a flourish he placed the key into the lock. The door opened and there, beneath some towels, was a laptop.

"That's it," I whispered. I cleared my throat. "We hoped we'd find a laptop."

"Go on, take it," Stavros said. "Tell Mr. Hollister, I will close his beloved Helmut's account."

I pulled the laptop out carefully, then rifled through the towels. There was nothing else. Not even a note.

"Thank you, Stavros. I'm sure Mr. Hollister will want to thank you himself."

"No need, my friend. I only hope this will bring you the information you need."

"Time and Nina will tell," said Luke.

* * *

Luke and I stood in the reception area. He had his messenger bag and I'd bought one of the Olympus gym bags to carry the laptop. Then I had a thought.

"You take the laptop to Nina." I handed it to him.

"Why? What's…" Luke took the laptop and stuffed it into his bag.

"Just a hunch. I want to collect Hollister. He'll need to be there when we look at the contents. He can tell what's important. He might even know passwords."

"Good idea."

"Go on ahead. I'll call Hollister." I flipped open my cell phone.

Luke pecked me on the cheek and left.

"Tim? I've got some good news." I explained the situation and he was more than eager to join in. I told him I'd drive by and pick him up since we were both anxious to get to work on the laptop.

It had grown dark and a cold breeze kicked the air around. There wasn't much foot traffic, rush hour was over and people were probably deciding what to do for the evening. Broad Street looked elegant and expectant, its buildings lit and waiting. The cold air was clear and City Hall had finally been sprung from its scaffolding, looking brand new.

I headed for the parking lot in my building. None of the crew was around when I arrived which wasn't unusual. Shift changes, bathroom breaks, and other things often kept the staff out of view. It would've been a problem if this were a strictly valet system. But it wasn't so I hoofed it up to the fifth level where my car was snug in its space.

I pulled out my keys and was about to open the door when someone mashed me face down into the hood. I felt a trickle of blood run from my nose and smelled gas fumes and oil. My assailant was rough and strong. He quickly twisted my arm behind my back, moving it up until a knife-like pain shot through me. I refused to make a sound. He leaned in on me heavily, making it difficult to breathe.

"Word of advice, Fontana." He tugged my arm up a fraction and the pain slashed through me. "Forget this case. There ain't nothin' more to find out. This arm," he said and tugged again for emphasis, "ain't the only thing's gonna hurt."

There was something familiar about his voice. Something I couldn't place. I wanted him to say more so I could figure out where I'd heard him before.

Then something heavy and hard whacked me and things went dark.

Chapter 18

I opened my eyes and there were three nurses staring at me. A set of triplets. All of them with short, dark brown hair, tortoise shell glasses, and light make-up. They were all past middle age and looked to be very kind hearted. They smiled at me and three pairs of hands pulled the thin blanket up to my chin.

"Welcome back, Mr. Fontana." When they spoke, their lips moved simultaneously and there was only one voice, a very motherly, comforting voice. I liked that, especially since my head felt as if it were split in two and lying half on each shoulder.

"I..." There wasn't much I felt like saying since when I attempted to speak my already shattered head felt as if it were developing more cracks. So I just stared at them and within moments, the three nurses melded into one smiling woman.

She told me that one of the parking lot attendants had found me lying next to my car. She also said that I was in the emergency room in Pennsylvania Hospital and some friends were waiting outside to see me.

I nodded and immediately felt the room spin.

"Should I let them in? Do you feel up to it?"

I nodded again and this time it felt marginally better.

She turned toward the door and I watched her open it. Luke, Anton, and even Hollister shuffled in and stood next to the bed. All of them looked down at me with mournful expressions of concern. Luke and Anton appeared to be sharing the pain I felt.

The throbbing ache in my head pulsed in time with my heartbeat and my eyes felt like grapefruits. But I tried to sit up anyway. The effort made me want to hurl.

The others backed off, horrified.

"Pain can make you sick to your stomach, Mr. Fontana. So can a knock on the head," the nurse said when she saw me place a hand over my mouth. "You're going to feel nauseous and dizzy for a little while."

I groaned.

"Don't worry." The nurse looked at them all. "He's had a bang on the head but there's no concussion. He'll be back to normal in no time." Easy for her to say.

"As for you," she said, holding up a small brown plastic bottle. "Pain killers. Just to get you through the next couple of days."

I lay back against the pillows and closed my eyes to stop the room from spinning. It kinda worked except now behind my eyes I was tossed on a stormy ocean.

"Your friends can take you home."

I kept my eyes shut.

"No sudden movements or changes of position and you'll be fine in a few hours," the nurse instructed, pressing the pill bottle into my hand. "See your doctor for a follow up. But I think you'll be fine in no time. Young man like you needs more than a bang on the head to cause damage." She quietly left the room.

I felt pretty damaged but it wasn't just my head. I'd let somebody get the drop on me in my own building's parking garage, which explained why I was off guard. But I still felt angry.

"Who's gonna help me up?" I looked at them. "We've got work to do."

"You're not going anywhere, tiger." Anton stood over me, his expression a mix of anger and concern. "Who did this to you? Is it related to the case?"

"I..." I tried to answer but the effort made me nauseous. I let out a breath and lay back on the pillows. "I must be making somebody nervous."

"This case isn't good for your health," Luke commented.

"It's getting too dangerous, Marco. I can't allow you to be harmed," Hollister said.

"I'm not about to let a two-bit thug force me off a case." I saw stars that time.

"He's right, Marco," Luke said. "It's not worth you getting hurt."

"I'm with them," Anton said. "In case you didn't get that earlier."

"But we just got a break." I chose to ignore the pain which was diminishing and the dizziness which wasn't. "We have the laptop. I've gotta be…"

"You've got to be at home," Hollister said. "This can wait."

"No it can't." I winced and shut my eyes. "This means we're getting closer. We can't stop." I kept my eyes shut and it felt like I was floating in a dark tank.

"We'll take you home. We can talk there." Hollister placed a hand on my shoulder.

* * *

Which is exactly what they did. Anton and Luke, together, helped push the wheelchair the to the door. Once there, Luke pulled his roomy Mercedes around.

"We don't have to talk business, Marco," Hollister said as the car made its way through the snarled center city traffic. The city needed new traffic engineers.

"We really need to see what's on the laptop," I insisted and my stomach did a sickening little dance. Riding in the car made the nausea worse but I was determined to tough it out. "We've come this far. I'm not about to stop because I have a headache bigger than Antarctica. So I got conked on the head, it doesn't matter. It's happened before. Besides, it's personal now."

"Nina's got the laptop. It's all in her hands," Luke said. "I was at her place when I got a call from that guy Carlos in your building telling me what happened."

"You need to rest, Marco," Anton said, his voice was low but his tone was firm. "Things like this, you never know the long term consequences."

"He's right," Hollister chimed in. "You could take a turn for the worse if you don't take it easy."

"That's not exactly what the nurse said. Call Nina, tell her we're coming."

"No." Anton insisted. "I'll take you up to your apartment now. Luke and Mr. Hollister can pick Nina up and take her here."

Anton tried to engineer some alone time with me but I knew it wouldn't work.

"We're not far from Nina's place," Luke said. He wasn't about to let Anton have time alone to baby me. He'd want to do that himself. "No sense me making two trips. We can fit Nina in the back seat with the two of you."

"Marco should get home," Anton insisted, annoyed. "He's not up to this."

"We're not taking him on a road trip. Just around the corner." Luke made a left at the next light. He zipped down Tenth Street, then down Pine and before long we were in front of Nina's place.

Luke eased out of the car and went to retrieve Nina. In moments they walked out, Nina carrying two laptops and moving gingerly to the car.

"Marco, how are you feeling?" Nina settled herself next to Anton. "I heard what happened."

"I'll be fine. I've got a pretty hard Italian head." I boasted as a wave of dizziness and nausea threatened to make a liar out of me. "Did you get to look at the laptop?"

"Well, when I heard what happened, I didn't know…"

"Just as well, we can start from the beginning when we get to my place. Tim can help, right?"

"I don't see how but I'll do what I can." Hollister sounded tired. He'd been running around for days, settling things, making arrangements and calls. Unable to live at his own place, the poor guy was under a lot of strain.

"You never know, Mr. Hollister," Nina said. "You may remember a key word or number. The laptop's probably encrypted. You might save me a lot of time.

* * *

I lay on the sofa in the living room, Anton attending to my every whim.
Nina had set her computers on the dining room table. She surrounded herself
with laptops, including mine, and got ready for what looked like it might be
a long night. I had a front row seat and could observe and comment.

Brandt's laptop was seductive. Slim silver case, looking serene, exuding
an aura of untouchability, as if it didn't care it'd been found because it knew
that only the magic words could obtain its contents. I blinked and looked
again. Just a pile of plastic and metal.

Nina gently slid the catch and lifted the screen.

"What's your plan, Nina?" I asked.

"It's encrypted. So..."

"There's no way to get into it?" Hollister asked.

"Normally. Most people would give up after a try or two."

"Of course, Wonder Woman can do anything, right?" Anton came up
behind Nina and placed an arm around her shoulder.

"Right, Batman. Or, are you really Robin?" Nina smiled. She liked
Anton, admired him, but never let him get the best of her. "Go back to the
Batcave and let a woman work."

"We're counting on you, Nina," I said as Anton returned to my side.

"We need to get around the password, jefe."

"Can you?" Hollister asked.

"I'll start it up with my magic DVD and we'll be in." Nina popped the
drive and placed a silvery disk on the tray. She concentrated silently.

Luke watched intently, as if memorizing her moves.

"Bingo!" Nina said. "The encryption is history."

"That's it?" Luke asked.

"Did you doubt me? That was the easy part. Removing the encryption
on the files will take time." Nina clacked the keys. "Take a look at this, Mr.
Hollister." She glanced at the older man and smiled encouragingly.

Hollister pulled a chair next to Nina's. He peered at the screen, the look
in his eyes softened. He placed one hand to his mouth.

"Look familiar?" Nina said

"Helmut's work. The names are familiar, all..." Hollister choked up.

"Take your time," I said. "This won't be easy."

"No. I've got to control myself. For Helmut's sake. This information might be what you need, Marco." He stared intently at the screen. "Why don't you open that one?" He pointed to a folder. I couldn't read names from where I lay.

"The 'Vatican Betrayal' folder?" Nina asked.

"We can start there," Hollister said.

"Here goes." Nina double clicked. "It's encrypted. We need the password."

"Try the usual, Nina," I suggested. "Birthdays, pet names…"

"Old telephone numbers," Luke chimed in. "Nicknames he might've had for things. Did you have pet names for one another, Mr. Hollister?"

"Not really. Just the usual. Honey, dear." Hollister paused. "Prosaic, I'm afraid."

"Can you write down the other stuff? Birthdays, pets, things like that?" Nina pushed a piece of paper in front of Hollister.

"I'll do what I can. Helmut had no pets, never did. I'll list his birthday, his old addresses, my birthday. Our old home towns, our schools. And his telephone number in Munich, I may be able to remember that." He scribbled words and numbers on the paper.

All of us went silent at the same time watching Nina's password program work.

"Any luck?" I asked when the screen went still.

"No." Nina said. "This could take a while."

"What about publication dates? Of his books." Anton said, his face lighting up with the idea.

"Those would all be on Helmut's website," said Hollister.

"It's worth a try," Nina answered.

"Start with the *Vatican Betrayal* book since that's the folder we're trying to open."

Nina clicked keys and searched.

"Got the pub date for that book," she said. "I'll let the program give it a try."

"Who wants something to drink?" Luke offered. "I can make coffee, tea… and… you have juice or something, Marco?"

"Look in the fridge and in the cabinets next to it. Whatever's there, use it. Anybody hungry? We can order in."

"Great idea," Hollister said. I'll take care of that." He was obviously having a hard time. It wasn't just the waiting. He was prying into his beloved's personal files, going through things he might never have seen if Brandt hadn't been killed. I wondered if he worried that he might discover something he really didn't want to see.

"Take-out brochures are in the drawer next to the sink," I said

Hollister stood slowly, as if his bones would crack.

"Got'cha!" Nina blurted out.

Hollister stopped, turned slowly back to the computer, and stared at the screen.

"That's his work. He showed the files to me whenever he needed help or advice."

"We're making progress," I said. "Let's see if he had something new. See anything promising?"

"First we'll have something to eat," Hollister announced, new strength in his voice. "I need some food. I'm sure you all do."

We did, but I knew Hollister was trying to keep himself together by keeping busy, avoiding the hard thoughts that would flood his mind as he viewed all of those files. It was like examining Brandt's soul or peering into his intellectual essence. All the thoughts and ideas he'd committed to paper or put into electronic files. It was like gazing at a snapshot of his mind. I was sure Hollister was disturbed at this necessary invasion of Brandt's privacy which he was no longer alive to protect.

Maybe a dinner break wasn't a bad idea.

* * *

After tofu and veggies for Nina, and moo shu pork, Chengdu chicken, beef satay, and pad thai for the rest of us – we were all in a better mood. My stomach had still signaled unhappiness so I wasn't sure I wanted food. But one taste of the fiery chicken and I knew things were fine. Nina inhaled her vegetarian meal and returned quickly to the laptop. The others ate at a more leisurely pace then went back to whatever they'd been doing.

Luke and Anton had little to do except fuss over me. Neither wanted to leave before the other, or that's the way it seemed. So I decided to enjoy the attention.

"I tried publication dates for the other titles and they worked on those folders," Nina said.

"So far nothing looks new or different," Hollister claimed.

"Make a list of the remaining folders and let's see," I offered. "You doing all right, Tim?"

"At first I thought this would be difficult," he said.

"And now?"

"Now… it's sort of comforting, like reacquainting myself with Helmut's wonderful mind. All of those things he did or wanted to do. It's all here. There's a lot he never got to publish. Maybe I can do something about that. He was a smart man. Smart, clever, and tenacious. That's what killed him. He wouldn't let go once he had an idea."

Nina turned to us waving a sheet of paper.

"Finished?"

"Finding passwords for these isn't going to be easy."

"Let's have a look." I held out my hand for the list. "Household, Ideas, Old Projects, Four Heads, Fiction, Italy, Finances."

"That's it. Anything ring a bell, Tim?"

"Well, 'Household' and 'Finances' seem obvious. I'll be grateful to get those folders open. He took care of all that for me." Hollister paused. "I knew he was working on fiction. Writing a novel was a dream of his. Helmut wanted his next project to fund a period of time for him to work on a novel. But I doubt he'd keep documents related to his newest project in there."

"We'll have to check them all. What about 'Ideas', 'Old Projects', 'Italy', and 'Four Heads'? Anything there?"

"Of course, 'Ideas' could be where he'd keep it. But I suspect it's only for things he hadn't yet developed. Still, I'd like to see it. 'Old Projects' wouldn't be it. He wouldn't mix the new with the old. But you should check."

"That leaves 'Italy' and 'Four Heads.' Sound like possibilities?"

"Italy, perhaps. The other… it sounds…" Hollister said, his voice taking on a dreamy quality as if he retreated into memories to try and grasp the meaning of the folder's name. "I don't know. There's something familiar about it. It's right there in my mind yet I can't grasp it. I know that I know what it means. But, I can't remember."

"Take your time," I said.

"Caffeine always helps me think," Luke offered. "How about I make some tea or coffee?"

"I'll have some," I said. Caffeine and I were old friends and I couldn't imagine a day without it. "I've got some nice strong Italian coffee in the cabinet, Luke. Brew some of that. What about you Tim?"

"Hmmm? Wha-what?"

"Italian coffee. One of my brothers sent it from Rome when he was there a while ago. It'll curl your toes."

Hollister was in some kind of thought trance, trying to reach old memories. Luke got busy in the kitchen and I smelled the coffee as soon as he opened the container.

"Tim? Coffee? From Rome. Strong stuff."

"Rome." Hollister uttered the word. "You said Rome?"

"Yes. Rome. Italy. The Popes. Hot men. High fashion."

"But that's it!"

"What?" Nina said. "What's it?"

"You remembered." I grinned at him.

"Yes, I remember now. The Bridge of Four Heads is in Rome. It connects the city to a small island in the Tiber river." He paused and gazed at the ceiling. "I wonder what he meant when he named the folder."

"His next book is… was… going to be about that Pope again, right?" Anton asked. "The one who died so quickly?"

"Yeah, John Paul the First," I said and realized Anton had been paying more attention than I thought. He was smart. I knew that, but I didn't think he was all that interested in this case.

"The Popes are in Rome and so is that bridge. Maybe that's the connection. It's worth looking into."

"Of course, you're right, Anton," Hollister said slowly as if trying to connect the dots of possibility. "But just what is the connection between that bridge and Albino Luciani? I mean to say there isn't any traditional connection between the bridge and the papacy. Except it was a Pope who had the bridge restored. Other than that, it's just a very old bridge."

"What's the four heads thing about?" Luke asked.

"As far as I remember," Hollister said, "it has to do with the four contractors commissioned with restoring the bridge. The Pope, at the time the temporal ruler of Rome, hired them and set them to work. They apparently argued and created quite a public scandal with their fighting. So, the Pope had them all beheaded. And then, the legend goes, he commissioned a sculpture with four heads, supposedly the likenesses of the contractors, and had the sculpture set on the bridge."

"Wow," Luke said. "I didn't know Popes were so bloodthirsty."

"They were… and are," Hollister answered. "Of course, it's partly legend. I believe the actual statue is from a much earlier time and was placed on the bridge for decorative purposes. But there's probably some truth in that story somewhere."

"And that would be connected to the recent work, how?" Anton asked.

"I have no idea," Hollister said.

"We might find an answer if we opened the file." Nina sounded impatient. "Any ideas on passwords?"

"Can't be a publication date," I offered. "It's not finished yet."

"And it may never be," Hollister said. "Unless… Well, maybe I could finish it for him. Sort of a tribute."

"Not unless we can get into the file," Nina insisted. "Are we thinking about passwords? I've tried all the other things while you guys were talking."

"Well, I don't know about all of you," Anton said getting up from where he'd planted himself next to me. "But I've got work in half an hour at Bubbles. So I'm going to have to leave this little party."

"I almost forgot," I said and tried lifting myself off the sofa. A wave of dizziness crashed over me. I sat back groaning. "Uh, I guess I won't be helping you tonight, Anton."

"Stay put. Take care of your head. I can handle things." Anton turned then shot a glance in my direction. "I guess Luke can help you out pretty well."

"I'll be taking Mr. Hollister home when we're through here," Luke said pointedly. I noticed he didn't say he wouldn't return to make sure I was going to be all right for the night. Which is probably what he had in mind.

"Just get things sorted out at Bubbles. I'll be there tomorrow unless someone surprises me with another concussion."

Anton bent down and placed a kiss on my lips. It wasn't his usual chaste peck, there was something more behind that kiss. Longing, sweetness. It was intoxicating and I wanted more. Then I realized Anton wanted me to feel just that. He'd succeeded.

I watched him pull on his soft-blue suede jacket and open the door. He waved at all of us, winked at me, then closed the door behind him.

The faint sweet scent of him lingered in the air around me and I took a deep breath. I stared at the door as if he'd come waltzing back in. He knew he had me hoping that very thing.

"I hate to pull you away from staring at the door," Nina said. "But we've gotta find a password. Unless you like paying me overtime?"

"Yeah, Marco. Back to earth," Luke said. He'd obviously noticed everything.

"I was lost for a minute. My head feels as big as New Jersey." I looked over at Hollister silently peering at the laptop screen. "Any ideas, Tim?"

"Nothing we haven't gone over already."

"Anton said the book was going to be about the same Pope." Luke asked. "The same Pope as the previous book?"

"Yes," Hollister said. "He claimed he had more information on the Pope's murder. Names, dates, documents."

"But there was no publication date set yet?" Luke pressed.

"He had two or three publishers after him. No one had bought the book yet."

"We're missing something that's probably right in front of us," I said.

"The book wasn't published but in a sense, something else was," Luke said.

"What could you mean?" Hollister asked.

Knowing the way Luke's mind worked, I guessed what he was going to suggest.

"Well, Mr. Hollister, it might be something simple or I could be flat wrong. The book wasn't finished and wasn't bought. So there's no publication date. But the Pope, in a sense, was published."

"You mean something the Pope himself wrote?"

"I don't think that's what Luke means. Do you, Luke?"

"What I mean is that the Pope himself was sort of published. Twice in a way. Like Ben Franklin's epitaph. He refers to himself as a book being published. So maybe…"

"Brilliant! I know exactly what you mean." Hollister shouted. He stood up and hugged Luke who blushed. But who, I knew, loved the accolades.

"So," Luke continued, once he'd wriggled out of Hollister's grip, "you can use his birth date and maybe the date he became Pope."

"I'm on it," Nina said.

"I'm surprised you know the dates," Hollister said.

"I didn't but while you were all celebrating, Wikipedia revealed it to me." Nina raised her eyebrows and laughed. "He was born October 17, 1912 and became Pope on August 26, 1978 according to them."

"That's correct," Hollister said.

"I'll try different combinations." Nina tapped away at the keyboard.

"Do you think this will work?" Hollister glanced from the screen to me and back again.

"We'll know in a…"

"Got it!" Nina said. She'd done this kind of thing a thousand times at least, but this must have been particularly satisfying because she sounded happy.

"Wonderful!" Hollister pulled his chair around so he could see the screen.

I eased myself off the sofa. I had to see the contents of that folder for myself. This could either break the case open or be another dead end.

Luke quickly pulled a chair out for me and I sat at Nina's side while Luke looked over my shoulder and massaged my neck, which was just what I needed.

The four of us peered at the screen. There were about twenty-five Word documents, several .pdf documents and even a video. Helmut had been a busy man.

"Can you tell anything from the titles, Tim?"

"It's Helmut's usual method of noting files. Some are named for the people I recommended to him. People who said they had documents, diaries, things like that. Perhaps those files contain what we're looking for?"

"Nina can you get my printer to make two copies of everything here?"

"Set your computer to share its printer and it'll work."

"Luke, can you handle that?"

He nodded and walked into my home office to make the necessary changes. Before long I heard the printer humming, turning out page after page of material.

"Nina?"

She turned from the laptop which she'd been tending.

"What's up?"

"I'd like you to make a couple of back-ups for all these files. I don't want anything happening to them."

"Got writeable CDs or DVDs?"

"And a couple of flash drives. Make several copies."

Luke knew where things were and got them for Nina.

After everything had been done, we sat around feeling pretty satisfied with ourselves. We'd cracked the codes and found a load of documents. The question now was whether or not the contents would help with the case.

"Gonna take you a while to go through all of that," I said. "Let's call it a night. I'm still feeling like I smacked a wall going ninety-five miles an hour."

"We can talk tomorrow," Hollister said. "What you need is sleep."

"Tomorrow? You may need a bit more reading time..."

"Nonsense. I never sleep much and having found all this, I couldn't sleep anyway. I'll call you some time tomorrow and let you know what I've found."

Luke volunteered to take them both home and after he shuttled them into the hall he turned around and gave me a kiss which made me dizzier than I'd been in hours.

"What was that for?"

"I'm just glad you're okay. When I saw you in the hospital today, I was kinda scared. I never saw you look so helpless."

"I'm fine. My head is harder than you think."

"Just watch your back from now on." Luke stared into my eyes, as if searching my soul.

"Don't worry."

He'd cleaned up everything before they left so there wasn't much for me to do but lie on the sofa and relax. Of course, the moment I did that, the telephone rang.

"Everything okay, Marco? How's your head?" Anton asked.

"I'm fine, Anton. Just relaxing. Everybody's gone."

"Just wanted to know," he said. I knew he also just wanted to know if Luke had stayed behind. "I wanted to tell you... that you'd better be more careful from now on. I can't manage these guys all by my..." He stopped.

"Everybody worries too much. I'll be fine. Everything okay at Bubbles?"

"Sure, except Nando hasn't shown up. He hasn't missed a night in six months."

Chapter 19

The clock said seven which meant I'd slept ten hours. I awoke to the blissful sense that I didn't have a headache. The pain from the whack on the head was gone. What I needed was a hot shower and a hotter cup of coffee. I rolled out of bed, opened the blinds and felt a stab of pain from the brightness.

* * *

"I am hearing news only this morning!" Olga opened the door for me. A first. "You are all right? All in one of the pieces? I am worrying until I am seeing you for myself."

"I'm fine, Olga. But it's nice to know you care."

"I am caring but I am also needing job." She moved back to her desk.

"Your job is secure. Any messages this morning?"

"I am placing them on desk. Why you are coming in to work? With knock on head, you should rest."

"Who would you have to bother you?" I walked into my office and sat down. I wasn't dizzy but the effects of being hit on the head weren't entirely gone either.

I picked up the phone and called Hollister.

"Is this that big, handsome detective again?" Bancrofft cooed before I even gave my name. Good memory for a voice and never shy.

"Well, it's Marco Fontana, anyway. I don't know about the handsome part."

"Modest as well as mannerly, strong, and sexy. You, sweetie, are a catch. Hold out for a good man."

"I'll settle for talking to Tim. How's that?"

"Coming right up, hon," Bancrofft said.

The phone was muffled a moment.

"Marco. I'm afraid I haven't got any news for you. Not yet."

"You finished that entire stack of papers?"

"No. I fell asleep in the middle of it all and Lyman found me slumped over the papers this morning. I was apparently snoring like a pig. His description."

"There wasn't anything in the documents?"

"Names. A long list of names. Men of the Church. All dead as far as I can tell. Three documents stood out because Helmut named them Head One, Two, and Three."

"The Bridge of Four Heads. But..."

"You're going to ask what about the fourth. It isn't there. At least I haven't seen it. Maybe Nina can help."

"Worth a shot. Get me that list of names. I'll have Olga do a search. You never know the connections we'll find."

"I've started a list. I've saved the longest documents for last. I want to be absolutely alert when I read them. Those, what did you call them, pee-dee-something files? I think those might hold the new information Helmut talked about."

"The .pdf files?"

"Yes. Yes, those. I'm a neophyte when it comes to computers. I'll read those files and add any names I find."

"I think it'd be good to have a second set of eyes go over things."

"My feelings exactly," Hollister said. "Who have you got in mind?"

"I'm hoping we can find someone knowledgeable about Church history and the workings of the Vatican. Maybe someone with personal experience."

"It's not a bad idea. Let me think about who," Hollister said.

"Call me before you make any moves."

* * *

It was way too early to try and corner Scanlan at Stella's. That would have to wait.

As much as I hated the thought of returning to Archdiocesan headquarters, I needed to confront Marlon. Something stuck in my craw about the phony way he'd responded when I questioned him and the way others characterized his reaction to Brandt. I also wondered if Quinn was a name he'd react to. Or Clifford and Navarro. I didn't trust Marlon and needed a better feel for the man behind that façade.

Lingering dizziness tempted me to take a taxi. The near-concussion and a still unsettled stomach sealed the deal. I hailed a cab in front of my building and zipped up to the Cathedral.

By the time I arrived, I'd decided that Monsignor Kusek might know the most about the reactions of people to Brandt's work. After all, as the Cardinal's adjutant, he was the eyes and ears of the head honcho and despite the nice guy appearance, I was willing to bet he kept good mental notes on everyone. He and I had never really gotten a chance to talk privately and, if he was around, I'd take the opportunity. The fact that he was a hot man with an angelic singing voice had nothing to do with my wanting to question him. Nothing at all.

I was directed to take an elevator to the top floor for Kusek's office. When you hold a lofty position, you need an office that soars over everything.

The elevator was filled with black-robed priests. All but one looked either jaded or tired. The youngest one had that devout, I'm-going-to-do-something-wonderful look that told you he'd just been admitted to the club and hadn't found out the real rules yet.

When I reached the top floor, I was alone. Probably none of my fellow passengers got to visit with the pooh-bahs very often. A thrill passed through me when I stepped into the cool and dimly lit corridor. This had to be where they hid the secrets. It was more elegant than other floors I'd seen, more serene and restrained. Gold-veined green marble flooring coexisted easily with walls clad in creamy marble shot through with rust-colored veins. Muted lighting in the ceiling cast a dignified glow over everything.

There was only one door. A solid, golden-oak color, it was imposing and solemn. I knocked and entered the stately reception area. A prim and proper woman in her sixties, sat behind an old, dignified, wood desk, one hand propped on a complicated-looking telephone. On an extension to the right a flat panel computer monitor held her attention. The carpet was red and thick, muted cream colored walls held paintings which were lit by tiny spotlights concealed in the molding around the ceiling. This was without doubt the outer office of an immeasurably important official. The office of the right hand man of a Prince of the Church.

The reedy receptionist eyed me suspiciously. I introduced myself and admitted to not having an appointment which didn't please her. I explained I was investigating a murder and that the Monsignor had spoken with me earlier. She didn't budge. I dropped hints that I was a good Catholic boy. An exaggeration, okay, but in a good cause.

"The Monsignor's schedule doesn't permit…"

"Could you tell him it's a Mr. Fontana? I only need a moment of his time? Like I said, he spoke to me a few days ago. He's aware of the serious nature of the case."

"But… if I…"

"I'll tell him I twisted your arm. He won't blame you. I'm sure he knows how persistent private investigators can be."

"Well… if you promise not to take too long." She picked up the phone and tapped a button, then spoke in low tones. As she placed the phone in its cradle, she looked up at me, a curious expression on her face. "Go on in. He sounded happy to be interrupted."

She followed me with her eyes as I moved, intensely interested in this person who'd been admitted so easily to her boss's presence.

I knocked and entered Kusek's office. It was as posh as the rest of the bigwig offices I'd seen, maybe more so. A sleek modernity marked the place, a cleaner set of lines and colors made it fresh. There was no hint of stuffiness. Lots of windows brought the sun into the room and there was no pious stained glass. Large, crystal clear windows gave you the sense you were standing on a pinnacle overlooking the city, able to survey several directions.

The room's style reflected Kusek's age which was probably close to mine. Of course, the fact he was a knock-out in the looks department made everything in the room appear happier and more alive.

He winced as he stood then smiled as if he were genuinely glad to see me.

"Mr. Fontana. How nice to see you again."

"Monsignor." I extended my hand.

"Call me anything else. Monsignor makes me feel ancient." He took my hand and held onto it. His hand was tender and warm; the hand of a man not used to heavy work, not accustomed to having to prove strength in his grip. There was comfort and confidence in that grip.

"In that case, call me Marco."

"Deal. Have a seat, Marco." He continued standing. "Can I get you some coffee? Just simple coffee-maker brew but it's got caffeine and that's all I need."

"Never passed up caffeine in my life and don't intend to start now." I laughed.

He poured two mugs of hot, aromatic coffee, set one next to me on a table and sat behind his desk. It may have been brewed in a coffee-maker but he used primo coffee.

"A Monsignor who plays with toy trucks?" I said, picking up a small scale-model delivery truck from his desk. It seemed out of place, as nothing on his desk was remotely playful or whimsical. It was all business except for the truck which was marked along the sides with "Augustine Pankowski, Butcher. Fine Meats and Poultry. Chicago, Illinois" in fancy script.

Kusek looked up from stirring sugar into his coffee.

"Playing...? Oh. My grandfather's business. It's the only thing left of him or his company. Poor guy went bankrupt and the family was destitute. That truck was a Christmas present he gave to all the grandchildren the year before the business failed. He died shortly after that."

"I'm sorry." I gently placed the truck back on his desk.

"It was a long time ago, in fact I never really knew the man." Kusek fumbled with papers on his desk. "I understand you've been a frequent visitor to the building," he said, letting me know he was aware of what went on under his roof.

"Not enough to rack up frequent flyer miles," I said. "But, you're right. This case has brought me here a few times. I'm still trying to get a handle on the effect Brandt's work had on people here. On how upset people were. Maybe still are."

"You want to fill your list of suspects from among our ranks." He smiled knowingly. "People here were understandably perturbed. But not enough to kill anyone." Kusek gave me a look as if he thought the whole idea of killing over Brandt's work was insane. "It would take someone with powerful hatred, or some real insecurity to resort to killing. Wouldn't you say?"

"I see all kinds of things in the work I do. You'd be surprised at the reasons people have for violence."

"I've got to admit that in my job, violence is kind of remote." Kusek took a long drink of coffee. "I've never come face to face with anything even close."

"I wouldn't find that hard to believe." I looked him in the eye and he stared right back, refusing to shy away. I felt him taking my measure.

"You might think I've had a sheltered life. I went into the seminary right after high school. Got assigned to the Cardinal when he worked in Rome and I've been working for him ever since. I've seen more than you think."

"You've traveled, you deal with people and organizations, you handle situations all over the diocese, and you lay the groundwork for your boss. You haven't been sheltered from everything. Just some of the nastier things."

"Managing a church-related organization or coping with trouble in a parish lets you see quite a lot and understand even more. Things can get rough."

"So how *did* Brandt's work affect people? When I saw you that first time, in Fr. Marlon's office, he laughed off Brandt's theories. Yet, someone told me he'd been livid, furious beyond words about Brandt's book."

Kusek laughed. "I told him his temper would get him into trouble one day." He took another pull from the mug and relaxed in his swivel chair. "But he's no murderer."

I remained silent.

"Fr. Marlon is a complicated character. People are all complicated in their own ways. No one is simply that shell you see when you look at them." He sighed. "Marlon generally explodes into a furious blur when something comes up. And then it's all over. He's quick to react and even quicker to retreat from his first reaction."

"Was that how he acted when Brandt's book was released?"

"And again when Brandt made headlines claiming he'd uncovered new material. Marlon is like fireworks – big splash and a quick finish into dark silence. He's harmless."

"Maybe." I stared at him.

"I suppose you have to be thorough. I like that."

"What about Wren? He seemed pretty upset when I spoke to him. Looked to me like Brandt's work really got under his skin."

"Wren is public relations. Those guys are only happy when everything goes their way. Nothing out of kilter, no bad spin, every bit of publicity a positive one."

"The pedophile scandals must've made him nuts."

"You can't imagine. He was crazed. Didn't know what to do. I swear, every time I saw him his hair was standing on end. His reaction to Brandt was mild in comparison."

"What about you?"

"And the sex scandals?" He laughed and it was a shy, boyish laugh, as if he were hiding from the realities of the secular world. "I wasn't…"

"No, no. I'm sorry. I meant what about you and Brandt's work? How did you take it? How did it complicate your life?"

"Personally, I take things like that with a large grain of salt. Everyone loves conspiracy theories. Who shot JFK? Who was really behind 9/11? How did Marilyn Monroe actually die? They never get tired of spinning theories."

"True. But the possible murder of a pope. That really wrinkled some shirts."

"Italians have been concocting theories about popes and murders for centuries. When a pope dies after only thirty-three days, you can bet your life savings that conspiracy theories will spin out of control within hours. That's just what happened."

"Looks like everyone wanted a piece of that particular conspiracy."

"Everybody's got a different spin. Believe me. I've read all the books. Even a few that were never published in English."

"But Brandt claimed to have new material."

"So he did. Except he never offered any. Besides, everyone involved is dead, so, who would he hurt anyway?" A sad smile crossed Kusek's lips. The soft sunlight in the room made his expressive face appear vulnerably beautiful.

"According to Wren, Brandt's work would hurt the Church in a more general way. Destroy people's faith in the institution's integrity," I said.

"After two thousand years, I think we can take the hit and survive."

"No doubt," I said. "So you didn't hold Brandt responsible? Didn't want him silenced?"

"I didn't give him much thought. I wanted it all to blow over."

"What about your boss?"

"Cardinal Galante? What about him?"

"How'd he react? The man's a powerhouse in the Church. I've heard him called the 'American Pope.' Right?"

"He's the one American cardinal with a good chance of getting elected. Others look up to him."

"Brandt's work must've angered him or at least worried him."

"To tell you the truth, the Cardinal dismissed the whole thing as hogwash. A manufactured series of publicity maneuvers to sell books. The Cardinal wanted Brandt to fade away. He felt the less publicity we gave him, the better. If we reacted, that would mean more ink for Brandt. Just like all those films people protest. The more they protest, the bigger the take at the box office. His Eminence understands that kind of thing. He chose to ignore Brandt and his attempts to goad a reaction out of us."

"Smart man," I said.

"Smart, wise, and kind." Kusek said, the look in his eyes softened. "He's been around a long time. And he's done a lot of good. I wouldn't be sitting here today if he hadn't come along and saved my life. If it happens that he becomes Pope, no one deserves it more. Of course, there's already someone sitting on the throne."

"I've heard rumors the Pope is not well, is that true?"

"He's not getting any younger, that's for sure. But I haven't heard there's any reason to believe he's not going to be around for a while," Kusek said. He drained his cup and looked at me. "Have I helped you any with your investigation? Do you need me to let people know you're welcome to interview them? Just say the word."

Before I could answer, the door to the office opened and in walked a short, stout, grandfatherly man. I recognized him immediately especially as he was dressed in a cassock trimmed in scarlet and wore a red zucchetto on his head. The scarlet sash around his waist emphasized his girth but, I had to admit to myself, he didn't look comical because of it. He had presence and an air of authority and at the same time gave off a feeling of benevolent gentility.

Cardinal Galante smiled as we both stood. He had a kindly face with just enough wrinkles to lend him the authority of age without making him look weak, a shock of white hair, brown eyes that held a happiness which spread to the rest of his expression. It was almost infectious but then I remembered his position on gays and I got over the warm and fuzzy feeling.

"Your Eminence. I thought you were getting ready for your trip to Rome."

"I've postponed for a few days. I still feel wobbly from the knee surgery. I apologize if I've interrupted your meeting. Gladys wasn't at her desk, so I took the liberty…"

"We were just finishing, Your Eminence," I said and the words nearly stuck in my throat. Calling someone Eminence was a little OTT as Anton might say. But over the top or not, I needed these guys to cooperate, so I'd call them 'honey buns' if it'd help. "The Monsignor was gracious enough to give me a few moments of his time."

"This is Marco Fontana, Eminence. He's investigating the murder of Helmut Brandt."

Galante hobbled forward with some difficulty, hand extended. I noticed the massive gold ring on his finger but was not about to kiss that ring. Some Catholics fall all over themselves to do that. I hadn't kissed a Cardinal's ring since I was an altar boy with stars in my eyes about becoming a priest. I stuck out my hand and we shook.

His soft pudgy hands packed a firm grip. He was a man of power and it was evident in his gracefully authoritative posture, the direct way his eyes met yours without wavering, and in the detached, confident way he spoke.

"Nice to meet you, Mr. Fontana. A familiar name. I grew up here. Did you know that? One of my grade school friends was Aldo Fontana. Any relation?" He gripped my hand as he spoke. He was in charge and would let go when he was good and ready.

"Not that I know. But I've got lots of uncles and there are branches of the family I've never met."

"You're investigating the death of the writer?" he said, finally releasing my hand.

"Helmut Brandt, yes."

"I'd heard it was a mugging."

"We want to be sure," I said. He'd 'heard' it was a mugging. It was difficult to believe he was that removed from daily events. But, Kusek did say the Cardinal chose to ignore Brandt. "There are a few loose ends his partner would like to tie up. Closure will help with his loss."

"Yes, yes. I'm sure. Tragic thing to be gunned down as if your life isn't worth a nickel. Life is more precious than that." He seemed genuinely disturbed by the state of the world. His eyes lost their happy gloss, his smile disappeared.

"Unfortunately, not everyone agrees. Sometimes all you can do is hope for justice. You can never make things right, exactly," I said.

"Quite right. And wise. You've obviously seen a lot of this kind of thing." He regarded me with amused curiosity. "Well, if there's anything we can do to help…"

"I've assured Mr. Fontana that he'll have our cooperation. If he needs anything he can see me any time." Kusek looked at me with something more than just a cooperative glance and I returned the favor. He smiled, a shy small smile that came and went as quickly as a shadow. His boss was here after all.

"I'll be going. I'm sure you two have business to discuss." I shook hands with Galante again. This time his grip was more gentle, less commanding.

"It was a pleasure. If Aldo is a relative, give him my warmest regards. Tell him I wouldn't mind reminiscing about Sr. Philomena and the other nuns who tortured us all through grade school!" He laughed and it was a sad hollow sound.

"Let me know if you need anything," Kusek said walking me to the door.

"I'll be sure to do that." We shook hands and he held on just long enough to let me know it was more than a good-bye handshake. "You've got my card, if you think of anything else."

∗ ∗ ∗

Marlon's office was a few floors below. Tony was not at his station. But Marlon was filling a mug with coffee and snatching a few cookies from a tray in the outer office when I entered. He looked up, guilt plastered on his pudgy nut-brown face, one hand lingering over the cookie tray.

"Wel-l-l, hello there." An unctuous smile spread across his face. "What brings you back? I must say, I thought we'd finished with your case." He took his mug and a handful of cookies and moved into his office. He beckoned with his chin for me to follow.

"I wasn't quite through, Father Marlon." I sat without permission. I didn't need his say so to get comfortable. I wanted him unsettled. He saw I'd taken a seat and seemed annoyed but said nothing.

He placed the mug on his desk and the cookies on a sheet of paper, brushed crumbs from his hands, and sat down. Once again, it was difficult to tell whether he was sitting or standing.

"What more can I tell you?" He slurped some coffee and popped a cookie into his mouth.

"What exactly do you think about Brandt and his work?"

"I already…" Flustered at first, his face became impassive and calm.

"I know what you told me. But maybe you weren't exactly forthcoming? Maybe because someone else was in the office with us?" I remembered sitting in the exact same chair with Kusek next to me. Marlon had laughed off Brandt's work as just so much nonsense.

"Whatever my reaction to Brandt's work, surely you can't suspect me of having anything to do with this tragedy."

"What did you think of Brandt and his work?"

I watched him carefully. I didn't fully suspect him but I wondered about his influence on people who worked under him.

"I believe I've already told you. But, if you insist… I thought Brandt was… misguided," he said. I was close enough to see that his pupils dilated as he spoke. He had rather large, slightly bulging eyes to begin with and they revealed a lot. He fought with himself on this point.

"That's a pretty mild assessment of a man whose work could have destroyed a lot of people or so Mr. Wren says."

"Wren? He was quite angry... furious... " He stopped himself realizing he'd cracked the door a little too much. "He was outraged. Who can blame him? We spoke several times. He knew Brandt was a publicity hound. It's Wren's business and he knows the type. But Brandt's life was less than perfect. He should have been more careful."

"He was a less than perfect, misguided soul? That all you felt?"

"Yes. But Wren wanted to take legal action. He was intent on getting an injunction."

"You felt that was wrong?"

"No... uh... yes. I mean... Brandt was wrong-headed but I saw no point in a lawsuit. That would make more headlines."

"So you convinced Wren to drop the idea?"

"Wren would never listen to me. He's in too exalted a position to pay attention to me. He only listens to his own voice unless he gets orders from higher up. And that's just what happened."

"Who? Monsignor Kusek?"

"Higher. The Cardinal refused to hear anything about a lawsuit. He told Wren exactly what I'd already said. Legal action would create unwanted publicity."

"Brandt was trying to sell books. Can't blame the guy."

"His book was all lies and innuendo. He rehashed discredited information and invented more lies. There was nothing new in the trash he promoted. Nothing new. The only thing he accomplished was turning people away from the Church and causing others to lose faith or hope in an institution that was for some the only lifeline they had."

"And getting at the truth? That didn't matter to you?"

"Truth? A decades old death which devious minds try to spin into a murder mystery. Even if Brandt could prove Church officials murdered the Pope, what would be the point at this late date? What would be the point? Is anyone left to pay for the crime?"

"I don't think Brandt cared if anyone paid for the crime. He was after the truth."

"The only ones who'd pay for that alleged crime would be the followers of the Church. They would pay with their faith. They would pay by losing something to hope for and believe in. No one in a lofty position will pay for that crime, if there was a crime. They're all dead. All gone." He sat back, breathing rapidly with his effort.

I kept silent.

"So, truth? The Truth is far more complex. The truth in this case is compassion for those who will suffer the most from hearing Brandt's version of the truth. The real story, the truth no one wants to accept is that Luciani was a sick man whose heart gave out. Will another truth serve to help or to hurt? That's what should concern us."

I hardly knew what to say. The man was passionate. Wrong but passionate. And angrier than he'd wanted to reveal. But there it was. Except, it seemed to me it was the kind of anger that would drive a man to despair not to murder.

"You make a good case, Father, though I can't say you've convinced me."

He stared, deflated, empty of his former passion. He glanced at the coffee and cookies on his desk as if they were something dirty he didn't want near him. The good mood he was in before I'd arrived had evaporated.

"Was there anyone you came across in your duties here, anyone under your authority or that you deal with who was angry enough to…"

"To commit murder? You don't give up."

"Not until I'm satisfied I've turned over every rock."

"I don't have people 'under' my authority. I have colleagues. None of them is capable of even thinking about murder."

I'd heard that line before. It was hardly ever true. But Marlon believed it. I saw that in his eyes, and heard it in his voice. He was also tired. Tired is when they let down their guard. I figured I should hit him with more.

"Maybe you can help with some other names I've come across."

"Haven't you learned enough?" His voice betrayed his surrender.

"Not about these guys," I said. "Francis Clifford. He works in this building, right?"

"A strange little man. Not someone I care to get close to. But he's not violent. Clifford is pathetic. His life is a sham and he has a bloated sense of his own importance. But violent? Murderous? I don't think so."

"How did he react to Brandt?"

"Mr. Clifford's agenda places his self interest first. If he chimed in on Brandt, it was because he wanted to be part of the crowd, part of the angry core, hoping it would give him credit among the higher ups. He cared more about his position than he cared about Brandt."

That's what I'd figured about Clifford, a lot of self-aggrandizing bluster. A showy man with not much to offer. But he also paid close attention to those in power and to those who could get him close to the center. His real value lay in the gossip he possessed.

"I assume you've heard of Tom Quinn?"

"Heard of him? Of course. And I do everything I can to stay out of his way. The man is psychopathic."

"To the point of murder?"

His sipped his coffee thoughtfully, apparently mulling over an answer.

"I'm no expert but I'd have to give a qualified yes."

"Qualified?" I asked.

"Well, I have no direct evidence. I'm not the man's psychiatrist. If he has one, and he should. All I can give you is the qualified opinion of an observer of people."

"You've seen a lot, I'd imagine."

"I have. You can't begin to know. I've been a parish priest. I've worked in some of the best places and some of the worst. I've been a chaplain in the Army and at a hospital. It was years before I landed this position and my experience stands me in good stead, I can tell you."

"Did Quinn ever threaten anyone or cause a problem here?"

"He made a nuisance of himself. Always in here for something or other, pestering people for nonexistent documents and inside information. He was convinced we were holding out on him."

"Did he threaten anyone?"

"He issued a veiled threat to me. Said I'd regret not helping him. Told me about a priest in Rome who'd refused to help him."

"What happened?"

"Disappeared, according to Quinn. He'd say anything, make up anything, to get what he wanted." Marlon stopped, took another drink from his cup. "This is cold, mind if I warm it up? Want some?"

"Thanks, no."

He waddled out the door and I heard Tony greet him. He was telling the truth about things. He was a pious, if a bit material, man.

"This is better," he said returning to his desk. He sighed and breathed in the steaming aroma. "Quinn threatened Tony once."

"Why's that?"

"Tony is not one to suffer fools gladly. Quinn made a scene wanting information on the death of Cardinal Krol. Quinn was convinced there was foul play. Something about the liberal faction wanting Krol dead. I asked Quinn why the liberals had waited until Krol retired before they supposedly killed him."

"Good question." I chuckled. Krol had been as conservative as they get but so were his successors. The liberal faction that Quinn fantasized, would've had their hands full. Quinn was a loon.

"He refused to believe me. He badgered Tony for documents, autopsy notes. Anything to prove his point. When Tony finally told him to leave or he'd call security, Quinn threatened him."

"Did you report that?"

"Of course. Quinn never actually did anything so there wasn't much the authorities could do. Tony looked over his shoulder for weeks because Quinn kept calling the office."

"How'd it stop?"

"Tony has some rather large relatives and a few friends who are, what word can I use? Unsavory? Yes, that's a good way to describe them. Tony has some unsavory friends. They told Quinn to leave Tony alone. We never saw Quinn here again."

"I think that about covers it." I stood and was about to extend my hand. "Wait, do you know a Mr. Navarro? A boarder at Clifford's home."

"Doesn't sound familiar," Marlon said. His eyes were droopy and I thought he'd doze off any minute.

"He's an Opus Dei adherent."

"Well that explains it. Opus Dei is its own prelature. They report to their own bishop."

I extended my hand to shake and Marlon stood, at least I thought he stood.

"You've been helpful."

"My pleasure," he said, smiling.

"I may call on you again. This is a tangled case."

"Warn me before, so I can leave town." He laughed.

Tony winked at me on my way out.

"Niko says you're OK. He likes you."

"Everybody likes me. Except the ones that don't."

"Well, Niko's a good judge of character. Anything you need, just ask," Tony said.

"That's an offer I'll take you up on some time."

"Hey. Anything but that, Fontana." Tony laughed. "Niko doesn't like you that much and he's not crazy about sharing."

"Well, how about some information, then?"

"Sure, anytime. Just call me. Take this." He handed me a card with his cell, home, and work numbers on it.

"How's Jared doing? He didn't look so great when I saw him."

"Jared's a mess. Losing Helmut like that. Scanlan beating him. His boss is giving him a hard time, too. Poor kid's a wreck."

"Take him to Bubbles some night. If you need me, just say the word."

"Gotcha," Tony said, then the office phone rang.

Back in the hall I snapped open my cell phone to call Kent. I had an assignment for him. He didn't answer.

I called Hollister and he agreed to meet for lunch. Said he was finished with the papers and we could talk. That was one of my objectives, that, and telling him I wasn't much further along on the case. I also wanted his take on Quinn and Scanlan.

Walking back to the gayborhood from the Archdiocesan headquarters, I felt more aware of everything around me. No one was getting the drop on me again. I thought about who might've sent the thug to bash in my head. Quinn was a leading candidate. According to Jane Palmer, he seemed generally prone to violent solutions. Of course, Scanlan wasn't a genteel soul either, judging from the beating he'd given Jared. Quinn wasn't an organized type and hiring someone took thought and organization. Scanlan was more likely the organized guy. But there were others just as capable.

If someone had hired a thug to bash me, they could easily have done the same to kill Brandt. Connections, money, planning, and organization. Whoever did it would have to have it all. I'd have to dig up more on Quinn, Scanlan, and others.

As I thought, I remembered something about the voice of the guy who took me by surprise. I'd recognized that voice just before all the lights had gone out.

Where had I heard him before?

Chapter 20

More Than Just Ice Cream is one of my favorite places to eat. Reasonable prices, good food, and cute waiters. Not a large place, it's comfortable and not overwhelming. A wall of floor to ceiling windows make it light and airy. I liked that. All that light made it seem like everything was right with the world even if it wasn't.

Hollister agreed to meet there. Said he'd never been there, another reason I'd never bumped into him in the neighborhood before.

I took a seat at the back. No one could look over our shoulders or overhear what we were talking about. Not that I thought anyone would understand what we'd be discussing. That knock on the head made me even more inclined to be wary. Besides, my uncle Fanuccio told me that it was good mafia practice to sit with your back against the wall. At least you knew no one would come at you from behind. I didn't want to know where or how he'd learned that rule and he never told me.

The waiter was new. He was cute, filled out his jeans like no one should be permitted to do in public, and was bouncy. He smiled so much I thought maybe he was a little off balance. No one smiles that much, not even the perkiest of wait-staff. But every time I caught his eye, he had a mile-wide smile plastered on his pretty face. And he was attentive. Brought me a cup of coffee quickly, gently placed two menus on the table, and kept checking to see if there was anything else he could do for me.

I was just about to tell him what else he might do, when Hollister walked in carrying a black leather briefcase. He smiled and headed over to the table.

"Tim. You look all business with that briefcase."

"You gave me homework and I did it." He laughed. "I hope the results are helpful. I have my doubts."

Bouncy the waiter came over to the table. It struck me that if he needed extra income, he was just the kind of guy the customers at Bubbles would love to see dancing on the bar. I decided to leave him my card.

"Can I get you anything?" He glanced at Tim then concentrated his gaze on me.

Hollister asked for black coffee and requested a moment to look at the menu.

We ordered when the waiter returned with the coffee. Hollister pulled a notepad from the briefcase and placed it on the table. It was filled with notes, arrows, rectangles, lines, and circles. He made notes the way I did and I liked that.

"Lots of names, a few dates and places. Whoever wrote it reports conversations he supposedly overheard." He emptied several packets of sugar into his coffee, stirred, then looked up. "It's interesting and even incriminating but I'm afraid all the names on the list are of men long dead. The most recent was Archbishop Marcinkus who died a year or two ago."

"Would he have been ruined if this information had leaked?"

"Not really. His reputation was already in tatters because of his involvement with the Vatican Bank financial scandal. Someone even wrote a novel implicating Marcinkus in the poisoning death of the Soviet Premier Andropov. If you can imagine that. Not that he wouldn't have been capable of doing it. To get that high up in the Vatican you've got to have ice water in your veins."

"Sounds like a handy person to have around when you want to get rid of someone. Say, like a Pope."

"Marcinkus sued the author but lost. His reputation had been tarnished by then anyway. Now he's dead. Reputations of dead men aren't worth a whole lot, especially dead churchmen."

"Have we hit a dead end with the documents?"

"There are some interesting things in what I've read and there are some larger documents I still need to scour."

"Anything we can use? Because it's feeling like a dead end to me."

"One major document is a kind of diary by a low level priest. He calls himself one of the *bagarozzi*."

"Beetles?" My Italian was a rusty but that word was easy. Except I wasn't sure about the reference. "He calls himself a beetle?"

"The Italians call them black beetles. The priests, the clerics who do the Vatican's daily business. You see them all over the city. Dressed in black from head to toe. Up one street and down another, they're all over the place. Like a crew of black beetles scurrying through the streets."

"Clever name. Italians are good at that. So, what's the *bagarozzo's* significance?"

"He describes the plot to murder the Pope," Hollister said and gave me a knowing look. "Helmut really did have his hands on something hot. It's amazing."

Bouncy brought our food and Hollister remained silent until the waiter was out of earshot.

"Whoever wrote this knew what those men were up to. He lists details."

"Yes, but…"

"You're still wondering how to connect this with Helmut's death."

"I usually follow the money, so to speak. It doesn't seem to me that anyone stands to lose or gain much with this information. But conspiracy nuts would love it."

"Is it possible that some pious fanatic thinks this information could destroy the Church? A person like that would think there's a lot to be lost if the documents were made public and a lot to gain if they're not." Hollister's eyes gleamed with his desire to find a connection between Helmut's death and the documents.

"Anything is possible. But, killing someone… that's the ultimate step. There's either got to be something very personal going on or something big at stake. Somebody's got to have a lot invested in keeping those documents secret. A run of the mill fanatic doesn't take the time to plot a murder for hire and make it look like a mugging. Your garden variety fanatic would take a gun and do it himself." I was sorry I said that as soon at the last word slipped my lips. "I apologize. I didn't mean to be callous."

"I understand. You're into the case, you're enthusiastic. I want you to be excited about it. I'm hoping you'll see something in these documents that will spark an idea."

"So far, all we've got is a bagarozzo who details a murder plot. Who are the plotters? How believable is he? Even more important, why didn't he warn the Pope or the authorities?"

"He claims he wasn't sure that what he'd heard was true until it was done. He couldn't believe it was real. When it actually happened, he says he was stunned. Then frightened out of his mind that they'd kill him if he said anything."

"Okay. He was probably too scared to tell anyone until they were all dead or unable to touch him. But why reveal anything now?"

"Maybe his conscience bothered him. Maybe he's just dedicated to the truth even if no one pays for their deeds."

"Who does he implicate?" I was still skeptical about connecting this to Helmut's death but I had to explore possibilities.

"The names are where it gets interesting. To me, anyway." Hollister took a forkful of omelet and savored the taste. He closed his eyes a moment then looked at me and smiled sadly. "Helmut loved omelets. I'd make him one every Sunday."

I bit into my turkey burger and allowed him to enjoy his memories. He probably had a difficult time conjuring up any good ones right now.

"Well," Hollister said breaking his reverie, "the names of the plotters are intriguing. From what I already know the bagarozzo's list sounds believable to me."

"And? They are?"

"Archbishop Marcinkus. It's not surprising to see him mentioned. So many others point the finger at him and that lends credibility."

"Okay." I held my skepticism to myself. Just because the black beetle mentioned the archbishop didn't mean squat to me. The name could have been added for the express purpose of making this document seem consistent with other theories.

"Did you know he was originally from Chicago? Marcinkus. He even went back there to work for a while after his disgrace with the Vatican bank."

"Didn't know that, but I wasn't wrapped up in that scandal."

"The interesting thing is that another of the plotters also had a Chicago connection. Cardinal Cody."

"Interesting but…"

"The Vatican's Secretary of State, Cardinal Villot is mentioned. There was also someone from P2, Archbishop Giovanni Martuzzi. He had connections to Licio Gelli, a financier and a big P2 man himself."

"Helmut mentioned P2 when he called me that morning. Truthfully, I don't know what it is."

"Propaganda Due is what it stands for and it's a shady Italian Masonic group. It was officially put out of business in 1976 but they say it operated covertly until 1981. If it was a covert organization, I have no doubt it still exists."

"But you can't be sure."

"It included some of the biggest names in Italian political, cultural, and economic affairs among its members. These are not people who fade away when told to do so by a government or a hierarchy they care nothing about. P2 was considered a shadow government in Italy for years. Who's to say they aren't still operating in Italy and elsewhere?" Hollister said.

"You're thinking they don't want word to get around about their possible participation in the plot?"

"Well…"

"Doesn't quite make sense. They supposedly don't exist anymore. So what if people suspect they were involved? So what if they actually know?" I asked

"On the surface you're right. But, think about it. There were some highly placed people in P2 and some of them are still alive."

"They'd have to have a long reach to harm Helmut. All the way from Italy," I said. "Can't say I'm buying the P2 story. The source has got to be closer to home. I like the Chicago connection. But they're all dead."

"The big names, yes. But what about possible assistants? The bagarozzo who produced this diary was an assistant to Villot, I think. They all had them."

"But even the bagarozzo wasn't sure about what he'd heard. Not until after the Pope had died. These assistants were all too low on the totem pole to be included in anything," I said.

"True."

"And would any of the big shots really want to risk having some flunky know what was really going on? Maybe one of the assistants would grow a conscience and the whole plot would be blown to hell and all their careers along with it."

"They could at least verify the truth of these documents," Hollister offered.

"If they knew anything. Which we both know they probably didn't. If they did know something, what would motivate them to tell the truth thirty years later?"

"You never know, Marco. Anything is possible."

"Does the bagarozzo give any indication who any of the assistants were?"

"No," Hollister said sounding genuinely sad. "It would be very difficult to find out who assisted whom thirty years ago. The Vatican guards its records with a ferocity you can't imagine."

Things looked bleak.

"I was really hoping these documents would tell us more," Hollister said. "Helmut was so certain."

"Is it possible Helmut knew something that isn't easy for us to see in the documents? Are there are other documents? Maybe we're missing something."

"Anything is possible."

"Did you figure out why he named the files after the bridge?" I asked.

"We got talking about P2 and I forgot to tell you." Hollister took a sip of his coffee and patted his lips with his napkin. "According to the bagarozzo, the conspirators met at a café on the other side of the Bridge of Four Heads in Rome. It's not a well traveled place. I suppose it made the perfect spot for a clandestine meeting."

"Send me the rest of the names you culled. I'll add them to Olga's research. She's good at background stuff like that."

"I'll get through all the documents and have a more complete list of names for you." He finished off the last of his omelet.

Bouncy was sharp and zipped over to the table the minute he thought we were through.

"Dessert? The chocolate cake is dreamy today," he crooned as if he'd just fallen in love. I was certain that neither chocolate nor any other flavor cake ever touched his lips. With a shape like his, sweets were not usually on the menu.

"What about it, Tim? They have great stuff here," I said.

"No, no. I'd better not."

"Just the check." I glanced up at Bouncy who looked at me as though he were disappointed I'd be leaving.

"You don't think these documents amount to much, do you, Marco?"

"Hard to say, Tim. Doesn't sound like they contain anything worth killing over. Of course, to me, there isn't much worth killing over. If you're right, and that information is why Helmut was killed, then it means something to somebody. But it's a big 'if' right now."

"I haven't changed my mind. This," he patted the papers and notes, "is the reason he died. I'm certain of it."

"Then we have to figure out who wants that information to go away."

* * *

Hollister walked with me as far as my office and promised again to drop off the list. I watched him shuffle away and noticed how bent over he was as he moved. I knew the walk. Grief bore down on him. He was strong but even the strongest people can be undone by grief. I resolved again to get to the bottom of the case.

I got into the rickety elevator. For some reason, the thought of taking the stairs wasn't so appealing. Maybe I didn't feel as good as I'd pretended.

"Boss is back from lunch. Now hired help can be having time to eat?" Olga looked at me as if I was on the verge of collapse. "You are feeling not so hot?"

"Go have lunch. I'll be fine." I opened the door to my office wanting peace and solitude.

"I am coming back soon. Since they are knocking you on head, there is more work to do."

"Well," I said, not understanding why my being hit on the head should increase her work, "I'll have even more work for you this afternoon. Mr. Hollister is bringing in a list of names. I need some deep research."

"Is my specialty," she said as she waddled out the door.

I sat in my comfy desk chair and lay back against it, forgetting the bump on my head. I winced, sat up sharply, then lay back, more gently this time.

Silence.

Not even a siren destroyed the moment. I felt the thoughts and concerns of the day slide away and I drifted into that state between sleep and wakefulness. It was a pleasant sensation, like rocking in a boat tethered to a dock, the sun high in the sky, a breeze caressing my skin. The gentle movement of the boat buoyed me as the water rocked it like a cradle.

After a while the phone warbled and for once I was grateful for Olga's insistence on that gentle ring tone.

"Fontana," I answered, the near-sleep state slurring my voice.

"Mr. Fontana, this is Jane Palmer. I have some information."

Chapter 21

"I'm leaving town, Mr. Fontana. And..." Palmer cleared her throat.

"Did Quinn harm you?"

"No. Nothing like that. I just can't work for the man any longer."

"Does he know you're leaving?" I already knew the answer. From her breathing and tone of voice, I knew she was clearing out before he found out.

"I'm moving back to New York. I've had... job offers. My family is there and that's where my heart is." I heard the sound of a boarding call in the background.

"You haven't told him, have you?"

"I left a letter. I don't want to be there when he finds it."

"You're doing the right thing. But, why tell me?"

"I heard Quinn planning something... He's insane. Someone will get hurt."

"I'm listening."

"I overheard a phone conversation Quinn had. Something about giving someone a warning. But it was the way he wanted the message delivered. He said he wanted to be sure the person would never be able to go through with whatever it was. He said he'd paid good money and expected results."

Quinn was more lethal than he appeared. He'd obviously use any means to get what he wanted. What Palmer had overheard could be about me but could easily have been about anyone else. Maybe someone not even related to this case.

"Why do you suspect it has anything to do with me?"

"I'm warning you just in case."

"You said you had a couple of reasons for calling."

"I have some information. Not much. Just some names Quinn gathered in his work on the conspiracy."

"How did you get…"

"I just did. I'm at a copy shop at the train station. I'll fax them to your office."

She hung up without a goodbye, after getting the fax number.

My office door swung open and Olga stood there, coat over her arm.

"I am back. You are still dizzy?"

I didn't quite know how to take that remark, so I let it slide. I tossed her a quick smile. As she waddled into the room, the fax machine started spitting out papers.

"You're just in time. Here are some names for you to hunt down." I indicated the fax machine with a thrust of my chin. "And Hollister will bring even more."

"And I am researching names to be finding… ?"

"A detailed background search. Anything and everything you can find. And if you can cross reference any of them, that would help."

"You are wanting everything? Everything?"

"Down to the kind of underwear they liked. Down to the most secret, private details you can hack your way into."

"Hacking. Is cruel word. I am not woman who is hacking. I am researching."

"Just get me as much as you can, Olga."

She scooped the papers from the fax machine, then pecked me on the cheek.

"What was that for?"

"Because you are good boss. And knock on head makes Olga worry."

"You're a peach, you know that?"

"Now I am fruit?" She shook her head and went out the door.

The phone rang and I took it knowing Olga was still settling in.

"Marco?" I recognized Kent's voice immediately.

"Where've you been? I could've used your help on some things."

"Something came up. I'm kinda stuck right now." He didn't sound like himself.

"Meaning you can't do any work?"

"For now. But I will. I promise. I will."

"What's going on, Kent? You sound…"

"Nothin' I can't handle. Don't worry. I'll call you as soon as I can."

The next thing I heard was dial tone. This was strange behavior even for Kent. Anton's warning about him nagged at me. I still felt I was right about the kid. I'm a pretty good judge of character or I'd have been eating dirt a long time ago. Something was up and I'd have to find out what.

Olga buzzed the intercom.

"Is Mr. Hollister, wanting to see you."

"Send him in."

Hollister opened the office door slowly and shuffled in. He looked beaten down.

"Tim. You okay?"

"It's all the arrangements, Marco. Everything is overwhelming." He sounded weary. "Helmut's family is flying in from Germany. I have to plan a memorial service. Helmut didn't want anything traditional. Except he expressly did not want to be cremated."

"I can get someone to help, if you like."

"Lyman is being a real support. I'll get through this. It's incredible how many things you never think about. Never realize you'd need to think about. Even though, when something like this happens, everything is painfully obvious. And you know that all your life you've just been avoiding and avoiding."

He held out a large manila envelope.

"The papers I promised," he said.

I took the envelope. "I'll add it to Olga's pile."

"Did Nina find anything more on the laptop?"

"I'll be calling her later," I said. Hollister looked lost and indecisive. "Listen, I know you want to be involved in the investigation, but you've got a full plate right now. I can keep you posted every step of the way."

"I need to be involved. It helps. Helmut's family is coming and they deserve the truth as much as I do."

I nodded.

"Call me any time, Marco. And for the love of God, don't get hurt again."

"I've got things under control. Let me know if you need anything."

He gave me a mournful look, turned, and left the office.

I opened the envelope and took out three sheets of paper. The first was a list of names I'd give to Olga. The rest was a synopsis of the documents and checklist of things Hollister thought Nina might be able to tease out of the laptop. Things that had been referenced in the documents but which weren't a part of files they'd already found.

The names included those Hollister had mentioned like Villot, Cody, Marcinkus, but there were others, none of whom were familiar and none, according to his notes, who he thought were still alive. I trusted Olga to do a deeper search that would yield something.

* * *

Anton had agreed to meet for dinner at the Bellini Grill which was a lot fancier than its name implied. Like a little bit of Italy transplanted to 16th Street, it was quiet, out of the way, and just right for talking. It was romantic which I knew Anton would like.

"Okay, what's up?" Anton said as he sat down. He picked up the white cloth napkin and spread it on his lap, then stared at me with those crystal blue eyes.

"Is that all you think of me? Do I only take you to nice places when I want something?"

"Yes." He teased. "Okay, no. But sometimes I can tell you've got an agenda. And this feels like one of those times."

I stared at him. The soft yellow glow of the candle on the table swathed him in otherworldly light. His blond hair and golden hued skin spoke of dreams and fantasies. The square cut of his jaw was strong. His lips were expressive and pink. I wanted to pull him to me and hug him.

But I didn't. Instead I gazed at him and wondered what it would be like to settle down, buy a bigger condo, and make a life together. Would it be a whole lot different than my life now? Yes. There was no getting around that. I looked at his face and there was an innocence beneath his unmitigated beauty. I knew that he cared for me, quite a lot. More than a lot. I knew life together could be good, it might even last. The look on his face made me understand that not everything had to be so up in the air for me. That maybe I could have an island of stability.

"Well," he said. "Do you? Have an agenda?"

The waiter placed a slivery basket of crusty rolls on the table and cruets with olive oil and thick balsamic vinegar. Anton took one of the rolls then promptly ignored it.

"Honestly? No. I just wanted to have dinner with you. I know I've been kind of wrapped up in this case and then getting knocked on the head… I haven't been at Bubbles enough."

"I assumed you wanted me to get used to handling things on my own." Anton took a piece of the roll and popped it into his mouth.

"I know you're handling things just fine. I'm happy about that. But this case has gotten to me and I'm spending more time on it than I thought I'd be." I jumped into every case with everything I had. You don't give it everything, you don't solve a case. But there was something about this one that took hold of me and wormed its way into my being. The memory of Brandt when I'd met him years before and the energy of his life force had stuck with me. Without realizing it, seeing him so alive and content with himself gave me the courage to come out and be myself all those years ago. It was nothing he said. We'd never actually spoken. It was his spirit.

"I can see the case has gotten under your skin, Marco. I know you. You feel the answer is just out of reach and that makes you crazy. I've seen it before."

"You're right. Problem is there are plenty of people who had some axe to grind with Brandt."

"None of them actually had an axe, though, so to speak. Right? Or, you'd have nailed them by now. You always get them."

"Yeah, sure," I said and broke my roll into pieces, choosing to skip the oil.

The restaurant wasn't yet crowded. Anton and I felt comfortably private in our little corner. We were able to enjoy each other's company without intrusions.

Our waiter was a plain-faced kid, kind of like the child in a family where the looks went to everyone else. All he got were facial quirks. Eyes too close together, thin lips, and no chin. Still he was attentive and gave us *tiramisu* on the house.

We lingered over coffee. Anton hadn't touched his *tiramisu*. When he looked at me, concern colored his expression.

"What?" I asked.

"Nando seems to be missing."

"Missing? You sure he's missing or just ducking work?"

"He hasn't shown for two nights. And," Anton paused and I could tell there was a bit of a zinger meant for me perched on his tongue.

"And? What?"

"And Kent hasn't been around either." His tone full of I-told-you-so.

"I'm sure Elton John and Boy George haven't been seen in Bubbles lately. You think there's some kind of group thing going on with the four of them?"

Anton harrumphed and took a large forkful of *tiramisu*, which I knew he didn't really like.

"Or, maybe…" I pressed.

"Okay! I get it. You think I'm jumping to conclusions." Anton took a long drink of water. "But I was trapped in the dressing room with Kent and his gun. Not you. I had to wait for you to come and do your hero thing. Then you took him under your wing and offered him a job. I was willing to go along with it, but now…"

I was amazed at his ability to keep his voice under control while effectively eviscerating me.

"I wasn't happy you hired him. And Nando was a little unnerved. But you're the boss. The padrone. Neither of us could say much. I knew Kent would be trouble. He's gone and so is Nando. That can't be a coincidence."

"All right, I'm not gonna minimize your suspicions. Wouldn't be the first time you were right about things like this," I said, practicing diplomacy. "Tell me what you'd like me to do and I promise I'll take care of it."

Anton's breathing slowed, he drank more water and looked at me skeptically.

"Very smooth, Fontana. No wonder all the boys fall over when you pass by. But this is Anton you're trying to con." He stared at me and smirked. "What should you do? Well, for starters you can help me find Nando. Kent I don't care about. But I'll bet a week's salary you'll find them together. I wouldn't be surprised if Kent has Nando against his will."

"Kidnapping? You're kidding, right?"

"No, I'm not. I'm willing to risk a week's pay that I'm right."

"Sounds good. You're on. This'll be easy money."

"Hold on, what're you putting up?" Anton asked.

"That you'll lose a week's salary and will have to dance to make up the loss."

"Not good enough, Marco. How about loss of a week's pay for me, if you win. And for you," Anton closed his eyes and thought. A smile slowly spread over his face. "For you, if you lose the bet..." He paused relishing the moment.

"What?" Suddenly I realized what he was thinking. "No. Oh, no. I'm not..."

"If you lose, you agree to strip for two successive weekends." He smiled broadly and it was a dazzler. "Well? Can't be a tough decision, Mister Private Eye."

"I don't think so." I saw the trap he was closing and I couldn't do anything.

"Afraid you were wrong about Kent?"

"Not at all. I have confidence in him."

"Then why not take the wager?"

He'd backed me into a corner. It'd become a matter of pride.

"All right. You're on. There's no way I'm losing anyway."

"I hope you still own a few g-strings."

The waiter brought the check and I took it.

"My treat for not being around as much as I should," I said.

"Don't be crazy." Anton placed his hand over the check.

"Let me pay, Anton, because when you lose the bet, you'll need all the savings you have to carry you through that week without pay."

"Oh, I'll get paid. And I'll see a lot more of the boss than I've been seeing lately."

"I'm heading over to Stella's to follow up on a lead. Wanna come along?"

"I'd rather clean toilets. Come to think of it, Stella's is a toilet."

"That may be true but someone there knows something about this case. And I'm gonna find out who it is and what they know."

Chapter 22

Stella's was nowhere near the gayborhood. It was a place for hustlers and johns, for guys on the lookout for sugar daddies, and for anyone seeking whatever they couldn't get elsewhere. It was especially the spot for guys who didn't want anyone knowing they were in the market for things no one would mention in public. The location had to be out of the way and off the beaten path.

To say Stella's represented the underbelly of gay life was both an understatement and a misstatement. There were lowlife types but there were also politicians, rich men, celebrities, and people who felt they didn't fit anywhere else. Of course, they often became prey for the lowlifes using Stella's as a hangout.

Sayda and Dora, who everyone called S&D, were the owners now, Stella having long before passed on to a much better bar. Tougher than nails, S&D, as far as anyone knew, were straight. They never spoke about themselves, if they ever spoke at all.

I knew I was close to Stella's when I noticed a few drug-soaked hustlers dotting the pavement. S&D never let obvious druggies muck up their place. If you even appeared to be high on something, you were forced to hit the bricks.

One young guy, wearing a torn and weathered coat two sizes too big for him, stood wavering on the sidewalk like a phantom. I'm not sure if he knew where he was or even who he was, but he knew he needed cash to feed his habit. That was the beast urging him on and it didn't matter who or where he was.

"Hey, whach'u up to tonight, man?" He placed a hand on my shoulder. His fetid breath smudging the air. "Need some company?" He stared as best he could while blinking away drug induced sleepiness and wavering to and fro trying to stay on his feet.

"Do I look like I need company?" I said shucking his arm from my back and moving off. Seeing the wasted potential made me angry then sad. Not that he'd remember I blew off his advance, he didn't respect himself enough to resent anything. I guess I thought maybe I should be a little kinder even if I didn't have to be.

Glancing over my shoulder, I saw he was already trolling for another prospect.

I saw the muted lights of Stella's bleak front entrance a block away. There wasn't much to identify it, no crackling neon, no sign. You just had to know where it was and, more importantly, what it was. This time of night, Stella's was the only thing happening on this shabby end of Mole Street, a low traffic area that was not at all welcoming. No one would accidentally wander into this bar. With all the shady dealings going on under Stella's roof which was virtually in the shadow of City Hall, I had the distinct impression it was allowed to stay in business so the authorities knew where they could find whatever they needed whenever they needed it.

Once you moved past the dull, time-worn entrance with its battered bricks and chipped stucco, you were confronted with a wide but shallow vestibule. A velvet rope prevented you from getting to the inner doorway. Behind the rope was an ugly hulk of a man, Bork by name, whose face had seen one too many illicit extreme-boxing matches. His nose was bent to the side, one eye stared into nothingness, its milky pupil useless. His shaved head showed a variety of unsightly lumps and scars. Despite his appearance, he was dressed impeccably. Not a stitch out of place. Black silk suit, white shirt, deep purple tie. And a blue carnation. The expression on his face was one of serene maliciousness. You didn't dare barge in. Bork would let you through as long as S&D didn't object. If they did, Bork would raise one of his tennis racket sized hands like a stop sign. If you resisted, he would wrap that hand around your throat and toss you out. Few gave him trouble. Those that did never gave him any more.

A faint glimmer of recognition crossed Bork's face when he saw me. What passed for a smile on that mug appeared and faded. He raised no objections as I moved past him into the club. I caught a glimpse of Sayda sitting at her desk in the front office. There were TV monitors allowing her to keep an eye on her domain. Dora was undoubtedly in the back office attending to the financial life of the club.

The first floor bar was all understated lighting with a lot of blacklight dusting the atmosphere. It gave the place a cool, almost stylish, air unless you knew the bar's reputation then you understood it wasn't about style.

Some of the older guys glanced furtively in my direction as I entered, then ducked their heads, either not wanting to be recognized or not interested in me as a type. Some of the hustlers looked at me as a new income possibility, others seemed to wonder if I was competition.

The long, rectangular first floor had a gracefully curved bar against each of the long walls. Littering the middle ground were tables occupied by hustlers and johns negotiating arrangements. I knew, from experience, there was an area to the back, off the main floor, that housed hidden alcoves for that private rendezvous everyone craved.

I headed for the curved bar to the left where Jimmy, one of my sometime dancers, tended bar. Few patrons sat at the bar. Most either hugged the walls or occupied tables. The hustlers scanned the place for clients.

"Marco, slumming again?" Jimmy laughed and placed a paper napkin on the bar in front of me. "What can I get you?"

"Molson's and some information."

He moved deftly behind the bar, pulled out a beer and set it before me. I plunked a twenty on the counter but he didn't move to touch it.

"What kind of information, Marco? Y'know, S&D don't like employees with loose lips. Bad for business." Jimmy leaned on the bar, propping his head on one hand.

"Murder's bad for business, too." I took a pull on the beer and set it back down. "I'm looking for a guy name of Scanlan. Seamus Scanlan. Know him?"

"Scanlan," Jimmy tasted the name and thought, eyes closed.

I described the man as best I could from the times I'd seen him.

"Yeah, he's in here a lot. Big tipper. He's in every weekend. You'll catch him here Friday for sure."

"Why's that?"

"It's when the workin' boys do their strip thing," Jimmy laughed. "I gotta hand it to them, they ain't professionals, not like you and your guys, but they do their best and they draw a crowd."

"Because they're for sale after the show," I commented and gulped more beer. "It's more like a commercial than a strip show."

"Shhh, not so loud," Jimmy said, half serious. "You never know when one of the Liquor Control Board freaks are snoopin' around."

"You ask me, the LCB geeks want a piece of ass like everybody else." I said.

Jimmy chuckled.

"Otherwise you'd have been shut down a long time ago. Stella's serves a purpose for people in high places."

"Well, Friday Stella's is gonna be servin' up some little hotties. And Scanlan'll be there."

"Does Scanlan hang with anybody in particular?"

"Usually comes in with…"

A customer interrupted, asking for a drink. Jimmy served it up with a smile and was back talking to me.

"What was I tellin' you?"

"Your phone number and when you can meet me." I smiled. Innocence personified.

"You already have my number and I know you don't wanna meet me later." He looked at me, then did a small double take. "Or do you? Wanna meet me, I mean? You do?"

"You were gonna tell me something about Scanlan."

"I know. I was gonna tell you who Scanlan hangs with. It's more like, who don't he hang with?" Jimmy pointed to my empty beer bottle and looked at me.

"Yeah, gimme another one."

"Scanlan mostly hangs with the youngest guys, but he's friendly with everybody. Buys drinks for people, especially the hustlers. Likes bein' a big shot."

"Nobody special stands out? Must be some guys who are special."

"Yeah, there's this kid he drags in with him. Not one of the guys for sale. I got the impression Scanlan and the kid were connected sorta. He's kinda cute. But never looks comfortable. Haven't seen the kid for a while. At first he was always trailin' behind Scanlan. Then the kid got friendly with some low life types. Who knows why? Probably bored and needed somebody to talk to because Scanlan usually ignored him."

The kid he was talking about had to be Jared. When Jimmy described him, I knew for certain that's who he meant. I wondered aloud if Tony or Niko, by description not name, ever tagged along with Jared.

"I've seen him in here with a few hot guys. Guys that don't look like they belong here on either side of the fence, if you catch my drift."

"I understand," I said. "Any of those friends become regulars?"

"Occasionally I see one or two of them come in. Sometimes the dark haired guys would come in, usually for the strip nights."

"Interesting."

"I think guys like that come in for excitement. Y'know, those clean cut types. Guys with decent jobs or a little money. This is like living on the edge for them."

"World hasn't changed all that much. Guys like that have been slumming since who knows when. They never get enough excitement." Of course, not all of them were slumming, some had more sinister reasons for being in Stella's. Like making connections with people who'd do anything for a buck.

"You know it, man," Jimmy said while washing some glasses in hot soapy water behind the bar.

"What about Scanlan? You remember anybody he got really cozy with?"

"Like I said, he was friends with everybody." Jimmy waved to another customer, brought him a rum and coke without being asked. "Scanlan got chummy with a few of the really tough ones. Guys I knew were packin' and they scared even me. It was like he wanted to know trouble. Always looking for the worst of the worst. Scanlan used to take home some kid called Little B. A runt. But tough. I saw Little B knock out a guy once. Right over there. Him and Scanlan left together lots of times."

"Little B still come in?"

"Yeah, almost every night. Especially when he don't have a sugar daddy takin' care of him. Except I heard he had his face rearranged by one of the other boys."

"Tough place."

"Tough life these kids have. I feel sorry for 'em," Jimmy said. "That's what was nice about the guy Scanlan dragged in here. He was good to the boys. Didn't make them feel like trash. He was actually nice to 'em."

"You remember any of the ones he was friendly with?"

"I'd have to think about it. I can see their faces but I don't remember names. There are so many of 'em in here. Sometimes it depresses me."

I saw Jimmy in a new light. He'd been dancing with StripGuyz for a couple of years and I thought he was a hard ass. But he seemed genuinely moved by the kids who sold themselves to get by. He made me think about the kids down at The Haven. I'd have to make a special effort for them as soon as this case was over.

"I know what you mean, Jimmy." I picked up my beer. "I'm gonna take a spin around. You remember anything else, let me know. I'll be back."

I left Jimmy to do his work, Stella's was getting busier and I needed to nose around. Even though Stella's was a treasure trove of contacts for anything you wanted, you still had to know how to ask.

I headed to the downstairs bar. Subdued lighting hardly ate the darkness. A bar occupied the center of the room and was lit from below and from recessed lighting in the ceiling. All the bottles shimmered with green light from beneath the shelving. The bartender was a tough-looking man with a scar the size of the Mississippi River running from his scalp to his neck and beneath his collar. Gave me the chills just looking at it.

Patrons hung around the bar, stood against the wall, or circulated through darkened alcoves in the back. A small staging area for strip shows occupied one end of the room. There was nowhere for a stripper to escape if the crowd got too close or too hands on. I'd never let my guys work in conditions like that.

Glancing around I saw buyers and sellers melting into the inky darkness. Some of the young guys gave me come hither looks, part of their sales pitch and nothing more. Now and then, though, I saw a pair of eyes that held a longing for more than cold cash.

"What're you lookin' for, man?" The guy was short and peered up at me when he spoke. "Got time to talk?" He had a sweet face, olive complexion, and the longest eyelashes I'd ever seen.

"Love to but I'm meeting someone." I can't remember just how many times I'd used that line.

"If your guy don't show up, come find me. If I'm still here." He stood on his toes and planted a delicate kiss on my cheek. His lips felt cold and he looked tired.

"I'll do that," I said and moved toward the back.

It was more crowded than the upstairs. People pressed in on all sides. I felt for my wallet after a few guys came particularly close. It was still there. I wondered how many people they packed in here on strip show nights. The words "fire trap" came to mind.

Just for the hell of it I ambled through the pitch dark back area. Whispers and sighs floated through curtained alcoves. The smell of stale beer and disinfectant hung in the air.

There were more of the privacy cubicles than was at first apparent in the deceptively large room. The oppressive stuffiness drove me out and as I passed a curtained room I heard a familiar voice. "Naw, man." The next words were muzzy, then, "I got another gig, man. No can do." Suddenly there was silence. I had the feeling one of them in the cubicle sensed someone was listening.

Now only whispered murmurs wafted through the stale darkness. The hair at the back of my neck stood on end as I moved back into the bar. The crowd had grown thicker, more noisy.

I ordered bottled water at the bar. Scarface plunked down a four-dollar bottle of water. For a few cents more I could've bought a whole case at ShopRite. I sighed, twisted off the cap, and downed half the bottle. All the while taking in the crowd, doing my own, human, version of facial recognition software I'd seen in operation at casinos and high security facilities.

People exited the back room. A tall, slender man, frowned his way to the bar and ordered bourbon and water. Behind him, a short guy ambled out wearing a baseball cap to shroud his face. He glanced around as if trying to find someone and, spotting an older man in a corner, shot over to him. Three other young guys walked out of the back room one at a time, all of them uniformed in tee shirts and jeans, two of them sporting baseball caps. None of them seemed to know the others. Once out they went separate ways, headed for different targets. Two older men plodded out, aimed for the bar. Then nothing. It was almost as if someone had rung a bell and told them to clear the back room. But I knew there had to be more guys back there from my earlier assessment.

I finished the water and took another turn around the floor. After being groped several times and getting a few more offers from hustlers wanting to score, I figured there was nothing left to learn at the downstairs bar that night. I decided to come back on Friday and corner Scanlan. He'd answer a few questions, I'd make sure of that.

Back on the first floor I headed for Jimmy who was busy with a load of patrons.

"Got anything else for me, Jimmy?"

"Another beer?" He laughed. "Yeah, actually I do remember something. There was one edgy guy who was real tight with Scanlan's boy. I don't know his name but he always wore a Phillies cap and a leather jacket that looked like it cost good money. Always looked kinda lost and real edgy. Whadda they call it? Attention-deficit malfunction? He musta had it. Always on edge except when he was talking to the boy who was nice to him. And Mister Phillies cap hung around him a lot."

The edgy description sounded familiar. Like the guy who was scoping out my apartment building and the video store. But a lot of these guys were edgy types, especially when they were trying to score a john.

"Anybody else?"

"He's the only one stands out. Scanlan's boy was friendly with a lot of the guys. But the Phillies cap was special."

"You're scheduled to work at Bubbles on Sunday. We'll talk then if you remember more."

"See ya then, Marco." He gave me a little salute and went back to his customers.

Leaving Stella's always felt like entering a different dimension. Some guys said they felt cleaner once they left Stella's. I always thought of it as an adventure in some exotic locale. You certainly never saw these types much anywhere else. My ears were ringing from the music and I felt cold.

I'd had enough of the exotic for one night and wanted to get home and sleep. I needed to be fresh in the morning.

When I put my hand into my jacket pocket, I felt something and pulled out what looked like a business card.

The front was scribbled over and crossed out. A Dr. Shubin would probably be mortified if he knew his business card was in the hands of someone from Stella's. On the other hand, he shouldn't have given his card to a street prostitute if he didn't want his peccadilloes known.

Turning it over I saw sloppy block letter printing. "Fontana, Meet me in 1 hour. 22nd and JFK. The Underpass. I got information."

It wasn't just another offer from a hustler. This guy knew my name. Sleep was a foreign country I'd have to visit another time. Right now I'd have to hoof it over to Twenty-second street.

Chapter 23

Arriving before whoever I was meeting was necessary for me to scope out the territory. The meeting place wasn't much traveled even in broad daylight. The underpass at Twenty-second was a sort of no man's land between Market Street and a newly gentrified area. During the day pedestrians didn't frequent that stretch of Twenty-second. After midnight, you had to wonder who might be lurking in the arched recesses of the underpass. It was a concrete nightmare.

Friends of mine lived three blocks away, so I knew the area. But the underpass held dead ends and dark hollows that could conceal just about anything. I suspected this might be a set up but I hoped I'd at least catch a look at him before he spotted me.

Several street lights were out on either end of the underpass creating deep shadows. I decided to circle around and double back onto Twenty-second to try and get the jump on him. Unless he was already waiting.

The air was brisk and before I knew it I was on Race and turning onto Twenty-second. I smelled burning leaves from off in the distance. The stillness in the air combined with the empty streets brought me to full alert.

I stopped half a block before the underpass. I waited as my eyes adjusted to the gloom. There were no houses, only a few shuttered businesses. A cold breeze kicked up and I peered ahead. The underpass was south of me.

Beyond, a lonely stretch led from the underpass to Market Street. Like a gauntlet I'd have to get through. I was alone and unarmed. Not the smartest move I'd ever made.

The clock on my cell phone indicated it was time. I took a few steps in the direction of the underpass. In the distance, the traffic speeding by on Market was a blur of light and sound. I listened for footfall, a voice, something. Only the indistinct whirr and rumble of cars filled the air. I almost missed the sound in the emptiness north of me.

A soft rumble, as if someone started a car a block away. The engine purred. I turned in time to see a car pull onto Twenty-second traveling the wrong direction. Blinding headlights shattered the darkness. Screeching wheels carried two tons of steel at me like a runaway truck.

I ran, zigzagging from side to side and let the shadows of the underpass swallow me. I had to avoid getting trapped in a dead end. I ran close to the massive concrete stanchions supporting the overpass.

The car gained on me. Its cold white headlights picked me out of the darkness. I kept moving. The driver floored the pedal and bore down on me. Tires screaming with the effort.

Running in the open would give him an easy target. I needed a plan. I zagged again and bought myself a few seconds behind a stanchion. The car idled in the distance, waiting to make me roadkill.

Then it came to me. I darted from behind the concrete shield and decided to play chicken.

Illuminated by the headlights, I backed myself against the stanchion. There was no way he could miss me. He must have realized the same thing.

He revved the engine. Tons of metal, plastic, and glaring headlights were about to plaster my insides all over the concrete. I'd be a grotesque mural added to the collection of graffiti decorating the underpass.

The car barreled on. I wanted to run but forced myself to wait. The car loomed large, loud, angry. I almost felt the heat of the roaring engine.

At the last possible second, I leaped to the side. The car smashed into the stanchion with a horrendous shriek. Sparks flew like fireworks. Glass shattered. Metal twisted. The headlights splintered and died. The car's horn blared. It filled my head as I ran.

I sped toward Market Street and heard gears grinding. Glancing back, I saw him back the car out and head unsteadily for me again.

It was a dark pursuit. No headlights. No streetlamps. Just the guttural growl of the mangled engine bearing down. Like a tank, mean and vicious.

He wouldn't fall for the same trick twice but without headlights the playing field was more even. I zigzagged and heard him scrape the walls as he gained on me.

A few more yards and I'd be at Market. He'd have to give up or risk running me down in front of traffic on Market Street.

I strained with everything I had. One more kick and I'd be there.

The lights and traffic of Market Street were just ahead.

Behind me the car groaned and growled.

I reached the corner nearly out of breath. The car skidded to a stop somewhere behind me. I didn't turn to see. I wanted to put as much distance between me and the maniac as possible.

* * *

"What the hell happened?" Anton shut the door to my office at Bubbles and backed me into my chair.

I winced. I hadn't felt the bumps and bruises until I'd gotten to Bubbles.

"Sit down. Let me look at you." Anton gently took my jacket. "Take off your shirt."

"I'm all right, really." My breathing was back to normal but my heart raced. "I outran him and he gave up."

"This was not just a warning, like the last time," Anton said, continuing to check for more damage. "Look at that." He pointed to a long abrasion on my left arm from the wrist to the elbow. "And your back. Did he throw you on the ground and stomp on you?"

"You think I'm a weak-kneed little kid? Ouch! Stop that." I vainly attempted to move out of Anton's reach. "Those bruises are all from me bumping into stanchions and walls. He never laid a finger on me."

"These people are serious. Who are they?"

"Good question," I said. "Got a paper towel?"

Anton handed me some paper towels. I wiped the sweat from my face with them and covered my eyes with my hands for a few moments.

"Maybe I upset somebody at Stella's tonight."

"I told you that place was evil. Nobody decent ever goes there."

"That's not entirely true," I joked. "I was there."

"That's different. You were on business."

"So are most of the guys there."

"Your business was legitimate," Anton insisted. "They're all thugs."

"Believe me, I don't think a simple thug was behind this tonight. Thugs don't think like that."

"Well, somebody at Stella's does."

"I'm getting close to something. I can't figure out what but I definitely rattled somebody's world tonight."

"Playing hero will get you killed, Marco. Then what?"

"I'll take protection next time. Maybe Kevin."

"The bouncer. Great idea. He can handle himself. So can I. Take me, too."

"Nah, it's a bad idea all around. I'd just be putting you and him in danger. I've gotta do this myself. It'd be a distraction having you guys along. I'd be looking out for you and that's when things go wrong."

"Were you distracted tonight?"

"It won't happen again."

"I'd like to believe you. But you're reckless."

"Kent still a no show?" I changed the subject not so deftly.

"And Nando."

"I'll see if Luke can do some snooping around."

"Oh sure, Luke. He'll be on your side. If he finds them for you, I'll never know if I actually win the bet we made."

"Luke doesn't even know about the bet. And I won't tell him. That way, whatever he finds, he finds and the bet is still good."

"Yeah, right." Anton glowered.

"Okay, how about if he reports to you before he tells me anything?"

"Yeah, have him report to me." There was a strange gleam in Anton's eyes.

"Well, I'm about to conk out. I've gotta get some sleep."

"You sure no one followed you?" Anton asked.

"Nah, I jumped into a taxi on Market and told the guy to drive around Rittenhouse Square twice before I made him drop me here. If anybody followed us around and all the way here, he deserves another chance at running me down. I'll be fine."

* * *

Next morning, I arrived at the office earlier than usual. The adrenaline that'd pumped through me the night before enabling me to escape the death car, had given me a restless night. So I'd gotten up, showered, took care of some email and left for the office.

At seven in the morning the streets had a quiet, underlying sense of the possibilities a new day brought. The pure potential floating in the morning air freshened everything and buoyed me.

I decided to head to a café for breakfast instead of eating alone in my office. There'd be nothing to do and no one to call for a couple of hours. So, I bought a Philly Inquirer and a Washington Post and headed over to the Village Brew.

Sean, who even his friends called Slutty Sean, was the barista. Curly brown hair ringed his head and made him look like a modern but sleazy Botticelli. His eyes sparkled with an inner glow and he smiled when I approached the counter.

"Marco! Haven't seen you in a while. Don't you like us anymore?" He mugged a sad face and curled his lower lip down as if he were ready to cry.

"You look familiar. What's your name again?" I kidded and stared at the list of coffees and teas on the wall chart. "Gimmie a venti coffee with a shot of vanilla. No cream."

"No cream? But cream, that's what makes the coffee, Marco. You gotta…"

"No cream, Sean."

"Black coffee with vanilla, comin' up." He turned to the coffee machine and I saw he wore jeans that showed his pert little ass to great effect. And his movements. It was no surprise where his nickname came from. I couldn't help but wonder if he was as bad as the nickname or if it was an image he enjoyed cultivating.

"Venti coffee, shot of vanilla. No cream!" Sean plunked the oversized container onto the counter and smiled again.

"And one of those blueberry muffins."

"There's less fat in the croissants," he said. "If you're worried about fat, I mean."

"Are you telling me I have to worry about fat, Sean? Never mind. Give me the fruit cup, nix the muffin."

It's a good thing the place was empty. I didn't need my body fat index calculated by casual observers.

Sean pulled a fruit cup out of the cold counter and placed it next to my coffee.

"Five dollars," he said and waited, smiling.

He took the five I proffered and I slipped a dollar in the tip jar. As I was about to pick up the coffee, Sean leaned over the counter, placed a hand on my shoulder, and whispered into my ear.

"Just so you know, I don't see an ounce of fat on you, but you've got clothes on. Maybe we can arrange for a closer inspection?"

I smiled slyly, took my coffee and fruit cup, and sat at a table facing the counter. Sean kept his eyes on me the whole time. The boy was forward and I saw now that his nickname was no accident.

The front page of the Post was filled with dire stories of atrocities around the world and news of political hopefuls for a presidential election more than a year away. I found an interesting story about a bizarre murder in upstate New York and hunkered down to read. The coffee was hot and harsh and I felt the caffeine rushing through me.

"Marco?"

I looked up and there was Hollister standing opposite me.

"Tim. Get some coffee, join me." I was happy to be interrupted. The gruesome details of the execution style murder of an entire family were not good breakfast reading.

"You don't mind?"

"Not at all. In fact, I'm glad you're here."

Tim bought coffee and sat across from me. I glanced at Sean who seemed intrigued by Tim's presence.

"Anything new, Marco?"

I debated telling him about the maniacal driver but I thought he should know. He could be in danger, too. It was a deadly can of worms he had me open.

"I don't know if I should tell you this…"

"Have you found something? Is it bad news? What?"

"Last night I went to a bar called Stella's."

"The hustler bar? I didn't know it was still operating. Well, if that's…"

"I was following a lead. But so far nothing. Except, on my way back someone tried to run me down."

"Run you down? With a car?" He was incredulous. "Have you called the police?" He stared at me in alarm. "I can't have you putting your life in danger. Nothing is worth your life."

"Look, this means we're getting somebody nervous. We're getting close to whatever it is someone wants hidden."

"Helmut's killer."

"Or someone connected to his death. We don't know and I have to keep digging."

"No. I can't let you take chances like that. You can't keep endangering yourself. I won't allow it. I'm calling an end to this."

"You want answers, don't you?"

"Not if it means you'll be hurt. No. There's been enough violence."

"This is the way the game is played. I can't drop the case. I don't like being intimidated and I don't respond well to threats. Besides," I said, staring at the dark liquid in my cup, "I feel a certain commitment to Helmut."

"You didn't even know him."

"Years ago, when I was just coming out, I saw Helmut here in Philly. At a reading. I don't know what it was, but he affected my life, made me change course. I'd never experienced a man who was so happy, even joyous, just to be himself."

"Helmut had that effect on people. It was a kind of magnetism. I felt it the first time I met him."

"So I kinda feel I owe him. Don't close the case down, Tim. Helmut deserves an answer."

"You're sounding like me now. How can I argue with you?" He massaged his temples with the tips of his fingers. The wrinkles on his face seemed deeper and sadder and he looked older than he had just a few days before. "I don't want you taking risks, Marco. Helmut wouldn't want that and it wouldn't honor his memory if you were hurt or... worse."

"I'll do my best, Tim. I'll do my best."

We were silent for a few moments, I heard the clink of cups and saucers as a few more people were served. Sean's throaty greetings rose and fell with different customers. The rich aroma of brewed coffee and pastry filled the air.

"Did you have a chance to finish reading the documents?" I broke the silence and Hollister raised his head, a wistful look in his eyes.

"I'd intended to call you later. I never expected to see you here," he said. "There wasn't much more in the documents other than an oblique reference to the fact that some of the people close to the plotters were on a track to higher office in The Church. But there were no names, no indication they were still alive."

"They wouldn't make it easy, would they?"

"No. Unfortunately. It doesn't give you much to go on." Hollister sighed.

"It's an interesting thought that there may be people around who might know about the plot. Assuming they were let in on the actual plans in the first place."

"What I read, admittedly it's not much and it's very sidelong, implies that some of these minions might have known something. I have no doubt Helmut was on their trail."

"If any of them are still alive," I said.

"If these people have risen to positions of power or importance, your chances of discovering anything or getting them to admit anything are less than zero."

"I don't give up that easily," I said.

"Getting them to admit knowledge of such a plot would be next to impossible. Killing a Pope is an abominable thing to think about let alone do, " Hollister whispered.

"We can only try to get to the bottom of Helmut's murder. Maybe the Pope's death is connected, maybe not. One way or another I'll find out."

* * *

"Boss is arriving early." Olga looked up from her work. "Is special occasion? You are having meeting with beautiful man?"

"No, I'm having a meeting with beautiful you."

"I have no meeting on schedule," she paged through her day book.

"I just want to know what you've found on those names I gave you."

"You are needing miracle working." Olga smiled. "Lucky for you, I am working miracles."

She spread out papers, each one headed by a name with a bulleted list of details below. All the names I'd given her were there but now complete with details of their lives and names of people connected to them in significant ways.

"This is wonderful, Olga. You outdid yourself." I beamed looking over the paperwork.

"Is nothing. Much more is possible but you give only names."

"This is marvelous. And all in one day. Worth a bonus. If I could afford a bonus."

"You are always not affording bonus." Olga frowned then smiled broadly. "I am not working for bonus. I am working for you."

"I'll look at all this material now. You're a gem. Take a three hour lunch today."

"Is better than bonus which does not exist."

I shut my office door behind me and heard Olga humming a tune which she'd once told me was an old Russian folksong. Something about a long-suffering peasant and a mountain of treasure.

Fresh coffee in the coffeemaker beckoned me with its strong aroma. I poured myself a cup and watched the steam rise like a ghost above the cup. Sunlight streamed in the window and, best of all, the office was quiet.

Olga's work stared up at me, page after page covered with dates, places, names. At the top of each, one name in large bold print. Olga had even included a picture of each of the people. None of them looked even vaguely familiar, all of them having been big shots in the Church or Italian finance at least twenty-five years before. Cardinal Villot was probably the biggest name on the list. One of the names associated with his was familiar: Navarro, the Opus Dei member I'd met with at Clifford's home.

Olga had neatly included as much information as possible about current locations of all the underlings associated with the bigwigs. Navarro was supposed to be located in Elgin, Illinois, near Chicago. But here he was in Philadelphia. That rated a red flag. So, I circled his name and put his sheet to the side. Turns out he was also on the P2 delegate's list. He'd worked double duty though probably not at cross purposes.

On the page headed up by Marcinkus, the discredited Vatican finance official, there were lots of associates but just about everyone was dead. The rest lived in Europe. It would take a long reach for them to be involved.

I combed through all the other lists, including those names supplied by Jane Palmer, and when I came to the sheet on Chicago's Cardinal Cody, lo and behold, there were two familiar names. That in itself meant nothing but it started me thinking.

First there was a John Wren, status unclear. Olga didn't note whether he was dead or alive. However, he was a Philadelphia native and I was willing to bet he was related to Peter Wren at the Archdiocesan office. John Wren had been a priest on the way up the administrative ladder. After the Pope's death, he'd eventually been made a bishop. Then something stopped his progress and there wasn't any further news about him. I'd ask Olga to try again once I'd confirmed he was related to the Wren I knew.

The other name I saw surprised me. Carlo Galante. The cardinal. As a young priest, he'd been assigned to Rome and had landed a position as an assistant to John Cardinal Cody. Galante had apparently been right in the middle of everything. Which proved exactly nothing. He'd been a young priest, one of many subordinates serving for the first time in Rome, like Wren. He'd been assigned to Cody who may or may not have been involved in a plot, if there actually was a plot. My head spun. There was no guarantee Galante had even been close to Cody, let alone close enough to be entrusted with the details of an assassination plot. My understanding was that Cody hadn't spent much time in the city.

Still, this was exciting. I'd have to question Galante. Not that he'd admit knowledge of the supposed plot. But, he could give me some insight into the bigger names on the list. Assuming he'd gotten to know them. Which, as a lowly young priest, wasn't too likely.

Kusek intimated that Galante would not want to discuss theories surrounding the Pope's death, since he thought it was all nonsense. Of course, if he knew that men had plotted to kill the Pope and he'd never said anything, what would that do to his reputation? If he did know anything, he'd be smart to deny everything, that was the safest route.

I picked up the phone and dialed Kusek's personal number, the one he'd slipped into my hand when I left his office. I wanted to invite him to dinner. Even if I got no information from him, it wouldn't be difficult staring at his face for the evening.

Chapter 24

Kusek agreed to have dinner without hesitation. He didn't flinch when I suggested the Venture Inn but seemed familiar with it and not concerned about being seen there. All of which I found interesting.

Even though I wanted more information about Galante, if I had to be honest, I also wanted to know more about Kusek himself. A stunning-looking man stuck away in the priesthood. Had to be a story behind that.

In the meantime, I had other leads to follow.

Jared topped the list. After what Jimmy, the bartender, had told me, it sounded like Jared knew more than he admitted. Finding out what he knew would get me closer to the truth. About him and Scanlan at least.

Anton stayed on my case about Nando and Kent. I needed Luke to take care of it for me. With his connections all over town and the large staff he employed, he might be able to find Nando faster than anyone.

I dialed his number, picturing him at his desk in the office he used at home when he didn't want to travel to his main headquarters.

"Clean Living. May I help you?" Luke sounded as if he were in the middle of something.

"You sound like you're... occupied. Who is he?" I joked.

"No one you know." Luke teased.

"Holding out on me?"

253

"I was just fixing my desk and had to crawl back out."

"Got some time for a small job?" I asked, peering around my office with its lived-in look. Newspapers and magazines overflowing the tables, shelves stacked with books and files. It was organized, Olga saw to that, but it wasn't spare like Luke's simple and Spartan quarters.

"I might," Luke was wary. "What are we talking about?"

"You remember Nando?"

"Your stripper?"

"Well, he works for me, he's not my property. And Kent? Remember him?"

"Yep, the gunslinger. I remember them both. Cute. Even hot. What about them?"

"They're missing in action, or at least that's what Anton thinks. He's bugging me to find them. Nando's probably just off with some guy. And Kent called to say he has things to take care of but that he'd be back."

"Maybe Kent's gone and done something else crazy. Is that what you're thinking?"

"It's what Anton is thinking. He's backed me into a corner. He wants me to find them or he'll call in a missing persons report. Which I think would open up a whole other box of problems. None of which anyone needs."

"And he also placed a bet with you didn't he?"

"He told you?"

"He knew you'd ask me to help and he wanted to make sure you'd play fair."

"Play fai… I'd never cheat," I tried sounding indignant. I knew full well I'd cheat like crazy not to have to strip at Bubbles for two weeks.

"Listen, Marco, I know the stakes but I'm playing by the book. No cheating."

"Collaborating with the other side, huh? It's not like I was gonna ask you to cheat a whole lot. I've helped you out of a few jams, if I remember."

"I kinda like the idea of seeing you bare-assed and twirling around that pole on stage. It's hot. Anton didn't have to convince me."

I groaned.

"But you'll help?" I asked.

"Of course I'll help. But I won't cheat."

"Let's have lunch," I said. "We can plan the search then."

My last chance to avoid a stint as a stripper had evaporated. But only if I was wrong about Kent and Nando. I didn't think I was.

Next, I called Navarro. It was time to stir up another hornet's nest and see what happened. I wanted to know just how his being a part of P2 fit into the scheme of things.

Franny Clifford answered and said Navarro was working. Like a good member of Opus Dei should be, I thought. I debated whether to give Clifford the message and have the blabbermouth spread the word all over Philadelphia, or to ask him to have Navarro call me. I decided to spill everything to Clifford. Then all I'd have to do was sit back and watch the fireworks. I mentioned P2, and Clifford drew in a sharp breath, and I mentioned the Bridge of Four Heads. To which he didn't react.

I needed to arrange one more meeting. Jared. I didn't know where to find the kid since he'd moved out of Scanlan's place, but Niko might know and he'd be working at the diner today. I'd take Luke there for lunch.

No sooner than I'd thought about it, Luke strolled into the office.

"Got your thongs ready? Didn't I give you one for your birthday a couple of years ago?" A mischievous smile played across his face. "It was royal blue with a yellow design right about where your..."

"That'll never see the light of day because as you're going to find out, I'm not wrong. I might be a lot of things but I know a good guy when I see one. And Kent's a good guy."

"So, you're banking on the hope that Kent, the guy who took a gun into Bubbles and held people hostage in order to win his lover back, would not make another attempt at getting lover boy back in some quieter way right under your nose? Is that about right?"

"I won't say I could've been wrong..." I mumbled.

"Did you miss the fact he was obsessed?"

"I thought he could handle it. In fact I know he can. Besides I had them work on separate nights."

"But he's disappeared and so has Nando."

"They could be missing for separate reasons. Making it only appear there's a connection. Why not?"

"Why not? I can think of one good reason. Obsession. He's a guy who can't take no for an answer. Besides, you don't believe in coincidences."

"I know." I felt glum. "Let's have lunch and make some plans to find them."

* * *

At the diner, Niko claimed Jared hadn't been heard from since the day he'd left Scanlan's place. Niko had tried to convince Jared to stay with him and Tony. But Jared had been afraid Scanlan would find him. Jared insisted he had other friends who'd keep him out of sight. But he'd never named those friends and Niko was worried.

It felt like a month had gone by since I'd found Jared bleeding in that Spring Garden Street apartment. In reality it'd only been a couple of days. I told Niko I'd do what I could. I needed to find Jared, too.

Luke and I plotted out the search for Kent and Nando. I gave him Kent's address and Nando's last known whereabouts after he moved out of Kent's place as well as any other information I had. I let Luke take it from there.

I'd handle searching for Jared myself since he was a lead in the Brandt case. Niko had given me a list of Jared's closest friends and people he might stay with. He also told me that Jared hadn't been at work either.

After lunch I set out for Rittenhouse Square. Jared's job was as good as anywhere to start. He'd worked with Belasco and Dalgliesh as an assistant for a couple of years and I figured they might know some friends that Niko wasn't aware of. Their ritzy design firm occupied a three story building near the Square.

Everything about the showroom was cool, calm, and expensive. There was no music, the clientele was classier than that. A receptionist's desk was off to the side in an unobtrusive alcove.

I showed her some ID and asked if she'd buzz whoever was in charge. She looked doubtfully at me but I asked her to tell them it was about Jared. At that, her eyes lit up and she pressed a button on the intercom.

She pointed to some stairs and told me Mr. Belasco would meet me on the second floor. I glanced at the expensive furnishings and stylish materials as I made my way to the stairs.

"Mr. Fontana?" A natty older gentleman with very tight skin and silver hair, held out his hand. He wore a forest green ascot. An ascot? His dark, undoubtedly expensive, suit was cut precisely to his figure. "I understand you have some news about Jared Beeton?" He looked worried, which seemed out of character for his type.

"Mr. Belasco?" I shook his hand which was cool and soft. "I'm here about Jared but I don't have any news. I'm sorry."

"I was so hoping." Belasco shook his head sadly. "It's not like him to disappear like this. He's a responsible young man. Everyone likes him. His clients depend on him."

"He hasn't called in?"

"Not since he called some days ago telling us he'd be taking a day or two to move. I thought surely he'd be back by now. Or that he'd at least have called."

"Do you know any of his friends outside the office? Anybody he might have relied on for help?"

Belasco stiffened his back and looked at me. "Who are you, Mr. Fontana? What's your connection to Jared? Is he in some kind of trouble?"

I didn't know what Belasco knew about Jared and I didn't want to lose him his job, although being gay in an interior design firm is kind of a given.

"Seems he had a disagreement with his former roommate. A conflict of interest, you might say."

"Are you here on behalf of that roommate?" The word roommate was said in a way that led me to believe Belasco knew all about Jared. "Because if you are, I don't have anything else to say."

I liked this guy. Protective. He must've known about Scanlan and the way he treated Jared.

"I'm gonna take a chance and be honest with you. I'm not here because of his former partner. I'm here because I need Jared's help and because his friend Niko is worried about him."

"You need Jared's help?"

"I can't go into detail, Mr. Belasco. But I'm working on a case and Jared might be able to give me some helpful information." I looked him in the eye. "Aside from that, I like Jared and I know what he was going through. So I want to make sure he's okay."

"We all do, Mr. Fontana."

"Any idea where he might be?"

"I don't know if this means anything but a few days before he said he'd be moving, this Latino boy came to meet Jared every day at closing time."

"Did you happen to catch his name?"

"No, sorry. I'm not the prying kind. Jared's always been a great asset to the firm. He'd never let anyone in who he didn't trust completely."

"What did this other kid look like?"

When he got through describing him, I knew it was Nando.

Chapter 25

He looked comfortable waiting against the red brick buildings on the quiet street. Kusek patiently examined his surroundings at Camac and Spruce. Dressed casually in jeans, he fit right in. He was even more attractive out of his priestly blacks, and I felt drawn to him.

"You made it," I said as I approached. "I was afraid you wouldn't find the place. It's kind of tucked away."

"Believe it or not, Marco, I've actually had dinner here before." He smiled. "Does that surprise you?"

Now I had to guess what might please him more, that I wasn't surprised or that I was. I don't like games. Subterfuge to solve a case is one thing but games between friends or potential friends or lovers is not how I work. Of course I wasn't surprised.

"Actually, no. Not surprised at all. Disappointed?"

"Not really disappointed. I was hoping… Let's get inside, it's chilly out here."

Thursdays were slow nights for most places and the Venture Inn was no exception, which allowed us to take a quiet table in the back near the fireplace. Not many prying eyes and ears. Even if Kusek felt comfortable, his official position had to make him a little gun shy in public. I got the impression from him of a man at odds with his position and his personal life. I wondered which would eventually win out.

"What'll it be, gents? A special occasion for the two of you? I didn't even know you were seeing someone, Marco. You cagey devil. How can you keep a drop dead gorgeous man like this under wraps?" Walt paused to take out his order book. "And you," he said turning to Kusek, "How could you take this hunk off the market? There's a line and you just butted your way to the front."

"Walt, Walt. You're the best," I said hoping to stop the torrent of words. "I'd like a mojito. What about you?" I looked over at Kusek.

"I'll have the same." Kusek smiled, unperturbed.

Walt appeared disappointed he was being shut out but I caught his eye and gave him a look saying he should go easy. He got the message. He was smart and I knew for the rest of the evening he'd make sure we had a lot of space.

"So," I said, feeling as if this were a date and I wasn't sure what to do next. Not that it couldn't be a date. But I had to remind myself of my primary purpose: information. After that, the night could be whatever it played itself out to be. The possibilities were interesting. I asked myself for the hundredth time if I were crazy, wanting to sleep with a priest. It'd happened before but I'd only found out afterward that the guy was a priest. Knowing in advance made this feel different.

"When are you going to call me by my first name? I notice that you kind of avoid doing that." Kusek asked.

"Too many years of Catholic school, I guess." I gave him a serious look then started to laugh. "Kidding. Just kidding."

His smile was a lot like Anton's. Which was unsettling.

"Your name's Tad. Short for…"

"Tadeusz. Traditional family. The English version is Thaddeus which is kind of dorky. So I settled on Tad. A long time ago."

"I like it. It's strong." I wondered about his coziness with the gay setting and about his seeming interest in me. Was it real or had he been ordered by his boss to take an interest in the investigation? I was sure the Cardinal was curious about my investigation, even if he didn't want to make a big deal of

Brandt's work. Anything that might make him look bad was something the Cardinal would want to know about in advance.

But I also read something in Tad's behavior and in his eyes. As if he wanted more but couldn't bring himself to ask.

"I'm kind've stuck with the name. Let me ask you something."

"You're wondering why the dinner invitation?"

Walt placed the drinks on the table and as he left, gave me an exaggerated wink.

"I assumed you wanted more information on people at the archdiocese. Right? None of them are killers but I don't mind spending time with you," he said. He lifted his glass and held it out to me. "What shall we drink to?"

"How about…" I paused. "How about we drink to new friends." I kept it innocuous and safe.

"To new friends, then." He clinked his glass with mine.

I nodded and took a drink. It wasn't half bad. Maybe the company had something to do with it. I found myself looking at Tad and seeing Anton. They were similar in looks and in movements. For a moment I felt a pang of disloyalty.

"Actually there is someone I want to know more about. His name turned up in some documents and I realized I didn't know much about him."

"Someone I know?"

"You know him well. The Cardinal."

"G? Cardinal Galante? Why would you need to know anything about him?" He made me feel he knew plenty but would protect the Cardinal first and foremost.

"Like I said, his name came up…"

"In your investigation? How's that possible, Marco? The man is a saint."

"Don't jump to conclusions. His name came up but not in connection to the investigation. Not directly anyway." I laughed, trying to smooth things over and change the mood. "Good thing you're not a detective or a doctor. You can't jump to the worst possible conclusion before you've heard everything."

"You seemed to suggest G was in some kind of trouble. I know the man and he's as far from trouble as anyone can get." He sipped his drink and stared at me with a look I couldn't read. "How did his name come up?"

"In some documents we found."

"When you rise to a position like his, you have a lot of people who want to tear you down." Tad was calm, his tone mellow, almost sad.

"You like him quite a lot."

"It's more than that," he said.

"Oh, I…"

"Get your mind out of the gutter, Marco. I didn't mean anything like that." He smiled to show me he wasn't really offended.

"It's just the way you said it."

"He saved my life when I was young. He's been like a father to me ever since."

"Saved your life? Literally?"

"A long time ago, when I was a kid. Before he became a Cardinal. If he hadn't come along when he had, you'd be having dinner alone right now. Or, with someone else."

"Do you ever talk about it? What happened back then, I mean." This might give me some insight into both Tad and the Cardinal.

"I'm sure a lot of people were in similar straits. The economy was bad in '89 and my father had been laid off. My mom worked as a waitress but that doesn't help much with five kids." He stared at his drink, seemingly transported back in time. "At fourteen I was a crazy kid. A daredevil. I did things which came pretty close to the edge. Maybe I just wanted to escape the realities of life at home."

"Normal for a fourteen year old, I'd say."

"Sometimes I went beyond normal into dangerous. Self-destructive dangerous."

"You don't strike me as the type."

"Go figure. I wasn't entirely a lost cause. I knew I had to get a job to help out at home. And I got one. But not any old job. I could've delivered newspapers or been a busboy in the restaurant where my mom worked."

"Not exciting enough for you?"

"Too dull. I signed on to work for a roofer on weekends. The pay was better than anywhere else and it was different."

"Dirty work, though," I said. "All that grimy stuff."

"It was fun. I got to run up and down ladders, walk all over rooftops, peek into other people's lives. I had a ball. I was the youngest worker so I was like their mascot."

"What went wrong?"

"One day we were roofing the St. Stanislaw parish hall, the rectory, and the convent. I played the crazy fool as usual, running back and forth. Except there was a slippery patch with my name on it and I went flying off a third story roof."

I saw the pain of the memory in his eyes. A grimace crept across his beautiful face like a shadow.

"You all right?" I asked and placed a hand over his. He didn't flinch.

"I'm… I still remember the thoughts running through my head as I fell. At first I felt as if I were flying. I was exhilarated. But once I realized what was happening I knew I was going to die. I just knew it. And I didn't want to. I flailed at the air but there was nothing to grab onto. I saw my mother's face and the pain I'd bring her. I saw my father. I heard voices. Then everything went black."

"Mygod," I said. "That must've been…"

"I was severely injured. I would have died. My family had no health care insurance. Even if the doctors managed to put me back together, the constant care I'd have needed and the rehab would've cost more than I was worth."

"And that's where Galante came in?"

"He was a bishop at the time. Charged with overseeing certain parishes. When he heard what had happened, he took over. Got me the care I needed and wouldn't let my family pay a cent. He was there through it all, even rehab."

"Like your guardian angel. He made sure you came through all right."

"I have lots of scars." He extended a leg and lifted the pant a bit to show an ugly scar. "And." He showed his hands, the left with one finger permanently crooked, and the right with a map-like scar.

"That was generous of Galante. Quite a guy."

"He never took any credit, never granted an interview. He never let it become news. That's the way he is. I wasn't the only person he helped. There were others."

"You said it earlier. He sounds like a saint. You don't see a whole lot of church officials rushing to help people like that."

"That's not really fair. G is an exceptional guy but there are a lot of generous men and women working in the church."

"Galante sounds different. More generous, more caring."

"He is but… I don't want to spoil the evening arguing church business. I know the man and there's a reason he might very well be the next Pope. He deserves it. The church could use a man like him."

"Is he the reason you entered the priesthood?" I asked, lamenting the fact that this beautifully sensitive man was not technically available. Except in a limited way, which wouldn't be enough for me, if I fell in love with a guy like him. Again, Anton came to mind and the similarities between the two. Except, of course, Anton was available.

"No and yes," Kusek said, pulling me from my thoughts. "I think the brush with death made me realize I needed to do something meaningful with my life."

"You could've been a doctor or a lawyer. They help people."

"Maybe it had something to do with all that time I hovered between life and death. I don't know. Something tugged at my soul and I knew. There was no confusion or doubt. It was as if something told me my life mattered and that's why I'd been pulled back from death. G backed my decisions. He sponsored me through the seminary, got me appointments in Rome."

I never thought I'd be having dinner with a guy who used phrases like "tugged at my soul." But on his lips it sounded genuine. This was no lie, I'd have known if it was. He was as real as they get. I couldn't believe I sat there lapping it up. His face had more of an effect on me than I wanted to admit to myself. His eyes drew me gently but with a force I wasn't prepared for. With some effort, I pulled my gaze from his and focused on my now empty glass.

"You worked for Galante in Rome?" I asked and signaled Walt to bring another drink for both of us.

"I studied at a theological school there, thanks to him. G accepted an appointment to the Vatican Secretariat of State around the same time. He became an advisor to the last Pope and now to this one. Eventually they gave him the red hat and this archdiocese. He took me with him."

"And he elevated you to Monsignor."

"Not a very heady height, that's for sure. Just a minor title. But being his adjutant, now that comes with benefits."

"I'll bet."

"I'd be happy just to clerk in his office. He gave me my life back. He saved me and I can't forget that."

"Sounds like there's more to it than that. Though, I've gotta admit, that would be enough to make me eternally grateful."

"Sure there's more. There's G himself. He's kind and generous. Not pretentious, not arrogant. A down-to-earth man. For somebody headed to Rome that's saying a lot. I'd like him as a person even if he hadn't saved me."

"You two look hungry," Walt said as he set down new mojitos. "Specials tonight are good. Don't even bother with the menu."

"What've you got?"

"Glad you asked," Walt said and exaggeratedly pulled out his order pad, flipped it over to where he'd noted the specials, and read them off.

"I'd like the salmon" Tad looked up at Walt. The candlelight caught the blue in his eyes and created an eerily beautiful effect.

"I'd say the salmon, too but the crab cakes sound too good to resist."

"I had 'em for dinner, hon. They're to die for."

"Well, I hope not."

"You're a funny man, Marco. Next time we have open mic night, drop in." Walt sashayed off to place the orders.

"How long since you've been to church?" Tad peered at me with something beyond curiosity.

"Funny you should mention that," I said. "Just last Sunday. With Tim Hollister. We all shook hands. Remember? I heard you sing. You've got a voice that sent shivers up my back."

"You know what I mean, Marco." He sipped his drink. "You don't like answering questions but you certainly ask a lot of them."

"Occupational hazard. I've made a lot of men uncomfortable with questions. Probably lost the chance at a few relationships because I can't keep my yap shut."

"So why do it?"

"In your case, I want to know more about you. Ever since you buzzed onto my radar, I've wanted to know more."

"Flattering," Kusek said. "I'm just a guy with a Roman collar."

"Yeah, just a guy." I sipped my mojito and looked him in the eye. There was a definite connection, the question was, did I want to pursue it? "Did you spend a lot of time in Rome?"

"A few years, I guess. If you add up all the time. Sometimes I'd be a few months here and the rest of the year there."

"Ever heard of the Bridge of Four Heads?" I waited for a reaction but his eyes betrayed only pleasant recognition.

"Yes, the Bridge of Four Heads." He smiled, probably reminiscing. "It's one of two bridges leading to an island in the Tiber. That's not the bridge's real name, you know."

"I didn't."

"It's called that because of a statue or rather a monument with four heads that Pope Sixtus the Fifth put there." And he launched into the same story Hollister had told. Not that I'd doubted Hollister.

"I'd heard something like that," I said. I really wanted to know if the bridge held any significance for Kusek. If maybe Galante had mentioned it or told him anything about working for Cardinal Cody. But it didn't appear Tad had anything more than fond memories of his time in Rome.

"Why do you ask? About the bridge, I mean?"

"We came into possession of some documents and parts of it are named after the bridge."

"Documents about the case you're working on?"

"Brandt's documents. The new information he'd been given." Now I'd see what his reaction was to this information.

"The stuff for his new book? Wow! You've got a real hot potato in your hands."

"Not really. It's all interesting, sure. A lot of details but nothing as explosive as we were led to believe. There are names, places, dates. Some information about a supposed plot. But there's no way to verify it. In any case, it doesn't seem to have anything to do with Brandt's murder. I'm thinking it was all hype to sell books." I gave him just enough to pique his interest or to send him to Galante with a report.

"It's what a lot of us thought. Brandt was just blowing smoke. It's all in the realm of loony conspiracy theories. G was right. He said if new information existed it was probably off the wall material spun by people with an axe to grind."

"I suppose I hoped the documents would be more exciting. Cloak and dagger stuff. Insider intrigue." I was also hoping Tad would ask to see the files, which might indicate he was worried they contained something damaging that we'd missed. So far, he didn't seem the least bit interested.

"Brandt's first book was as exciting as it gets," Kusek said. "G worried about what that kind of scandal would do to the Church, to people who believed in the Church. But he refused to make a public fuss because it would bring more publicity and do more harm than good. He was upset that people felt the need to tear down the whole Church to prove a smaller point. That they were willing to let a lot of people lose their faith over something that was probably not true and even if it was, it's all history. Long dead. None of it can be undone."

"Marlon said something similar. I guess you're all in the same boat in a way."

"Well, I wouldn't be happy if those theories proved true, if that's what you mean. I'd hate to think of my Church as a nest of murderers. I also wouldn't want to see millions of people suffer a crisis of faith over something that no one can do anything about."

"Wouldn't it be better to know what really happened? All people want is the truth." I really didn't want to argue with him. I'd begun to like him too much.

"Yes." He sighed. Looking over at me, his blue eyes glistening, he stared for a moment, then focused on me. "But I often wonder exactly what Truth is."

"How do you mean that? Truth is Truth. No matter how you cut it."

"Is it? Is it better to know the truth when it leaves you in a barren place with no hope and no relief from life's pain?"

"That's not the way I see it."

"Maybe you think the truth will set you free," Kusek said, "What happens then? You're free to do what? Find another way to cover over the drabness of life with some pretty falsehood? Free to find some lie to make you hold on for another day when you've got starving kids and nothing to feed them with?"

He stopped and I wanted to hug him.

"I'm sorry," he said. It was a whisper. "Didn't mean to spoil dinner."

"You didn't spoil anything."

"I see a lot of suffering. Traveling with G, sometimes everywhere you look people are in need, desperate, hopeless."

"Hot plates," Walt's voice cut through the moment like a foghorn. "Make some room. You get the salmon, right, handsome."

"Yes. Thank you," Tad said, his voice unsteady.

"Hey, what's the matter? This bruiser upsetting you? Listen, hon, he's gorgeous but he's not worth crying over. You tell Uncle Walt if he makes you cry again. I got a paddle in the back that has your name on it Marco Fontana. You be nice to this man. He's too pretty to cry." With that he plopped my crab cakes in front of me and walked away.

I glanced up and saw him scowl at me over his shoulder.

"Honestly, it wasn't you, Marco. I don't really know what's gotten into me."

I had an inkling. Maybe he was berating himself about a truth he wasn't facing. The truth about himself. Maybe just being in a gay restaurant with a man who paid attention and seemed interested, made Tad think about a different kind of life he could be leading. If only he'd faced his own truth.

But I wasn't about to open that can. He was in bad enough shape as it was.

"How'd you like to help me out?" I asked.

"You mean on this case? What can I do?"

"If I can get Tim Hollister to give permission, maybe you can read over the documents for me and see if there's anything we missed?"

"Oh, I don't…"

"Don't say no yet. Look, you know Rome. You know the Church. Maybe something in those documents will make some sense to you that it didn't to us. I'm not trying to bring anybody down. And I don't intend to do anything with the information, unless it helps solve the case. But at least it might bring Hollister some closure."

"You really believe I can help?"

"Maybe you'll just tell us once and for all there's nothing there. That the nothing we've already found is all we're gonna find. Whaddaya say?" I knew it was a gamble. Perhaps he'd find something and he'd never tell us because the implications were overwhelming. But we'd be no worse off than we were now.

"If it'll bring him some peace."

"And one more favor."

"You're really pushing your luck." He smiled and laughed. It was like the sun breaking through clouds.

"Can you get me a meeting with Galante?"

"Oh. That's it? A meeting with G? That's why you invited me to dinner."

"You sound disappointed." Did he want more than just dinner?

"Not exactly. I guess...," he paused and looked at me again. "I don't know quite what I was thinking. You want a meeting with G. I'll see what I can do."

* * *

We stood inside the small, glass enclosed vestibule at the Venture. Sort of a decompression chamber from the warmth and conviviality of the gay world inside and the harsh realities of the world outside.

"Thanks for getting me out of the rectory, Marco. I had a great time. I'm sor..."

I stopped him from apologizing by planting a kiss on his lips. He flinched, then pulled back, resisting and kissing at the same time. His scent was intoxicating. I placed a hand alongside his cheek and held his face as I pressed my mouth to his. His tension melted and he leaned into me, returning my kiss with what seemed all the force in his body. It was warm, electric. I was taken aback and wanted more all at the same time.

We moved apart slowly. I tried to catch my breath and noticed he was doing the same.

"I… I uh, I didn't expect…," he stuttered and glanced at the floor.

"I want to see you again, Tad."

"Um, my day job kinda frowns on things like this." He drew his thumb across my lips.

"I won't take no for an answer," I said. "I'll call Tim Hollister tomorrow and then I'll call you. I'll get you the documents. That's a nice official reason to meet, isn't it?"

"Call me and we'll see." Tad smiled so sadly I wanted to hug him. Except I was afraid if I did, I might not let go.

He pushed the door open and stepped out into the cold night air.

"I've got to get up early tomorrow. You've made me forget it's a workday and I have meetings all morning."

"I'll call you as soon as I hear from Hollister," I said. "See you…soon."

"I'll wait to hear from you." He smiled and made a tentative step toward me then halted and turned to walk away.

He waved at me as he ambled down Camac Street with that funny tilted walk of his. I headed to Spruce debating whether or not to stop into Bubbles. I didn't want Anton to think I didn't trust him to handle things. But I wanted to see him. Kusek had made me think about Anton. Maybe it was Anton I wanted and not another date with Tad. But Tad was vulnerable, sweet. And so was Anton.

I felt light-headed, disoriented. This guy had thrown the proverbial monkey wrench into my night. Maybe into my life. I took a few tentative steps and decided the noise and lights of Bubbles would help distract me. If I felt this way after another meeting with Tad, I'd deal with that wrench then.

Before I entered Bubbles, my cell phone rang. I flipped open the phone.

"Fontana." I said.

"I told you I'd call again." That voice. The guy who'd called before. The guy who'd mugged me in the garage. The guy whose voice I'd heard in Stella's.

"Listen, pal, I'm getting' tired of this. Whadda'you want?"

"I got information. About the shootin' and things."

"You've got thirty seconds. Talk."

"Meet me in an hour. I know who the shooter is."

"So you can try to run me down again? Listen up…"

"Wasn't me tried to run you down. But I know who. I'll tell you everything. One hour. Washington Square. The tomb."

Chapter 26

"Y ou can't be serious," Anton said, eyes wide.

"Washington Square. How bad can it be? Last time was a different story."

"Last time he didn't get you, this time he might."

"I'll plan better."

"In an hour? He wants to meet in one hour and you're going to plan better. I'm coming with you."

"No." I couldn't look him in the eye. It'd be dangerous for him to come along.

"Because it'll be dangerous. Right? I'm not letting you go." He stood with his back to the door of the tiny office. Admittedly it would have been more pleasant, not to mention satisfying, staying cheek to cheek with him here but I had a job to do.

"I promise I'll be careful. And I'll be back in one piece."

"They have a lot of people in one piece at the morgue. I don't want to have to identify your body."

"You won't have to. Everybody down there already knows me." Humor didn't work. Anton's golden face was etched with sadness. "Kidding. Just kidding. I promise I won't take chances."

"Just going is taking a chance. It's late. There won't be anyone in the park and there are too many places for someone to hide."

"I'll keep my eyes open." I looked at my watch. "Gotta go. I want to get there early. Scope it out."

"That plan didn't work last time."

"I'll be extra careful."

Anton took me in his arms and hugged me as if this were the last time he'd see me.

"You'd better be back here before we close."

"Don't worry so much. I can take…"

He stopped me from speaking with a kiss. I was caught off guard by Anton's intensity. I felt consumed by his embrace. His warm, soft lips seduced me to linger, dared me to forget what I had to do. I reluctantly pulled back and gazed at him.

"I… I've gotta… go." I said catching my breath."

"Come back to me, Marco," he whispered."

"Count on it."

* * *

Washington Square, a large park just outside the boundaries of the gayborhood, was one of five original city squares laid out by Billy Penn. Lots of trees, including a moon tree which is really just a tree grown from a seed taken to the moon, make it a green oasis. There are plenty of bushes and monuments. And dead bodies. Thousands of Revolutionary War soldiers buried in mass graves.

At night it's dimly lit, rarely visited, and has plenty of places for people to hide.

After I picked up my gun, I headed for the square. A short walk down Walnut, past jewelers row, through an area only lightly populated at night, took me to the northwest entrance. I could almost make out the back of the wall of the monument to Washington, like a huge shadow near one corner of the park. On the other side of that wall was a statue of Washington, an aboveground tomb containing an unknown Revolutionary War soldier, and an eternal flame. And maybe the guy who'd called me.

There was minimal light and I steeled myself for a cautious, nearly blind approach. My anonymous caller could be hiding anywhere in the shadows. I decided to walk a block and enter from the southeast. I'd use the cover of shadow and approach head on, keeping things in view as much as possible.

All my senses on alert, I moved slowly into the square. There was no one around. A small breeze rustled the leaves. I could hear nothing else and saw even less. Something made the hair at the back of my neck stand on end. More a feeling than a sound. A feeling that someone I couldn't see was there.

The square's layout was familiar to me. The monument and tomb were just ahead. The closer I came to the tomb, the more I felt something was wrong.

Eventually I saw him. Or, at least I saw someone in the thin light cast by the eternal flame. Someone stood waiting. I had to believe it was the caller.

I kept moving but didn't make a sound.

A twig snapped across the square and the dark figure pivoted around. A low, indistinct voice said something unintelligible from this distance.

A shot broke the silence, then two more, and the shadowy figure in front of the tomb collapsed to the ground. Someone broke from the cover of the trees to my left and darted toward the street.

"Stop!" I pulled my gun. There was little time to think. I sprinted toward the fleeing dark figure.

A shot rang out and whizzed past my face. I saw him bolt the last few yards toward the wall. Adrenalin kicked in and I chased him.

Under dim street lamps, I saw him turn and fire again. Muzzle flash briefly lit the darkness. The shot went wide. He turned and tore through some bushes. I wasn't close enough. He hurtled over the short brick wall and was out of sight down a side street.

I turned back to the guy at the monument. As I neared, I saw a limp figure sprawled on the ground. There was blood, lots of it, pooling around him.

He had a faint pulse and was still warm, his breathing ragged. I tried not to look at the holes in his chest or the blood around him. I concentrated on his face. Young, filled with fear and pain, he grimaced, eyes wide. A tear trickled down the side of his face.

He moaned and his hand clutched at my arm. Bending closer, I realized he was trying to speak. I removed his hat and gently brushed back his hair. He was a lot younger than I thought and very pale. The fearful look on his face disappeared at my touch but he winced with pain. His lips moved but his breathing was labored and he spoke indistinctly.

"I'll call 911, kid. Hang on. You'll be all right." I knew he wouldn't be all right. He was bleeding out on the paving stones which were already filled with blood.

"F-Fontana?" His voice was a wheeze.

"It's me. I'm here like I promised." I caressed his head then placed my palm against his cheek. No one deserved to suffer alone like this. "Who did this to you?"

"I... ki-killed Br-brandt." He exhaled a long breath and I thought he was gone. His eyes fluttered and he spoke again, "Shot...sh-shot him."

"Why? Why'd you do it?"

"J-job...they... paid... m-me."

"Who paid you?"

"Stel-ste-stella's."

"Somebody at Stella's?"

"A-ask... Colt..."

"Colt?..." I stroked his cheek. "Hang in, kid. I'll call the..."

"Ja-jared... help. S-stop... Scan..." Another long exhalation. He closed his eyes and lapsed into silence.

I pulled out my cell phone and dialed 911. My hands shook not because I was afraid but because of what he'd said. Jared needed help? And who was Colt?

I waited with the kid, stroking his hair, just letting him know someone was there. Not much else I could do. I didn't think the EMTs would be able to help either.

The park was still, the light of the eternal flame fluttered in the cold breeze. The boy's blood oozed more slowly now. Behind him was the Tomb of the Unknown and Washington's statue silently observing everything. He'd seen thousands of young men die for nobler things. Their bodies beneath this boy whose blood seeped into their graves.

Sirens cut the silence. The first car rolled onto the pavement, siren blaring, lights wildly flashing red, white, and blue. I heard car doors slam shut and other sirens in the distance. Another car, with a slap-on strobe, pulled onto the sidewalk.

When I saw her walking toward me, I swore to myself. Giuliani would grill me, even if I had nothing to do with this. She'd find some reason to waste my time. She enjoyed making me miserable.

One of the officers felt for a pulse on the boy and just as he stood the ambulance arrived. The EMTs jumped out, rushed over to the kid, and worked on him. The one kneeling over the boy signaled for a stretcher and the other EMT ran to get it.

"Is he...?"

"It's bad. I don't know if he'll make it." The EMT was all business. He must've seen hundreds of things like this and it probably gave him a bleak, matter-of-fact outlook. "Okay, step away, please, we've got to get him onto the stretcher."

The stretcher was placed by the body and they gently lifted him onto it, holding IV bags high, making him as comfortable as they could. Then they trundled him off.

There was a pause before the ambulance revved to life. It began moving slowly. There was no siren. I knew what that meant.

Suddenly Giuliani stood in front of me.

"Fontana. You find your way into a lotta funny situations."

"Yeah, a real laugh, this one." I took out my cell phone again. It was getting close to closing time at Bubbles and Anton would be frantic if I didn't show up.

"Put that away, Fontana. I've got questions for you."

"You arresting me, Giuliani?"

"Not unless you've done something to be arrested for. From the looks of it I might have a case."

"All due respect, detective, I gotta make a call. Your questions can wait." I didn't mind pissing her off, she'd never minded making me wait when I needed something.

I turned, walked away, and called Anton.

When I got back to Giuliani, she looked like she'd blow a gasket.

"You done?"

"For now. What can I do for you?" I looked at her deep brown eyes and raven black hair and wondered what hostile thoughts she harbored against me.

"What happened here? Start with that."

So I did. But without telling her what case I was on or why the kid had contacted me or that he'd told me anything as he lay there. She listened, a puzzled look on her face. She was perfectly made up, even for this late hour. Lip gloss, perfect eyes, smooth complexion. And lots of venom. Just for me.

"I don't get it." Her usually perfectly modulated voice was laced with uncertainty. "You're gonna meet this kid who you claim is a lead in a case. A case you don't wanna talk about. But before you get here some joker puts a couple of holes in your boy."

"I think you get it," I said.

"No. No, I don't. Are you telling me somebody wanted this kid dead because he was comin' to see you? Or, are you telling me this was just a random shooting?"

"You got a third choice, Giuliani. Could be the shooter was after me and missed. But seeing as you've got nearly five hundred shootings in the city so far this year, the 'just-another-random-shooting' thing sounds good."

"There's something you're not telling me, Fontana. I can tell. Just like your brother. Your family is all secrets. You like it that way."

"Hey, I'm telling you what I'm telling you. I get here and the kid is bleeding out on the ground. I wanted him alive not dead. I have no motive for shooting him."

"Says you," Giuliani snapped. She made some notes on her pad and looked up at me. "You know the drill, Fontana. Don't go where we can't find you. I'm gonna need to talk to you again."

"You know where to find me."

It was after two and Anton would be waiting at Bubbles while the staff cleaned up. I headed that way.

The kid was dead but he'd given me a lead. Maybe that made him feel better about himself in the end. I hoped so.

But he'd also made me realize I had to act fast. The fact that he'd mentioned Jared meant Jared could be the next target. The dead kid had known too much and maybe Jared did, too. Whoever shot the kid might want him dead.

I had to find Jared before the shooter did.

Chapter 27

The morning sun blasted through my bedroom and tore me out of the fitful sleep I'd finally sunk into. My head ached, my mouth was dry.

The phone rang and I glanced at the clock. Eight AM. I'd slept three hours and my eyes felt as if they'd grown fuzz.

I reached for the phone.

"Fontana," I mumbled.

"You sound great," Luke said. "Heard you had a close call last night. You okay?" He'd obviously talked with Anton and both had gone into mothering mode.

"And you decided to call me at," I checked the clock again since I thought maybe the fuzzy covering on my eyeballs had distorted my vision, "eight in the morning?"

"Thought you might want to get an early start figuring things out." Luke had probably been at his desk for an hour. The housecleaning business was an early riser's game.

I had to admit he was right, but it didn't make me feel any more awake.

The night before came into focus. I'd left Washington Square and gone to Bubbles. From there, Anton and I went to the all night diner to talk. All of a sudden it was four AM. I was amped. A shooting tends to wire you like nothing else. I could've yapped for hours. But I knew underneath I was bone tired and needed sleep. Which is eventually what I managed to do. Until Luke's call.

"You're right, Luke. Make any progress finding Kent?"

"Not much. But I've got eyes and ears all over the place." His eyes and ears were the men and women who worked for him in houses, condos, apartments, and office buildings for miles around. If Luke told them he needed something, they were like army ants in their drive to find it. Their loyalty had nothing to do with the fact he paid well. Something about him inspired their allegiance and none of them wanted to let him down.

"It's all more urgent now."

"Because of the shooting?"

"Yeah, the kid mentioned Scanlan and Jared. If that boy knew something, others know that same something. Could be Jared's in deep shit unless we find him first."

"Right."

"Nando knows Jared. Maybe he knows where to find him. If we ever find Nando."

"I'll step up the search." Luke sounded grim.

I lay back on my pillow. The memories of that kid dying in the park were still vivid. Nothing seemed right. How did anyone know we were meeting? If I knew that, I'd know the answers to a whole lot more.

Then it hit me and I sat straight up.

I'd have to tell Hollister about the kid. He'd admitted shooting Brandt. But I had no idea who he was, or why he'd done it. All I had was what he'd whispered as he lay there. This was guaranteed to send Hollister into overdrive. I wasn't looking forward to that.

Instead of waiting, I decided to get it over with.

"Bancrofft residence." For some reason, Hollister answered the phone.

"Tim, just the one I want," I said.

"What is it? Are you all right?"

"I need to talk with you, Tim."

"What's wrong? Have you…"

"Meet me in two hours at Rouge. You know it?"

"I'll be there. But isn't there anything you can tell me?"

"I need some advice and I want to bring you up to date. Things seem to be moving and I need to bring you into this."

Hollister reluctantly hung up and I dashed to get out to the office.

* * *

"He is alive," Olga greeted me in typical Olga fashion. "There is talking you were involved in shooting. But you are here. No holes in chest or head."

"Only the ones I was born with." I laughed. "Good morning to you, too, gorgeous."

"Getting shot in park is affecting eyes. No one is gorgeous here."

"Not even me?"

"Handsome. Movie star face. Stunning. But gorgeous, no." Olga resumed typing.

"I'm wounded."

"What?! Is true? Where is wound?"

"By your words, Olga. Wounded by your words. I'll be in my office licking my wounds."

"Coffee is made. Strong like poison," she said. We had two coffee makers, one was Olga's and only for tea. In mine, she made powerful, hair raising, coffee.

The intoxicating aroma of coffee permeated the room and my nostrils tingled. I'd already had some at home, but more caffeine never hurt. I filled a mug and sat at my desk.

If I were inclined to make To-Do lists, I'd put finding Scanlan and Jared at the top. Next would come Quinn, Navarro, and Wren.

The kid had mentioned someone named Colt at Stella's. That'd have to wait for the bar to open.

The phone stared me in the face. Scanlan was hiding and Jared was missing. I decided to start with Navarro and called him at work.

"Navarro."

"Mr. Navarro, Marco Fontana. I think it's time we talked again. Your name's come up in some documents. Before I turn the information over to the authorities, I want to get your side of things." I wasn't about to turn anything over to anybody but he didn't know that.

"I have no idea what you're talking about and I resent you calling me at work."

"Just wanted to give you an opportunity. I guess you won't mind sitting in the precinct office once I turn this stuff in. They'll want to hear your story." I paused a moment. "Won't be as nice as I am but…"

"There is no story to tell. There is no reason for the police to see me. I'm a simple man. I work, I go to church. I serve my God. There's no more to my story than that."

"A simple man? You're a simple man?"

"I live a Spartan life, Mr. Fontana. You've seen my home. It isn't even my home, really. Just a place to pray and sleep. A place to house my earthly shell. It doesn't get much more simple."

"But…," I wanted to sound innocent. "Aren't you the same John Navarro who worked for Silvio Calvino? In Rome? Calvino the communications and financial mogul? You're not that John Navarro?"

Silence.

"Weren't you there at the Bridge of Four Heads?" I pressed. "The place of the plotters, isn't that what some people called it? The documents say Navarro was there."

Silence again.

"The documents might be wrong, I suppose. I'll let the police sort that out. The bio on this John Navarro sure sounds a lot like you. I guess you'll be able to explain that to the police."

"What documents? Why would my name appear in any documents?"

"Remember what we talked about at your home? I was thinking maybe Opus Dei had something to do with Brandt's murder."

"I remember your ridiculous assertions about Opus Dei. There isn't a more dedicated group…"

"Save it, Navarro. I was off-track when I thought it might be them. Actually it was you. A different organization but the same John Navarro. You were involved in P2."

"I was nev…"

"You were one of the interns working for Silvio Calvino. He kept good records and you probably kept a pretty nifty set of records of the meetings he attended. Including the ones at The Bridge of Four Heads."

"What is it you want, Mr. Fontana?"

"Meet me and I'll tell you all about it."

"I'm at work. I can't just…"

"They let you out for lunch, don't they?"

"But…"

"Yes or no, Navarro."

"Noon. At the Clothespin."

"You got it."

The Clothespin, a gigantic Claes Oldenburg sculpture set in front of a skyscraper across from City Hall, had become an instant hit as a meeting point for people. Who could miss a forty-five foot high clothespin?

Making guys like Navarro squirm was almost better than a shot of caffeine, so I decided to stir another pot. After what Palmer had told me about Quinn, I wanted to coax him out and see if he'd trip himself up. I wouldn't have to pressure the egomaniac. He'd be only too happy to meet and puff up his profile even when he had no idea what he was walking into.

His phone rang ten times before sending me to voicemail.

"Professor Quinn is not here to take your call. Please leave your name and… yadda, yadda, yadda."

I asked him to call me as soon as he could about important new information I had. Quinn would fall for that before he could think it through.

It was nearly time to meet Hollister. I gulped some coffee, picked up my jacket, and headed for the door.

"You are just arriving and now boss is leaving?"

"A P.I.'s work is never done, Olga. I won't be back until later this afternoon. If you need me…"

"I am having your cell number."

I headed down the stairs and out into the fresh air. I needed to think about the case. There were still missing pieces. Not to mention missing people. And I wasn't sure what I was close to discovering.

Aside from telling Hollister about the kid, I dreaded asking him about allowing Kusek to read the documents. It was like asking him to give everything over to the enemy. Hollister was smart enough to understand that Kusek might see something we missed, might recognize names or places we didn't. Anything could help get us closer to a solution.

But why would Kusek tell us anything? What would motivate him to help us if it made the Church look bad? Would he tell the truth if he did find something? All questions Hollister might ask. And I didn't have an answer that weighed more than a slice of prosciutto.

Walking on Walnut Street was good if you wanted lots of people without being overwhelmed. It was early enough so the city felt fresh and the air was cold. People hurried to their offices or strolled into cafés. Some looked stolid and resigned, as if they couldn't wait to retire. Others resembled worker bees on their way to help the hive survive.

The high fashion shops weren't open yet and I imagined their oh-so-fashionable clerks readying themselves at home, donning too-tight clothes, or whacky name brand outfits to impress fashion snobs. I noticed yet another clothing store was being outfitted: all glass, chrome, and lacquered wood.

When I got to Eighteenth Street, I stood by the bank at the corner and took in the scene. Rittenhouse Square to my left, old magnificent townhouses turned commercial properties to my right. And people. Walking dogs, jogging, strolling the Square. Some weighed down with briefcases and papers, others burdened with whatever troubles clouded their dour faces.

The Square was still green, the weather not cold enough to wither the leaves. Tall oak, maple, locust, and plane trees sheltered dozens of people. Someone once told me the Square had been a notorious gay meeting place years before and I smiled thinking how it must've been.

I headed to Rouge, a café people frequented in order to see and be seen. From the famous to the unknown, well-heeled men and women came to sit at the faux rattan tables and sip outlandishly expensive espresso, cappuccino, or more pricy drinks. The food was overpriced but good, the service efficient. But the reputation was everything. And everyone wanted to sit outside no matter what the weather. How else could one be seen by the hoi polloi?

There were a few tables available, in less than prime locations. A waitress in a slinky black dress approached. You'd never know she was a server but that was the idea, all the waitresses were required to look as high class as their customers. After all, if you were a nobody wanting to be thought a somebody, would you want a frumpy waitress in a stained smock taking your order? Of course not. You'd want a classy woman in a tight, black, low cut dress to make it appear you were worthy of just that type of attention.

I smiled and asked for a table. She smiled back, with a little wink thrown in, and showed me to the best of the remaining tables. I asked for espresso and told her I was expecting someone. She looked mildly disappointed but the smile reappeared as she turned to leave.

She returned quickly with the espresso and placed it in front of me. And, there was that wink again. I smiled.

The bitterness of the espresso was like the taste of a long-held grudge. Savoring the feeling, I looked up to see Hollister standing by the table.

"You look right at home. One of the beautiful people." Hollister laughed and sat in the chair opposite me. "My host will never forgive me for not inviting him along. He is absolutely fascinated with you and I don't think it's merely the type of work you do. If you know what I mean."

"He'll get over it." I chuckled. "Besides, we're talking business. He'd be bored."

"Not as long as he could stare at your face. That's what he said when I told him this was a business meeting."

"I'm flattered and when this is all over, we'll all go out for a drink."

"In that case, he'll insist on helping you solve the case."

"I'm getting closer. Last night…" I hesitated not knowing exactly how to tell him.

"Go on, last night… what?"

"I got a call to meet someone who said he had information on the shooting."

"Good! This is progress."

"He wanted to meet in Washington Square. When I got there, I found he'd been shot."

"Marco!" Hollister drew a breath sharply. "This is terrible! How could this happen?"

"You've gotta keep this under your hat, Tim. Because I didn't tell the police."

"What've you done?"

"Tim…" I paused then decided to just tell him. "Before he died, the kid told me that he'd shot Helmut."

Hollister gasped and his already pale face turned paper-white.

"Are you all right, Tim?"

He nodded, his eyes glistening with tears. Hand over his mouth, he shut his eyes for a moment and remained silent. When he opened his eyes, he looked more composed.

"Who… who was he? Why did he do this?"

"Two questions he didn't answer, Tim. But before he died, he gave me a lead. I think he was trying to make up for what he did."

Hollister was quiet again.

"I thought I'd want him to rot in hell. You know, Marco? I thought I'd be satisfied if I ever got news like this. But I'm not."

"I understand."

"You say he was just a boy?"

"Young. Probably nineteen or twenty."

"And now he's dead." He looked at me. "There's too much death. Too much."

I allowed Hollister a moment to absorb it all. A dog barked in the Square and Hollister, hand trembling, picked up his water glass.

"Now we'll never know why he killed Helmut."

"That's what I'm working on. I keep thinking those documents have more in them than we've found. Something neither you nor I have noticed."

"I gave you every name I squeezed out of them. I don't think there's any more useful information in them."

"I was thinking…" I paused and downed the rest of my espresso.

The waitress sidled up to the table again.

"What can I get you, sir?"

Hollister glanced at the menu.

"A cappuccino and a croissant," he said.

"Anything more for you?" She turned her green eyes on me and waited, smiling.

"I'll have the same."

"What were you about to say?" Hollister asked once the waitress left.

"I was going to ask if you'd mind someone else looking at the documents."

"Someone else?" Hollister was wary.

"I've read them, Tim. I don't see anything more than you've found. I was hoping someone with a different perspective might have more luck."

"Well…" Hollister mulled over what I'd said. "It's basically a sound idea, I suppose. It would all depend on the person. I'm pretty well acquainted with all this material, all the background, and everything that Helmut's already done."

"True."

"You have someone in mind, don't you? Someone who might have a different sort of insight?"

"Yes, but I want your approval."

"All right, Marco. At this point I'm at my wit's end. Planning the memorial, waiting for Helmut's family to arrive. Just trying to get my life back in order. Right now I think I'd jump at any chance for a resolution."

"I've met a guy. Connected to the Church."

"Connected? You make it sound like he's mafia. Who is he?"

"He's a monsignor named Kusek."

"The Cardinal's right hand man?" Hollister couldn't disguise his shock. "You're asking to let…"

"He's worked in Rome and.."

"Under the tutelage of one of the more conservative members of the hierarchy. In the bosom of the enemy, as it were."

"But he's not…"

"The enemy? Is that what you were going to say?" Hollister's breathing became rapid. He was interrupted by the waitress with our orders, then busied himself with adding far too much sugar to his cappuccino.

"Okay, maybe he's in the enemy camp but he's willing to help," I said.

"What makes you so sure? What makes you think he'll give us the truth about what he finds in the documents?"

"I can't say for sure he'll give us anything at all."

"Why would he do anything to damage the Church? It's his bread and butter. I'm sure he likes the privileges he has as the Cardinal's adjutant. If he helps uncover something that gives credence to Helmut's work or that leads you to the answers you're looking for, he could face a bleak career outlook. He might be assigned to a crumbling parish in some backwater town on the edge of oblivion. A far cry from the champagne and glitter of Rome."

"Who knows what his motivations are? I get the strong impression the guy is gay. Maybe that has something to do with why he wants to help. Who knows?"

"You're hot for the man, aren't you?" Hollister said, sounding amused. "I've seen him, he's handsome and that's putting it lightly."

"Busted!" I laughed and sipped my cappuccino which was almost as bitter as the espresso. "But I'd never let that get in the way of an investigation. Ask anyone. I never let a hot man keep me from getting at the truth."

"But this is different, isn't it? I can see it in your eyes."

"How so?"

"He's a man of God. He's almost unattainable. Like an angel you can wrestle with but never really have. But you'd like to try, wouldn't you?"

"I can't say what I'm looking for. But he's fascinating."

"Because he's a priest. You want what you can't have. That's what's so alluring."

Hollister was perceptive, I'll give him that. But he wasn't always right. I felt something for Kusek but it wasn't love and it was only minor lust. What I was feeling was pity. The man had reached his thirties and hadn't even fully admitted to himself that he was gay. Never mind all the other trappings, he hadn't even gotten to the basics yet.

"Maybe you have a point, but..." I looked him in the eye. "If it were me, I'd let the guy have a crack at the documents. He can't steal Helmut's work or destroy it. You'll still have a chance to do something with that research. What'll it hurt?"

"I want to hear everything he has to say. I want to know everything he tells you."

"Deal."

"One more thing," Hollister stared at me. "Next time you have dinner with Kusek..."

"Yeah?" I was wary about more conditions.

"I want you to invite me along for a drink with the two of you."

"So you can ream the poor guy for his involvement with the Cardinal?" I laughed.

"No, because he's a hunk and I want to see him up close." Hollister smiled sadly, then glanced over at the trees in the Square, teary-eyed and lost in thought.

I concentrated on my croissant.

* * *

I was glad Hollister agreed to let Kusek read the files. Not just because it gave me another opportunity to talk with Tad but I thought he might actually help. Hollister had read those files and his judgment was clouded by grief, anger, and a sense of responsibility to the memory of his beloved Helmut. I read them with a detective's eye but without the detailed background Kusek or Hollister had. Both knew the Church well. All its workings, all its arcane ways. Cardinals and camerlenghi, conclaves and catechisms. I had knowledge but they had proximity and connections inside.

I'd call Kusek and tell him he'd be getting the documents then cajole him into setting up a meeting with the cardinal for me.

There was plenty of time before my meeting with Navarro. Sitting at Rouge was easy on the ego. Passersby looked at Rouge patrons as if they were peeking at Philadelphia society. In truth, all they were seeing were minor lights, wannabes, and the showy. True Philadelphia society was tucked away on the Main Line, sitting on its cash, and wondering how they could keep their private clubs private and their piles of money from getting into the hands of the less worthy. Philly's real, old-money elite was a collection of characters stretching back to before Philadelphia was a Tory stronghold. Most customers at Rouge probably didn't know or care what the word Tory even meant.

* * *

Meeting Navarro outdoors wasn't the optimal setting for discussing murky things. I'd spotted a small lunch dive across from the Clothespin on an unfriendly concrete plaza which mirrored the sterile concrete areas around City Hall.

I waited at the Clothespin and before long, a bald man with pink skin and bulging eyes approached me.

"Mr. Fontana." His eyes bulged even more when he stared.

"Navarro. You hungry?"

"Let's get this over with, I've got work to do."

"How about a little lunch, my treat? We can talk."

"I… this…"

"There's a little place tucked between those buildings." Without looking back I started walking. Navarro hesitated, like a magnetic force his doubts held him in place until he willed himself to follow.

The luncheonette didn't deserve the title. It was small, just a sandwich, salad, and soup establishment. Perky young women behind the counter took orders and gave them to sullen, dark-haired, male workers who put the salads and sandwiches together.

Navarro opted for coffee. Probably part of his Opus Dei asceticism. Mortifying the body by denying it sustenance. I wasn't, however, going to deny myself, so I ordered a turkey sandwich and a bottle of cranberry juice. We found a table in a corner.

"Well?" Navarro asked after a few moments of silence.

I made him wait. Waiting and silence make good conversation starters. I munched on my sandwich and fiddled with opening the bottle. I took a long swig of the ruby red juice and patted my lips with a napkin.

"You've gotten me here to talk about some idiotic Propaganda Due fantasy of yours. So, talk."

I made as if to take another bite of the sandwich, then stopped myself midway and placed the sandwich back on the plate.

"I don't get it," I said looking him square in the eye. "I just don't get it."

"Don't get what? What are you talking about? Why did you drag me into this awful place?" He made a point of looking at his watch.

"Why would you deny working for a guy like Calvino when the records are so readily available?"

"Records can be wrong," he said sounding harsh but not defensive. "People make mistakes. Names are similar. My name is not uncommon."

"But biographies aren't usually exactly the same, other details aren't usually duplicated along with a name. So, I'll ask again, why would you deny working for Calvino?"

"I'm not denying anything. It's simply not true."

"Okay then," I made as if to rise from my chair. "I'll let the police sort it out."

There was silence. I scraped my chair noisily on the floor as I moved.

"It means nothing, you know."

"The police can decide," I said.

"I... I didn't work for him for very long." Navarro sighed with resignation. "I quit just after he broke off ties with the group you mentioned. The Bridge of Four Heads cabal. He left in disgust. I quit working for him days later."

"So, you're telling me he quit the group of plotters? He didn't stay to see it through? And you expect me to believe this, why?"

"He was disgusted by it all."

"Weak stomach or did Gelli replace him with another P2 heavyweight?"

"Mr. Fontana." He addressed me as if I were a deficient pupil and he a frustrated teacher. "How much do you know about P2?"

"Enough to know it's not an organization I'd belong to. Not that they'd have me." I figured he'd give me a Masonic history lesson and deflect the conversation to something other than himself. I played along.

"You know how it started?" He asked.

"As a Masonic lodge. Common knowledge."

"What do you know about the Masons?"

"Not a whole hell of a lot. Unless you're telling me they had something to do with the plot, in which case I'm gonna start boning up on them."

"Masons pride themselves on integrity, character, and steadfastness."

"Okay, they're a bunch of Boy Scouts. So what?"

"They take oaths, Mr. Fontana. They're serious about keeping their word."

"This is not news, Navarro. What I want to know is how deep was Calvino, how deep were you? Do you know more than you've admitted about the plot to kill the Pope?"

"One of the oaths they take," he pushed on as if I hadn't said a word, " is that they would never divulge the secrets of their brothers."

"What's your point?"

"They hold those secrets sacred. Except if those secrets concern criminal activity especially murder or other serious crimes. They would never condone anything remotely like that. And certainly not a plot to kill the Pope."

"Yet Calvino never spoke a word about this to anyone. Are Masons in the habit of keeping the secrets of non-Masons?"

"Neither did he continue with the group after he learned of their plans. He washed his hands of the whole mess. Never reported any of it because he feared for his life."

"That so?" I saw that Navarro knew how to spin a story. After denying everything, now all the details are in order. "You're expecting me to believe this?"

"They killed Calvino anyway. At least that's the impression they wanted to leave whether they actually did or not. Calvino died not long after the Pope. Found dead at his home. The police say it was an accident. Though they've never revealed the details."

"Why didn't they kill you? They knew you'd been Calvino's messenger boy."

"I don't think they realized I knew anything. Messenger boy is just about what they thought of me, just like all the other assistants to the big men of the group. All we did was carry messages, run errands. Nothing more. Calvino didn't entrust me with details. He forbade me to make notes of any kind."

"Still, you could've been a danger to the plotters."

"Which is why I left Calvino's employ before they could act. I wanted to believe they were a bunch of old men playing at being assassins. They talked about killing the Pope but did they really do it? There was talk of a plot but I don't believe there was any follow through. They were talkers, Mr. Fontana. That's all. Besides, after so many years the details are fuzzy."

"Consorting with a bunch of men planning to kill a pope is not something I'd imagine you'd ever forget. Details like that don't grow fuzz."

"I want to put it all behind me. Whatever happened then, it's all in the past."

"But it isn't. Brandt was writing about it and Brandt is dead. I'd call that very much in the present."

He stared silently at his coffee cup, never lifting his eyes to mine.

"What did you do after you left Calvino's employ?"

"I couldn't think what to do. I was lost, in every way you can be lost. Physically, spiritually, emotionally. All I knew was that I wanted to get away. That's when I discovered Opus Dei. I joined, returned to the U.S., and never looked back. I don't keep a steady residence, never own much of anything. If they'd wanted me dead, it wouldn't have been easy to track me. And Opus protects its members."

"You've never had contact with any of the plotters since that time? Not one of them tried to find you, communicate with you?"

"No. Which is why I believe they saw the evil in their plans and never really went through with them. I'm sure they wanted to forget it as much as I did."

"So they just let you be? I find that hard to swallow, Navarro. If I find out that you've been in contact with them, everything I have is going to the police. You get no second chances."

"I've told you, my life is doing God's work now. The taint of having worked near those men is something I still need to wash from my soul. Whether or not they were serious about their plans, they were evil men."

"Calvino thought they were serious."

"Calvino, like all Italians, had a flair for the dramatic."

I bristled but I realized that I was being dramatic. Maybe he was right.

"So you aren't even sure he was telling the truth?" I asked.

"Oh, he was telling the truth, filtered through the dramatic lens of an Italian too long practiced in seeing conspiracy where there is none."

"Well, tell me this, then. If you were so unsure of everything, why did you hold Brandt in such contempt? The first time we spoke, you as much as said his death was Divine retribution."

"Whether or not the plotters actually carried out their plans, Brandt made it seem as if they did. On the flimsiest evidence. He branded them with the sign of murder."

"He was looking for the Truth. Isn't that something worth pursuing?"

"It was his truth, spun from threads of fantasy. He had a desire to bring down the Church because they didn't see things his way."

"And there isn't room for healthy debate?"

"There isn't room for falsehood which a lot of misdirected people are hungry to disseminate. I'm ashamed of my feelings about his death. But the world is better off without Brandt."

* * *

Navarro gave me a lot to think about. I moved him to the bottom of my suspect list. He wasn't lying, that much I could tell. He wasn't telling the whole truth, that much I could tell.

I strolled down Chestnut Street where hordes of workers rushed to and from lunch. People chatted, charter school students screeched, and traffic rumbled. Amid the tumult I tried to sort things out.

My cell phone rang, disrupting my thoughts.

"Fontana."

"Is Olga." Her voice was shaky. "Men are in office. Angry men. They are wanting you. One has baseball bat but is not wanting to play."

Chapter 28

I took the stairs two at a time. Drew my gun as I reached my floor. Everything was silent.

I approached cautiously. There was no possibility of surprising these guys. There was only one way in. They'd be expecting me anyway.

Placing my hand on the doorknob, I swiftly opened the door and swept the room with my gun.

Olga was at her desk typing, ignoring the two men standing over her. One was Quinn. He was accompanied by a ragged, thuggish-looking kid with spiky hair and one of those almost-beards that kids who can't grow a beard often have.

Skimpy Beard held a bat and his grip tightened when he saw me. But the look in his eyes was all confusion at the sight of my gun.

"Put it down, kid." I motioned with the gun.

Skimpy Beard hesitated. His eyes darted from side to side. I guessed he was making the quick calculation that his bat wouldn't be a match for my Smith & Wesson.

"Got a hearing problem?" I pointed the gun at the kid's head.

He looked from me to Quinn and back again.

"Tell the kid to beat it. Or, after I shoot him, I'll take the bat and hammer you with it."

The kid's hands shook and he dropped the bat. It hit with a solid pock! sound on the old wood floor. His right leg wobbled and shook. He looked ready to piss himself. Next thing I knew, he flew past me out the door.

"Worthless little shit," Quinn said.

"Some protection you got there, Quinn." I smirked.

Quinn clutched a briefcase to his chest, looking every bit as wild-eyed and insane as the first time I'd seen him. His thick, black-framed glasses were askew and his hair stood out in different directions. But he wasn't fazed by the sight of my gun.

"Drop the briefcase and put your hands behind your head," I ordered.

Quinn scowled.

"Do it!" I motioned with the gun.

Quinn let the briefcase slip to the floor. Slowly he placed his hands behind his head. I watched his anger building up, like an old steam engine on overload. His eyes were furiously wide, his lips so tightly drawn together they were white and bloodless.

"Good boy," I said.

Quinn said nothing.

"I thought you said there were angry men here, Olga."

"Angry men, da. I am saying this," she commented without looking up. "You are seeing anger in eyes, no?"

I took my jacket off and placed the gun back into its holster. Then I sauntered past Quinn and into my office. The man reeked of tobacco and onions.

"Got something you need to tell me?" I said as I moved past.

He grunted, a rough animalistic sound, then turned to follow me.

"I need my briefcase."

"No, you don't."

Quinn fumed silently.

"Come in and shut the door. Or, leave. I don't give a rat's ass what you do." I sat at my desk.

Quinn entered and shut the door.

"What's got your fur up, Quinn?"

"You called me, remember? You have new information. Or, are you just jerking me around?"

"Not my style."

"What's the new information? You're still trying to pin Brandt's murder on me." He huffed. "Prove it. You're gonna hafta prove it." He moved closer.

"Prove what?"

"Prove I had anything to do with that fraud's murder. Prove it!" He pounded a fist on my desk.

"I can prove you'll owe me money for a new desk if I find any cracks. But who said anything about Brandt or murder? Unless... wait, are you telling me you wanna make a confession?" I loved pulling this guy's chain.

"You are infuriating! You call me. Make provocative remarks then expect me to react calmly."

"All I said was I have new information. I didn't say, 'Come on over with a bat- wielding freak to scare my secretary.' Or, did I?"

"New information could mean anything. That could be code for, you think you have the goods on me."

He sounded like something from a '30s movie. I tried not to laugh.

"I won't admit to anything."

"We've managed to find Brandt's documents."

"Brandt's... you've found... how could you find anything? He had nothing."

"Guess you didn't look close enough, Quinn." I wanted to hear him say it. "When you were in the house you didn't look everywhere."

He was silent.

"Of course, a thorough guy, a real researcher would have looked and found this. A guy who knows his stuff would have made a real search and found the answers he was looking for. But I guess..."

"I did no such thing." He said.

"Just when I thought you'd get interesting." I leaned back in my chair.

"You think you're clever. But you're just a thug."

"If you say so. Aren't you gonna tell me how you searched Brandt's house? And you came up empty. Even though any fool could have found what we found." He'd probably never have found that key but he wouldn't know that. I wanted to see how much he'd tell me.

"Any fool…?I don't have to put up with your insults." He half rose from his seat.

"Sit down, Quinn. Get it off your chest. I've got a private lab working the place and they'll come up with prints, a stray hair, something."

"Prints." He laughed. "They'll never find a thing."

"Right. I imagine you'd be careful. You may be a dolt when it comes to research but breaking and entering, stealing other people's work, you've got that down. Right?"

"I stole nothing. If you know as much as you say, you know that. Brandt was the thief. He stole my work. Work I'd been doing for decades. He comes along and with his pretty face, takes all my research, and publishes a book of his own."

"By 'steal' do you mean he did his own research and came up with the same set of facts and documents you'd found and done nothing with?"

"I… that information was my property. I have been compiling it for years. Brandt used the same information. He stole my ideas, my work. And twisted it to his own ends."

"Okay, let's call that stealing, if you want. So, you figure it's just fine to break into the guy's house and ransack it to steal his new findings?"

"I did no such thing."

"How'd you know Brandt and Hollister wouldn't be there? Did you know because you murdered Brandt and then ransacked his house?"

"Murder? You have no right to accuse me."

"That's not much of a denial."

"I'm denying it in every possible way. I had nothing to do with that. It was others. Brandt made many enemies. The conspirators, the Church authorities, there are many who wanted to see him dead. I just wanted him to tell the truth about stealing my work."

"So, you only broke into his house?"

"Never." Quinn fumed. "Have you investigated elsewhere, Mr. Fontana? Have you? Am I the only one you are investigating? There are others. People with power, people who can pick up a phone and in the next moment anyone they want will disappear. I fear such people. They haunt my days and nights, Mr. Fontana. I live in fear. And so should you."

"They didn't have someone knock me out to warn me off the case. You did."

"That wasn't me," he said loudly. "I don't need to resort to that."

"You act indignant, invade my office with your bat boy, and that's supposed to make me believe you? You're a liar from top to bottom. You're a thief. You like to bully people. Give me a reason to believe anything you say."

He was silent.

"That's what I thought. You've got nothing. Your so called work is just a pale copy of what Brandt had been doing. That's why you broke into his house and that's why you had him killed. I'll be going to the police with everything."

He glared at me, his eyes bloodshot, his hair tangled and dirty.

"You can't leave well enough alone, can you, Fontana?" Quinn stood, placed a hand in one pocket of his voluminous coat.

A tingle of alert thrilled up my neck.

"Stand up, Fontana," he ordered. The hand in his pocket apparently held a gun, or at least he wanted me to believe that.

"You'll have to do better than that, Quinn. That's one of the oldest tricks in the book."

"Stand up and come around to the front of the desk." He pulled a pistol from his pocket and pointed it at me.

"What? Are you gonna kill me here? And my secretary?" I stayed put.

"Get up," his voice was calm and low.

I stood slowly. I figured it'd be better to play along rather than set him off.

"Now come around to this side."

Slowly moving from behind my desk, I stood within a foot of him and noticed something.

"You got a plan, Quinn?"

"You'll give me the documents or both you and your secretary will suff…"

I put out a hand and snatched the gun. It was a fake which I realized when I got close. I wanted to smack him across the face with it but I tossed it into the trash can instead.

"Sit down, dirt bag." A well-placed shove and he was down.

Letting out a sigh, which, like the rest of him, was laden with the odor of onions and tobacco, he slumped in the chair.

"You broke into Brandt's house, right?"

"No. No, I... did not," he stammered.

"Save it. I've heard enough."

Silence.

I picked up the phone and buzzed Olga.

"Place a call to Lt. Giuliani. When you've got her, switch it to me."

I waited, phone in hand.

"All right, all right... no need to call the police, Fontana."

I didn't budge.

"Enough!" He rose from his seat. "Stop!... Please."

"Cancel the call, *carina*. But keep the number handy." I placed the receiver in its cradle. "Well...?" I stared at him. He sank back into his chair.

"All right, I... I may have broken into Brandt's home." He sat back, closed his eyes, and sighed. It was as if he were unburdening himself. "I may even have had someone call to warn you off the case. Call, you understand. Not hit you or touch you. Just a phone call. That is the extent of it." He feebly slapped a hand on my desk. "I draw the line at anything worse than that. No violence. And murder... never."

"No violence? That's where you draw the line?"

"Absolutely. Violence is not my way. I'm a researcher, an historian."

"So pulling a gun is not violence?"

"It was a fake as you saw."

"And the kid with the bat was an illusion? I just fantasized a young man wielding a baseball bat." I looked at him. "Quinn, lemme tell you, I have fantasies but that's not one of 'em."

"It was a show of force. He'd never have used the bat. I instructed him to stand there and look tough. He couldn't even accomplish that. You see how he ran when you arrived. He's street scum, not worth the time of day."

"Nice attitude. You're a lying scum bucket yourself. A thief and a liar."

"But not a murderer. Never a murderer. I could never do that. They could. But not me. I'm not like them."

"They?" This guy was losing cards from his deck as we spoke. "Who is this 'they' you're talking about?"

"The ones with all the power. The ones who control everything. They're the ones you need to seek out. Though if you do, you'll be finished."

"Whatever."

"That flippant attitude, Fontana. That is what will get you killed. They murdered the Pope. They murdered Brandt. Because he was getting too close to the truth."

"Which Truth is that?"

"That powerful men murdered the Pope and Brandt may have known their names. That's what I want to find out. That's why I need to see the documents."

"Never gonna happen."

"Your life... and others may depend on it."

"If these powerful men are anything like you, I'm not worried."

"Remember what I've said, Fontana. Something will happen. Keep looking over your shoulder. They'll come after you, I can see to it."

"But you're not a violent man, right?"

"One word to them and you're dust."

"Get out, Quinn. And remember, you're not off my list yet."

"You won't go to the police? They'll know if you go to the police..."

"I'm making no promises."

He stood.

"When you find the real killer you'll know I was telling the truth." He ran a hand through his zany hair and it looked no better.

"When I find the real killer he might be you."

He gave me one last wild-eyed look, turned, and stomped out the door.

I sat back and thought about what he might be capable of. I've seen murderers, thieves, rapists. You could never really tell what they might or might not be capable of. Usually, I got a feeling. Listening to them talk, looking into their eyes. I'd get a sense for just how far they'd go. If you knew what to look for, you'd see it. My instinct was good.

Quinn was a loon but his eyes said he wasn't as crazy as he pretended. He was a bully and a bluffer. But a murderer? I got the feeling he wasn't. But I wasn't ready to let him off the hook.

I stepped out to see Olga.

"You all right?"

"Me? I am tough like snails."

"They didn't touch you?"

"I am telling them everything is on camera. Touching me will be on film and they will be stars at police station."

"Clever. Maybe I ought to get that surveillance system I've been thinking about."

"Maybe is good for Olga's health. And for you. You would be mess without secretary."

"I'll do it. Now I've got some calls to make." I went back to my desk.

She was right. I'd be a mess without a secretary and she was the best.

I picked up the phone and dialed the private number Kusek had given me.

"Kusek, here." His voice was as smooth as I'd remembered.

"It's Marco."

"Marco! I had a lovely time last night. I wanted to thank you."

"I enjoyed it, too, Tad. You made quite a hit with the waiter. He gave me a look on the way out as if I'd hit the jackpot. I noticed a lot of other eyes trained on you, too. We should do it again. Soon."

It wasn't empty flattery. For some reason he had stirred something in me. But I also felt guilty. Anton and Luke were more important to me, more integral to my life. And here I was getting dreamy about a priest. A priest! Maybe all I wanted was a quick roll in the hay, then this priest thing would just go away.

"Flattery will get you nowhere, Marco."

"How about a guy who keeps his promises, then? Will that earn me points?"

"You bought me the Tuscan villa?" He laughed and I wanted to be there with him. I remembered his smile, the way his eyes crinkled when he laughed. It made me think of Anton. They were remarkably similar.

"Wow, I must have had more to drink than I remember. Actually, I was thinking about a smaller promise I'd made."

"Okay, hit me. I can't remember."

Always nice to have them remember your conversation and your promises. That helped to dampen the embers a bit.

"About reading some documents? I hoped you'd read them to see if you could help with the case? Remember that?"

"Documents. Documents. Oh! Brandt's documents. Yes! I remember now."

"Well, I've gotten permission and I'd like to email them to you."

"I'm here at the computer. Mail away."

"You'll keep this under your hat, right? Hollister doesn't want anyone else to see this material. But we're hoping that you'll see something we missed."

"If there's one thing a priest knows how to do, it's keep a secret. Remember the seal of the confessional? From when you were still a practicing Catholic? Don't worry. The documents will be my eyes only."

As he talked, I attached the files to the email I composed.

"Sent. Let me know when you get them."

There was a brief pause during which I heard a keyboard clacking.

"They're here. Thanks for trusting me with this, Marco."

"Here's your turn to have some faith in me. How about returning the favor?"

"I knew there'd be a catch. Italians have a quid pro quo mentality. It was that way when I lived in Rome, it's that way with G. You have the same trait."

"Should I feel insulted or flattered?"

"Flattered. I like that quality. What is it you want?"

"You mentioned Galante would be meeting the mayor at the Marriott tomorrow."

"That's true," he said, suddenly wary.

"You also mentioned I might be able to get a little face time with the Cardinal."

"I knew it! As I recall, it was you who mentioned you'd like to have a meeting. I never said I might be able to arrange it."

"Well, maybe my memory isn't clear. After all you remember me promising a villa and I have no recollection of that."

"He's got a tight schedule."

"Nobody's schedule is that tight. Even the president has time to spare when it's something consequential."

"It's that important to you?"

"Important enough, Tad. I need to close this case. Give Hollister a little peace. Maybe Galante can help."

"Well…"

"I'll never know unless I can talk face to face."

"If you upset him, he'll eat me for lunch."

"I've got your life in my hands?" I said.

"My life, my career, my everything. I'm sticking my neck out for you."

"In that case, I'll be extra gentle. I'll leave the brass knuckles and rubber hose at home. You think he'll mind if I grill him under a bright light, though?"

"I'm serious. G is a great guy but he's a stickler and he never forgets a slight or someone who makes him look foolish or worse. If you're not careful I'm as good as assigned to some parish in Idaho."

"But you'll do it?"

"You don't give up, do you?"

"Not when there's something I really want."

"Be at the Marriott at noon. In the main lobby. And remember what I said."

I picked up the phone again, Kusek's voice still in my head, and dialed Detective Giuliani.

"Giuliani."

"It's your favorite P.I." I tried sounding cheerful.

"No such thing. What do you want now, Fontana?"

"Just wondering if you'd managed to ID that kid yet?"

"Who wants to know?"

"It's related to the case I'm working. Remember?"

"I remember a certain arrogant P.I. telling me he couldn't let me in on a case. Private. Hush hush. Bullshit."

"You know how it is, Gina." I tried being friendly.

"It's Detective Giuliani. And I know exactly how it is."

"So how about a break?"

"They haven't identified the vic. If and when they do, you won't be the first to know. In fact, you won't get to know at all."

She left a wave of dialtone in her wake.

Chapter 29

The cool air washed over me as I stood on my balcony but it couldn't wipe out the annoyance I felt at Giulani's refusal to cooperate. I'd have to use up favors doing an end run around her.

I diluted the feeling with some merlot and turned to get ready.

Luke had agreed to tag along at Stella's. Luke never shies away from helping even when it involves the sleazy underbelly of the community. Though he'd never engage that element on his own, he's not cowed by it. I liked his intense curiosity and the more I thought about him, I realized there were a lot of things to like about Luke.

* * *

Stella's was more crowded on Fridays. We squeezed our way through packs of men and hustlers searching for a compatible match up. From the looks of things, everyone was holding out for something better because not many people were chatting with one another.

They'd lowered the lights to legal blindness level and the music pounded out sounds that vibrated my whole body. Few people responded to the music, most stood locked in search-stare mode, surveying the room for a face they liked, a body that entranced them, a friendly look.

Strategically placed black lights heightened the atmosphere. Some of the hustlers, wearing white tank tops or t-shirts, stood out like beacons, as the blacklight intensified their white clothing. I laughed to myself thinking if all the hustlers did the same thing, it would look surreal, like a bunch of buoys floating on a sea of old otters.

Luke went to question the bartender as planned. I'd decided to scope out what passed for a strip show on the lower floor where Scanlan would most likely show up.

I fended off wayward hands and guys asking how much I charged as I moved. Finally pushing my way to the top of the stairs, I sensed a different mood downstairs. The sex-drunk tension floated up the steps.

Before you noticed what they stared at, you saw the audience itself. It was like peering at a congregation in a church. They were mesmerized by something happening in front of them, all together, all in rapt attention. Sexually charged thumping music cascaded over the spellbound men united in concentrated attentiveness.

I knew what gripped the audience. As I moved down the stairs, the small stage came into view and I saw the object of everyone's desire. Average height, the dancer had a naturally muscular body. He had a wholesome kind of beauty that only comes with youth. Muscle definition without work, a bubble butt that looked soft as a pillow and just as inviting, and a g-string with enough heft to enthrall even the casual observer. His best feature by far was his face, a mix of angelic and sleazy. Full pouty lips, a finely sculpted nose, deep dark eyes, and a clear creamy-pink complexion that begged the spectator to taste. All framed by luxurious, dark, curly hair.

Staring at his face, I almost missed a step, on my descent to the bar. He was that enchanting. I considered asking him to join StripGuyz. He'd be a real draw for the group. Problem is this kid was a hustler and hiring a hustler would be bad for business. He'd have the patrons at Bubbles eating out of his hand his first few minutes onstage. Just like he was doing at Stella's. Except here, he was also conducting a silent auction. The highest bidders would have him for their hour of pleasure.

The dancer's routine was pure sex. He'd chosen slow, sexy, music which gave him the opportunity to roam the stage, engaging with customers and drawing them in. He moved his long legs slowly and spread them wide, inviting the men to look and hope. He slid to his knees close to the front row of spectators but when they reached out to touch, he deftly pulled back refusing them even a hint of what his skin felt like.

Upended and balancing on one hand he rotated himself, giving everyone a topsy-turvy view, until he arched his back and lowered his feet to the stage. Standing again, he began a new tantalizing round.

Hot as he was, I tore my eyes away and scanned the crowd. According to my information, strip nights were when Scanlan was most likely to show. The dying kid had implicated him. I wanted to see his reaction to that.

So far, there was no sign of the guy. But it was early.

The lights dimmed and the music stopped momentarily. I moved to the rear of the room near the curtained alcoves.

When the lights came up again, a different dancer had taken the stage, undulating suggestively. Not nearly as attractive as the first.

I kept an eye out for Scanlan but there was still no sign of him.

"Hey, you." The voice was smoky and seductive.

I turned to see the first dancer standing next to me. We were as alone as you could be in the place and he pushed himself close to me. The fragrance of delicate cologne mixed with sweat swathed his body, filled my nostrils.

"I know you," he said. "You own StripGuyz."

"And you're one of the best dancers I've seen in a long time." I smiled.

"Beto," he said, holding out his hand.

His name was instantly familiar as the one Niko mentioned.

"Marco." I felt strength in the softness of his hand.

"How about I audition for you?"

"We have rules, Beto. Auditions are once a month."

"I mean… now." And with his chin Beto indicated the darkened rooms beyond the curtain.

"It's not the way we do things."

Beto took my hand. I didn't resist partly because I didn't want to and partly because I suspected there was something more than an audition going on.

He led me through the curtains and into one of the rooms at the back. Weak, crumbly light from a single amber bulb gave everything a dreamlike quality.

Beto gently eased me into a soft chair, then stood before me wearing only his thong.

The music filled the room through a hidden speaker and Beto began to tempt me. His gyrations and turns, his nimble moves showcased every inch of his flesh. Supple muscles layered with pink skin, emphasized his elegantly proportioned form. Running his hands over his body, he dared me to touch, taste. He moved seductively close, brushing my face with his chest. His soft flesh smelled like sex and sweat.

Every nerve in my body came to attention. The room temperature rose and I felt my breath come short.

Pulling my hands, he placed them on the firm round cheeks of his ass as he continued to swivel his hips slowly. Leaning back his head he encouraged me to taste his chest, lick his nipples.

I felt sweat slide down my forehead. My heart raced as I kissed his chest.

"You're beautiful, Beto."

"Then, hire me. Make me one of your boys." He emphasized that with a long slow motion dragging his semi-hard cock over my torso.

"We don't work like this at Bubbles," I said, my hands roaming the smoothness of his ass and legs.

Beto took my face in his hands and moved so I looked him in the eye.

"Maybe I like your way better," he said. "Maybe I am tired of this way."

He bent his face to mine and kissed me, thrusting his tongue deep into my mouth. I didn't resist. His flesh pressed against me, his mouth on mine, the fragrance of his skin combined in a hypnotic mix. My head swam.

Suddenly he pulled back.

"This can be a dangerous place, Marco." He drew his hand down my chest to my crotch and I felt myself respond again.

"You're pretty dangerous, Beto."

"Not for you. For you I am whatever you want. But there *are* dangers here."

My senses returned to alert status.

"A friend has told me to warn you. To take care with you."

"Who is this friend?"

"He's dead. He don't want you to die, too."

"I'm listening."

"He says to talk to Colt."

"That's all?"

"This is all he tells me, Marco."

"Is Colt here?"

"Sometimes. Often. You need to find him."

"What's he look like?"

"Like me a little. But he has something I would never have." Beto nuzzled my neck as he spoke, his tongue flicking in and out sending little electric thrills through me.

"W-what's he got that you don't?" I said holding Beto close.

"A tattoo."

"Oh?"

"A large tattoo. It runs up," Beto opened my shirt, placed his tongue just below my nipple, and licked up, up, up to my neck. "From there…" He continued licking from my neck to my cheek. "To there. A lizard. With a long tongue."

Beto covered my mouth with another passionate kiss.

"Look for him, Marco. And be careful here."

Slowly, Beto peeled himself from me, making the separation sweetly painful. He stood before me again and I felt a longing to have him back. To have that warm flesh, that raw sexuality crushed against me.

"I will come for an audition," he said. "And I will play by your rules, Marco."

I blinked and in that moment he was gone. I sat alone and breathless in the dimly lit room where the memory settled like dust over me.

Stumbling my way through the darkness, I entered the bar again. I still reeled from my encounter with Beto, but I took control and got back to work.

Coolly detached, heavily muscled bouncers raked the crowd with their gaze. Their only mission, to maintain control. The crowd at Stella's wasn't as well-behaved as the guys at Bubbles. Stella's needed brutish bouncers.

I moved to where I could observe the stairs and the crowd and waited for Scanlan. If I'd judged Scanlan correctly, he'd be the kind who loved to show his insider status. To prove he knew dancers personally, maybe had even slept with them, and could command their attention. He probably spread around plenty of cash to ensure that status.

Guys of every stripe filled the audience. One short, squat man stood at the front waving cash in the air like bait to attract a wild animal. Others did the same and the kid onstage cleaned up. But he never looked as if it was the money that urged him on. He made it appear it was the men and the pure joy he received from dancing for them.

Every so often men came down the stairs and melted into the crowd. From my corner, I saw them all. It was a far cry from a cold morning stakeout sitting in my car watching some guy emerge from a bathhouse fresh from cheating on his partner. At least here I could enjoy the show.

Patience paid off, Scanlan swept down the steps eventually. I almost didn't recognize him. He carried himself with an arrogance he hadn't displayed before. He stood straighter, wore a sleazy smile, and dressed in clothes that said he had money. People greeted him deferentially, some nodding in his direction, some shaking his hand. The security guards turned toward him and nodded curtly.

People actually made a path for him to get closer to the stage. One guy, who objected was rudely shoved out of the way by others. Scanlan took his position near the stage and the crowd closed around him. I saw why he never failed to attend these nights.

The dancer, losing none of his cool, gracefully made his way to Scanlan. He gyrated his hips and thrust his crotch in Scanlan's direction, then turned his back and offered his pink bubble-butt, bending over and thrusting a hand between his legs to caress his own cheeks. Scanlan took a twenty and placed it in the crack of the dancer's ass. Squeezing the twenty between his cheeks, the dancer turned to face Scanlan again. The kid continued to gyrate and sway, he squatted down and slowly rose to his feet, then turned his back and waggled his rear, the twenty still between his cheeks. Turning to face Scanlan again, he bent forward and placed a kiss on Scanlan's lips, something he had not done for anyone else.

A murmur of approval rippled through the crowd. The music continued and the dancer moved to other customers.

Scanlan stood there, loving himself, happy others were envious of his power. He turned, and the crowd parted again. Obviously bored for now, he headed to the bar. I moved to beat him there.

So full of himself, Scanlan didn't notice me standing there. He leaned down, one elbow on the bar, and ordered a Courvoisier. He took no notice of me, as if I were just another peasant in his domain. He didn't need to pay attention. I moved closer.

"They said you'd be here tonight."

Scanlan turned and looked at me. For a brief moment there was no recognition, then I watched his eyes grow wide with a mix of fear and anger.

"You!" He drew in his breath sharply and stood straight up. He scanned the room.

"Got a few questions I need to ask you, Scanlan."

"I've got nothing to hide and nothing to say. Get out. I won't answer questions."

"Take it easy. You got nothing to hide, then why not answer my questions? I'm just looking for information. Big cheese like you, hell, you should be able to help me, no sweat. Am I right?"

Scanlan stood there, his head panning back and forth looking for an excuse to evade me.

"How about we go into one of those private rooms and talk? Someone told me you were the one to talk to." I didn't tell him the kid had been shot and was dead.

"I don't know what you want and I don't really care. Get lost."

"Even if it's about you and Jared?"

"Where is Jared? You know where he is?" Now he advanced on me. Out of the corner of my eye I noticed one of the security guys turning his head to look at us.

"I thought you could help me with that." I stood my ground. "After all it was you who beat him, right? You're the one left marks on the kid's face, right?"

I was in Scanlan's face now. He was shorter but puffed up with anger. His eyes betrayed him though, they were filled with fear.

"Get out!" He was loud. Loud enough to attract attention which was probably what he wanted.

The security goons headed over. Scanlan must have noticed because he grabbed my jacket and pulled me toward him. I pushed him off me.

"Stop! Get away!" He shouted. "Are you crazy? Keep your hands off me!" He jerked back and against the bar, pretending I'd knocked him back. In the dim lighting that's undoubtedly what people thought they saw.

"All right, break it up." A tall bouncer, sporting a blond buzz cut and a face like a weathered fence post, placed his hands on our shoulders to hold us apart.

"How about you get your hands off me?" I shrugged him off. "I'm just talkin' to the man."

"Maybe he ain't in a talkin' mood," he snapped and edged us gently away from one another. "You all right, Mr. Scanlan?"

"Get him away from me, Den."

"Time for you to leave, Mister. Show's over. Beat it."

"I'll track you down, Scanlan," I said in a low voice. "You'll talk to me one way or the other."

"Get him out of here," Scanlan ordered.

"Beat it, or I'll beat you." The blond bouncer scowled.

I slowly turned my back on them and walked casually to the stairs.

"See you around, Seamus," I called out as I climbed the steps.

The erotically charged music from the downstairs bar was obliterated by the blaring sound upstairs. Beto and the other dancers were happy memories. Reality was once again hustlers and johns searching for hook ups.

I looked around for Luke and spotted him chatting with the bartender.

"Ready to go?"

"Marco!" He turned to smile at me. "This is Rob."

The bartender, a slightly older, suave-looking man, smiled and extended his hand.

"Rob's a gamer. Loves Lifeonline and is thinking of starting his own company."

Now I knew why Luke was so engaged. Sophisticated businessman and savvy entrepreneur, Luke had a passion for online games. From a purely business angle. He was considering getting involved with the business once he'd had enough of his housecleaning venture.

Rob was called to get a drink for a customer who looked as if the last thing he needed was another drink.

"Did Rob happen to mention anything helpful? About the case?"

"He says he knows your guy Colt but hasn't seen him tonight. Says Colt's a shadowy guy. But popular."

"He give you a description?"

"Short, swarthy, shaved head. He's got piercings. One over his eyebrow and an earring. And Colt has a big tattoo. He says Colt is attractive if you like rough, thuggish, and pierced."

"I'm not looking for a date. I just have to find out what he knows. Maybe he can ID the dead kid. Did Rob say anything else?"

"He knows Scanlan because he comes in all the time but he never spends any time at the bar. So they never talk. He remembers Jared, too. Says a lot of guys here would do anything to get with Jared. Even Colt was interested. But Scanlan keeps him on a short leash. Colt made a pass anyway."

"How'd that turn out?"

"Colt and Scanlan argued. Scanlan paid a couple of goons to warn Colt off."

Rob came back to chat.

"Rob, Luke tells me you know a few things that might help."

"I keep my eyes open. You gotta watch your own back in here. Nobody's gonna do that for you."

"Colt got into it with Scanlan?"

"I wouldn't say they fought. Colt made a pass at Jared and Scanlan wasn't happy. He made sure Colt knew about it. Money always wins, especially in a place like this. A few bucks to security and they gave Colt a warning for Scanlan. Nothing rough, S&D won't have that kinda thing here. The goons made sure he knew Jared was off limits. Of course, Colt's got his own connections. He doesn't scare easy. He's just like the rest of 'em. Think they'll live forever. It's not gonna end good. You can take that to the bank."

"So Colt keeps hitting on Jared."

"Not so's you'd notice. But I've caught 'em out of the corner of my eye. Edging their way back to those booths. Talking together. Never when Scanlan's around, of course."

"I was under the impression Jared never came in here without Scanlan."

"That's the way it used to be. But I seen the kid in here a few times on his own. That's when he was talking to Colt. Coupl'a times he was with Colt and another guy, tall dude, hat and lapels up coverin' his face. Never could see that face. But they all seemed friendly."

"No idea who the other guy is?"

"Could be one of Colt's connections. Colt and the other guy were in here once without Jared. Went into one of the back rooms and stayed there a while. Coulda just been sex for all I know."

"Other than that you don't know the guy?"

"Like I said, never saw his face. I don't know if I ever saw him before. Lotta guys in and outta here. They all blend after a while."

"Didn't you tell me one night Scanlan talked to that tall guy, too?" Luke said.

"Well, sorta. Damned if I know what was goin' on that night. The tall guy looked like he was avoidin' Scanlan. Kept turning away from him. Never really talked to him."

"Jared started coming in on his own after that night?"

"Yeah. That's when he and Colt started talkin' real tight. Damned if I know what goes on here half the time. There's too many come in here for me to remember everything."

"Scanlan never knew Jared was talking with Colt?" Luke asked.

"Who knows?" Rob answered. "Colt didn't seem worried. You ask me, Jared wanted Colt as much as Colt wanted Jared. Go figure."

Go figure is right. I had to wonder if Scanlan used Jared and Colt for his own purposes. Especially since he knew Colt wanted Jared.

I left Rob a nice tip.

"Wanna head over to Bubbles with me, Luke? Unless you've got to get home."

"I'm all yours, Marco. I haven't been to Bubbles in a while." He started for the door. "Did Rob help any?"

"Maybe." I pushed the door open and we were out on the sidewalk. "But Scanlan won't let me get close and Jared is missing. It's a dead end."

"What about this guy Colt?"

"I'll have to come back to Stella's, now that I know what he looks like. But, Jared's the key. I've gotta find him. I'm probably not be the only one looking for him. The sooner I find him the better."

The sidewalk was empty. The lights illuminating Stella's sputtered and buzzed. And I had one of those odd feelings.

"What about the documents? Did you guys get anything out of them?"

"Names. Places. Stuff we can spin ideas from. And I've got a guy, ha! Not just a guy. He's a monsignor. I've got him looking over the documents for us. He's the Cardinal's right hand man. We'll see what he comes up with."

"He won't find anything. I'd bet on it. If he's so close to the top, why would he want to get his church in trouble?"

"Oh, ye of little faith," I joked. "Maybe I was drawn in by the Monsignor's hot exterior. Maybe he was captivated by my charming personality. I think he knows a lot. He just might see something in those documents and feel compelled to tell, just for the sake of the truth."

"Yeah. Sure. Hellooooo? He's a priest. And not just a priest. A highly placed priest."

"Maybe he'll help me to connect some of the dots. And Colt can connect a few more and then…"

Before I could finish, a bedraggled young guy stepped out of the shadows of a doorway and stood in front of us.

I instinctively pushed Luke behind me and stood face to face with the stranger. He was average height and thin, a light-skinned black guy whose drooping eyelids gave him a vaguely threatening, drugged-up appearance.

"Hey," he said, his voice thick. "Saw you guys inside and…"

"Not interested, pal," I snapped and hoped he'd get the hint.

"Hey, man, it's not like that…"

"What's it like then?" I said. Though the guy appeared harmless, I wasn't taking chances.

"I hear you're lookin' for Colt." He waited.

"You know Colt?"

"I know where to find him."

"And how much is this gonna cost me?" I knew what his game was. But I had no other leads on Colt.

"A hundred bucks," he stared with those dull, half-closed eyes. "Cheap. If you really wanna find the dude."

"How do I know you're on the level?"

"You don't, man. You ain't never heard'a trust?"

"Yeah, I have. Have you?" I paused. "What if I told you to give me the information and you just trust me for the cash?"

"I say, fuck you, dude." He turned to go.

"How do I know you're telling the truth?"

"You don't. But a Benjamin ain't much to find out if I am." He waited patiently.

I pulled out my wallet.

"You're gonna pay him?" Luke whispered.

"Cost of doin' business, Luke."

I fished two fifties out of my wallet and held them so the guy could see them.

"Okay, let's have it." I noted everything about him, just in case I had to hunt him down later.

"He live in a dive hotel on Arch Street. Up in the twenties. You know it?"

"I know it. Got a room number?"

"Naw, man. I juss know he live there."

"How do you know?"

"He owe me money, man. I followed him home one night. Got my money, too."

"If this doesn't pan out, I know where to find you. And I will."

I handed him his money and he disappeared around the corner.

Chapter 30

A hundred bucks lighter, I led Luke to Bubbles to commiserate.

"Paying a hundred dollars for information you don't even know is good," Luke clicked his tongue.

"You're the big spender. Who just bought a seventy-five inch LCD TV?"

"I make a lot. I can afford it," Luke said without any pretense. "But I don't throw it away."

Luke spent a lot but was also generous. He'd never had much money when he immigrated to the U.S. He'd struggled for everything, including school and setting himself up in business. His business and smart investments had made him rich and able to live comfortably. He enjoyed expensive restaurants, vacations, lots of technology, and anything he decided he wanted. He had a second home at the beach and was considering another condo in Florida. But none of that stopped him being generous with his friends.

"Sometimes you've gotta trust these guys. Besides, I could tell he wasn't lying. I'm good. You know that." Still, I'd be happier when the information panned out and I'd found Colt.

"Problem is, he could've thought he was telling the truth. He looked pretty tweaked."

"I don't wanna seem callous or anything but Hollister's gonna pay for all of this. It's part of expenses."

"I figured as much."

"Tell you what, I'll buy you a drink," I said holding the door for him. "But we've gotta make a stop at my office first."

"You mean you're going to force me to look at all the naked guys hanging around outside your office?"

"Oh, no. Not at all." I smiled. "You can stay down here. Please, get comfortable. I'll be down and we can…"

"Not on your life. I'll put up with the naked guys." Luke laughed. His smile lit up his entire face. "The things I put up with for friends."

He followed me up the stairs and we found Anton herding dancers and reminding them who was up next.

"Did you have a fun time at the sewer called Stella's?" Anton tucked his clipboard under his arm and smiled.

"Had a ball," Luke said. "Boss man here wouldn't let me downstairs to see the strippers." Luke turned to gawk at Zeb and Jeb, twin dancers, who were adjusting their thongs and not embarrassed about what was exposed as they worked. The twins were one of the hottest tickets I had.

"You didn't miss anything, Luke. The classy strippers work for us," Anton boasted.

"They do," I said. "I'm being honest when I say that. But tonight I saw a dancer at Stella's whose face…" All I could do was utter a small moan.

"Bet you he sells more than the dance," Anton said. "Not that I have anything against prostitution, but we can't run a whore house here."

"Anyway, the visit paid off. I had a run-in with Scanlan, saw a beautiful dancer, and got a lead on where Colt lives. Not to mention, I got a clear description of the guy."

"Yeah, he got a hundred dollar lead that he doesn't know will really pay off." Luke rolled his eyes.

"Tell me about it. I know how he operates," Anton said. "It's easy to see why he works two jobs to keep himself clothed and fed."

"Just came up to see if you needed help here," I said, changing the subject before Ma and Pa started in on other aspects of my life. "Any sign of Nando or Kent?"

"No, as a matter of fact. I'm worried. Haven't you made any progress?" Anton said.

"I'm sorry, Anton. We've checked their apartments. I even put a guy on stakeout at both their places. No dice."

"How about your guys, Luke? They haven't come up with anything?" Anton asked.

"Something's bound to turn up. We'll find them."

"As long as it isn't a dead body you find. That's what I'm worried about. You almost had me fooled into thinking I could trust Kent."

"C'mon down and have a drink with me and Luke. My treat," I said. "No use worrying about what you can't control."

"Let me finish up here first. I'll join you in a minute."

I placed an arm around Anton's shoulders and gave him a squeeze. He melted into me and it felt good. But I also felt a lot of tension in his body.

"No more than five minutes. That's an order. From the Boss. C'mon Luke." I headed toward the stairs. "If I don't see you in five, I'll send Curly up after you."

Curly was one of the patrons who had a crush on Anton. Except in Anton's presence all Curly ever did was stutter and mumble, which drove Anton crazy.

"I'll be there." Anton called down as we made our way back to the bar.

Cal was dancing. A baby-faced, blond heartthrob. He knew exactly how to tease the dollars out of patrons. In fact, I saw he already had more than a few twenties sticking out of his g-string.

Across from where we sat, Tony chatted with someone I didn't recognize.

"Order whatever you want," I said to Luke. "Be right back."

I went around to approach Tony, who saw me and smiled.

"Have you heard anything about Jared?" Tony asked.

"That's what I was about to ask you."

"Niko is frantic. We're both worried sick. I've put feelers out but nothing so far."

"He's not making it easy, I'll tell you. You're aware Jared is friendly with one of my dancers?"

"Nando? Sure, I knew that. They've been friendly for a while. What's that got to do with anything?"

"Nando is missing. And so's one of my workers, Kent. In fact Kent and…"

"Yeah, I know. Jared told us." Tony sipped his drink and looked at me. "Jared likes Nando. They're really close."

"You think Nando and Jared are involved?"

"Not a chance. They're girlfriends. Nando turned to Jared when he was having doubts about Kent. But it never went further than that."

"Why so sure?"

"Because Jared would've told Niko. He tells him everything. Besides, Jared's in love with someone else."

"Helmut," I said. "That much I know. But Helmut is dead. Isn't it possible that Jared found some comfort with Nando?"

"Not from what Jared told us. He and Nando became friendly before Helmut was shot. They had things in common. They were girlfriends, like I said. The idea of them sleeping with one another just doesn't compute." He gulped the rest of his drink and signaled for another. "And falling in love. That's a whole other level. No. It's just not them."

"They're both missing. That's no coincidence. And it's more than a little suspicious."

"Could be a coincidence. Stranger things have happened," Tony said. His tough demeanor had totally melted away as the liquor washed through him. We talked like old friends and I liked that.

"I don't believe in coincidences," I said. "In my line of work there's no such thing."

"What're you saying, then? They ran off together? They eloped?" Tony started laughing. "Or, what?"

"You tell me. The way they think is not exactly linear. I mean, have you ever had a conversation with Nando? Anyway, they're not the only ones missing."

"You don't think Kent did something? Do you? Like maybe he found them together and just assumed Jared was stealing Nando… and… and… maybe he…"

"Whoa, pull up on that horse before he runs away with you." I placed a hand on his shoulder. "I may not be sure about a lot of things, but I'm pretty sure about Kent. He's a nice guy. Romantic. Crazy in love. But not violent."

"Not the way I heard it."

"Well, you hear a lotta things that don't turn out to be true. Listen to the news some time. I'm bettin' this is all some big misunderstanding and it'll be all right." I silently berated myself again for literally betting this was going to work out in my favor.

"I wish you could tell that to Niko. The guy's going nuts. Maybe if you talked to him he'd calm down."

"I will. I'll stop by the diner tomorrow."

"Jared was... I mean... is... that's right, isn't it? Nothing bad has happened?"

"Jared is gonna be fine. He'll be back and he'll be fine."

"He's like a little brother to Niko and he's my best friend. He's like family."

"We'll find him."

Luke was busy chatting with one of the customers. I heard him mention cleaning rates and knew he was drumming up more business.

"Marco. You know Mr. Tabouleh?" He turned to the swarthy older man, smothering his barstool with his generous bottom.

"Don't think I know you." I extended a hand. "Nice to meet you. Enjoying the show?"

"Oh, very much, indeed. And the company is even better." He beamed at Luke.

"Mr. Tabouleh owns a couple of apartment buildings and needs a cleaning service. I told him this was his lucky day." Luke smiled at me and I knew that once he turned that smile on Tabouleh, the poor man would be signing a lifetime contract with Luke's company.

* * *

Luke left well before closing and I stuck around to help Anton. By the time I started walking home it was past three. Keeping hours like this was bound to show up in my face sooner or later. But I didn't always have a choice.

When I reached Broad, my cell phone rang. I fished it out of my jacket pocket and glanced at the screen. It said: "Restricted."

"Fontana."

"This is… Jared." His voice was soft, the words tentative.

"Jared! Where are you? Are you all right? I've been looking for you. Niko is going nuts." I wanted to jump through the phone and pull him out.

"I'm all right," he said, his voice quavered.

"Where are you? I'll come get you. Stay put and don't worry."

"I'm not worried, Marco. But you've got to stop looking for me."

"What are you talking about?"

"Just what I said. Don't look for me. I'm safe. I don't want to be found."

"Look, Jared, it's not just about you." I was angry. Sure I was happy he was safe, if he really was, but if he knew something, I was obligated to find out what. I wasn't about to give up. "Niko is crazy with worry and so's Tony. Besides which, I need to talk with you. You can help put a killer away. Think about it."

"I have. That's why I don't want to be found." He sounded scared but resolute. "I'll be in big trouble if I say anything to you." He paused. I thought the call had been dropped.

"Hello? Jared?"

"In a few days I'll be out of the city altogether. I'm leaving." There were tears in his words. "You're not the only one who wants me. I can't let them get to me. You've got to stop looking. You understand?"

"No. No, I don't understand. People are dead. You might be able to help catch a killer. You're being selfish." I regretted talking to him this way. I'm sure Scanlan had treated him badly and I didn't want to add to that. But I needed him. Maybe this was the exact wrong way to go about it but being reasonable hadn't worked.

"Maybe I am selfish but that's because I've gotta look out for myself. No one else does. You've gotta stop looking for me. They'll find me if you keep looking. You know it's true."

"Just tell me if you're all right."

"I'm fine. I said I was safe. No one's gonna find me and then I'm leaving town."

"Who are you with?"

"I'm st… very clever. You're a smart guy, Fontana." He sighed. "But I'm not telling you. I'm fine and I don't want to be found."

"But… you've got to let me…"

"You'll hear from me."

Then the phone went dead.

Chapter 31

I decided on casually dressy for my meeting with the Cardinal. I probably wanted to impress Tad with my civility more than I wanted to show the Cardinal any deference. I harbored no innate respect for that Prince of the Church. Not this Italian. Galante was just a man with a title and a red sash. On the other hand, my Aunt Yolanda would be scandalized if I was anything less than respectful, on the surface. Italians are supposed to know how to hold their enemies close and keep them off guard.

Settling on regulation black slacks and a blue, rayon, CabanaNick shirt, I looked myself in the mirror and saw an off duty cop. Sleek, neat, up-to-date. But a cop. Maybe the Cardinal would get a subliminal message from my clothing choice. Nah, he was too cagey for that.

I fished my best leather jacket out of the hall closet and stuffed my notepad in the pocket along with two pens. I waltzed out of the apartment and headed for the elevators. Before long I was waving to Carlos in the lobby.

"Got you working on Saturday, Carlos?" I watched him come to life.

"Buildin' up some comp time, man. Holidays are comin' and I want some time off," he answered. "Where you off to all dressed up?" His deep brown eyes sparkled with a happiness I envied.

"Got a meeting with the Cardinal," I said.

Carlos laughed as if he thought I was joking. "Yeah, kiss his ring for me, man." He chuckled as I went out the door.

Tell the truth and they don't believe you. Tell a lie and they eat it up.

The Marriott was a few blocks away. It was cloudy and colder this morning but the October chill was filled with the promise of holidays and cozy times. The sky, though, was overcast with the potential for colder weather and it seemed to signal danger. There was something exciting in never knowing what to expect. I walked to Market Street and the Marriott's blocky structure loomed up ahead. Its pink granite exterior gave it a pale washed-out appearance.

I was to meet Tad under the faux rotunda in the middle of the quietly elegant lobby. Plants and leather seating made a quiet oasis. I sank into one of the chairs and reviewed my questions for Galante while I waited. I'd have to approach things carefully if I wanted him to talk. I needed information on Wren and Scanlan particularly, then I could launch into his association with Cody and the plotters.

Galante was at the hotel speaking to a national conference of mayors about the fate of big city parochial schools. Then he was scheduled to meet with Philly's mayor and explain the closing of several city schools. The Cardinal was presiding over the downsizing of inner city Catholic education. But he did it with a cheerfully resigned attitude. The Church's philosophy of periodic retrenchment meant survival which meant they'd live to expand another day.

I had a lot to ask but I knew he'd cut me off at the knees once I started down Conspiracy Road and John Paul the First. But I'd have to ask. It might help with the case or it could just help Hollister know whether Brandt had really been on the right track. If he was, then even someone like Galante could be a suspect in the Pope's murder. Odds were Galante had been just another clerical flunky assigned to work for an American Cardinal in Rome, the holy grail for all new priests. Living and working in the bosom of the Vatican was the ideal. If you got assigned to an important Cardinal, all the better.

Do your job well, do as you were told, kiss the right hierarchical butts, and you'd be on a career path that ultimately led to the red hat. That had apparently been Galante's course. He'd worked for Cody, had done a good job and kept moving up. He'd put himself on the path to that brand new red hat he was finally awarded. I wondered if Tad wanted that same career path? He didn't strike me as the ambitious, be-a-cardinal-at-any-cost type. It was difficult picturing Tad, tall, blond, tan, and windblown, dressed in the robes of a Cardinal. But Galante was grooming him for just that.

A stray thought made me sit straight up in my chair. Imagining myself in bed with a priest... a monsignor who might easily become a cardinal. This was like nothing I'd ever envisioned doing. Me and the Church in bed together? Easier to imagine myself as a nun. But Tad had been flirty with me and that's often the first signpost on the way to the land of Between the Sheets.

I could hear my Aunt Yolanda wailing, "Scandaloso!" Of course, she'd want to know every detail of the dirty deed.

Before I thought another lascivious thought, Tad stood in front of me. From where I sat he looked like a blond colossus towering over my comfortable leather chair. I was still a bit tired from the night before and his presence had a dreamlike quality. For a moment I wasn't sure he was real.

"I see you made it." He smiled nervously.

"Disappointed?"

"Just nervous about your meeting," he said.

"It's not everyday I get to grill a Cardinal."

"Your jokes will backfire one day, Marco," Tad said. "Unless you really do want to make my life difficult."

"That's not what I want," I said. Of course, if I had to grill the old man, I'd grill him nice and slow. If it meant getting to the bottom of things, I'd grill anybody. But Tad had stuck his neck out getting me face time with Galante. I didn't want to make trouble for him but I had the case to think about.

"There's a conference room off the lobby. I told him I'd have you there when he finishes with the Mayor." He beckoned me to follow.

"How's that meeting going?"

"So far, so good. No arguments," Tad said.

"Maybe Galante will be in a good mood," I said.

"Don't expect too much. If he thinks you're trying to blindside him, he won't cooperate."

"Me? Blindside someone." I feigned shock. "That's not me at all."

"Yeah, well, I don't know you that well, now do I?"

"That's easy to fix." I smiled at him as we walked.

"I haven't had a chance to read those files you sent."

"I was hoping you'd get to them soon. It could help." I looked at him and he seemed genuinely sorry. "But I know you're a busy man."

"I've got some free time coming up, Marco. I'll get to the files in a day or so. There's quite a lot of them. But I'll do it. That's a promise."

"It's a lot to ask, I know. I'll treat you to dinner as a thank you. Deal?"

"Deal," Tad said coming to a stop. "Here we are." He pushed open a door.

The windowless pastel green room had several paintings of pastoral scenes on the walls. The conference table was made of honey-colored wood and on it was a tray with bottled water and several glasses.

"Do me one favor." He smiled mischievously.

"What's that?"

"I know this doesn't fit your personal views or anything, but as a favor to me…" He teased with a look.

"What? You want me to kiss his ring?"

"Nothing like that. Well, something like that. Could you address him as 'Your Eminence'? It'll get you off on the right foot with him. Make him happy and you'll get to ask your questions."

Tad was matter of fact and not apprehensive, but I detected a note of something other than procedural advice in what he'd said. As if my potential lack of cooperation in even a small detail could have consequences.

"Just remember, I'm doing it for you." I smiled. "And for my Aunt Yolanda. She called to make sure I behaved myself around you guys. She knows all about this case."

"Thanks for understanding," he said. "And I haven't forgotten about reading the documents."

I sat facing the door, which Tad closed quietly behind him, and the silence felt good. I needed to gather my thoughts. I had memorized details of the supposed plot against John Paul the First, and knew all the key players. I wanted to see what Galante knew or how he might slip up in pretending not to know. If he allowed me to get that far. The thoughts and facts swirled through my head and I closed my eyes.

Before long there was a soft knock at the door. I stood, shaking off the sleepiness which had begun to spin its web around me.

Tad entered followed by Galante. The squat, grandfather of a man filled the room with his presence, obviously used to being the center of attention. But there was something contradictory about him. The genial grandfather, smiling, laughing, and making you feel good was the first impression he gave. He brightened the room with that persona. At the same time, however, there was an air of condescension about him, as if he were deigning to do something for the little people. That contradiction swirled about him like dust motes.

The peaceful silence was shattered by the disturbing sound of the Cardinal's presence.

Today he dressed in a plain black clerical suit, Roman collar, with not a hint of scarlet. The severe cut of the suit presented an incongruous contrast with his plump, avuncular face and brilliant white hair.

Tad followed him, not obsequiously but not with the absolute confidence I'd seen in him earlier.

"You've met, I know, but this time I'll make it formal.… Allow me to introduce His Eminence Carlo Cardinal Galante."

I extended my hand and inclined my head slightly, as much deference as I was willing to offer.

"Your Eminence," I said. It nearly stuck in my throat but I said it.

"Your Eminence, this is Mr. Marco Fontana."

"Good to see you again." He shook my hand. His pudgy hand had the firm grip I remembered from that day in Tad's office. He held on just long enough to show this was a favor he was doing and not an obligation.

"I don't know about you, Mr. Fontana, but I've got to sit. The knee surgery was successful but they didn't tell me how painful it would be." His smile was broad and warm, but didn't make it to his eyes.

He placed a hand at my back gently pointing me to a chair.

"Please have a seat, Mr. Fontana." He turned to Tad, nodded and said only, "Monsignor."

At which point, Tad, his face solemn, gave a curt bow and left the room, pulling the door shut. I imagined him standing, like a sentry, outside.

Galante, favoring his right leg, sat delicately in one of the chairs and exhaled a sigh of relief.

"So much better. Now, young man, what can I do for you? I confess I don't have a lot of time but Tad… the Monsignor… is a wonderful assistant and asked that I speak with you. He's like my right arm, really. So, when he asks a favor, which is rare, how can I refuse? You have a powerful ally in him, Mr. Fontana." The smile again. But there was a disingenuous quality behind that smile.

"He speaks of you in glowing terms, Your Eminence," I said. "He's a compassionate man. He'd like to see this situation resolved so people can get on with their lives."

"The monsignor has a compassionate nature," he said, as if it were an unfortunate flaw. "He feels for the people he ministers to and that's not a bad thing for a priest." He delivered the line without much conviction.

"He's lucky to have you as a patron. Also not a bad thing for a priest. You're a real power in the Church from what I understand, and a close advisor to the Pope." These guys are human, too, and love to think their importance is impressive to others. "My Aunt Yolanda will be thrilled to hear I had a personal meeting with you."

"Please give her my regards." His smile was not as broad or as warm. "Flattery aside, I'm sure you didn't ask for this meeting so you could impress your aunt." Now, he was getting down to business and his persona tweaked itself ever so gently to the darker side of his personality. He glanced at his wristwatch.

"That's right. I didn't." I produced my notebook, opened it, and took out a pen.

"I understand you wish to discuss the unfortunate death of Mr. Brandt. Again," he emphasized the last word. Picking up one of the bottles of water, he offered it to me. I declined. He twisted off the cap and poured himself a glass. "I don't think I can add anything to what I've already said. But ask your questions. Let's get this out of the way."

"I've heard you dismissed Mr. Brandt's work as just so much nonsense."

"Not nonsense." He sipped some water. "Dangerous nonsense. His work is meant to further erode the confidence people have in the Church. After the unfortunate recent scandals, all the Church needs is some lunatic theory being given credence."

"You didn't believe Brandt when he claimed to have new, more damning evidence?"

"I gave his work the attention it deserved. That is to say, none." Galante sipped more water.

"True. Why fan the flames of curiosity? That would only bring more attention to his accusations."

"Exactly!" Galante said. "I refused to be an unwitting part of the promotional plan for his books."

I made a show of flipping through some pages in my notebook.

"Did you know you were mentioned in the latest documents? The ones he claimed had new information."

I watched the Cardinal's face, his eyes, his body language. There was a slight and passing reaction. His eyes shifted, he pulled himself in defensively, ready for battle.

"I can't imagine why, but I can't say I'm surprised."

Now that was a lie. The signs were there in his eyes. Of course he was surprised. I'm certain he knew he was listed as a clerical functionary. But the mere appearance of his name as a small time flunky for one of the conspirators proved nothing. And he knew, that, too. Which made his reaction more interesting.

"So you had some notion that your name might come up in documents? Is that why you aren't surprised?"

"Not at all, Mr. Fontana. I am not surprised because Brandt searched for excuses to trap anyone and everyone in the snare he set. It didn't matter to him who he smeared. His real target was the Church itself, not any one individual or group. Don't you see?"

"You're familiar with Seamus Scanlan?"

"He works for us. Beyond that, I have no association with him."

"You've never spoken with him about his work?"

"I'll say this, Mr. Scanlan does his work well. What he does on his own time, is his own business. He's not a man I care to know very well."

"Did you know a John Wren or a John Navarro?"

"Wren? Mr. Wren works in Public Relations for us."

"John Wren, not Peter. John worked in Rome assigned to Cardinal Villot at the same time you were there."

"I don't recall." Galante's eyes drew down to a squint. He tried his best to conceal his lies. "Peter does have a brother, John, who is a bishop in some diocese in Montana or Utah or somewhere like that. Whether he was in Rome, I have no idea."

"What about John Navarro? Attached to Silvio Calvino. At exactly the same time as you and Wren."

"No recollection. Mr. Fontana, your questions make no sense. What have these men to do with Brandt's death?"

"You had a pretty heady assignment as a young priest." I said tacking away from my other direction.

"Heady? Not really. My assignment to Rome was the same opportunity given to many seminarians and newly ordained priests."

"You're being modest, Eminence." I smiled and took a bottle of water from the tray. "In Rome, you were assigned to Cardinal Cody of Chicago."

"For the few times he visited. It wasn't a permanent assistantship. I had other duties."

"But you had to stick with the Cardinal whenever he was in Rome?"

"I don't see what this has to do with anything."

"Cody was kind of controversial, if I remember correctly." I should remember since I'd just read a lot about him in Brandt's documents and on the Internet. "The man had money problems, was involved with the Vatican Bank, had what seemed to be a mistress, and was asked several times to resign. He was even reported to be on a list of Cardinals the new Pope, John Paul the First, was going to force to step down."

"Rumor and hearsay," Galante snapped without looking at me. "The man was controversial because he demanded a lot of those who worked under him. He saw to it that things got done. Men of action, like Cardinal Cody, are often disliked, even despised. But that doesn't mean they…" He paused, then glanced at me. It felt to me as if he thought he'd said more than he wanted to.

"You worked for him in Rome at the time John Paul the First was elected and died in office. Is that right?"

"All right. And that proves...?"

"That you were associated with Cardinal Cody when he and a group of others within the Church, like Cardinal Villot and Bishop Martuzzi, met to plot the Pope's death."

"This is appalling." He glared at me. "I think, Mr. Fontana," he said and began, with some effort, to lift himself out of his chair. "I think, this interview..."

"They met at the Bridge of Four Heads. Do you recall that name?"

"I recall nothing of which you are speaking." He stood and grimaced with pain. "I've had enough of your vile insinuations. This interview is over."

Like hell. I thumbed through my notebook.

"The Bridge of Four Heads, Eminence, do you recall that? Did you assist Cody at those meetings?"

"Paranoid, disgusting fantasy. What has this got to do with alleviating the grief of Brandt's friends? What good can come of your questions?"

He straightened his back and stared at me imperiously. The grandfatherly image was submerged and he became a formidably angry and powerful man. His smile was replaced by a thin-lipped expression of disdain. The warmth he'd radiated on his entrance had become an icy wall of contempt.

"Your confirmation that these men plotted to kill a pope would let Hollister know Brandt's death had some meaning. That his search for the truth wasn't in vain."

The Cardinal peered at me. He twisted his episcopal ring a few times, then folded his hands.

"I cannot confirm what I do not know. I cannot admit that lies are truth just so someone will feel comforted. Lies and the clouded judgment of a vengeful man are what Brandt has left his loved ones. I won't be complicit in continuing his deceitful fantasy."

"You were there, Your Eminence. You knew those men. You watched them operate. You must have had some suspicions at the time."

"I have no knowledge of plots. Nor am I aware of anyone who does."

"Did you attend any of those meetings yourself? Is that why you're afraid to answer?"

He raged silently. His face took on a rosy hue as his fierce gaze raked the room. He wanted to leave, anyone could see that, yet he couldn't make the move.

"How dare you? How dare you malign my good name and that of others? What right have you?"

"You're familiar with details of the plot those men devised. Isn't that right, Your Eminence?" I pushed.

"You know nothing. Nothing!" He raised his voice and it was like the rumble of thunder. The storm was yet to break.

"I have documents. They mention you. In detail. I know more than you think." Which is what I wanted him to think even though he was only peripherally mentioned. I needed to get under his skin.

"You couldn't possibly have anything because there is nothing!" He bellowed like a wounded bull. "There is nothing to know. No plots were devised. No one was murdered." He pounded a fist on the table and the glasses jumped and clinked as if they'd been intimidated.

I held his stare.

He regained control in seconds, a huge feat considering his shuddering rage. The transformation was something to watch. Once again calm, Galante peered at me, his lips formed a mockery of a smile.

"I'm sorry for you, Mr. Fontana." He turned toward the door. "I'm even sorrier for Hollister. He lived a lie even before he met Brandt. That lie was compounded because he felt he'd been rejected and abandoned by his Church. In truth, the Church never hurt him. He rejected the Church, he abandoned his vows. When he met someone who had presence and a connection to the media, Hollister did his saddest, dirtiest work. He filled Brandt's head with distorted ideas, connected him to deluded individuals who lived only to ruin the lives of others. He forced Brandt down the road which got him killed. Now he seeks comfort." He paused, turned toward me. "I can't give him any. He ruined his life and that of Brandt. The hell he created for himself will have to be his only comfort now."

"Is that why you wanted Brandt silenced? Because he might ruin your life?"

"I wanted no such thing." Galante fumed silently.

"Is that it, Your Eminence? Were you afraid of losing everything? Losing your reputation. Maybe even losing that shot you imagine you have to become the next Pope."

"I could no more silence anyone, than I can keep you from asking questions, Mr. Fontana. And if you knew anything about my life, you would know how wrong you are."

"I know that some men never have enough power or control. Capturing high office is what they live for. An office like the papacy, for instance."

"One does not choose the papacy. You don't set your sights on it as if it's some prize to collect. God chooses His servants. The Holy Spirit moves a conclave to decide. I could never get myself elected, no one can. The selection is in greater hands than ours."

I knew this was false. The Papacy was as political as the Presidency. Men campaigned, made deals, and voted.

"But you did want Brandt stopped. You wanted him and his work to go away."

Galante snorted his contempt, opened the door and stormed out, hobbling along with his painful knees faster than I imagined he could. I saw Tad trailing behind Galante, his off-kilter stride emphasized by his speed. He never turned to look back at me.

I felt sorry for Tad. He'd done me a favor and I'd gotten under Galante's skin. I'd have to make it up to him somehow. If he'd even talk to me after this.

Chapter 32

Stepping out of the Marriott, I wondered if Tad was waiting to whack me for turning his boss into a raving maniac. I wouldn't blame him. I'd really ticked off the Cardinal who would, no doubt, come down on Tad.

Galante nearly slipped up. He said more in what he didn't say about the plotters. He'd also confirmed that John Wren was connected to Peter. It was clear he didn't like Scanlan but that could just have been an act. The interview didn't get me as far as I'd have liked.

Navarro and Quinn were still on my list. But what I needed to do was find Jared and Scanlan.

I couldn't drop my hunch that Scanlan was behind things. I wasn't buying Galante's story about not knowing Scanlan. He was too in control not to know him. That made me think there was something going on that might include Galante. Maybe he took advantage of his relationship with Scanlan. Connecting the Cardinal and Scanlan wasn't much of a stretch. It was all circumstantial but I couldn't escape connecting the two in my mind. Marginally linking them was easy. Putting them together as co-conspirators and figuring out how they did it would be the hard part.

Both had a motive for wanting Brandt out of the way.

Scanlan had lost Jared to Brandt and Scanlan didn't like to lose or seem weak. I had no doubt he'd do what he had to in order to keep what he assumed was his.

Galante wanted Brandt silenced to avoid any hint of scandal, even an off the wall scandal few people believed. Talking to the Cardinal reinforced my impression of him as the kind of man who tightly controlled every aspect of his public image. He enjoyed being known as the American Pope and the shoo-in as successor to the current Pope.

But violence made no sense in Galante's case. It would have served his purposes equally well to neutralize Brandt's work by discrediting him so thoroughly no one would take him seriously. I had a difficult time believing he would want Brandt murdered to solve his problems. The Cardinal was an ambitious man who was also careful and too smart to be sloppy.

Compelling as the idea of a connection between Galante and Scanlan was, there was nothing solid binding them together. Not yet. Finding Scanlan would help.

The key to Scanlan was Jared and the path to Jared was through Colt. All I had to do was find Colt.

* * *

The café at Bubbles bustled at lunchtime but Dolph always had a table for me at the back. He knew I liked privacy in case I had business to do. Today I just needed time to think.

The place was crowded and I recognized a few faces I knew. I waved, winked, and nodded hellos to them then pretended to concentrate on my menu. I already knew what I'd order. Bubble's kitchen makes the best cheesesteaks outside of South Philly and I was in the mood for the greasy mess that tasted like heaven. It came with salty shoestring fries which I needed like a hole in the head. Add a Coke and you've got a perfect coronary confection but one that sends your taste buds into overdrive. When the waiter arrived, that's just what I ordered.

It meant spending more time on the treadmill, but I needed comfort food. The case made me feel like I was using a teaspoon to dig a hole in a concrete slab.

"Look who's here. Taking a break from harassing innocent people?" The voice over my shoulder sounded familiar.

I turned to see Franny Clifford. Slightly subdued today, wearing a blue blazer with a lime green vest sweater underneath and loud plaid pants. The lack of sleep was evident on his puffy, pasty face. He reeked of cheap cologne.

"Even us evil guys gotta eat, Franny," I said. "Harassing the innocent takes energy."

His cackling laugh drilled right through me.

"Mind if I join you?" he asked. "Only for a moment. Got a hot date with a young thing. A rare occasion for me these days. Dates are no doubt nothing special for you."

"I wouldn't say that," I answered and waved him to the seat opposite. "After the last time we met, I didn't think you'd want to give me the time of day."

"Taking to a hunk like you is good for my image," he said, scouring the crowd for his date. "Besides, you've got the people at the Archdiocese buzzing. Somebody even said you were gunning for the Cardinal."

He stared at me with his watery eyes, as if trying to read my thoughts.

"Are you? After the Cardinal, I mean."

"I don't see it's any of your business."

"You're right. But I like to know what's going on. It comes in handy."

"Like when you deal with Scanlan?"

"Deal with… are you kidding me?" He made an extravagant gesture with his hand. "I would never be caught dead with that man."

"He's that bad?"

"Do you know," Clifford said, leaning in closer, "do you know he goes to that bar… Stella's?"

"It's a wonder they allow him to work at the Archdiocese," I coaxed.

"He's got protectors."

"You said he worked for Wren."

"He's shadowy. I don't really know what he does for Wren. I just know he's on the payroll."

"How can a guy like Scanlan come and go as he pleases? Can they afford to pay a guy for doing nothing?"

"Oh, honey, I don't think he does nothing. I think he does a whole lot of something. I just don't know what that is. Wren's fierce about him. Won't let anyone even think about criticizing the man." He fidgeted and kept scanning for his date's arrival. "He's got free rein in the office."

"Does Scanlan meet with the Cardinal often?"

"Maybe." He became more wary. "Still full of questions, aren't you? But I guess that's what private eyes do. Ask questions. People like me get pulled into your pretty brown eyes and we'll answer anything you ask."

"Not you. You're way too smart for that."

"You bet I am, mister pretty boy detective."

"So?"

"You want me to vacate?" Clifford huffed.

"Not at all."

The waiter brought my lunch.

"Be right back with the fries," he said and moved off.

"You're going to eat that?" Clifford's eyes went wide. His mouth worked as if he were salivating at the thought of gobbling a cheesesteak. He licked his lips. "It's a cholesterol nightmare. How can you do that to your beautiful body? You need someone like me to take care of you. I'd see to it you eat right."

"You'd cook for me?"

"Didn't say I'd cook. I said I'd see to it you ate right."

"Aw, and I was just getting all warm inside."

"Sarcasm never makes a pretty boy prettier."

"You never did answer my question about Scanlan and the Cardinal. I guess I'm not all that pretty if I can't squeeze an answer out of you."

"You can squeeze all kinds of things outta me. But you just want information. I'm old enough and wise enough to know that."

"Am I gonna get the information?"

"Like I said, I don't know all his comings and goings."

"You're on top of everything at the office. You help keep that place humming and you know everything everybody does. Am I right?"

"I know what I know. True."

"So what about Scanlan?"

"Scanlan pretty much sees whoever he wants to see whenever he wants to see them. I'll bet Scanlan can even see the Cardinal without a problem."

"What gives a guy that much juice?"

"If I knew, hon, I'd be dining with the Cardinal, myself. I know plenty, but Scanlan, he's like the wind."

"Tell me about it."

"Oh! There he is…." Clifford stood and waved wildly at someone who'd just come through the door.

"Have fun, Franny."

"Call me, sometime." He blew a kiss at me as he left.

The waiter dropped off my fries. But before I had a chance to bite into my cheesesteak, Anton sat down across from me.

"I see you're back on your health food kick," Anton quipped.

"Like someone just told me, 'Sarcasm doesn't make a pretty boy prettier.' And this is the first cheesesteak I've had in two or three months." I popped a french fry into my mouth for emphasis. "What're you doing here so early?"

"It's not that early and we've got a special show tonight. Remember? Or have you totally forgotten those of us toiling in the fleshpots of the city?"

"Tonight Cal and Bruno are sharing the spotlight. See, I haven't forgotten."

"Right, but it's also Top Cheeks night and I've got a lot to get ready. Not that you should be concerned or anything. I have it all under control."

"As I knew you would." I ate some of the sandwich, popped a few more fries, and swilled some Coke. My taste buds were singing. "Which dancers are scheduled?"

"Mostly the bigger names. More tips on Top Cheeks nights. Too bad we can't let them show more than their cheeks."

"The Liquor Control Board would be delighted to slap us with numerous citations and close down the place for a few days. Stan wouldn't be happy."

"I know." Anton sighed. "Just letting you know everything's under control."

"I was gonna come up after clogging my arteries. How'd you know I was here?"

"Word gets around when the boss strides into town. You get noticed," Anton peered at me as if he hadn't seen me in ages. "Will you be here tonight?" There was a wistful quality in his voice.

"Sure. If you don't need me now I'll go home and be back at showtime."

Before he responded, his cell phone rang.

"It's marked 'Restricted' I hate that." He tapped the screen. "Hello?" He paused, listening. His face contorted into a look of pain or fear or both. "Nando? Nando! Are you all right?... What are... Are you crying?... Nando, talk to me."

"Let me listen in." I grabbed his hand and placed my head next to his.

"I'm sorry..." It was Nando's voice. He was sniffling. "Anton... I wanna... be there... for the show... but...I can't... not right now." That teary voice didn't sound sincere.

"Nando! This is Marco." I gently pulled the phone from Anton's hand.

"Marco? It's you? I thought... but... Anton..."

"I'm with Anton. Where are you Nando? I can help. I can come get you."

"No!" He cleared his throat. "No, it's not necessary. I am all right... No one hurts me... We... I will be back... yes, some time...I will be back."

"Are you being held against your will?"

Silence. A few sniffles and a cough. I heard other sounds in the background. Distinctive sounds.

"Nando?"

"I'm all right. I must go now. Tell... Anton... I wanna perform... I am happy at Bubbles... I..."

"Then let me come get you, Nando." I soaked up the background sounds.

He sobbed a few times and the phone went dead.

"I told you, Marco. He's in trouble. It's Kent. Your protégé with the gun. Damn it, Marco. When you find him, I'll beat him to a pulp."

"Nando was hiding something, Anton."

"Sure he was hiding something!" Anton snapped. "He's being held against his will and that gun-crazy kid won't let him tell you where he is."

"No. He wasn't being truthful. That much was in his voice. Something's not right."

"That's a goddamn understatement," Anton said. "I'm going upstairs." He left without looking back.

I had to let him cool down. No use running after him right then.

My cheesesteak was soggy and the fries were cold. I didn't have much of an appetite left anyway. Nando's call was on my mind. And it wasn't the fact that he'd been lying about something.

There were sounds in the background. Familiar sounds. Very familiar. Identifying them and putting them all together might help locate Nando.

Chapter 33

“We’ve gotta limit the crowd. Firecode regulations,” Stan complained.

Bubbles was packed to overflowing and Stan paced the hall outside my office. Top Cheeks Night was always a crowd pleaser but tonight there were lines out the door.

“Don’t worry, Stan. Your guys’ll keep a line outside. As people leave, we let people in.” I thumped him lightly on the shoulder. “Relax. It’s good for business.”

“Yeah, yeah.” Stan’s voice trailed off as he went down the stairs.

My closet of an office was my only refuge and muffled the music and noise. I enjoyed the almost-quiet before I plunged into hosting the contest.

My workout at the gym earlier left me feeling sore but good. That half-eaten cheesesteak kept me on the treadmill an extra forty-five minutes. At least Grant, my trainer, had been easy on me, claiming I’d surpassed his goals.

“No rest for the wicked,” Anton said as he entered the office. “You’ve got to get down there. Get somebody to take names of potential contestants, and tell Bruno and Cal your plans.”

I kept my eyes closed and let his words wash over me. It was kind of nice letting him arrange the schedule. After the past few days, it was like a mini-vacation.

"You're listening, right? Your eyes are closed but I know you're listening."

"I have heard your every word, sir and I shall obey." I teased. "Of course I'm listening. So, tell me again what you just said."

I waited for his reaction which I saw building on his face.

"Just kidding. I'll get down there now. The contest starts in fifteen, right?"

"Right," Anton said and blocked my way. "Are you all right?" He placed a hand against my cheek. It sent a shiver through me and I wanted to kiss him.

So, I did. And he didn't object. In fact, he leaned into me and kissed me so fiercely I wondered if something was wrong. I let that thought die as I backed Anton to the wall and nuzzled his neck.

"Y-you've… got to get downstairs… now… Marco." He was breathing heavily as he pulled away but it felt like he wanted to stay right where he was. I know I did. We'd been down this path before. He'd let it go so far and no further.

"You're beautiful. You know that?"

"Almost showtime," he said, avoiding my eyes.

Crowd noises and music filtered up the steps as I moved to the main floor. There was an anticipatory thrum in the air. Everyone waited for the show to begin. I heard footsteps on the stairs behind me and turned to see Bruno and Cal, dressed in military fatigues, clomping down the steps in army boots.

"Ready for your big night?"

"Good one, Fontana," Bruno said. "The big night belongs to all the amateur asses that are gonna get exposed. Not us."

"But they won't be collecting the tips. You will."

"I hope so," Cal said. "I saw a new leather jacket that I have to have."

"It'll be a good night. You guys'll be on in five."

"We're ready," Bruno growled.

Instead of hitting the main floor, we turned down a hall to reach the stage door. I snatched the mike from its stand, took a deep breath, and stepped through the tinsel curtain.

The crowd erupted in cheers, applause, whistles, and catcalls.

"Ready for Top Cheeks?"

Cheers, whistles, hoots.

I recited rules and procedure. Contestants, otherwise known as audience volunteers, would come to the stage and, behind a specially made curtain, expose their bare ass to the crowd through a convenient opening. The crowd would, through applause and cheers, choose the top five. Through more applause they'd choose first to fifth places. But before those results were revealed, three lucky patrons would come to the stage and, after a closer inspection, try matching asses with the faces of their owners.

At the end, the winners would be announced, the top five would flash their faces and their asses, just to show whose was whose. Prizes would be distributed and more dancers would come out to continue the show.

It was simple, fun, and relatively cheap to produce. Often the most unlikely people volunteered along with some of the hottest guys. Sometimes audiences chose surprising winners and a lot of hotties went home disappointed. Mostly, everyone had a great time.

"Travis, the cute guy in the orange thong, will be circulating throughout the bar collecting names of people who want to put their ass on the line."

I noticed a few guys pushing their friends to sign up.

"Give him your name, and yes, you can use a phony name, then walk out that door, up the hall, and come backstage. We'll take care of your cheeks from there on out.

"When you gonna show your buns, Marco?" Someone shouted from way at the back.

"Play nice, boys, and you never know," I winked.

"C'mon. We wanna see the boss! We wanna see the boss!" Others joined the original guy in his chant.

I held up my hands to quiet them.

"This is my night off, guys. Come on up and volunteer. I promise you never know what'll happen or what you'll see backstage!"

More cheers and suggestive catcalls.

"Let's get it started!" I bellowed. "To warm you up for what's to come, here's Bruuuunooooooo! and Caaaaaaaalllll! Give it up for Bruno and Cal."

The music thumped and pounded as Bruno and Cal burst through the tinsel in an obviously well choreographed act. They were good, bumping and grinding against one another. Whirling and stripping off their shirts at the same time. The fog machines at either side of the stage billowed soft white smoke that spotlights turned gold and pink.

Backstage, while Anton, Stan, and a couple of off-duty bartenders handled set-up, I watched the parade of nervous contestants enter. Some cute, some shy, some bold. One guy on overdrive began stripping off his pants until I told him to wait for the right time.

"Gonna take a spin around the floor and see what's going on," I said to Anton. I liked to mingle with the customers and keep an eye on things. The bouncers were good but it never hurt to have an extra set of eyes on the crowd. Which made me think about Kent.

"We'll start as soon as we have fifteen or twenty contestants," Anton called out.

"I'll be back." I walked into the bar.

Music pounded through my chest. Bruno and Cal transfixed the men. Customers' faces were tilted upward, their eyes on him only. Patrons came in all shapes and sizes, ages, and colors. Everyone loves a stripper. Business was good.

"Marco." Someone grabbed my arm.

I turned and saw Grady, one of the regulars. Grady was in Bubbles almost every night. Middle-aged, with salt-and-pepper hair, his refined look said money. But his eyes said loneliness and that trumped money every time.

"Grady. Everything cool?"

"I just want to thank you. You've made this place a thousand times better than it was before you arrived with your group."

"I appreciate that, Grady." I signaled the bartender to give him a free drink by placing a shot glass I'd snatched from the bar upside down in front of Grady.

"I really enjoy your guys and I'd love to treat the whole group, and you, of course, to dinner some time."

"We'd be delighted, Grady. Let's talk after the show. I've gotta MC."

"You should do more than that, Marco." Grady winked.

I made my way around the entire bar, trading greetings and jokes with the men. They were a great bunch of guys, and they were generous with my boys.

On the way back around, I spotted a guy with a tattoo running up his neck and onto his face. A lizard tattoo, tongue flicking onto the guy's cheek. Yes!

Colt! Just the way Beto had described him. I needed to talk to him. I glanced around. Bruno and Cal, stripped to their g-strings, and finished rounding the bar, were on their way to the stage. My cue to get back there. But I couldn't let Colt get away. And there was no time to tell Anton.

Clusters of people obstructed my view of Colt for a moment. Fixing him in my sights again, I moved quickly through the crowd. He turned and saw me. We locked stares for a moment. Short and swarthy, Colt's shaved head gave him a fierce look. As I moved closer, he whipped his head around searching for a way out.

Roughly knocking a few people to the side, Colt shoved his way to the door.

There was no time to apologize as I shoved aside the same startled guys.

He was fast. Faster than I expected in the tangle of customers. He slipped through one more knot of men and blasted through to the exit. I pushed myself, like a runner leading with his chest to break the tape at the end of a race.

I was out the door.

It had started raining and customers attempted to crowd themselves into Bubbles. I tried to figure which way Colt had run. I doubted he'd go to Stella's because he knew I'd track him there easily.

Taking a chance, I sprinted toward Broad as the rain pelted down. He could be heading anywhere. The rain soaked streets were nearly deserted. I glanced to the right and saw someone running about a block away. Had to be him. I took off, scattering raindrops. He was fast but I was just as good. When he turned onto Chestnut Street, I was barely a block behind. I pounded the ground trying to make up the distance. Chestnut was just ahead. I dodged traffic crossing Broad. Angry horns blared. Drivers shouted. I kept my eyes on Colt.

Half a block behind him, I saw him slow down. He turned right at Fifteenth Street making it appear he was going to Stella's. Instead, when he reached Market, he dashed west and kept going.

I guessed he was headed home.

I stayed on his tail all the way to Twentieth Street, where he turned, but it wasn't toward Arch. He ran south again and I followed. I was panting hard but he must have been tiring even faster. His pace was lots slower. But he kept going and I kept chasing.

Until Chestnut. Colt was just ahead. I'd have been on top of him a moment later. But when I hit the corner, a large man sheltering himself under an even larger black umbrella, appeared almost out of nowhere. I bowled right into him.

"What the fuck," he said as the air rushed out of him. The poor guy went ass over heels onto the wet pavement. His umbrella blew away and he lay sprawled on his back. I glanced from him to Colt who turned right and disappeared.

"I'm sorry." I reached out a hand to pull him up. I was still panting. "Are you... all right?"

"Winded, thanks to you," he said as he attempted to get to his feet with my help. "What's the rush, asshole?"

"Stay right there I'll get your umbrella." It was a few feet away, lodged in a storefront grate.

He stood there dripping and I handed him the umbrella.

"Thanks for nothing." He opened the umbrella and stalked off.

My clothes were soaked through. I felt chilled but I couldn't just turn around, not after all that running. I stood close to the building on the corner and thought.

Colt had turned right on a street up ahead. Sansom Street. The block he'd chosen held The Lockerroom bathhouse and Rudy's Place, a porn emporium. Both were well known and well used. Colt could have ducked into one of them. Getting lost in Rudy's dark rooms would be easy or he could get himself a room at the baths and keep the door shut. That was the same gambit used in the movie *The Ritz* and if I ever had to keep out of sight, it's what I'd do.

I decided Colt would opt for Rudy's Place. Entry was faster and cheaper, and the darkness afforded great cover.

When I got to the door, I fished fifteen bucks out of my wallet and entered feeling like a drowned rat. It wouldn't be easy finding Colt but the possibilities were interesting.

Sounds of feet shuffling across floors whispered in the dark. A cough punctuated the air now and then. My own shoes made a squishing sound from the rain water they'd soaked up.

Feeble lighting filled the place with heavy shadows and dark corners. Barely enough light filtered through to prevent someone tripping. It took my eyes a while to adjust. I nudged my way past people moving slowly from one area to another. The smell of disinfectant mixed with an odd stale odor assaulted my nose. Tinny eclectic music floated on the musty air. Layered beneath the music were moans and grunts some from the movie on screen, some from the booths where patrons met to satisfy cravings. With so many rooms to choose from, Colt could be anywhere. If he was actually in Rudy's Place. The screening room was a logical place to start. I could maneuver myself to the front then surreptitiously explore the faces lit by light reflected from the screen.

A muscled couple locked lips in the porn flick. Both were still dressed so the main event was yet to be and I felt the anticipation in the audience.

Some heads turned when they heard me enter. I was new meat. One or two stared until they saw me clearly enough to cruise me and beckon me to sit with them. I kept moving. A few more signals to sit were tossed my way as I eased myself forward. Finally reaching the front, I kept my movements subtle, not wanting to be overly intrusive. I had no desire to ruin anyone's evening. People needed to find what they craved where they could. I needed to find Colt.

None of the faces I saw belonged to Colt. A few heads bobbed up and down in some of the rows. When one or two surfaced for air, I saw none of them was Colt.

I decided to go to the next room. As I edged up the side of the screening room, a hand reached out and grabbed me right in the family jewels. I flinched but the guy didn't keep his hand there long.

"Honey, if you're that wet, it's time to go home," he whispered.

I almost laughed. There's nothing more deflating than laughter in these situations and I imagined a room full of flaccidly disappointed, yet still horny, men groaning in anger.

Stumbling my way to the basement playroom, I took a few steps down into darkness. The absolute murkiness existed for obvious reasons. You could be hooking up with Medusa but fantasize any hunk you wanted in the dark. Halfway down I rethought my strategy. Why was I going to fumble around in a lightless pit of men drugged with lust and hunger? Okay, maybe under other circumstances that might sound inviting. But this was not the optimal way to find Colt. There'd be no way I could pick him out in the dark madness which was the theme down there.

So, angering another man close behind me, I turned around and made my way back up the stairs to revise my plan.

I could wait outside and try to catch Colt when he left, if he left. That would probably lead to another chase down wet streets and my bones were already soggy. There wasn't much choice, I'd have to wait him out.

Colt was undoubtedly planning his next move. He'd have two choices. He could assume I'd left and then head for his apartment, unaware I had any idea where he lived. Or, if he was a smart boy, he'd hook up with somebody in Rudy's Place, convince the guy to take him home, and hide there. That'd be his most effective maneuver.

I turned to look back into the dark recesses of Rudy's Place and saw lonely shadows floating back and forth. My skin felt clammy under my wet clothing. The cold air would turn me blue as soon as I stepped out.

At least the rain had stopped. The air smelled fresh and clean. The asphalt glistened, reflecting streetlamps and neon signs. A few ragged gray clouds scudded across the sky as I searched for a vantage point that would keep me hidden. Up the street was an all night parking garage that would provide cover and good sightlines. I slogged over, shoes squishing water as I moved, and found a place behind a sign listing the lot's pricing.

After an hour, during which every part of my body went numb with cold, someone stepped out of Rudy's Place. A tall man, flaccid gray hair, nondescript clothes. Jerky, hesitant movements said he was nervous. He glanced around cautiously as if wondering who might catch him at his illicit games. Stepping onto the sidewalk he looked expectantly back at the door.

A moment later, Colt appeared. Clever boy. He was going home with someone to hide out for the night. Colt was smart but I was one up on him. I had him. He was as good as cooked.

Colt said something to the tall man who bristled at Colt's words. From this distance I heard only indistinct voices. Colt said something again. The man responded, his voice elevated. Colt raised his voice in response. They argued but all I heard was an angry murmur.

The man thrust out his hands like a soccer referee calling a foul. He seemed finished with Colt and turned his back on him. As the man walked away, he glanced over his shoulder at Colt. I suspected he wondered what he was missing by not taking Colt home. Far as I was concerned, he'd just dodged a bullet.

Colt, for his part, didn't waste time. He turned toward Twentieth and started walking. Obviously sure no one followed, he didn't walk fast. I wanted to keep him feeling secure, so I followed from a distance. I was pretty sure he'd go back to his apartment.

He wrapped his arms around himself, undoubtedly cold, and kept trudging. He looked like a man headed home. I wondered how I'd corner him back at his building. Even flop houses want things orderly and peaceful. They weren't going to like me throttling Colt in the lobby.

Best thing would be to get there first. I hustled to Market and found a cab.

"Let's see yer money," the cabbie said. I obviously looked like a deadbeat in my disheveled, wet clothes.

"Here." I pulled out my wallet and flashed a twenty which was four times more than the ride would cost. "Get me there in five minutes and I'll double it."

He turned the key in the ignition and roared off without starting the meter. He zipped me to the Arch Street residential hotel lots quicker than I could've run. I gave the man his money and exited the cab.

Sure that I looked the part, wet, wrinkled and downtrodden, of someone who belonged in a hotel like that, I approached the desk. I needed to work fast, having no idea when Colt would come through the door.

Pulling a fifty from my wallet, I tapped on the desk and cleared my throat to get the attention of the rather broad-bottomed woman concentrating on a computer terminal.

No response. She was probably tuned out.

"Excuse me." I slapped the desk.

"Hold your horses. Lemme finish this," she said. Her voice was familiar.

"I'm in kind of a hurry."

"Everybody's in a hurry." She turned around and I realized I knew her. Only it wasn't a her. It was Lotta Tush, one of the city's more popular drag performers. "You! I thought that voice was familiar, you bad boy."

"Lotta. This is fantastic."

"If you think I'm cheap and easy, you can just put that fifty away right now, Marco Fontana." She smiled and broke into a hearty laugh. "You were expecting someone else? Hmmmm?"

"I'm trying to catch a guy," I said and regretted the word choice.

"Who ain't, honey? But lemme tell you about the guy I caught last night."

"I wanna hear all about it, Lotta. I really do. But I'm on a case and I need to move before this guy comes through that door. I need to get the jump on him."

"Who you lookin' for, hon?"

"Guy named Colt. Short. Shaved head. Lizard tattoo."

"Oh, him." A look of displeasure planted itself on her face. "That little weasel keeps teasing me, sayin' he's gonna give me a freebie one of these days. Sayin' he's the best lay since who knows when? But he's just talk. And if you take my advice, you'll stay away, Marco."

"Trouble is, I need to talk to him. But he doesn't wanna talk to me. If you catch my drift."

"Who wouldn't wanna talk to you? Whattaya need?"

"His room number."

"Easy, he's in 201. That's it? You don't ask much, do you?"

"Well… if you have a pass key, that would save me havin' to break in…"

"Break... now, you're worryin' me. What's he done? Why do you gotta break into his place?"

"It's a long story and I've gotta get up there now."

She turned away, dipped her hand into a drawer and pulled out a key.

"You didn't get this from me. Understand?"

"You're a doll, Lotta." I took the key and left the fifty on the desk. It was the least I could do.

I took the stairs and found 201 down a threadbare hall badly in need of cleaning and a paint job. Gun in hand, I knocked at the door. I knew he wasn't there but someone else might be. I knocked again. No answer.

The door opened onto a dark, musty smelling room. Shades drawn over windows. The darkness was nearly complete except for light spilling in from the hall. I took a moment, allowing the hall light to give me a sense of the place. It was small, no more than a converted hotel room. A bed, a chair, a table, a nightstand. The bathroom off to the right.

Waiting inside behind the door, I knew he'd have nowhere to run once he entered. I'd be between him and his only escape route. I closed the door and waited in the silent darkness.

It wasn't a long wait.

He fumbled with the key, then entered as if he didn't have a care in the world. I remained still. He tossed the key onto the table. Then there was a click and soft yellow light filled the room. He stood stock still, as if he sensed something was not quite right. Turning around, he saw me and his face was a jumble of emotions. Anger, fear, sadness, frustration. He opened his mouth but no sound came out.

"Why'd you run, Colt?" I didn't move.

Silence. His lips worked but he said nothing.

"I didn't come here to hurt you," I said. "Unless you give me a reason..."

"I..." He began and I almost thought he'd be cooperative but I saw his face harden as he recovered from his initial shock. "I got nothin' to say, Fontana. I heard about you. You ain't gonna hurt anybody with that toy gun."

"Well then," I said and advanced on him. Colt backed up and fell into the chair. I moved in and loomed over him. The kid began to shiver and I knew it wasn't the cold.

"I don't know nothin' about what you want." He looked up at me, brown eyes signaling fear and anger, face marked with a few scars and a pimple here and there. I could see he was just a kid who'd grown up too fast. That made him hard on the outside. But I also saw the scared, soft, little kid crouching down, hiding inside.

"You know more than you think."

"I don't. I got nothin' at all. You can beat me or shoot me…"

"I was never gonna hurt you, kid. Why'd you run? Makes you look like you've got something to hide."

"They told me you was crazy. You was looking to pin some murder on anybody. They said you was askin' about me. So, when I saw you, I just thought, y'know, you was comin' after me for that murder."

"You didn't commit that murder, but I'll bet you know something."

"Knowin' is just as bad to the police. If I know something, they'll put me away just like I did the crime myself."

"Do you see a badge on me?"

"You don't work with the cops?"

"Put it this way, they don't work with me."

He stared at me. Despite his tough exterior, the tattoo, the scars, the mean expression he affected, he was a scared kid trying to cobble together a life the best way he knew how. It wasn't pretty and I didn't want to make things worse. But he knew something I needed to know.

"Somebody gave me your name."

"They told you I did the murder? I didn't. I don't get into that. He was lyin' about me. Honest."

"The kid who gave me your name wasn't lying either."

"How do you know that? People lie. That's what they do. Lie. They tell you one thing then they do somethin' else."

"People don't usually lie when they're dying, Colt. This kid died right in front of me. Nice-looking kid, red hair, baseball cap. Told me to find you, that you knew what was goin' on. You know him?"

"Little B, they... they said he was dead but I didn't believe them. Said he was shot. Little B should'a been careful. I told him..."

"Why would he put me onto you? He said you'd know things. You and somebody named Jared."

"Jared? He mentioned Jared? Little B?"

"Said you and Jared and somebody else knew what was goin' on. Do you?"

"Naw, man. I got nothin' for you." Fear edged his voice.

"Even if Little B spent his last minute on Earth telling me to find you? You can't even talk for him?"

"Who shot him?"

"You were gonna be my number one suspect. But I'm thinking there's gotta be somebody else. Whaddaya think?"

"I think my ass is dead if I say anything."

"Why's that? If you did nothing, like you said. You got nothin' to worry about. Am I right?"

He was silent.

"Of course, if you did something, people are gonna find out. One way or another. You ever hear about crime scene people and forensics? They can find you without even trying. A bit of hair, a little snot, something you brushed against. Anything. Crime's not what it used to be."

"I got nothin' to worry about then."

"The police aren't the only ones you're worried about. Am I right?"

"So?"

"I'm just sayin'. Like, if I went out and spread the word that you talked to me. Told me everything you knew. Whaddaya think these other people are gonna think?"

He kept his mouth shut.

"Maybe I'll find you shot one night, like Little B. Maybe you'll have enough air in you to spill one more name before you die, like he did."

"I didn't tell you nothin'. I didn't. How you gonna lie?"

"Easy. I put the word out that you ratted and it's done. I go home and have breakfast. Maybe you get to have breakfast, too, maybe you even get to have lunch. Maybe not. They'll find you."

"Shit, 'ats wrong, man. I thought you was a good guy. They said you was a pushover."

"They lied," I said. "So, I guess, since you got nothin' for me, I'll be goin' 'cause I got people to talk to." I stepped back without taking my eyes off him. He might be scared and just a hurt kid deep down, but I wasn't about to turn my back on him.

"All… all right. Whaddaya wanna know?"

"Everything. From Little B to you sittin' in that chair."

"Little B's dead because of me. I got him that job and he fucked up, man. Went overboard. He wasn't supposed to kill nobody. I don't know what happened."

"Start at the beginning, Colt. What job we talking about? How'd you find out about it?"

"That guy who they said was mugged. That was Little B doin' the work. He was just supposed to scare the guy. 'Ats all he was bein' paid for. Just throw a scare into the guy." Colt's leg jumped up and down in a nervous dance. He rubbed his chin.

"Who wanted the job done?"

"Some dude. I don't know. Found me in Stella's. Tall dude, wrapped up in a long overcoat, floppy hat down over his face. Called himself Augie. He had cash. A lot of it. Told me he didn't wanna know who was gonna do it or anything. He just wanted a guy scared off. He said, 'Make sure you shake him up. Tell him to drop what he's doing.' I took the cash and went to find Little B."

"Anything else you remember about the guy? His voice, the way he talked."

"He was nervous," Colt said, his own nervous leg pumping like a piston. "He talked kinda funny. Said words funny. Like he was a foreigner."

"Did you see his face at all?"

"Naw, he was all wrapped in that hat and the coat collar was up with a scarf. It's dark in Stella's. He had a smooth voice. Real smooth. I was hopin' he'd ask me to go home with him. He had a lotta money. Smelled nice, too. Like oranges."

"How did he know to find you?"

Colt was silent again.

"Who brought him to you? How would he know you'd do something like this?"

The kid stared at the floor and his nervous leg got more nervous.

"Okay, well at least I don't have to lie when I spread the word you told me everything I wanted to know."

"He didn't know what was gonna happen."

"Who?"

"He's... he's special. I don't wanna get him in trouble. He don't really know nothin' about all this. He was just makin' a connection."

"Who? Look, Colt, he could be in a lot of trouble anyway. If they got to Little B, they can get to your friend, too. If I know who it is, maybe I can help."

Colt was silent.

"You're just gonna sit there? He might be in danger and you're gonna sit there. I thought you said he was special?"

"He is... he's... I love him, man. I love him. But he don't know that. And don't you tell him."

"What's his name, Colt?"

"Jared."

Chapter 34

I was right, Jared was the key. But I figured Colt knew more.

Colt had crumpled into his chair, all the fight gone out of him. The lizard flicking at his cheek seemed tired and unenthusiastic. But I had more questions.

"Do you know where Jared is?"

"No. Last time I saw him he was scared, man. Said Scanlan had beat him again. I wanted to knock Scanlan's fuckin' head off, but Jared said not to. Said he was gonna move out. I haven't seen him since. Can you find him?" He eyes welled up.

"I have to find him. He may be targeted. Like Little B. He knows too much. You have any idea who killed Little B?"

"No. I didn't even know for sure the dude was dead. You gotta find Jared."

"This Augie, what exactly did he tell you when he hired you?"

"He wanted to send a message. That's what he said, 'I want to send a message.' He wanted to scare that guy. Tell him to stop what he was doin' and leave town."

That was too vague. Lots of people wanted to send Brandt a message for different reasons. Scanlan, Quinn, Wren, Navarro, Galante. Any of them. Hell, even Hollister might've wanted to get Brandt to stop seeing Jared.

Scanlan certainly wanted to keep Brandt away from Jared. The thought occurred to me that the tall stranger might have been Scanlan, heavily disguised, since people at Stella's knew him. He could have forced Jared to play along, just to be cruel knowing how much Jared loved Helmut.

"Did Augie give any information other than who to scare and how to find him?"

"No, just asked me to make sure the guy got a good scare. Rattle his cage."

"You're sure he didn't say anything else?"

"He said somethin' about books and papers and shit. But," he paused, swiped a hand over his face. "But, man, I can't remember this shit now."

I grabbed him by his collar and brought him close to my face. The veins on his neck popped. Even the lizard seemed more lively.

"Listen, asshole, this is no time to forget. You want me to help Jared? You gotta do better." I shoved him back in the chair.

"He... yeah... he said something about books. To tell the guy to stop writin' his shit and leave people alone."

That could still include any of them. Scanlan could be fronting for someone who wanted Brandt stopped. Quinn, Wren, and Galante would still be on the list.

"And Augie gave you money?"

"Ten big ones. Half up front."

"You met him again for the other half?"

"He never showed. Never paid the rest. The job went wrong. Guess he didn't wanna pay."

"He give you a way to contact him?"

"Naw, he said he'd contact me."

"All Jared did was hook the stranger up with you? He didn't know anything about the guy being targeted?"

"Yeah, he kne... well, no... he just hooked us up."

"He knew? Knew what?"

"He knew me and knew I had connections. He didn't know nothin' else."

"But he also knew Brandt. Jared knew him really well, right?"

"I don't know, man," Colt said. I knew he was lying it was in his voice.

"You said you love Jared. A guy who loves somebody knows if that somebody loves him back. Does Jared love you?"

Colt was silent.

"Forget it. I already know the answer. Jared was in love with Helmut. And you knew that, right?"

"He was confused. That Helmut dude was older. He confused Jared."

"Even if Jared only thought he loved Helmut, there was still no room for you, right?"

"I was hopin'…"

"That's why you wanted to help scare Helmut away. Maybe you even saw to it that Helmut got scared permanently. Dead permanently. Am I right?"

"No!" Colt tried to stand. I pushed him back into his seat. "No, that's not the way it went down."

"You just played your part and hired Little B to play a mugger? That's it? You did nothing else?"

"I…"

"I think you pushed Little B into killing Helmut."

"No. I wanted Helmut scared. That's true. But I knew Jared thought he was in love with the guy. So, I…"

"You what? What did you do?"

"I told Jared about the plan. In case he wanted to warn Helmut. I figured if he saw how nice I was bein' maybe he'd like me. If I helped him protect Helmut maybe Jared would see that I loved him and Helmut didn't really care."

I felt for Colt. Being in love makes you do crazy things. Makes you see the world differently. In his own way he was being noble about it. He loved Jared that much.

"Did Jared warn Helmut?"

"Said he was gonna call him and warn him. Later he told me he could never get past that old guy livin' with Helmut. The geezer told Jared they had all kinds of threats all the time and thank you and good-bye. That's just the way Jared said it."

"Tell me again about Augie. Tell me everything you remember."

"I don't…"

"You remember. Just think. Close your eyes and think back. He's near you at Stella's and talking to you."

"Okay, yeah…" Colt said, his eyes shut.

"What's he look like? Old, young, what?"

"Can't tell, his hat, the coat collar, and that scarf covered his face. His eyes though, they was shiny. Like, they was reflectin' all the light."

"Eye color?"

"It was dark at Stella's. All I saw was they were shinin' like, I don't know."

"What about his voice. Did he seem old or young?"

"He had like an accent or something' that's all I remember. Could'a been foreign. Used funny words sometimes, too."

"Like what?"

"It's no use, man. I can't remember. He was a soft kinda guy, though."

"Soft?"

"Yeah, nice. It didn't feel like he really wanted to be doin' what he was doin' if you know what I mean. He was gentle and nervous when he talked with me. If you ask me, he ain't never done anything like this before."

* * *

Colt agreed to stay put. He finally realized that he was in danger from whoever shot Little B. And Jared was in equally deep shit. I left Colt sitting alone and scared.

The cabbie who picked me up whistled when I got settled in his cab.

"Looks like you had a rough night, my man," he said and chuckled. "Your girlfriend throw you out?"

"Don't ask. You wouldn't believe me," I said, resting my head on the seat.

It'd been a long night. I smelled like wet chicken feathers and felt as if I'd run a marathon without any prep. At least I'd found Colt. It was more than I'd had before. One thing was certain, Jared was not only a key to things, he was in real danger.

I entered my building and Grace was on the desk. She looked at me and nodded. She probably thought I didn't see her eyes widen at the sight of me. But I was past caring what gossip she'd pass around to the rest of the staff.

The elevator couldn't get me to my floor quickly enough and the key just wouldn't unlock my door as fast as I wanted. But eventually I was inside, the door was locked, and the silent darkness enveloped me. I closed my eyes and stripped off my clothes one wet piece at a time. I felt clammy and shivered in the coolness.

The shower beckoned and I turned on the water full force, adjusted it to the hottest setting, and stepped in. The hot water pelting my skin soothed my jangled nerves swirling the tension away down the drain. I stood under the hot steady rush of water for a long while, steam building and drifting around me. Jared, Colt, Hollister, Quinn, Scanlan, Galante haunted my thoughts.

Jared knew he was in danger. He wasn't just running from Scanlan, he was also ducking whoever wanted to keep him quiet about what he knew.

It had to be connected to this stranger Colt remembered. Gleaming eyes and funny accent. It didn't ring any bells, didn't raise any alarms. But it did prove someone was behind Brandt's murder even if it hadn't been meant as a murder. It could be anyone.

The strangest thing was the accent. Might've been phony, just part of the disguise. Could have been real or just a mistake on the kid's part. Jared might be able to give me more information.

My mind was swimming in details, names, and faces. I needed sleep. I finished showering and tumbled into bed. I must have fallen asleep immediately. Next thing I knew it was light out and my phone was ringing.

Chapter 35

"Any breaks in the case?" Luke asked as we walked to Nina's.

"No but I have something Nina might be able to help with."

"Aside from the laptop?"

"Yes. Something entirely different." I explained the phone call Anton had gotten from Nando and what I thought Nina could do.

We arrived at the Fortress and I rang the bell.

"You guys again?" Hallie stared at us, neither hostile nor happy. "It's Sunday."

"And that means what?" Luke asked. "My guys work on Sundays. And I know Nina never takes a day off either."

"We're just here to pick up the laptop." I attempted to head off a battle. "Nina said she'd be here."

"Don't you guys like having business?" Luke said. "Whatever happened to good customer relations?"

Hallie glowered and grudgingly opened the door to let us pass.

"It's not like we don't have lives, you know," she said.

"You..." Luke started and I poked him with my elbow.

"We'll just get the laptop and give Nina a check," I said.

"Hey guys!" Nina emerged from the interior of the Geek Cave. "We squeezed everything we could from the laptop. We cleaned it up for him. Operates faster now."

"He'll be grateful. Thanks for doing this so quick."

"No problem." Nina shrugged it off.

"Here's what we agreed on and a little something extra for getting it done so fast." I handed her an envelope.

"While I've got you here," I said. "Maybe you can help with a little problem?"

"Sure and I won't even charge." Nina smiled. She was actually stunning-looking.

"You can help, too, Luke, like I explained."

"Shoot," Luke said.

"It's about a phone call Anton got from Nando."

"Can't trace calls anymore. I got in trouble last time," Nina said.

"No call tracing. But maybe the three of us can figure out something that's nagging at me. When Nando called I heard sounds in the background. I was hoping we might take a stab at locating him based on that."

"Cool," Nina said.

"It all depends on what you heard." Luke said.

"Three things, gulls. Seagulls. Construction noises. Like jackhammers and things. The third I'm not exactly sure about, but it sounded like a boat or boats of some sort."

"We might be able to triangulate a general location. But I'm not sure about a specific spot." Nina said.

"General is good. If we get close I can do some old-fashioned legwork."

"You're assuming Nando is still in Philly?" Luke asked.

"We've gotta start with that assumption."

"Okay, let's pull up some maps." Nina worked with the surface computers. Maps of Philadelphia's rivers appeared on the huge screen. "Gotta be a building on one of the rivers."

"Why's that?" I asked.

"The gulls. They hang around the rivers."

"But I've encountered them in a lot of places," Luke added. "Like the parking lot at Home Depot. Gulls are all over there."

"It's near the Delaware," Nina said. "Nothing's far from rivers in Philly."

"Okay," I said. "Let's add the other details. What do we get then?"

"You're also assuming Nando was in a building when he called. Not out on the street at a pay phone," Luke said.

"Nando's hiding. He probably wouldn't be out on the street. There aren't many pay phones anymore, anyway."

"Okay, let's limit to places where there are seagulls and apartments or condos," Nina said, peering at the map. "It's gotta be one of the rivers."

"Most likely the Delaware," Luke said. He had to know where potential cleaning clients were for his business to thrive. "There's very little right on the Schuylkill, unless they're holed up in one of the boathouses."

"Unlikely," I said.

"There's a few residential buildings and a couple of new condo towers going up on the Delaware waterfront."

"That could be it." Nina pulled up the riverfront map on the computer. The Delaware spread out, blue and beautiful, across the surface of the huge table-like screen. "Waterfront and new construction. Let's see."

She made some deft moves with her hands over the surface, all of which looked mysterious and magical, and the map changed to include existing and future buildings along the waterfront.

"Look there," Luke said. "There's only one building located next to new construction. Pier Four."

"Yep, and Penn Place construction is bound to be noisy," Nina added.

"We'll center the search around Pier Four," I said. "Luke, any of your staff work there?"

"Several. I'll get on it now." He took out his phone and got to work.

"I owe you big time, Nina." I placed an arm around her shoulder. "What would I do without you?"

"You'd make a bigger profit." Nina laughed.

Once we were on the street, I called Anton to see if we had pictures of Nando and told him I'd be by to get whatever he had. I remembered we had Kent's picture, too. From his application. I always photocopied an applicant's driver's license, for legal purposes. It wouldn't be a great picture but it'd be better than nothing.

Hollister might not be happy about this detour I was taking from the case. But sometimes the living take precedence over the dead even in the work I do. Besides, Nando might know where Jared was. And that would get me back on track.

Chapter 36

"Marco!" Chip rushed over to me, face flushed, smiling broadly. I hoped he'd found some information at Lobster Plaza.

The riverfront was windy and cold but the sun was out and people strolled the plaza. Motorboats zipped by on the river, their rumbling propellers churning the water. A sizeable tug muscled through the water, its horn ripping apart the quiet. Those were some of the sounds I'd heard on the phone. I felt we were close.

"Anything?"

"No, sorry, Marco," Chip said. "But this beats housecleaning gigs."

"I like it better when there are results." We were taking a gamble on someone noticing something near the Pier Four Condos. Just north of the Penns Landing plaza, it wasn't a tall building. Couldn't be more than twenty or thirty apartments in the place.

Luke, Chip, and I had split up the businesses neighboring the condos. A couple of giant restaurant-bar complexes and two or three chain restaurants. We each had pictures of Nando and Kent.

I'd had no luck with the restaurants. None of their workers remembered Nando or Kent. Chip had also struck out. We waited for Luke. The only thing left was the Pier Four itself.

Everything depended on what had actually happened to Nando. I pinned my hopes on the idea Nando just wanted to get away from everything for a while. Anton was betting Kent had spirited Nando away against his will.

I refused to believe Kent would betray my trust. But he was crazy in love, as they say, and that can make you betray even yourself. If Kent had kidnapped Nando, my goose was cooked. I'd be dancing nearly bare sooner than I could say 'g-string.'

I hoped we'd find Nando all by his lonesome. After all, there was no proof Kent had done anything other than disappear at the same exact time as Nando. And there was plenty of proof that Santa Claus and The Easter Bunny were in charge of the World Bank. I reminded myself that I didn't believe in coincidences and saw a vision of myself dancing on the bar at Bubbles.

"I've got zip," Luke said sauntering over to us. "Now what?"

"We check out the Pier Four."

"Just remember, Marco," Luke said. "The Pier Four is a secure building. The residents like their privacy. My guys are bonded and it wasn't easy for me to get the Pier Four contract. Management won't give you carte blanche."

"All they can do is say no. I'll show them Nando's picture. If they say no, we go to Plan B."

"Plan B?" Chip asked.

"Yeah, Marco, what's Plan B? You never mentioned it."

"I haven't put it together yet. Let me try the front desk first. Wait here."

I went through the wrought iron gates leading into the building. The developers had transformed an old pier into a palatial residence. These condos started at a million and a half. Now I saw why.

The lobby desk was green marble and mahogany. Muzak filled the air and huge vases spilling over with flower arrangements were placed strategically around.

The man at the front desk was an anachronism with silver hair, wire-framed glasses, waxed moustache, and a three piece pin-striped suit.

"May I help you, sir?" His voice was tight and controlled.

"Good afternoon. My name is Marco Fontana." I smiled and pulled out Nando's picture. "I'm investigating a missing persons case."

I didn't show a badge and he didn't ask. Too discreet for that here.

"Have you seen this man?" I handed him the picture.

He inspected it. Placing a hand to his chin, he tapped one finger just below his lower lip as he thought.

"I can't say I have but I'm not on the desk all the time. Have you reason to believe the young man is in this building?"

"I can't go into details, sir, as you might imagine," I said in deadpan fashion, which always made a good impression. "We were given to believe he might be here. It's urgent we move quickly, sir."

"Yes. Yes, I know. I watch television, you know. I understand the urgency in missing persons cases."

"What about other members of the staff?"

"Charles is in the back and is on duty much more often than I. There's also Jerome, the head of security. Wait here." He took Nando's picture with him.

As if I'd be going anywhere else in this locked down fortress. There were cameras everywhere, if you knew where to look.

A moment later, a small man with a pencil thin moustache and slicked back hair, emerged from a door behind the counter. He had Nando's picture in hand.

"Mr. Fontana?" He said, his dark suit lending him authority.

I nodded.

"This picture. It is recent?" He held it lightly.

"Yes, pretty recent." Nando had only been working a year. The photo was recent enough. "It's a photocopy of a photo from a flyer. It's grainy but should give you some   idea."

"I ask because the face looks familiar." His nose twitched, like a rabbit. His pencil moustache moved side to side. "This appears to be the young man who was here some days ago. He claimed to be waiting for a friend."

"Did you see this friend? Do you know where they went?"

"That just the thing." His nose twitched again. "I turned away from my work at the counter for just a moment. When I turned back, the young man was gone."

"Could he have gotten past you and into the building somehow?"

"I should say not." Charles looked ruffled. "We are quite secure here."

"Suppose he had help from someone in the building? Someone who lives here?"

"No. Absolutely not. Our residents would never do that. This building is home to judges, members of the state legislature, the city council. It would be unheard of for anyone here to breach our security."

"Unheard of, but possible?"

"Anything is possible," said a voice behind me.

I turned and saw a man in a uniform looking like a military officer who'd wandered away from his base. Tall, young, and intense, he stared at me.

"That's what I thought." I looked him up and down. "You must be Head of Security."

"Are you from the Police Department, Mr. Fontana?"

I wasn't going to lie outright. Having them assume was one thing. But I wasn't about to mislead them.

"I'm a private investigator. That doesn't make the case any less urgent. Missing persons cases are time-sensitive. I'm sure you know that."

"I do. But why aren't the police involved?"

"The family doesn't want that." Okay, so that was a lie but StripGuyz was Nando's family, too. And Anton didn't want the police involved.

"I see," Jerome said. "I'm afraid you'll have to take this up with management. Tomorrow."

"You've got to be kidding. Anything could happen. He could die. Do you want that on your conscience?"

"I'm going to have to ask you to leave." With that he maneuvered himself between me and the counter and began, ever so subtly herding me out the front door. "Ask for Mrs. Winters. Tomorrow."

In a building like this, you don't make a fuss.

On the sidewalk again, Luke and Chip stared at me.

"You have clients in this building, right?"

"A few. My guys love this gig. They're big tippers," Luke said. "The apartments are large, I get to charge higher fees. It works out all around."

"Can you get a crew in today?"

"Sunday? Building staff might think that's odd."

"If we tell them it's an emergency?" Chip said.

"No. They wouldn't believe their residents would call my company about an emergency without notifying the front desk."

"Any of your clients in this building on vacation?"

Luke checked the schedule in his smartphone and smiled.

"Two of them. The schedule says we're to skip those apartments this month."

"I have an idea," I said. They leaned in to listen.

* * *

Less than an hour later, we returned. Luke and three of his guys who worked Pier Four regularly. Chip and I were also in uniform. I had a hat pulled down over my forehead and I'd stuck on a pair of sunglasses.

"All set?" Luke said. Like a military commander leading us into battle, he looked us over, nodding approvingly. He moved forward and signaled we should follow.

Luke marched up to the counter where Mr. Waxed Moustache was stationed.

"Clyde!" Luke said. His professional demeanor firmly in place, he oozed authority. Clyde gave him a submissive look. His waxed moustache seemed to droop.

"Mr. Guan. So nice to see you." His smile appeared forced. "What brings you here on a Sunday? Surely your company doesn't work Sundays, too."

"Not normally, Clyde, but I received a call from Mr. Beglighter."

"The penthouse. He's away. On vacation." Clyde's eyes widened. "Is everything all right?"

"Everything's fine. He thought he might return early and asked if I could have his place cleaned in advance."

"I understand completely, Mr. Guan." Clyde gave the rest of us a perfunctory glance, as if looking at us might contaminate him. "Will you be needing anything?"

"I've got my staff. We shouldn't be very long. As I recall the place was immaculate. Mr. Beglighter just wants to be sure."

"I won't be on the desk when you leave, so I'll wish you a good day." Clyde gave a slight bow.

Luke nodded and motioned for us to move to the elevators.

We entered one of the ornate elevators and were zipped to the sixth floor where we huddled to make our plans.

"Should be one of the apartments that faces the water," I said. "It'd be easier to hear both the sounds of construction and boats from those. We'll limit ourselves to them."

"You know this could cost me my contract here," Luke said.

"I won't let that happen, Luke. I promise." I squeezed his shoulder. "You've all got the script and the photos. We're checking reports of leaks. No embellishment."

They mumbled assent.

"I'll take the second and third floors. Chip you take four. Luke will take five and six. If you encounter a situation, call me. Let me take care of it. Got it?"

They all nodded.

"If you do find Nando don't rattle him. Say you made a mistake and call me. Then wait by the door till I arrive. Don't let Nando out."

We paired up with Luke's workers and made our way to our assignments.

The second floor was quiet. A bright, crisp October day, not many people were likely to be at home. I went to the first of the apartments facing the river and knocked.

Silence.

Knocked again. Nothing.

I nodded to the guy with me and we moved to the next place.

Knocked and waited. After a few moments we heard the shuffling of feet.

"Who's there?" The woman's voice had a wary tone.

"There've been reports of leaks in some units and we'd like to assess the damage."

"I've got no water damage," she said. Then the sound of feet shuffling away.

I decided we shouldn't push it since she could easily call the front desk and find out the truth.

"Thank you, ma'm," I said.

One more apartment on the floor fit the bill and no one was at home.

The third floor was much the same, with the exception of a guy who answered the door in his bathrobe. Medium height and overweight, he smiled broadly when I mentioned water damage.

"Damned building. Been like living under a friggin' waterfall." He cheerfully led us through one room after another where leaks had caused damage. "Can't believe management is finally taking this seriously."

"No guarantee they'll do anything," I noted. "This assessment will take a while. Management will outsource the work. Best you wait until they contact you. You know how it is."

"Oh, I know. Next time they hear from me it'll be through my lawyer." He smiled. "How long do you think I should wait?"

"Give it three, four months. Contractors, what can you do?"

There was no one other than the man in the apartment. He kept the place tidy but with all the leaks, it was depressing. We left him to his watery Sunday morning.

"Now what?" My mostly silent partner looked at me.

"We head to the next floor." I pressed the elevator call button. The doors swooshed open and as we entered my phone rang. "Fontana."

"Sixth floor. I think he's in an apartment up here," Luke whispered.

I hit six on the panel and called Chip to meet us there.

"The apartment belongs to Dr. Wentworth. Sound familiar?" Luke said as soon as we got there.

"Wentworth. Sugardaddy Wentworth? One of the regulars at Bubbles?"

"One and the same. He's a client of mine." Luke moved toward the apartment. "He's away for the season. He's got a place in Florida and one in Tuscany and another one or two."

"And he lives here?"

"Well, it's not his only condo in the city. This is one he uses in the summer. I'm thinking Nando broke in."

"I saw Nando giving Wentworth a few little extras at Bubbles, if you know what I mean. I had to warn Nando to play by the rules."

"He must've made an impression on Wentworth."

"How do you know he's in the apartment?"

"I knocked and someone answered but wouldn't open the door. The voice was familiar. Slight accent. I questioned him about Wentworth. He said the Doctor would be back later. He's probably lying to get rid of us. I'm guessing it's Nando."

"Maybe Sugardaddy gave him a key," I suggested. "Especially since this isn't Wentworth's primary residence."

"We'll never know if we don't go in," Chip mumbled.

"Let's do it," I said. "He'll know my voice. Chip, how about you coax him to open up?"

"What should I say?"

"Make something up. Like the computer wiring needs to be checked or the place will short out and the building will have to be evacuated. Sounds good and serious."

"Who'd fall for that?" Chip looked incredulous.

"You'd be surprised," Luke said.

He knocked on the door so lightly, I didn't even hear it.

"Gotta make some sound. Gotta make it look urgent, remember?"

Chip pounded on the door.

"Wh-who is it?" A soft voice, quavering with fright. I recognized Nando immediately.

"We've got an emergency here," Chip lied. He sounded authentic. "Faulty wiring needs to be repaired or we'll have to evacuate the whole building. We've got to check the wiring in your apartment."

Silence.

"Sir?" Chip pressed. "Sir, this is urgent. Can you open the door, please?"

I heard mumbling, as if Nando were talking to someone. My heart beat faster both at the thought of finding Nando and with the idea that my bet with Anton might have me dancing on the bar. In my skivvies. Soon.

Chip pounded once more for effect, I supposed. But it did the trick.

Slowly the door opened.

And there was Nando, all five-feet-six, dark sleepy eyes, thick brown hair. Dressed in a translucent silk lounging robe, he appeared happier than I ever remember.

"You got to be quick, I'm just a guest here and…" Nando looked around as he spoke and stopped when his gaze fell on me. "M-Marco? What are you doin' here?"

"Finding you. There's a lotta people worried, Nando. You all right?" I stepped forward. "Call Anton, Luke. Let him know."

I moved quickly but gently into the apartment and Luke followed.

"Who is it this ti…" Kent wandered into the living room, bare as a bird. His eyes widened and he dropped the red apple he'd been eating. It bounced once then rolled into a corner.

I felt the others behind me staring as if they'd never seen a naked man. I was sympathetic, though. Kent was perfect. Lightly muscled, everything in perfect proportion, light brown eyes offset by chestnut hair, his skin grazed by a summer tan which had never left.

"Get some clothes on, Kent. We're going back to my office. You, too, Nando," I ordered before they spoke a word.

I followed them both back through the apartment. I wasn't about to lose track of them again. The apartment was long, narrow, and had lots of windows facing the river. As we walked I heard a tugboat as it passed by churning water.

The place was decorated in an understated yet elegant way. A seaside theme, with lots of blue and beige. We passed empty rooms, doors open. Kent looked back at me nervously as did Nando. They were hiding something and they looked desperate to prevent me from finding it.

"Can we have some privacy?" Kent asked, positioning himself in front of the bedroom door.

"You've had plenty of privacy for days now. So, no."

Neither of them moved.

"What's it gonna be, boys? If I have to dress you myself I will." I stepped forward and they flinched.

"You gotta…" Nando started.

"Don't say anything, Nando," Kent interrupted.

"All right, I don't have all day." I placed my hands on their shoulders, gently turned them around, and pushed them lightly into the bedroom.

The master bedroom was large and bright, one wall of windows gave it a spectacular view, it was as if you were dangling over the river as it flowed beneath you.

I heard the shower running in the bathroom.

"Who's in there?" I demanded.

"Nobody," Nando fumbled. "I… I was gonna take a shower."

"Well, I'll shut the water while you two get dressed," I said, figuring that whoever they were hiding was in the shower. I could guess who it was.

"No!" Nando said. "I mean, I can do it. Don't bother."

"No bother at all." I moved quickly to the bathroom and cut them off. The steam floating in the bathroom obscured my view. I pushed forward to the tall glass doors. A slender figure stood soaking under the noisy showerhead. Head back, pelvis thrust forward, he was letting the warmth seep in.

Tapping on the glass didn't get his attention. He was on another planet. I didn't want to yell and I didn't want to yank him out so I rolled up my sleeve, stuck my arm in, and reached for the controls. With one move I shut the water.

For a moment he didn't react. Eyes shut, standing as if he expected the water to continue, he was still in a trance. Then his eyes shot open and he looked around. Seeing me he tried to cover his genitals with his hands as he backed into a corner of the spacious shower stall.

"Jared." I kept my voice calm and didn't move other than to dry my arm on a towel and roll my sleeve back down. "I kinda thought I might find you here. We need to talk." I tossed him a white towel.

Chapter 37

Luke dropped us all at my office where Anton was waiting. The place was eerily quiet. It was Sunday morning and the whole neighborhood was on hold until evening.

"Nando! Are you all right?" Anton placed an arm around his shoulder and guided him to a soft chair. "Did he hurt you?" He turned toward Kent who looked confused. "What kind of twisted mind do you have?"

Anton was about to grab Kent by the collar when Nando's cry stopped him.

"No, no, Anton. You got it all wrong." Nando said.

"He kidnapped you," Anton insisted. "We've been searching for days. You've had us all crazy." He turned to glare at Kent. "You'll spend a lot of time in a cell for this. I'll see to it."

"But, I didn't do anything. Honest. Ask Nando. He..."

"I think you might want to hear him out," I said.

"Tell us what happened, Nando. You don't need to be afraid just because he's here. I won't let anything happen," Anton said.

"I'm not afraid, Anton. I'm happy." Nando went to stand with Kent. "After that night, you know, when Kent came in with the... you know... I began to think how much he must love me." Nando paused. "To do that... is a lot of love."

Kent placed his arm around Nando.

"I didn't know what to think. And Kent, he was being so nice. He stayed away. Never bothered me. Just like he promised to Marco."

"So why did he take you away with him? Why was he hiding you?" Anton demanded.

Kent flinched, closed his eyes, and waited.

"It was…" Nando hesitated. "It was me. I took Kent away. I told him about the Doctor's condo, that I could use it any time. We needed time together without anything else. Not my job, not anything. I'm sorry if I made you worry. I am."

"This was all your idea, Nando?" I asked, smiling. I'd won the bet but I wasn't about to gloat just yet. "You're sure?"

"Yes. How would Kent know about the condo? It was all me. I realized I need Kent. We needed to talk. But we were ready to come back," Nando said. "We… we can come back, Marco? We can have our jobs back?"

"Only if Anton agrees." I turned to him. Better to let him make the decision.

"If it's all right with you, Marco," Anton answered. "But…"

Everyone waited for Anton's conditions.

"The next time you two decide to run away together, let us know in advance." He frowned but I saw he was relieved.

"Then you guys are back on the payroll. But I have one question, Nando."

"Yes?"

"If the two of you wanted to be alone, why was Jared there? Or is this a three-way relationship?"

"Three… oh, Marco… you play with me. No. There is no three-way," he looked over at Jared and giggled. "Jared is a friend. He was running away from that monster. He needed a place to stay. Can I refuse a friend?"

"Clears that up," I said and gave Nando a peck on his cheek. "Glad you're back and all in one piece."

"I'll take the lovebirds to Bubbles and we'll discuss Nando's schedule," Anton said.

"And Kent?" Nando said.

"And Kent's schedule." Anton relented.

On their way out, I heard Anton ask Kent, "You think you want to dance for us?" and I knew things would be fine.

I was alone with Jared and he looked uncomfortable.

"Jared. Boy, do I have questions for you."

He shifted uneasily in his chair and his eyes didn't meet mine.

"You've had some bad times lately. Scanlan, Helmut."

"Like you care."

"I care about my case," I said. "I talked to Colt. He tells me you helped him with a client he had.

"I didn't."

"Why would he lie, Jared?"

"He lies. He's a lowlife."

"Seemed like a kid who had a lotta bad breaks. I don't think Colt lied. Be straight with me or we just go down to the police."

"I… didn't do much. Just introduced a guy to Colt," he said. Jared was smooth and intelligent. But he was a bad liar. He wasn't telling me the whole story.

"I need to find that guy."

"I don't see how you're gonna find him. He was wrapped like a mummy. Couldn't see his face."

"What about his voice?"

"He had an accent. Like he came from somewhere else. It was a nice voice but maybe he disguised that, too."

"Did anything at all that strike you as familiar about him?"

"When you say that, it makes me think there was something about him that maybe I'd seen before. But it can't be. I couldn't see his face."

"What did he want?"

"Colt didn't tell you?" Jared said.

"I want to hear it from you."

"He said he needed to throw a scare into somebody. Nothing serious, just scare him. Wouldn't say more than that. He asked if I knew anybody who'd do that," Jared grew uneasy. He sat on his hands but his foot began to tap nervously.

"Did you ask him who'd sent him to you? I mean why would he pick you out?"

"I assumed it was Seamus. I know a lot of guys. They have rough neighborhoods where I come from, too. I grew up in one. You learn quick who can get things done. Seamus doesn't like to get his hands dirty." Jared squirmed now.

"You think Seamus knew the guy?"

"Probably not. I think the guy had been asking around for a while. Kind've indirectly. Eventually somebody turned him on to Seamus. Seamus threw him my way."

"So Scanlan had nothing to do with any of this?"

"That's a laugh. Seamus is a coward and a bully. He only likes to hit people like me. There's nothin' inside him but sawdust. He brings his dirty work to other people. Like with that stranger."

"Then you hooked the stranger up with Colt? And that was the end of it."

"I washed my hands. I've gotten beyond my background. I'm in design now. I've made a better life for myself. Seamus is the one who dragged me to places like Stella's and made me deal with people like that. I never wanted to bother with that ever again." He didn't look at me when he said this.

"That's not what Colt said." I stared at Jared.

"He's lying. He wants to drag me down." Again refusing to look me in the eye.

"Colt says he's in love with you. Did you know that?"

"He's crazy."

"That's why he told you who the target was. Remember now?"

"I don't know what you're talking about."

"Let me refresh your memory. Colt knew you were in love with Helmut. So, he told you Helmut was the target. He thought you'd want to warn Helmut."

"No. Colt didn't tell me anything."

"If you ask me, Colt really does love you. To give you that information even though it could help his rival. Colt has it bad for you."

"He's unbalanced. You can't believe anything he says."

"Colt told you and you didn't warn Helmut. Instead of warning him, you got in touch with the shooter and told him to shake Helmut up really good. Maybe you even asked him to kill Helmut."

"I'd never do that!" Tears spilled over onto Jared's cheeks as he protested. "I loved Helmut. I loved him. I'd have done anything for him. But he wouldn't leave that old man. He was in love with me but he loved Hollister, too. He could never even think about leaving him. No matter how much he loved me."

"So you told Little B to kill him."

"Why would I do that? I loved Helmut. I still love him." Jared cried openly now, his words tangled in tears and sobs.

"You didn't tell Little B to kill Helmut? You didn't tell Little B anything?"

"I'd never want him to kill Helmut. Then there'd never be a chance."

"You wanted him hurt though. Right? You told Little B to hurt him."

"I never told him anything. You can't prove I said anything."

"You were hurting. You felt abandoned. Helmut said he loved you. But he didn't mean it."

"He did love me. It wasn't just words."

"But he wouldn't come through for you. Wouldn't leave Hollister for you."

"He told me I made him happy."

"But…" I coaxed.

"But Hollister made him happier. That hurt. You know? It hurt me."

"So you wanted to hurt him back. Really hurt him. Maybe kill him?"

"Hurt not kill. There's a difference. I wanted him hurt not dead. Maybe it was that guy in Stella's. Maybe he wanted Helmut dead and he told Little B."

"The stranger never hinted at that to you?"

"Why would he? Little B came to me later looking for Colt. He wanted to get paid. He bragged to me how he'd done what I…" Jared stopped.

"Don't stop now. You were just gonna admit what you did."

"I didn't do anything. You can't prove anything."

"Little B came bragging to you that he'd done what you asked. He'd hurt Helmut. Hurt him real good. Right?"

"No!"

"That's what happened isn't it? It's easy to find out."

"How? Little B is…" He stopped again. There was no way he could know Little B was dead.

"Little B is dead. That what you were going to say?"

"I didn't know Helmut was dead until I saw it on the news." Jared drew in a breath and sobbed. "Then… it was too late and I wanted Little B to pay. I wanted them both to pay. Little B and the creep who hired him."

"Did you kill Little B?"

"When I saw Colt I had a fit. I told him I wanted to kill Little B, make him pay for what he did. But I didn't kill him."

"How'd you know he was dead, then?"

"I… I didn't… Colt… Colt must've told me."

"No, Colt didn't know where to find you. He didn't know Little B was dead. You killed him. Somebody told you where to find him and you killed him."

"I…"

"You're in deep shit here, Jared. The police don't take kindly to murder for hire." I knew he wasn't the only player in the game. I had to find out who the stranger was. "If you told me more about the stranger, maybe that'll help your case."

"I don't know what else to tell you." Jared's voice was low and soft. He was broken. The reality of his part in Helmut's death was dawning on him.

"Anything might help. Think. His voice. Did you see anything at all familiar about him? The way he handled himself. What he was drinking?"

"He had a glass of wine. He shook my hand when we met. He wore a ring but not a wedding ring. There was a scar on his hand. An old scar on the back of his hand."

"A scar." That sounded familiar. But I couldn't remember right then where I'd seen it. "Did he give you a name?"

"Augie. Said his name was Augie. And when he got up from the barstool, he acted like he was in pain. That's all I remember."

Unfortunately that was enough. I remembered now. And it didn't make me happy.

Chapter 38

My office was oddly still. Sundays were always quiet but today the silence was woven of something stronger, sadder, heavier. From what Jared and Colt had told me, I was certain I knew who the stranger was and who'd ultimately been responsible for Helmut's death. What I didn't know was whether or not he'd acted alone.

I needed one more piece of information before I settled the case and gave it to the authorities. I called the one person who could help me with that.

The phone felt like a lead weight in my hand. I didn't want to destroy people's dreams and make a ruin of their lives. But no one has the luxury to operate under the illusion that life is fair. If they thought so, they were in for a horrible surprise.

Tapping in the numbers and waiting for him to answer seemed to take forever. "Kusek." His voice was a buttery whisper.

"It's Marco," I said.

"Marco," Kusek sounded exhausted, frightened. "I was about to call you. I've read the documents… I need to talk with you."

"I need some information from you, too."

"Why don't you meet me here at the Cathedral rectory?"

"When?"

"Now." There was a finality in his tone.

* * *

The unassuming, grey stone building sat short and squat in the shadow of the immense cathedral at its back. I approached slowly, carefully choosing the words I'd use, trying to subdue the feelings that had begun to well up inside me.

I rang the bell and a small, pale attendant came to the door. I told him the Monsignor had called me to a meeting and he led me to a waiting area.

After a moment, he returned to show me to the Monsignor's quarters on the second floor. The inside of the building was elegant. Wood paneling, crown moldings, the works. The oak staircase was polished to a high gloss and the carpeting was a rich sage color. We climbed the stairs noiselessly and the attendant left me at a tall, solemn-looking oak door.

I knocked and before my knuckles left the wood, Kusek opened the door. He looked tired. His eyes red, his hair uncombed, and his face unshaved. Even disheveled, he was still one of the most beautiful men I'd ever seen. His unkempt condition added a vulnerability that was not usually present.

"Marco, I've got so much to tell you. So much I need to say. The documents have been a revelation. I'm still reeling."

He waved me into his suite and shut the door. The main room was large, nicely furnished, and painted in restful colors. There was a sofa, a couple of soft chairs, a desk with a computer, a flat panel television, sound equipment, and more. The walls were hung with paintings and photographs. Doors led to several other rooms in the apartment.

Kusek sat on the sofa as if he were weighted down. Papers were strewn everywhere. The soft yellow light creating a glow around Kusek made him appear ethereal. But he also looked drained and defeated.

"Have a seat." He waved to the chairs.

I was too edgy to sit but I did. None of this would be easy.

"I've got a few questions for you, Tad." I felt a deep pang of sadness. "But you said you had things to tell me."

"Ask your questions. What I've got to say will take a while." The spark of animation that had filled him previously was absent now.

"I've talked to a lot of people the last few days," I said and paused. "There's no easy way to put this, Tad."

He looked at me, then away. He must've known what I would say.

"You hired someone to scare Brandt. That much is clear. What I want to know is if you took it a step further."

"I must've left an easy trail. It's not something I ever dreamed of doing."

"You hid your tracks fairly well. But little things eventually added up. Like your accent. Sometimes people think you're foreign, don't they?"

Tad said nothing.

"That Chicago accent and whatever little flourishes you picked up in Italy gives some people the impression you have a foreign accent. And the ring and that scar on your hand. They got noticed."

"I thought I'd covered all the bases. All amateurs think so, don't they?"

"And that pain in your back. The one that makes you wince and limp sometimes. I'd noticed but it never fully registered."

"From the accident. The one I told you about. That accident was my salvation and my undoing. Funny how things work out."

"You used the name Augie. Didn't register either at first, but it made sense eventually."

"You even recognized that name?"

"I remembered it was your grandfather's name. I'll bet no one ever called him Augie."

"Oh." He hung his head and I heard him choking back tears.

"Did you, Tad?"

"Did I...?" He looked up, eyes red.

"Did you ask the kid to kill Brandt?"

"No. No." He shuddered. "I didn't want Brandt to die. I wanted him scared off his project. I'd sent him an e-mail threat knowing the kid would follow up with the attack."

He hunched over now, head down, talking to the ground. A few tears fell, making a small pocking sound on a sheet of paper on the floor.

"He wasn't supposed to hurt him. Just scare him." There was no anger in Kusek's voice, just remorse. He seemed resigned, acutely aware of his guilt, and ashamed. "But I have to take responsibility."

"One other question, Tad." Sadness blanketed me. "Was there anyone else in on this? Did anyone ask you to do this? Force you?"

"No. It was only me."

"The Cardinal didn't have a hand in this?"

"No." He took a deep breath. "I respected that man."

"Did he make you do this?"

"No, I did it. All myself. I felt sorry for Galante."

He paused, cleared his throat and shuddered as if he'd rid himself of something and regained his composure. He wiped his eyes and stood, then moved to his desk.

"G worried that Brandt was ruining his life with his books on the Pope's death. He'd said even though it was all lies, it might wipe out any chance he had to be elected pope. The first American pope."

I nodded.

"He's a good person. He can be arrogant, even imperious but he truly believes in the mission of the Church. He goes out of his way to help people. I owe him everything. And I'm not the only one. He believes it's his duty to help the poor and those in need." Kusek sat at his desk and faced me.

"So Galante had no part in this?" I felt there had to be more.

"He kept saying he wished Brandt would go away," Tad murmured. A fresh bout of tears overtook him. I let him cry. Eventually, he stopped and took hold of himself. "He hoped Brandt's work would quickly sink into obscurity. But it didn't. Brandt was a publicity hound. He kept things going. G never took action against Brandt, though. He cursed his own luck. For having been in Rome when John Paul the First died. Then having Brandt exploit the conspiracy theories and implicate people even without naming them. G became more depressed each day. It hurt to see him that way. I couldn't stand watching the man who'd saved my life suffering from Brandt's poisonous treatment."

"So you decided to do something about it?"

"I didn't come to it lightly. I saw G going downhill, saw his dreams evaporating. I had to do something," he said. "He gave me my life back. You understand? I owed him."

"How did you know what to do?"

"I'd heard about Stella's indirectly from Scanlan. I overheard a conversation in my outer office. Scanlan thought I was away. He tried to convince Tony that Stella's wasn't a bad place. I heard Tony say Stella's was filled with druggies and lowlife types. I remember he said you could get anything you wanted there. I knew it was probably the opportunity I was looking for."

I shook my head. I felt for him and I felt horrified.

"Then you came along," he continued. "You appeared and something inside me changed again. I began regretting everything I'd ever done. Every step I'd taken, every choice I'd made up until I met you. Especially hiring that man. But mostly not being myself." He remained silent, his hands covering his face. "Then you asked me to read those documents."

"And?"

"That changed everything again. It was as if I was standing on sand. My whole world was a sham. I'd managed to make it worse by dirtying my hands in the service of someone who didn't deserve it."

"What're you saying, Tad? What did you read in those documents? I went over them, Hollister went through them. Neither of us found anything that made sense."

"You didn't know what to look for. I'd heard G tell stories of his years in Rome a thousand times. Each time he added more details, more names. He told me about a nickname Cody and his friends had for him, Piccolo Titta. When I read the documents, it made sense."

"I don't understand," I said.

"Titta refers to Mastro Titta, a Nineteenth Century Papal executioner in Rome who was never allowed to cross the bridge from Trastevere into Rome unless he was going to do his job. In the documents, the men gathered at the Bridge of the Four Heads referred to a Piccolo Titta and said he helped them in their work. Who else could they have meant?"

I was beginning to get the picture and I didn't like it.

"G was one of the black beetles scurrying around Rome then, but he was more like a lethal spider. He'll undoubtedly say he was following orders, but he knew what those orders meant." Tad paused and shuddered. "No matter how wrongheaded you think someone is, you don't kill him. G must have been a zealot back then just like the men who plotted to assassinate the

Pope. I'd never seen that side of him before. Not until I read those documents and then things made sense."

"Are you saying he had something to do with the death of the Pope?"

"He was like the bullet they fired. He brought the poison to the man on the inside. G helped poison the Pope's tea. The documents clearly say that Piccolo Titta was the go between. That no one would know what he was doing. He'd have been viewed as a messenger boy for Cody. He allowed the Pope to be poisoned that night. He did it and lived with it all these years."

"Son of a bitch." There was no joy in learning this. Especially seeing how it ripped Kusek apart.

"It's not something I can live with, Marco. Not now. Not ever. So, I had to tell you first." He pulled open a drawer as he spoke. "Galante has made a mockery of everything I ever believed. I can't wear the collar any more."

I'd been watching his face but suddenly I noticed he had something in his hand. Something metallic, dull, and deadly.

"Tad." I rose from my chair and faced him over his desk.

"Don't worry. I feel good now, Marco. I've made a choice and I feel good about it. For once I'm doing something for myself."

"Tad. Put that away. Please," I kept my voice low and calm. "There's no need to do this. We can talk. We can have dinner and talk. Like we did…"

"But there is a need, Marco. I need to pay for what I did and I can't pay with prison. That wouldn't be enough." He held the gun to his head. The cold gray metal against his golden hair. His hand trembled as he moved, then his resolve took hold.

"Tad! Please. Don't do this." I moved toward him.

"G will know why. He'll have to remember that he saved me and he killed me."

"Put it down, Tad. Let's talk. Just a little more."

"There's nothing left to say, Marco."

I reached over the desk trying to stop him. I felt my muscles tighten as I stretched.

His determination made him quicker. He placed the gun in his mouth and pulled the trigger before I could do anything more.

The sound in that small space was deafening. His head exploded in red spray, spattering blood and brain everywhere. His body flew back throwing over the chair and spilling him onto the floor with a crash and a thud.

A millisecond later the silence was complete.

Chapter 39

I watched him approach. The sun was high overhead and he was just another elderly man in casual clothes making his way down the street. The sight of him was jarring and satisfying at the same time. Galante didn't look like the embodiment of evil. Didn't look like much of anything to tell the truth. Just a broken old man whose dreams had just been thrown down a sewer.

He'd been obstinate and dismissive when I confronted him after Kusek's death. But faced with the documents and with what I'd learned from Kusek, he had little choice but to agree to terms. He agreed to resign claiming poor health. It was either that or public humiliation and condemnation or worse. He chose the course of least resistance for himself and for the institution he professed to love.

Afterward, he'd asked to meet in Kahn Park, in the middle of the gayborhood. Appropriate. It was the most sterile park in the city – devoid of anything resembling friendliness or beauty. It matched Galante's life. I didn't know why he wanted to talk face to face but it was his last wish, you could say.

When he approached me, I stood, more out of habit than respect.

"Mr. Fontana." He nodded curtly.

"Mr. Galante." I refused to use a title he had no business bearing.

"It's done," he said, sitting wearily. "Everything you've asked has been done. I'm sure you're a happy man now."

"Too many people are dead for me to be happy. As for everything I've asked for…"

"I have resigned my position as Archbishop of Philadelphia. The Church is allowing me to spend the rest of my life at The Monastery of the Holy Cross in Idaho. You've effectively destroyed my career. My life."

"You destroyed your own career, Galante. I just wanted to save a lot of people from losing what little faith they have left in your institution. Don't ask me why."

"I could have made a difference in the Church. I could have…"

"Why did you want to meet? I could've heard all about it on the news."

"I wanted to look you in the eye, Mr. Fontana. I know we've met before but I never really took your measure and I realize I underestimated you."

"I get that a lot. So, are we finished?" I wanted to go. Sitting with this guy gave me the creeps.

"And I wanted you to know just what it is you've done by destroying me. You need to know what the Church has lost. I would have brought it back to where it should be in people's lives, in the world. I would have made a difference."

"I think you did that thirty years ago, Galante. And you'll be doing it again once people learn you've resigned."

He glowered at me. There was little he could do and no spells he could cast that would turn me into the lump of shit he obviously thought I was.

"I've got things to do. I won't wish you luck, you seem to make your own wherever you go." I stood up, turned, and walked out of the ugly little pocket park. The sun was shining although while I sat with Galante, something had obscured the light.

Walking back to my office I had to pass Giovanni's Room, where Helmut had entranced me so long before and where he'd made his last public appearance. Camac Street, where he'd been killed, wasn't far either. I ambled past that place, too. I don't know why exactly, maybe I just wanted to pay my respects. Say goodbye to him once and for all. People had been placing small bouquets at the spot where he died. At least one fresh bouquet every day. I'd been told someone also placed a single red rose there, a new one every day. Red as the blood he'd shed.

Maybe I let Galante off easy for the same reason that Helmut wanted to hang him. Even if I didn't believe in the Church and all its works, some people did. It was the least of them, the ones who had little left in their lives but faith in that Church, it was those people I worried about. If the whole sordid story had come out and Galante had been exposed publicly, it might have been the last straw for those people after the sex abuse scandals, the financial misconduct, and all the other misdeeds and wrongdoings of people they were supposed to trust.

The Church was a hornet's nest. Thirty years before, John Paul the First had wanted to fix it and he was dead. Helmut had wanted to save it in his own way. And he was dead. Even Kusek's sincere beliefs led him to think he was doing the right thing. And he was dead, too. It was all such a waste.

We'd at least gotten to the truth about Helmut's murder. Kusek had paid the ultimate price. Little B was dead. Jared and Colt would do time in prison. I didn't want more people hurt.

Hollister was satisfied with the fact that Galante would resign his position. The Trappist monastery where he'd contemplate his sins for the rest of his life would not be an easy place to live. Being removed from the limelight, from the power, and from any possibility of a future in the hierarchy was a terrible price for a man like Galante. Considering there was no actual eyewitness to his part in the plot to kill the Pope, I'd thought it was a good compromise. He would be punished and no one had to learn that men who were supposed to be doing God's work had devolved into murderers.

Sometimes Truth has to stay hidden. Its light is too bright. Too many people would be wounded if certain truths were known. So I buried it this once. I could live with that.

Camac Street was empty and quiet. The late October sun filtered in between tall buildings and a chilly breeze blew down the street driving dead leaves and paper before it. I could hear gun shots in my imagination, cries for help, confused shouts. Memories still haunted the place.

The colorful flowers leaning against the wall were a mute testament to both the kindness and cruelty of people. I bent down to look at the red rose near the wall where Helmut died. The blossom was so fresh a crystal clear drop of dew still caressed one of the petals. I felt a tear wanting to push its way out of my eye, so I cleared my throat, swiped a hand over my face, and stood up.

It was time to get back to the office. There were cases, there were always more cases. I walked away from that place of death and didn't look back. I placed one foot in front of the other and thought about what I had to do next. Each step took me toward feeling a little better. Things would never be the same for some and would never change for others. I looked around and took a deep breath.

The gayborhood looked good, everything was right where it should have been and so was I.

About the Author

Joseph R.G. DeMarco lives and writes in Philadelphia and Montréal. Several of his stories have been anthologized in the *Quickies* series (all three volumes) published by Arsenal Pulp Press, in *Men Seeking Men* (Painted Leaf Press) and in *Charmed Lives* (Lethe Press). His essays have been published in anthologies including *Gay Life* (Doubleday), *Hey Paisan!* (Guernica), *We Are Everywhere* (Routledge), *BlackMen WhiteMen* (Gay Sunshine), *Men's Lives* (Macmillan), *Paws and Reflect* (Alyson)), *The International Encyclopedia of Marriage and Family* (Macmillan) the *Encyclopedia of Men and Masculinites* (ABC CLIO), and *The Gay and Lesbian Review Worldwide* among others.

A current travel columnist for XXFactor Magazine online (www.xxfactor.com), he has written extensively for the gay/lesbian press. He was a correspondent for *The Advocate, In Touch, Gaysweek,* and his work has been featured in *The New York Native,* the *Philadelphia Gay News* (PGN), *Gay Community News, The Philadelphia Inquirer, The Welcomat, KLIATT, Chroma,* and a number of other publications.

In 1983, his PGN article "Gay Racism" was awarded the prize for excellence in feature writing by the Gay Press Association and was anthologized in *We Are Everywhere, Black Men, White Men,* and *Men's Lives.*

He was Editor-in-Chief of *The Weekly Gayzette* (Philadelphia); Editor-in-Chief of *New Gay Life,* a national magazine; and has been an editor or contributing editor for a number of publications including *Il Don Gennaro,* a national Italian-American magazine, and *Gaysweek* (NY).

Currently his is the Editor-in-Chief of *Mysterical-E* (www.mystericale.com) an online mystery magazine and has won the Preditors and Editors Reader's Choice Award for Best Editor in 2005 and 2007.

One of his greatest loves is mystery (all kinds) but he also has an abiding interest in alternate history, speculative fiction, young adult fiction, vampires, werewolves, science fiction, the supernatural, mythology, and more.

Murder on Camac is the first in his Marco Fontana Mysteries series

You can learn more at www.josephdemarco.com and at www.murderoncamac.com

LaVergne, TN USA
01 December 2009
165584LV00001B/184/P